Richard Malcolm Johnston

Dukesborough Tales

By Philemon Perch

Richard Malcolm Johnston

Dukesborough Tales
By Philemon Perch

ISBN/EAN: 9783337343897

Printed in Europe, USA, Canada, Australia, Japan

Cover: Foto ©Andreas Hilbeck / pixelio.de

More available books at **www.hansebooks.com**

DUKESBOROUGH TALES

BY

PHILEMON PERCH.

BALTIMORE:
TURNBULL BROTHERS.
1871.

DEDICATED

TO

MEMORIES OF THE OLD TIMES:

THE GRIM AND RUDE,

BUT HEARTY OLD TIMES IN GEORGIA.

PREFACE.

These Sketches, which I have ventured to call TALES, drawn partly from memories of incidents of old times, but mostly from imagination, were written for the sake of my own entertainment, in the evenings when I had nothing else to do. And now I am going to let them be published in a little book, having been persuaded, perhaps too easily, that they may amuse others, enough at least to have me excused both for the writing and the publishing. I know very well that such words as these, which are meant for a Preface, may be regarded rather as an apology. Let it be so ; and if it be thought not sufficient, even as such, it is as much, I insist, as ought to be expected from a man of my age.

P. P.

CONTENTS.

		Page.
THE GOOSEPOND SCHOOL,		1
JUDGE MIKE'S COURT,		36
HOW MR. BILL WILLIAMS TOOK THE RESPONSI-		
BILITY,	.	75
THE PURSUIT OF MR. ADIEL SLACK,	.	97
THE EARLY MAJORITY OF MR. THOMAS WATTS,		133
THE ORGAN-GRINDER,	. .	145
MR. WILLIAMSON SLIPPEY AND HIS SALT,	. .	160
INVESTIGATIONS CONCERNING MR. JONAS LIVELY,		176

THE GOOSEPOND SCHOOL.

"You call this education, do you not?
Why, 'tis the forc'd march of a herd of bullocks
Before a shouting drover."

CHAPTER I.

THE incidents which I propose to relate in these sketches, and those which may follow hereafter, occurred, for the greatest part, either at or in the neighborhood of Dukesborough, once a small village in Eastern Georgia. For many years it has ceased even to be mentioned, except by the very few persons now living who knew it before the Dukes, from whom it was named, moved away. It has suffered the most absolute decay that I have known ever to befall any village. It had not been laid off in its beginning according to any definite plan. Dukesborough seemed indeed to have become a village quite unexpectedly to itself and to everybody else, notwithstanding, that instead of being in a hurry to become so, it took its own time for it, and that amounted to some years. The Dukes first established a blacksmith shop. This enterprise succeeded beyond all expectation. A small store was ventured. It prospered. After some years other persons moved in, and buying a little ground, built on both sides of the road (a winding road it was), until there were several families, a school, and a church. Then the Dukes grew ambitious and had the place called Dukesborough. It grew on little by little until this family had all gone, some to the counties farther west, and some to the grave. Some-

I

how, Dukesborough couldn't stand all this. Decay set in very soon, and now a small mound or so, the site of an ancient chimney, is the only sign of a relic of Dukesborough.

It would be useless to speculate upon the causes of its fall. The places of human habitation are like those who inhabit them. Some persons die in infancy, some in childhood, some in youth, some at middle age, some at threescore and ten, and some linger yet longer. But the last, in their own times, die as surely as many of the former. Methuselah, comparatively speaking, was what might be called a very old man ; but then *he* died. The account in Genesis of those first generations of men is, after all, a melancholy one to me. The three last words closing the short history of every one are very sad — " And he died."

So it is with the places wherein mortals dwell. Some of them be-come villages, some towns, and some cities : but all — villages, towns, and cities — have their times to fall, just as infants, youths, men, and old men, have their times to die. People may say what they please about the situation not being well chosen, and about the disagreeableness of having the names of their residences all absorbed by the Dukes whom few persons used to like. All this might be very true. But my posi-tion about Dukesborough is, that it had lived out its life. It had run its race, like all other things, places, and persons, that have lived out their lives and run their races : and when that was done, Dukesborough *had* to fall. It had not lived very long, and it had run but slowly, if indeed it can be said to have run at all. But it reached its journey's end. When it did, it had to fall, and it fell. So Babylon, so Nineveh. These proud cities, it is highly probable, had no more idea of their own ruin than Dukesborough had immediately after its first store was built. But we know their history, and it ought to be a warning.

Ah, well ! It is not often, of late years, that I pass the place where it used to stand. But whenever I do, I feel somewhat as I feel when I go near the neglected grave of an old acquaintance. In the latter case, I say to myself, sometimes, And here is the last of him. He was once a stout, hearty, good-humored fellow. It is sad to think of him as having dropped everything, and being covered up here where the earth above him is now like the rest all around the spot, and the grave, but for my recollection of the place where it was dug, would be indistinguishable even to me who saw him when he was put here. But so it was. It could not be helped, and here he is for good. So of Dukesborough. When I pass along the road on the sides of which it once stood, I can but linger a little and muse upon its destiny. Here was once a smart village ; no great things of course, but still a right lively little village. It might have stood longer and the rest of the world have suffered little or no harm. But it is no use to think about it, because the thing is over and Dukesborough is no more. Besides myself, there may be two or three persons yet living who can tell with some approximation to accuracy where it used to stand. When we are dead, whoever may wish to gather any relic of Dukesborough must do as they do upon the supposed sites of the cities of more ancient times : — they must dig for it.

These reflections, somewhat grave I admit, may seem to be unfitly preliminary to the narratives which are to follow them. But I trust they will be pardoned in an old man who could not forbear to make them when calling to mind the forsaken places of his boyhood, albeit the scenes which he describes have less of the serious in them than of the sportive. If I can smile, and sometimes I do smile at the recital of some things that were done and words that were said by some of my earliest contemporaries, yet I must be allowed a sigh also when I remember that the doings and the sayings of nearly all of them are ended for this world.

CHAPTER II.

" Books ! " There is nothing terrible in this simple word. On the contrary, it is a most harmless word. It suggests quiet and contemplation ; and though it be true that books do often produce agitations in the minds of men and in the state of society, sometimes even effecting great revolutions therein, yet the simple enunciation of the word, even in an elevated tone, could never be adequate, it would seem, to the production of any considerable excitement. As little would it seem, in looking upon it from any point of view in which one could place oneself, to be capable of allaying excitement however considerable. I never could tell exactly why it was, that, as often as I have read of the custom in England of reading the Riot Act upon occasions of popular tumult, and begun to muse upon the strangeness of such a proceeding and its apparent inadequacy for the purposes on hand, my mind has recurred to the incidents about to be narrated. For there was one point of view,

or rather a point of hearing, from which one could observe this quieting
result by the utterance of the first word in this chapter twice a day for
five days in the week. It was the word of command with which Mr.
Israel Meadows was wont to announce to the pupils of the Goosepond
schoolhouse the opening of the school morning and afternoon.

The Goosepond was situated a few miles from Dukesborough, on
the edge of an old field, with original oak and hickory woods on three
sides, and on the other a dense pine thicket. Through this thicket
there ran a path which led to the school from a neighboring planter's
residence where Mr. Meadows boarded. The schoolhouse, a rude hut
built of logs, was about one hundred and twenty yards from this thicket
at the point where the path emerged from it.

One cold, frosty morning near the close of November, many, very
many years ago, about twenty-five boys and girls were assembled as
usual at the Goosepond waiting for the master. Some were studying
their lessons, and some were playing; the boys at ball, the girls at
jumping the rope. But all of them (with one exception), those studying
and those playing, the former though the most eagerly, were watching
the mouth of the path at which the master was expected. Those
studying showed great anxiety. The players seemed to think the game
worth the candle: though the rope jumpers jumped with their faces
toward the thicket, and whenever a boy threw his ball, he first gave
a look in the same direction. The students walked to and fro in
front of the door, all studying aloud, bobbing up and down, exhibiting
the intensest anxiety to transfer into their heads the secrets of knowledge that were in the books. There was one boy in particular, whose
eagerness for the acquisition of learning seemed to amount to a most
violent passion. He was a raw-boned lad of about fifteen years, with
very light coarse hair and a freckled face, sufficiently tall for his years.
His figure was a little bent from being used to very hard work. But
he had beautiful eyes, very blue, and habitually sad. He wore a round-
about and. pants of home-made walnut-dyed stuff of wool and cotton,
a seal-skin cap, and red brogan-shoes without socks. He had come up
the last. This was not unusual: for he resided three miles and a half
from the schoolhouse, and walked the way forth and back every day.
He came up shivering and studying, performing both of these apparently inconsistent operations with great violence.

"Halloo, Brinkly!" shouted half a dozen boys, "got in in time this
morning, eh? Good. You are safe for to-day on that score, old fellow."

"Why, Brinkly, my boy, you are entire*lee too* soon. He won't be here for a quarter of a hour yit. Come and help us out with the bull-pen. Now only jist look at him. Got that eternal jography, and actilly studyin' when he is nigh and in and about friz. Put the book down, Brinkly Glisson, and go and warm yourself a bit, and come and take Bill Jones' place. It's his day to make the fire. Come along, we've got the Quses."

These words were addressed to him by the 'one exception' before alluded to, a large, well grown, square-shouldered bóy, eighteen years old, named Allen Thigpen. Allen was universally envied in the school, partly because he had once upon a time been to Augusta, and knew, or was supposed to know, all the wonders of that great city, and partly because he could go to Dukesborough whenever he pleased, and above all, because he was not afraid of Mr. Israel Meadows. But it was the boast of Allen Thigpen that he had *yit* to see the man that he was afraid of.

Brinkly paid no attention to Allen's invitation, but came on up shivering and studying, and studying and shivering.· Just as he passed Allen, he was mumbling — "A-an em-em-pire is a co-untry go-overned by a-an em-per-or."

Now ordinarily, the announcement of this proposition would be incapable of exciting any uncommon amount of risibility. It contains a simple truth expressed in simple language. Yet so it was that Mr. Allen burst into a roar of laughter; and as if he understood that the proposition had been submitted to him for ratification or denial, answered, "Well, Brinkly, supposin' it is. Who in the dickence said it weren't? Did you, Sam?"

"Did I do what?" answered Sam Pate in the act of throwing the ball.

"Did you say that a empire weren't — what Brinkly said it was?"

"I didn't hear what Brinkly said it was, and I don't know nothin' about it, and I haint said nothin' about it and I don't keer nothin' about it." And away went the ball. But Sam had thrown too suddenly after looking toward the mouth of Mr. Meadows' path, and he missed his man.

Brinkly scarcely noticed the interruption, but walked to and fro, and studied and shivered. He bowed to the book; he dug into it. He grated his teeth, not in anger, but in his fierce desire to get what was in it. He tried to fasten it in his brain whether or not by slightly

changing the hard words, and making them as it were his own to command.

"An yem-pire," said he fiercely, but not over loudly, "is a ke-untry-
ge-uvend by a ye-emperor."

"And what is a ye-emperor, Brinkly?" asked Allen.

"Oh Allen, Allen, please go away from me! I almost had it when
you bothered me. You know Mr. Meadows will beat me if I don't
get it, because you know he loves to beat me. Do let me alone. It
it just beginning to come to me now." And he went on shivering and
studying, and shiveringly announcing among other things that "an
yem-pire was a ke-untry ge-uverned by an ye-emperor," emphasizing
every one of the polysyllables in its turn : sometimes stating the
proposition very cautiously, and rather interrogatively, as if half inclined to doubt it; at others, asserting it with a vehemence which
showed that it was at last his settled conviction that it was true, and
that he ought to be satisfied and even thankful.

"Poor fellow," muttered Allen, stopping from his ball-play, and looking towards Brinkly as the latter moved on. "That boy don't know
hisself; and what's more, Iserl Meadows don't." Allen then walked
to where a rosy-cheeked little fellow of eight or nine years was sitting
on a stump with a spelling-book in his lap and a pin in his right hand
with which he dotted every fourth word, after reciting the following :

"Betsy Wiggins; Heneritter Bangs; Mandy Grizzle; Mine!"
(Dot).——"Betsy Wiggins; Heneritter Bangs; Mandy Grizzle;
Mine!" (Dot).

"I-yi, my little Mr. Asa," said Allen, "and supposin' that Betsy Wiggins misses her word, or Heneritter Bangs hern, or Mandy Grizzle hern,
then who's goin' to spell *them*, I want to know? And what'll you give
me?" continued Allen, placing his rough hand with ironical fondness
upon the child's head, "what'll you give me not to tell Mr. Meadows
that you've been gitting your own words?"

"Oh, Allen, please, please don't!"

"What'll you give me, I tell you?"

"Twenty chestnuts!" and the little fellow dived into his pockets and
counted twenty into Allen's hand.

"Got any more?" Allen asked, cracking one with his teeth.

"Oh, Allen, Allen, will you take all? Please don't take all!"

"Out with 'em, you little word-gitter. Out with the last one of 'em.
A boy that gits his own words in that kind o' style aint liable, and
oughtn't to *be* liable to eat chestnuts."

Asa disgorged to the last. Allen ate one or two, looking quizzically into his face, and then handed the rest back to him.

" Take your chestnuts, Asa Boatright, and eat 'em, that is if you've got the stomach to eat 'em. If I ever live to git to be as afeard of a human as you and Abel Kitchens and Brinkly Glisson are afeard of Iserl Meadows, drat my hide if I don't believe I would commit sooicide on myself — yes, on myself, by cuttin' my own throat ! "

" Yes," replied Asa Boatright, " you can talk so because you are a big boy, and you know he is afraid of you. If you was as little as me, you would be as afraid as me. If I ever get a man —— " The little fellow, however, checked himself, took his pin again, and mumbling,

" Betsy Wiggins ; Heneritter Bangs ; Mandy Grizzle ; MINE ! " — resumed his interesting and ingenious occupation of dotting every fourth word.

Brinkly had overheard Allen's taunt. Closing his book after a moment's pause, he walked straight to him and said :

" Allen Thigpen, I am no more afraid of him than you are ; nor than I am of you. Do you think that's what makes me stand what I do? If you do, you are much mistaken. Allen, I'm trying all the time to keep down on mother's account. I've told her of some of his treatment, but not all ; and she gets to crying, and says this is my only chance for an education, and it does seem like it would break her heart if I was to lose it, that I have been trying to get the lessons, and to keep from fighting him when he beats me. And I believe I would get 'em if I had a chance. But the fact is, I can't read well enough to study the jography, and my 'pinion is he put me in it too soon just to get the extra price for jography. And I can't get it, and I haven't learnt anything since I have been put in it, — and I am not going to stand it much longer ;— and, Allen Thigpen, I'm not going to pay you chestnuts nor nothing else not to tell him I said so neither."

" Hooraw ! " shouted Allen. " Give me your hand, Brinkly." Then continuing in a lower tone, he said, " By jingo ! I thought it was in you. I seen you many a time, when, says I to myself, it wouldn't take much to make Brinkly Glisson fight you, old fellow, or leastways try it. You've stood enough already, Brinkly Glisson, and too much too. My blood has biled many a time when he' been a beatin' you. I tell you, don't you stand it no longer. Ef he beats you again, pitch into him. Try to ride him from the ingoin'. He can maul you, I expect, but — look at this," and Allen raised his fist about the size of a mallet.

Brinkly looked at the big fist and brawny arm, and smiled dismally. " Books ! " shouted a shrill voice, and Mr. Israel Meadows emerged from the thicket with a handful of hickory switches. In an instant, there was a rushing of boys and girls into the house — all except Allen, who took his time. Asa Boatright was the last of the others to get in. He had changed his position from the stump, and was walking, book in hand, apparently all absorbed in its contents, though his eye was on the schoolmaster, whose notice he was endeavoring to attract. He bowed, and digged, and dived, until, just as the master drew near, he weariedly looked up, and seeing him unexpectedly, gave one more profound dive into the book and darted into the schoolhouse.

It was a rule at the Goosepond, that the scholars should all be at their seats when Mr. Meadows arrived. His wont was to shout '*Books*' from the mouth of the path, then to walk with great rapidity to the house. Woe to the boy or girl who was ever too late, unless it happened to be Allen Thigpen. He had been heard to say, " Ding any sich rule, and he wasn't goin' to break his neck for Iserl Meadows nor nobody else." If he got in behind the master, which often happened, that gentlemen was kind enough not to notice it, — an illustration of an exception to the good discipline of country schoolmasters which was quite common in the times in which Mr. Meadows lived and flourished. On this occasion, when Mr. Meadows saw Allen, calculating that the gait at which himself was walking would take him into the house first, he halted a little, and stooped, and, having untied one of his shoe strings, tied it again. While this operation was going on, Allen went in. Mr. Meadows, rising immediately, struck into a brisk walk, almost a run, as if to apologise for his delay, and then entered into the scene of his daily triumphs.

But before we begin the day's work, let us inquire who this Mr. Meadows was, and whence he came.

CHAPTER III.

Mr. Israel Meadows was a man thirty-five or forty years of age, five feet ten inches in height, with a lean figure, dark complexion, very black and shaggy hair and eyebrows, and a grim and forbidding expression of countenance. The occupation of training the youthful mind and leading it to the fountains of wisdom, as delightful and interesting as it is, was not in fact Mr. Meadows' choice, when, on arriving at manhood's estate, he looked around him for a career in which he might the most surely develop and advance his being in this life. Indeed, those who had been the witnesses of his youth and young manhood, and of the opportunities which he had been favored withal for getting instruction for himself, were no little surprised when they heard that in the county of——, their old acquaintance had undertaken, and was in the actual prosecution of the profession of a schoolmaster. About a couple of days' journey from the Goosepond, was the spot which had the honor of giving him birth. In a cottage on one of the roads leading to the city of Augusta, there had lived a couple who cultivated a farm, and traded with the wagoners of those days by bartering, for money and groceries, corn, fodder, potatoes, and suchlike commodities. It was a matter never fully accountable, how it was that Mr. Timothy Meadows, during all seasons, had corn to sell. Drought or drench affected his crib alike — that is, neither did affect it at all. When a wagoner wished to buy corn, Timothy Meadows generally, if not always, had a little to spare. People used to intimate sometimes that it was mighty curious that some folks could always have corn to sell, while other folks couldn't. Such observations were made in reference to no individual in particular ; but were generally made by one farmer to another, when, perchance, they had just ridden by Mr. Meadows' house while a wagoner's team was feeding at his camp. To this respectable couple there had been born only one offspring, a daughter. Miss Clary Meadows had lived to the age of twenty-four, and had never, within the knowledge of any of the neighbors, had the first beau. If to the fact that her father's always having corn to sell, without his neighbors knowing exactly how he came by it, had to a considerable extent discouraged visiting between their families and his (though it must be owned that this was not the fault of the Meadowses, who had repeatedly, in spite of their superior fortune, shown dispositions to cultivate good neighborhood with all the families around)—if to this fact be added the further one, that Miss Clary was bony, and in no respect possessed of charms likely to captivate a young gentleman who had thoughts upon marriage, it ought not to be very surprising that she had, thus far, failed to secure a husband. Nevertheless, Miss Meadows was eminently affable when in the society of such gentlemen of the wagoners who paid her the compliment to call upon her in the house. So that

2

no person, however suspicious, would have concluded from her manner
on such occasions that her prolonged state of single blessedness was
owing to any prejudice to the opposite sex.

Time, however, brings roses, as the German proverb has it, and to the
Meadows family he at last brought a rose-bud in the shape of a thriving
grandson.   As it does not become us to pry into delicate family matters,
we will not presume to lift the veil which the persons most concerned
chose to throw over the earlier part of this grandson's history ; suffice
it to say that the same mystery hung about it as about the inexplicable inexhaustibility of Timothy Meadows' corn crib, and that the
latter — from motives, doubtless, which did him honor — bestowed
upon the new-comer his own family name, preceded by the patriarchal
appellation of Israel.

There were many interesting occurrences in the early life of Israel
which it would be foreign to the purposes of this history to relate.   It
is enough to say that he grew up under the eye and training of his
grandfather, and soon showed that some of the traits of that gentleman's
character were in no danger of being lost to society by a failure of
reproduction.

In process of time, Mr. and Mrs. Meadows were gathered to their
fathers, and Miss Clary had become the proprietress of the cottage
and the farm.   Israel had the luck of the Meadowses to be always able
to sell corn to the wagoners.   But unluckily, the secret which lay hidden in such profundity during the lifetime of his grandfather, of how
this wonderful faculty existed, transpired about six months previously
to the period when he was introduced to the reader — a circumstance
which would induce one to suspect, in spite of the declaration of the
law in such case made and provided, that there was something in the
blood of Israel which was not all Meadows.

One Saturday night, a company of the neighbors on patrol found a
negro man issuing from the gate of Miss Meadows' yard with an empty
meal bag.   Having apprehended him, they had given him not more
than a dozen stripes with a cowhide before he confessed that he had
just carried the bag full of corn to Israel from his master's corn crib.
The company immediately aroused the latter gentleman, informed him
what the slave had confessed, and although he did most stoutly deny
any and all manner of connection with the matter, they informed him
that they should not leave the premises until they could get a search-
warrant from a neighboring magistrate, by which, as their spokesman, a

shrewd man, said, they could identify the corn. This was a ruse to bring him to terms. Seeing his uneasiness, they pushed on, and in a careless manner proposed that if he would leave the neighborhood by the next Monday morning, they would forbear to prosecute him for this as well as many similar offences, his guilt of which they intimated they had abundant proof to establish. Israel was caught; he reflected for a few moments, and then, still, however, asserting his innocence, but declaring that he did not wish to reside in a community where he was suspected of crime, he expressed his resolution to comply with their demand. He left the next day. Leaving his mother, he set out to try his fortune elsewhere, intending by the time that the homestead could be disposed of, he would remove with her to the West. But determining not to be idle in the meantime, after wandering about for several days in search of employment, it suddenly occurred to him one night, after a day's travel, that he would endeavor to get a school for the remainder of the year.

Now, Israel's education had been somewhat neglected. Indeed, he had never been to school a day in his whole life. But he had at home, under the tuition of his mother, been taught reading and writing, and his grandfather had imparted to him some knowledge of arithmetic.

But Mr. Israel Meadows, although not a man of great learning, was a great way removed from being a fool. He had a considerable amount of the wisdom of this world which comes to a man from other sources besides books. He was like many other men in one respect. He was not to be restrained from taking office by the consciousness of parts inadequate to the discharge of its duties. This is a species of delicacy which, of all others, is attended by fewest practical results. Generally, the most it does is to make its owner confess with modesty his unfitness for the office, with a 'he had hoped some worthier and better man had been chosen,' and then — take it. Israel wisely reflected, that with a majority of mankind the only thing necessary to establish for oneself a reputation of fitness for office is to run for it and get into it. A wise reflection indeed ; acting on which, many men have become great in Georgia, and, I doubt not, elsewhere, with no other capital than the adroitness or the accident which placed them in office. He reflected further, and as wisely as before, that the office of a schoolmaster in a country school was as little likely as any he could think of to furnish an exception to the general rule. Thus, in less than six weeks from the eventful Saturday night, with a list of school articles which he had picked up in his travels, he had applied for, and had obtained, and had opened the Goosepond school, and was professing to teach the children spelling, reading, and writing, at the rate of a dollar a month; and arithmetic and geography at the advanced rate of a dollar and a half.

Such were some of Mr. Meadows' antecedents.

CHAPTER IV.

IT was the custom of the pupils in the Goosepond, as in most of the other country schools of those times, to study aloud. Whether the teachers thought that the mind could not act unless the tongue was a-going, or that the tongue a-going was the only evidence that the mind was acting, it never did appear. Such had been the custom, and Mr. Meadows did not aspire to be an innovator. It was his rule, however, that there should be perfect silence on his arrival, in order to give him an opportunity of saying or doing anything he might wish. This morning there did not seem to be anything on his mind which required to be lifted off. He, however, looked at Brinkly Glisson with some disappointment of expression. He had beaten him unmercifully the morning before for not having gotten there in time, though the boy's excuse was that he had gone a mile out of his way on an errand for his mother. He looked at him as if he had expected to have had some business with him, which now unexpectedly had to be postponed. He then looked around over the school and said:

"Go to studyin'."

It was plain that in that house Mr. Meadows had been in the habit of speaking but to command, and of commanding but to be obeyed. Instantaneously was heard, then and there, that unintelligible tumult, the almost invariable incident of the country schools of that generation. There were spellers and readers, geographers and arithmeticians, all engaged in their several pursuits, in the most inexplicable confusion. Sometimes the spellers would have the heels of the others, and sometimes the readers. The geographers were always third, and the arithmeticians always behind. It was very plain to be seen that these last never would catch the others. The faster they added or subtracted, the oftener they had to rub out and commence anew. It

was always but a short time before they found this to be the case, and
so they generally concluded to adopt the maxim of the philosopher, of
being slow in making haste. The geographers were a little faster and
a little louder. But the spellers and readers had it, I tell you. Each
speller and each reader went through the whole gamut of sounds, from
low up to high, and from high down to low again ; sometimes by regular ascension and descension, one note at a time, sounding what musicians call the diatonic intervals ; at other times, going up and coming
down upon the perfect fifths only. Oh ! it was so refreshing to see the
passionate eagerness which these urchins manifested for the acquisition of knowledge. To have sliced out about five seconds of that
studying, and put the words together, would have made a sentence
somewhat like the following :

"C-d-e twice e-an c-three r-ding-i-two l-v-old. My seven vill times
a-de-l-cru-i-l coin-g-f-is man o-six-h-nin-four ni-h-eight cat p-c-a-t-r ten
e-light is ca-light i-light x tween-by-tions fix de-a-bisel-cru-fa-cor-a-light-
bisel-rapt-double-fe-good ty-light man cra-forn-ner-ci-spress-fix-Oh ! ! ! "

To have heard them for the first time, one would have been reminded of the Apostles' preaching at Pentecost, and it might not have been
difficult to persuade a stranger, unused to such things, that there were
then and there spoken the languages of the Parthians and Medes,
Elamites and the dwellers in Mesopotamia, and in Judea and Cappa-
docia ; in Pontus and Asia ; Phrygia and Pamphylia ; in Egypt and
in the parts of Syria about Cyrene ; and strangers of Rome, Jews and
Proselytes, Cretes and Arabians. Sometimes these cloven tongues
would subside a little, when it might be half a dozen would stop to
blow ; but in a moment more, the chorus would swell again in a new
and livelier *accrescendo.* — When this process had gone on for half an
hour, Mr. Meadows lifted up his voice and shouted " Silence ! " and all
was still.

Now were to commence the recitations, during which perfect silence
was required. For as great a help to study as this jargon was, Mr.
Meadows found that it did not contribute any aid to the doing of *his*
work.

He now performed a feat which he had never performed before in
exactly that manner. He put his hand behind the lappel of his coat-
collar for a moment, and then, after withdrawing it and holding it up, his
thumb and forefinger joined together, he said :

"There is too much fuss here. I'm going to drop this pin, and I shall whip every single one of you little boys that don't hear it when it falls. Thar!"

"I heerd it, Mr. Meadows! I heerd it, Mr. Meadows!" exclaimed simultaneously, five or six little fellows.

"Come up here, you little rascals. You are a liar!" said he to each one. "I never drapped it; I never had nary one to drap. It just shows what liars you are. Set down and wait a while, I'll show you how to tell *me* lies."

The little liars slunk to their seats, and the recitations commenced. Memory was the only faculty of mind that underwent the smallest development at this school. Whoever could say exactly what the book said was adjudged to know his lesson. About half of the pupils on this morning were successful. The other half were found to be delinquent. Among these was Asa Boatright's class. That calculating young gentleman knew *his* words and felt safe. The class had spelled around three or four times, when lo! the contingency which Allen Thigpen had suggested did come to pass. Betsy Wiggins missed her word; Heneritter Bangs (in the language of Allen) hern, and Mandy Grizzle hern; and thus responsibilities were suddenly cast upon Asa which he was wholly unprepared to meet, and which, from the look of mighty reproach which he gave each of these young ladies as she handed over to him her word, he evidently thought it the height of injustice that he should have been called upon to meet. Mr. Meadows closing the book, tossed it to Asa, who, catching it as it was falling at his feet, turned, and his eyes swimming with tears, went back to his seat. As he passed Allen Thigpen, the latter whispered:

"What did I tell you? You heerd the pin drap too!"

Now, Allen was in no plight to have given this taunt to Asa. He had not given five minutes' study to his arithmetic during the whole morning. But Mr. Meadows made a rule (this one with himself, though all the pupils knew it better than any rule he had), never to allow Allen to miss a lesson; and as he had kindly taken this responsibility upon himself, Allen was wont to give himself no trouble about the matter.

Brinkly Glisson was the last to recite. Brinkly was no great hand at pronunciation. He had been reading but a short time when Mr. Meadows advanced him into geography, with the purpose, as Brinkly afterwards came to believe, of getting the half dollar extra tuition. This morning he thought he knew his lesson; and he did, as he understood it. When called to recite, he went up with a countenance expressive of mild happiness, handed the book to Mr. Meadows, and putting his hands in his pockets, awaited the questions. And now it was an interesting sight to see Mr. Meadows smile as Brinkly talked of is-lands and promonitaries, thismuses and hemispheries. The lad misunderstood that smile, and his heart was glad for the unexpected reception of a little complacency from the master. But he was not long in error.

"Is-lands, eh? Thismuses, eh? Take this book and see if you can find any is-lands and promonitaries, and then bring them to me. I want to see them things, I do. Find 'em if you please."

Brinkly took the book, and it would have melted the heart of any other man than Israel Meadows to have seen the deep despair of his heart as he looked on it and was spelling over to himself the words as he came to them.

"Mr. Meadows," he said, in pleading tones, "I thought it was is-land. Here it is, Is-l-a-n-d-land : is-land ;" and he looked into his face beseechingly.

"Is-land, eh? *Is-land!* Now, thismuses and promonitaries and hemispheries —"

"Mr. Meadows, I did not know how to pronounce them words. I asked you how to pronounce 'em, and you wouldn't tell me ; and I asked Allen, and he told me the way I said them."

"I believe that to be a lie."

Brinkly's face reddened, and his breathing was fast and hard. He looked at the master as but once or twice before during the term he had looked at him, but made no answer. At that moment Allen leaned carelessly on his desk, his elbows resting on it, and his chin on his hands, and said, dryly :

"Yes, I did tell him so."

Mr. Meadows now reddened a little. After a moment's pause, however, he said :

"How often have I got to tell you not to ask anybody but me how to pronounce words? That'll do, sir ; sit down, sir."

Brinkly went to his seat, and looking gloomily towards the door a minute or two, he opened his book, but studied it no more.

CHAPTER V.

MR. MEADOWS now set about what was the only agreeable portion of the duties of his new vocation, the punishment of offenders. The lawyers tell us that, of all the departments of the law, the *vindicatory* is the most important. This element of the Goosepond establishment had been cultivated so much that it had grown to become almost the only one that was consulted at all. As for the *declaratory* and the *directory*, they seemed to be considered, when clearly understood, as impediments to a fair showing and proper development of the vindicatory, insomuch that the last was often by their means disappointed of its victim. Sometimes, when his urchins would not "miss," or violate some of his numerous laws, Mr. Meadows used, in the plenitude of his power, to put the vindicatory first — punish an offender, and then *declare* what the latter had done to be an offence, and then *direct* him that he had better not do so any more. This Mr. Meadows seemed to owe a grudge to society. Whether this was because society had not given him a father as it had done to almost everybody else, or because it had interfered in the peaceful occupation which he had inherited from his grandfather (as if to avenge itself on him for violating one of its express commands that such as he should inherit from nobody),— did not appear. But he owed it, and he delighted in paying it off in his peculiar way ; this was by beating the children of his school, every one of whom had a father. Eminently combative by nature, it was both safest and most satisfactory to wage his warfare on this general scale. So, on this fine morning, by way of taking up another instalment of this immense debt, which like most other debts seemed as if it never would get fully paid, he took down his bundle of rods from two pegs in one of the logs on which he had placed them, selected one fit for his purpose, and taking his position in the middle of the space between the fireplace and the rows of desks, he sat down in his chair. A cheerful, but by no means a gladsome smile overspread his countenance as he said :

"Them spellin' classes and readin' classes, and them others that's got to be whipped, all but Sam Pate and Asa Boatright, come to the circus."

Five or six boys and as many girls, from eight to thirteen years old, came up, and sitting down on the front bench which extended all along

the length of the two rows of desks, pulled off their shoes and stockings. The boys then rolled up their pants, and the girls lifted the
skirts of their frocks to their knees, and having made a ring around
Mr. Meadows as he sat in his chair, all began a brisk trot. They had
described two or three revolutions, and Mr. Meadows was straightening
his switch, when Asa Boatright ran up, and, crying piteously, said:
"Please sir, Mr. Meadows — oh pray do sir, Mr. Meadows — let me
go into the circus!"

Mr. Meadows rose up and was about to strike; but another thought
seemed to occur to him. He looked at him amusedly for a moment,
and pointed to his seat. Asa took it. Mr. Meadows resumed his chair,
and went into the exciting part of the exhibition by tapping the legs,
both male and female, as they trotted around him. This was done at
first very gently, and almost lovingly. But as the sport warmed in interest, the blows increased in rapidity and violence. The children began to cry out, and then Mr. Meadows struck the harder; for it was a
rule (oh he was a mighty man for rules, this same Mr. Meadows) that
whoever cried the loudest should be hit the hardest. He kept up this
interesting exercise until he had given them about twenty-five lashes
apiece. He then ceased. They stopped instantly, walked around him
once, then seating themselves upon the bench they resumed their shoes
and stockings, and went to their seats. One girl, thirteen years old,
Henrietta Bangs, had begged him to let her keep on her stockings;
but Mr. Meadows was too firm a disciplinarian to allow it. When
the circus was over she put on her shoes, and taking up her stockings
and putting them under her apron, she went to her seat and sobbed as
if her heart was broken.

Allen Thigpen looked at her for a moment, and then he turned his
eyes slowly around and looked at Brinkly Glisson. The latter did not
notice him. He sat with his hands in his pockets and his lips com-
pressed. Allen knew what struggle was going on, but he could not tell
how it was going to end. Mr. Meadows rested three minutes.

It has possibly occurred to those who may be reading this little history that it was a strange thing in Asa Boatright, who so well knew all
the ways of Mr. Meadows, that he should have expressed so decisive a
wish to take part in this last described exhibition,— an exhibition
which, however entertaining to Mr. Meadows as it doubtless was, and
might be perchance to other persons placed in the attitude of specta-
tors merely, could not be in the highest degree agreeable to one in the

3

attitude which Master Asa must have foreseen that he would be made to assume had Mr. Meadows vouchsafed to yield to his request. But Asa Boatright was not a fool, nor was he a person who had no care for his physical wellbeing. In other words, Asa Boatright knew what he was about.

"Sam Pate and Asa Boatright!" exclaimed Mr. Meadows, after his rest. "Come out here and go to horsin'."

The two nags came out. Master Pate playfully inclined himself forward, and Master Boatright leaped with some agility upon his back. The former, gathering the latter's legs under his arms, and drawing as tightly as possible his pants across his middle, began galloping gaily around the area before the fireplace. Mr. Meadows, after taking a fresh hickory, began to apply it with great force and precision to that part of Master Boatright's little body which, in his present attitude, was most exposed. Every application of this kind caused that young gentleman to scream to the utmost of the strength of his voice, and even to make spasmodic efforts to kick, which Master Pate, being for the occasion a horse, was to understand as an expression on the part of his rider that he should get on faster, and so Master Pate must frisk and prance and otherwise imitate a horse as well as possible in the circumstances. Now, the circumstances being that as soon as Master Boatright should have ridden long enough to become incapacitated from riding a real horse with comfort, they were to reverse positions, Master Boatright becoming horse and himself rider, they were hardly sufficient to make him entirely forget his identity in the personation of that quadruped. He did his best, though, in the circumstances, such as they were, and not only frisked and pranced but actually neighed several times. When Asa was placed in the condition hinted at above, he was allowed to dismount. Sam having mounted on his back, it was truly stirring to the feelings to see the latter kick and the former prance. This was always the best part of the show. A rule of this exercise was that, when the rider should dismount and become horse, he was to act well his part or be made to resume the part of rider,—a prospect not at all agreeable, each one decidedly preferring to be horse. Sam was about three years older and fifteen pounds heavier than Asa. Now, while Asa had every motive which as sensible a horse as he was could have to do his best, yet he was so sore, and Sam, with the early prospect of butting his brains out, was so heavy, that he had great difficulties. He exhibited the most laudable desire and made the most faithful efforts to prance, but he could not keep his feet. Finding that he could do no great things at prancing, he endeavored to make up by neighing. When Sam would cry out and kick, Asa would neigh. He would occasionally run against the wall and neigh as if he was perfectly delighted. He would lift up one foot and neigh. He would put it down, lift up the other and neigh. Then when he would attempt to lift up both feet at once, he would fall down and neigh. But he would neigh even in the act of rising, apparently resolved to convince the world that, notwithstanding appearances to the contrary, he was as real and as plucky a little horse as had ever trotted. Never before had Asa acted his part so well in the Horsin' at the Goosepond. Never had horse, with such odds on his back, neighed so lustily. Sam screamed and kicked. Asa pranced and neighed, until at last, as he stumbled violently against the bench, Sam let go his hold upon Asa's neck, in order to avoid breaking his own, and fell sprawling on his belly under a desk. This sudden removal of the burden from Asa's back made his efforts to recover from his false step successful beyond all calculation, and he fell backward, headforemost, upon the floor. Mr. Meadows, contrary to his wont, roared with laughter. His soul was satisfied; he dropped his switch, and ordered them to their seats. They obeyed, and sat down with that graduated declension of body in which experience had taught them to be prudent.

CHAPTER VI.

AFTER the close of the last performance, Mr. Meadows seemed to need another resting spell. This lasted five minutes. He always liked to be as fresh as possible for the next scene. The most interesting, the most exciting, and in some respects the most delightful exercise was yet to follow. This was the punishment of Brinkly Glisson. It was curious to see how he did enjoy it. He was never so agreeable at play-time or in the afternoon as when he had beaten Brinkly in the morning. If he recited well, and there was no pretext for beating him, Mr. Meadows was sadder and gloomier than usual for the remainder of the day, and looked as if he felt that he had been wronged with impunity.

Now, Brinkly was one of the best boys in the world. He was the only son of a poor widow, who, at much sacrifice, had sent him to

school. He had pitched and tended the crop of a few acres around
the house, and she had procured the promise of a neighbor to help her
in gathering it when ripe. Brinkly was the apple of her eye, the idol
of her heart. He was to her as we always think of him of whom it
was said, 'He was the only son of his mother, and she was a widow.'
And Brinkly had rewarded her love and care with all the feelings of
his honest and affectionate heart. He was more anxious to learn for
her sake than his own. He soon came to read tolerably well, and was
advanced to geography. How proud was the widow when she bought
the new geography and atlas with the proceeds of four pairs of socks
which (sweet labor of love!) she had knit with her own hands. What
a world of knowledge she thought there must be in a book with five
times as many pages as a spelling-book, and in those great red, blue,
and pink pictures, covering a whole page a foot square, and all this
knowledge to become the property of Brinkly! But Brinkly soon found
that geography was above his present capacity, and so told Mr. Meadows.
That gentleman received the communication with displeasure; said that
what was the matter with him was laziness, and that laziness, of all the
qualities which a boy had, was the one which he knew best what to do
with. He then took to beating him. Brinkly, after the first beating,
which was a light one, went home and told his mother of it, and intimated his intention not to take another. The widow was sorely dis-
tressed, and knew not what to do. On the one hand was her grief to
know her son was unjustly beaten, and his spirit cowed; for she knew
that he studied all the time he had, and though uneducated herself, she
was not like many other parents of her day who thought that the best
means to develop the mind was to beat the body. But on the other
hand would be the disappointment of his getting an education if he
should leave the school, there being then no other in the neighborhood. This, thought the poor woman, was the worse horn of the
dilemma; and so she wept, and begged him, as he loved her, to submit to Mr. Meadows. He should have the more time for study; she
would chop the wood and feed the stock; he should have all the time
at home to himself; he could get it, she knew he could; it would
come to him after a while.

Brinkly yielded; but how many a hard struggle he made to continue
that submission, no one knew but he, — not even his mother, for he
concealed from her as much as he could the treatment which he had
received and the suffering which he had endured. Mr. Meadows could

see this struggle sometimes. He knew that the boy was not afraid of him. He saw it in his eye every time he beat him, and it was this which afforded him such a satisfaction to beat him. He wished to subdue him, and he had not succeeded. Brinkly would never beg nor weep. Mr. Meadows often thought he was on the point of resisting him ; but he knew the reason why he did not, and while he hated him for it, he trusted that it would last. Yet he often doubted whether it would or not ; and thus the matter became so intensely exciting that he continually sought for opportunities of bringing it up. He loved to tempt him. He had no doubt but that he could easily manage him in an even combat ; but he did not wish it to come to that. He only gloried in goading him almost to resistance, and then seeing him yield.

Have we not all seen how the showman adapts himself to the different animals of the menagerie? How quickly and sharply he speaks to the lesser animals who jump over his hand and back, and over and back again, and then crouch in submission as he passes by ! But when he goes to the lion, you can scarcely hear his low tones as he commands him to use and perform his part, and is not certain whether the king of the beasts will do as he is bidden or not. Doubts like these were in the mind of Mr. Meadows when he was about to set upon Brinkly Glisson ; but the greater these doubts, the more he enjoyed the trial. After a short rest from the fatigues of the last exercise, during which he curiously and seriously eyed the lad, he rose from his seat, paced slowly across the room once or twice, and taking a hickory switch, the longest of all he had, he stopped in the middle of the floor, and in a low, quiet tone, said :

" Brinkly Glisson, come."

Allen had been eyeing Brinkly all the time since the close of the circus. He saw the conflict which was going on in his soul, and when Mr. Meadows had burst into the paroxysm of laughter at the untoward ending of the ' horsin',' he thought he saw that the conflict was ended.

Slowly and calmly Brinkly rose from his seat, and walked up and stood before Mr. Meadows.

" Why, hi ! " thought Allen.

" Off with your coat, sir," — low and gentle, and with a countenance almost smiling. Brinkly stood motionless. But he had done so once or twice before, in similar circumstances, and at length yielded. " Off with it, sir," — louder and not so gentle. No motion on Brinkly's part, not even in his eyes, which looked steadily into the master's, with a meaning which he nearly, but not quite understood.

" Aint you going to pull off that coat, sir?"
" What for?" asked Brinkly.
" What for, sir?"
" Yes, sir; what for?"
" Because I am going to give you this hickory, you impudent scoun-
drel ; and if you don't pull it off this minute, I'll give you sich a beatin'
as'll make you feel like you never was whipped before since you was
born.   Aint you going to pull it off, sir?"
" Not now, sir."
Allen wriggled on his seat, and his face shone as the full moon.   Mr.
Meadows retreated a step, and holding his switch two feet from the
larger end, he raised that end to strike.
" Stop one minute, if you please."
Mr. Meadows lowered his arm, and his face smiled a triumph.   This
was the first time Brinkly had ever begged.   He chuckled.   Allen
looked disappointed.
" Stop, eh?   I yi!   This end looks heavy, does it?   Well, I wouldn't
be surprised if it warn't sorter heavy.   Will you pull off your coat now,
sir?"
" Mr. Meadows, I asked you to stop because I wanted to say a few
words to you.   You have beat me and beat me, worse than you ought
to beat a dog," (Allen's face getting right again); " and God in heaven
knows that, in the time that I have come to school to you, I have tried
as hard as a boy ever did to please you and get my lessons.   I can't
understand that geography, and I aint been reading long enough to
understand it.   I have asked you to let me quit.   Mother has asked
you.   You wouldn't do it; but beat me, and beat me, and beat me,"
(there is no telling whether Allen wants to laugh or to cry), " and now,
the more I study it, the more I don't understand it.   I would have quit
school long ago, but mother was so anxious for me to learn, and made
me come.   And now I have took off my coat to you the last time."
(Ah! now there is a great tear in Allen's eye.)   " Listen to me," (as
the teacher's hand makes a slight motion); " don't strike me.   I know
I'm not learning anything, and your beating aint going to make me
learn any faster.   If you are determined to keep me in this geography,
and to beat me, just say so, and I'll take my hat and books and go
home.   I'd like to not come to-day, but I thought I knew my lesson.
Now, I say again, don't, for God's sake, don't strike me."   And he
raised up both his hands, pale and trembling.

It would be impossible to describe the surprise and rage expressed on the face of Mr. Meadows during the delivery and at the close of this little harangue. He looked at the boy a moment. His countenance expressed the deepest sadness; but there was nothing in it like defiance or threatening. It was simply sad and beseeching. The master hesitated, and looked around upon his school. It would not do to retreat now, he thought. With an imprecation, he raised his switch and struck with all his might.

"My God!" cried the boy; but in an instant sadness and beseeching passed from his face. The long pent-up resentment of his soul gushed forth, and the fury of a demon glared from his eyes. He was preparing to spring upon Mr. Meadows, when the latter, by a sudden rush, caught him and thrust him backward over the front bench. They both tumbled on the floor, between the rows of desks, Mr. Meadows uppermost.

"It's come," said Allen, quietly, as he rose and looked down upon the combatants.

Mr. Meadows attempted to disengage himself and rise; but Brinkly would rise with him. After several attempts at this, Brinkly managed to get upon one knee, and by a violent jerk to bring Mr. Meadows down upon the floor, where they were, in the phraseology of the wrestling ring, cross and pile. Mr. Meadows shouted to two or three of the boys to hold Brinkly until he could rise. They rose to obey, but Allen, without saying a word, put out his hand before them, and motioning them to their seats, they resumed them. And now the contest set in for good, Mr. Meadows struggling to recover his advantage, and Brinkly to improve what he had gained. The former's right arm was thrown across the latter's neck, his right hand wound in and pulling violently his hair, while his left hand pressed against his breast. Brinkly's left leg was across Mr. Meadows' middle, and with his right against a stationary desk, his right arm bent and lying under him like a lizard's, and his left in Mr. Meadows' shirt-collar, he struggled to get uppermost; but whenever he attempted to raise his head, that hand wound in his hair would instantly bring it back to the floor. When Mr. Meadows would attempt to disengage himself from underneath Brinkly's leg, that member, assisted by its brother from the desk, against which it was pressed, held it like the boa holds the bullock. Oh, Mr. Meadows, Mr. Meadows! you don't know the boy that grapples with you. You have never known anything at all about him, Mr. Meadows. You blow, Mr. Meadows! See! Brinkly blows not half so hard. Remember, you walk a mile to and from the school, and Brinkly seven, often running the first half. Besides, there is something in Brinkly's soul which will not let him tire. The remembrance of long continued wrongs, which cannot longer be borne ; the long subdued but now inextinguishable desire of revenge ; every hostile feeling but fear — all these are now dominant in that simple heart, and they have made of him a man, and if you hope to conquer you must fight as you never have fought before, and never may have to fight again.

Your right hand pulls less vigorously at the hair of Brinkly's ascending head. Look there ! Brinkly's leg has moved an inch further across you ! Wring and twist, Mr. Meadows, for right under that leg, if anywhere for you, is now the post of honor. Can't you draw out your left leg, and plant it against the desk behind you, as Brinkly does with his right. Alas ! no. Brinkly has now made a hook of *his* left, and his heel is pressing close into the cavity behind your knee. Ah ! that was an unlucky move for you then, Mr. Meadows, when you let Brinkly's hair go, and thrust both of your hands at his eyes. You must have done that in a passion. But you are raking him some now, that is certain. But see there, now ! he has released his grasp at your shirt-collar, and thrown his left arm over you. Good morning to you now, Mr. Meadows !

. In the instant that Mr. Meadows had released his hold upon his hair, Brinkly, though he was being gouged terribly, released his hold upon his collar, threw his arm over his neck, and pushing with all his might with his right leg against the desk, and making a corresponding pull with his left, he succeeded in getting fully upon him ; then, springing up quick as lightning, as Mr. Meadows, panting, his eyes gleaming with the fury of an enraged tigress, was attempting to rise, he dealt him a blow in the face with his fist which sent him back bleeding like a butchered beast. Once more the master attempted to rise, and those who saw it will never forget that piteous spectacle of rage, and shame, and pain, and fear. Once more Brinkly struck him back. How that brave boy's face shone out with those *gaudia certaminis* which the brave always feel when in the midst of an inevitable and righteous combat ! Springing upon his adversary again, and seizing his arms and pinioning them under his knees, he wound his hands in his shaggy hair, and raising his head, thrust it down several times with all his might against the floor.

"Spare me! for God's sake, spare me!" cried Mr. Meadows, in tones never before heard from him in that house.

Brinkly stopped. "Spare you!" he said, now panting himself. "Yes! you who never spared anything that you could hurt! Poor cruel coward! You loved to beat other people, and gloried in seeing them suffering, and when they begged you to spare them, you laughed — you did. Oh, how I have heard you laugh, when they asked you to spare them! And now you are beat yourself and whipped, you beg like a dog. Yes, and I will spare you," he continued, rising from him. "It would be a pity to beat any such a poor cowardly human any longer. Now go! and make them poor things there go to horsin' again, and cut 'em in two again; and then get in the circus ring, and make them others, girls and all — yes, girls and all — hold up their clothes and trot around you, and when they cry like you, and beg you to spare 'em, do you laugh again!"

He rose and turned away from him. Gathering up his books, he went to the peg whereon his hat was hanging, and was in the act of taking it down, when a sudden revulsion of feeling came over him, and he sat down and wept.

Oh, the feelings in that poor boy's breast! The recollection of the cruel wrongs which he had suffered; of the motives, so full of pious duty, which had made him endure them; the thought of how mistaken had been the wish of his mother that he should endure them; and then of how terribly they had been avenged. These all meeting at once in his gentle but untaught spirit, overcame it, and broke it into weeping.

Meanwhile, other things were going on. Mr. Meadows, haggard, bruised, bleeding, covered with dirt, slunk off towards the fireplace, sat down in his chair, and buried his face in his hands. The pupils had been in the highest states of alternate alarm and astonishment. They were now all standing about their seats, looking alternately at Brinkly and Mr. Meadows, but at the latter mostly. Their countenances plainly indicated that this was a sight which, in their minds, had never before been vouchsafed to mortal vision. A schoolmaster whipped! beat! choked! his head bumped! and that by one of his pupils! And that schoolmaster, Mr. Meadows! — Mr. Meadows, who, ten minutes before, had been in the exercise of sovereign and despotic authority. And then to hear him beg! A schoolmaster! — Mr. Meadows! — to hear him actually beg Brinkly to spare him! These poor children actually

4

began to feel not only pity, but some resentment at what had been done. They were terrified, and to some extent miserable at the sight of so much power, so much authority, so much royalty dishonored and laid low. Brinkly seemed to them to have been transformed.   He was a murderer! a REGICIDE!!   Talk of the divine right of kings!   There was never more reverence felt for it than the children in country schools felt for the kingly dignity of the schoolmaster of fifty years agone.

CHAPTER VII.

ALLEN THIGPEN was the only one of the pupils who did not entirely lose his wits while the events of the last few minutes were taking place. While the contest was even between the combatants, he stood gazing down upon them with the most intense interest.   His body was bent down slightly, and his arms were extended in a semicircle, as if to exclude the rest of the world from a scene which he considered all his own.   When Mr. Meadows called for quarter, Allen folded his arms across his breast, and to a tune which was meant for ' Auld Lang Syne,' and which sounded indeed more like that than any other, he sang as he turned off,

" Jerusalem, my happy home."

When Mr. Meadows had taken his seat, he looked at him for a moment or two as if hesitating what to do.   He then walked slowly to him and delivered the following oration :

"It's come to it at last, jest as I said.   I seen it from the fust ; you ought to a seen it yourself, but you wouldn't, ur you couldn't, and I don't know which, and it makes no odds which you didn't.   I did, and now it's come, and sich a beatin', Jerusalem !   But don't you be too much took aback by it.   You warn't goin' to keep school here no longern to-day, nohow.   Now, I had laid off in my mind to have gin you a duckin' this very day ; and I'll tell you for why.   Not as I've got anything par-ticklar agin you, myself ; you have not said one word out of the way to me this whole term.   But, in the fust place, it's not my opinion, nor haint been for some time, that you are fitten to be a schoolmaster. Thar's them sums in intrust — intrust is the very thing and the onliest thing I wanted to learn — I say, thar's them sums in intrust, which I can't work and which you can't show me how to work, or haint yit, though I've been cypherin' in it now two months. And thar's Mely Jones, that's in the same, and she haint learnt 'em neither, and dinged if I believe all the fault's in me and her, and in course it can't be in the book. But that aint the main thing ; its your imposin' disposition. If this here schoolhouse," he continued, looking around, "if this here schoolhouse haint seen more unmerciful beatin' than any other school-house in this country, then I say it's a pity that thar's any sich a thing as education. And if the way things has been car'd on in this here schoolhouse sense you've been in it is the onliest way of getting of a education, then I say again it's a pity thar's sich a thing. It haint worth while for me to name over all the ways you've had of tormentin' o' these children. You know 'em ; I know 'em ; everybody about this here schoolhouse knows 'em. Now, as I said before, I had laid off to a gin you a duckin' this very day, and this morning I was going to let Brinkly into it, tell I found that the time I seen was a comin' in him was done come ; and I knowed he wouldn't jine in duckin' you on account of his mother. Now I've been thinking o' this for more'n two weeks, bekase— now listen to me ; didn't you say you was from South Calliner ? "

Pausing for, but not receiving an answer, he continued :

" Yes, that's what you said. Well now, I've heern a man — a travel-lin' man — who staid all night at our house on his way to Fluriday, say he knowed you. You aint from South Calliner ; I wish you was, but you aint ; you're from Georgy, and I'm ashamed to say it. He ast me, seein' me a studyin', who I went to school to, and when I told him," (Mr. Meadows appearing to be listening) 'Meadows,' says he, 'what Meadows?' 'Iserl,' says I. 'Iserl Meadows a schoolmaster?' says he, and he laughed, he did ; he laughed fit to kill hisself. Well, he told me whar you was raised, and *who you was.* But you needn't be too bad skeered. I aint told it to the fust human, and I aint going to, tell you leave. Now, I had laid off, as I told you, to gin you a duckin', but I hadn't the heart to do it, and you in the fix you are now at the present. Nuff sed, as I seed in a bar-room in Augusty on a piece of pasteboard, under the words 'No credit,' when I was thar. Wonder if thar's going to be much more schoolin' here ? "

Saying which, Allen puckered up his mouth as if for a whistle, and stalked back to his seat.

Mr. Meadows, during the last few sentences of this harangue, had exhibited evidences of a new emotion. When Allen told him what the traveller had said, he looked up with a countenance full of terror, and on Allen assuring him that he had not mentioned it, he had again buried his face in his hands. When Allen went back to his seat, he rose, and beckoning to him imploringly, they went out of the house together a few steps and stopped.

"I never done you any harm," said Mr. Meadows.

"You never did, certin, shore," answered Allen, "nor no particklar good. But that's neither here nor thar; what do you want?"

"Don't tell what you heard tell I git away."

"Didn't I say I wouldn't? But you must leave toler'ble soon. I can't keep it long. I fairly eech to tell it now."

The schoolmaster stood a moment, turning his hat in his hands, as if hesitating what sort of leave to take. He timidly offered Allen his hand.

"I'd ruther not," said Allen, and for the first time seemed a little embarrassed. Suddenly the man hauled his hat on his head, and walked away. He had just entered the path in the thicket, and turning unobserved, he paused, and looked back at the schoolhouse. And oh, the anger, the impotent rage, the chagrin and shame which were depicted on his bloodshot face! No exiled monarch ever felt more grief and misery than he felt at that moment. He paused but for a moment; then raising both his hands, and shaking them towards the house, without saying a word, he turned again and almost ran along the path.

After he had gone, and not until he had gotten out of sight, Allen, to whom all eyes were turned (except Brinkly's, who yet sat with his head hidden in his hands on the bench), took Mr. Meadows' chair, and crossing his legs, said:

"Well, boys and gals, the Goosepond, it seem, are a broke-up school. The schoolmaster have, so to speak, absquatulated. Thar's to be no more horsin' here, and the circus are clean shot up. And the only thing I hates about it is, that it's Brinkly that's done it and not me. But he wouldn't give me a chance. No," he continued, sorrowfully and as if speaking to himself, "he wouldn't give me a chance. Nary single word could I ever git him to say to me out of the way. I have misted lessons; 'deed I never said none. I never kept nary single rule in his school, and he wouldn't say nothin' to me."

Then rising and going to Brinkly, he put his hand upon his shoulder.

"No, its jest as it ought to a bin; you was the one to do it; and in the name of all that's jest, Brinkly Glisson, what *is* you been cryin'

about? Git up, boy, and go and wash your face. I would rather have
done what you've done than to a bin the man that fooled the tory in
the Revolutionary War, and stoled his horse in the Life of Marion.
Come along and wash that face and hands."

And he almost dragged Brinkly to the pail, and poured water while
he washed.

The children, recovering from the consternation into which they
had been thrown by the combat and its result, now began to walk about
the house, picking up their books and laying them down again. They
would go to the door and look out towards Mr. Meadows' path, as if
expecting, and, indeed, half-way hoping, half-way fearing that he would
return; and then they would stand around Allen and Brinkly, as the
latter was washing and drying himself. But they spoke not a word.
Suddenly, Allen, mimicking the tone of Mr. Meadows, cried out:

"Asa Boatright and Sam Pate, go to horsin'!"

In a moment they all burst into shouts of laughter. Asa mounted
upon Sam's back, and Sam pranced about and neighed, oh, so gaily.
Allen got a switch and made as if he would strike Asa, and that young
gentleman, for the first time in the performance of this interesting exercise, screamed with delight instead of pain.

"Let Asa be the schoolmaster," shouted Allen. "Good morning,
Mr. Boatright," said he with mock humility. "Mr. Boatright, may I
go out?" asked timidly, half a dozen boys.

Asa dismounted, and seizing a hickory, he stood up in the middle of
the floor, and the others formed the circus around him. Here they
came and went, jumping over his switch, and crying out and stooping
to rub their legs, and begging him to stop, "for God's sake, Mr. Boatright, stop."

Suddenly an idea struck Mr. Boatright. Disbanding the circus, he
cried out :

"You, Is'rl Meadows, come up here, sir. Been a fighten, have you,
sir? come up, sir. Oh, here you are."

Mr. Boatright fell upon the teacher's chair, and of all the floggings
which a harmless piece of furniture ever did receive, that unlucky chair
did then and there receive the worst. Mr. Boatright called it names ;
he dragged it over the floor ; he threatened to burn it up ; he shook it
violently ; he knocked it against the wall ; one of its rounds falling out,
he beat it most unmercifully with that ; and at last, exhausted by the
exercise and satisfied with his revenge, he indignantly kicked it out of
doors, amid the screams and shouts of his schoolfellows.

CHAPTER VIII.

" FAR you well ! " said Allen, solemnly, to the fallen chair.
They had all gathered up their books and slates, and hats and
bonnets, and started off for their several homes. Those who went the
same way with Brinkly, listened with the most respectful attention as
he talked with Allen on the way, and showed how bitterly he had
suffered from the cruelty of Mr. Meadows. They had already lost
their resentment at the dishonor of that monarch's royalty, and were
evidently regarding Brinkly with the devotion with which mankind
always regard rebels who are successful. Each one strove to get the
nearest him as he walked. One little fellow, after trying several times
to slip in by his side, got ahead, and walked backwards as he looked
at Brinkly and listened. He was so far gone under the old régime
that he felt no relief from what had happened. He had evidently not
understood anything at all about it. He seemed to be trying to do so,
and to make out for certain whether that was Brinkly or not. The
voice of those young republicans, had Brinkly been ambitious, would
have made him dictator of the Goosepond. Even Allen felt a consideration for Brinkly which was altogether new. He had always expected that Brinkly would at some day resist the master, but he did
not dream of the chivalrous spirit of the lad, nor that the resistance
when it should come would be so terrible and disastrous. He had
always regarded Brinkly as his inferior ; he was now quite satisfied to
consider him as no more than his equal. How we all, brave men and
cowards, do honor the brave ! / And Brinkly had just given, in the
opinion of his schoolfellows, the most brilliant illustration of courage
which the world had ever seen. /

But Brinkly was not ambitious nor vain ; he felt no triumph in his
victory. On the contrary, he was sad ;/ he wished it could have been
avoided./ He said to Allen that he wished he could have stood it a
little longer.

"Name o' God, Brinkly Glisson, what for ? It is the astonishenist
thing I ever heerd of, for you to be sorry for maulin' a rascal who beat
you like a dog, and that for nothin'. What for, I say again ? "

"On mother's account."

Allen stopped — they had gotten to the road that turned off to his
home.

" You tell your mother that when she knows as much about the villian as I do, she will be proud of you for maulin' him. Look here, Brinkly, I promised him I wouldn't tell on him tell he had collected his schoolin' account and was off. But you tell your mother that if she gets hurt with you for thrashin' him, she will get worse hurt with herself when she knows what I do."
. Saying this, Allen shook hands with him and the others, and went off, merrily singing 'Jerusalem, my happy home.' Soon all the rest had diverged by byroads to their own homes, and Brinkly pursued his way alone.

It was about twelve o'clock when he reached home. The widow's house was a single log-tenement, with a small shed-room behind. A kitchen, a meat-house, a dairy, a crib with two stalls in the rear, one for the horse the other for the cow, were the out-buildings. Homely and poor as this little homestead was, it wore an air of much neatness and comfort. The yard looked clean ; the floors of both mansion and kitchen were clean, and the little dairy looked as if it knew it was clean, but that was nothing new or strange. Several large rose-bushes ·stood on either side of the little gate, ranged along the yard-paling. Two rows of pinks and narcissus hedged the walk from the gate to the door, where, on blocks of oak, rested two boxes of the geranium.

The widow was in the act of sitting down to her dinner, when hearing the gate open and shut, she advanced to the door to see who might be there. Slowly and sadly Brinkly advanced to the door.

" Lord have mercy upon my soul and body, Brinkly, what is the matter with you ? and what *have* you been a doing, and what *made* you come from the schoolhouse this time o' day ? " was the greeting he met.

" Don't be scared, mother ; it isn't much that's the matter with me. Let us sit down by the fire here, and I'll tell you all about it."

They sat down, and the mother looked upon the son, and the son upon the mother.

" I was afraid it would come to it, mother. God knows how I have tried to keep from doing what I have had to do at last."

" Brinkly, have you been and gone and fought with Mr. Meadows ? "

" Yes, mother."

" And so ruined yourself, and me, too."

" I hope not, mother."

" Yes, here have I worked and denied myself ; day and night I have pinched to give you an education, and this is the way you pay me for it," and she fell straight to crying. |

"Mother, do listen to me before you cry and fret any more, and I believe you will think I have not done wrong. Please, mother, listen to me," he entreated as she continued to weep, and rocked herself, in order, as it seemed, to give encouragement and keep time to her weeping. But she wept and rocked. Brinkly turned from her and seemed. doggedly hopeless.

"Say on what you're going to say — say on what you're going to say. If you've got anything to say, say it."

"I can't tell you anything while you keep crying so. Please don't cry, mother; I don't believe you will blame me when I tell you what I have been through." His manner was so humble and beseeching that his mother sat still, and in a less fretful tone, again bade him go on.

"Mother, as I said before, God knows that I've tried to keep from it, and could not. You don't know, mother, how that man has treated me."

"How has he treated you?" she inquired, looking at her son for the first time since she had been sitting.

"You were so anxious for me to learn, and I was so anxious myself to learn, that I have never told you of hardly any of his treatment. Oh, mother, he has beat me worse than anybody ought to beat the meanest dog. He has called me and you poor, and made fun of us because we were poor. He has called me a scoundrel, a beggar, a fool. When I told him that you wanted me to quit geography, he said you was a fool and had a fool for a son, and that he had no doubt that my father was a fool before me."

. The widow dried her face with her handkerchief, settled herself in her chair, and said:

"When he said them things he told a — what's not so; I'll say it if he is schoolmaster." And she looked as if she was aware that the responsibility of that bold observation was large.

"He said," continued Brinkly, "that I should study it, and if I didn't git the lessons, he'd beat me as long as he could find a hickory to beat me with. I stood it all because it was my only chance to git any schoolin'. But I told him then — that is when he called you a fool, and father one, too — that it wasn't so, and that he ought not to say so. Well, yesterday, you know you sent me by Mr. Norris' to pay back the meal we borrowed, and I didn't get to the schoolhouse quite in time. But he wasn't more than a hundred yards ahead of me, and when he saw me, he hurried just to keep me from being in time. When I told him how you had sent me by Mr. Norris', he only laughed and called me a liar, and then — look at my shoulder, mother."

He took off his coat, unbuttoned his shirt, and exposed his shoulder and back, blackened with hideous bruises.

"Oh, my son, my poor son," was all that mother could say.

She had not, in fact, known a tenth of the cruelties and insults which Brinkly had borne. He had frequently importuned her to let him quit the school. But she supposed that it was because of the difficulties of learning his lessons which got for him an occasional punishment, and such as was incident to the life of every schoolboy, bad and good, idle and industrious. These thoughts combining with her ardent desire that he should have some learning, even at the risk of receiving some harsh and even unjust punishment, made her persist in keeping him there. Seeing her anxiety, and to avoid making her unhappy, Brinkly had concealed from her the greater part of the wrongs which he had suffered. But when she heard how he had been abused, and saw the stripes and bruises upon his body, her mother's heart could not restrain itself, and she wept sorely.

"Well, mother, I stood this too, but last night I couldn't sleep. I thought about all he had said and all he had done to me, and I made up my mind to quit him anyhow. But this morning, before day, I thought for your sake I would try it once more. So I got up and studied my lesson here and all the way to the schoolhouse; and I did know it, mother, or I thought I did, for he wouldn't tell me how to pronounce the words, but Allen Thigpen did, and I pronounced them just like Allen told me. When I told him that, he called me a liar, and afterwards I begged him not to strike me, but to let me go home. But he would strike me, and I fought him."

"And you done right. Oh, my son, my poor Brinkly! Yes, you are poor, the poor son of a poor widow; but I am proud that you have got the heart to fight when you are abused and insulted. If I'd known half of what you have had to bear, you should have quit his school long ago; you should, Brinkly, my darling, that you should. But how could you expect to fight him and not be beat to death? Why didn't you run away from him and come to me? He wouldn't have beat you so where I was." And she looked as if she felt herself to be quite sufficient for the protection of her young.

5

"Mother, I didn't want to run; I *couldn't* run from such a man as he is. Once I thought I would take my hat and books and come away; but I could not do that without running, and I *couldn't* run; *you* wouldn't want me to run, would you, mother?" The widow looked puzzled.

"No; but he is so much bigger than you, that it wouldn't a looked exactly like you was a coward; and then he has hurt you so bad. My poor Brinkly, you don't know how your face is scratched."

"I hurt him worse than he hurt me, mother."

"What?"

"I hurt him worse than he hurt me; I got the best of it."

"Glory!" shouted Mrs. Glisson.

"In fact, I whipped him."

"Glory! glory!"

"When I had him down —"

"Brinkly, did you have him down, my son?"

"Yes, and he begged me to spare him."

"Glory be to — glory be to — but you did not do it, did you?"

"Yes, mother, as soon as he give up and begged me to stop, I let him alone."

"I wouldn't a done it, certin, shore!"

"Yes you would, mother; if you had seen how he was hurt, and how bad he looked, you would a spared him, I know you would."

"Well, maybe I might; I suppose it was right, as he was a man grown, and schoolmaster to boot. Maybe it was best — maybe it was best — maybe I might a done it too, but it aint quite certin."

She had risen from the chair and was pacing the floor. This new view of Brinkly's relation to his tyrant was one on which she required time for reflection. She evidently felt, however, that as Brinkly had so often been at the bottom in the combat, now when he had risen to the top, there was no great harm in staying there a little longer. "But maybe it was best; I reckon now he won't be quite so brash with his other scholars."

"He will never have another chance."

"What?"

"Allen has found out all about him, and where he came from, and says he's a man of bad character. He begged Allen not to say anything about it until he got his money and could git away. So he is quit, and the school is broke up."

"Glory! glory! hallelujah!" shouted again and sung the mother.

Let her shout and sing. Sing away and shout, thou bereaved, at this one little triumph of thine only beloved ! Infinite Justice ! pardon her for singing and shouting now, when her only child, though poor and an orphan, though bruised and torn, seems to her overflowing eyes to be grand and beautiful, as if he were a royal hero's son, and the inheritor of his crown.

JUDGE MIKE'S COURT.

"And then the Justice :
And so he plays his part."

CHAPTER I.

ONCE upon a time, in this glorious country, a respectable but uneducated woman, who had taken to her home an orphan child of poor parents, had brought her up with great care and tenderness, and, though reluctantly, allowed her to receive, at the hands of some other benevolent persons, a year's schooling, had the misfortune to lose her *protégée*. The girl, who was very pretty, being offered a home in a family where she thought she could have better society and more enjoyments than were to be had in the house of her first benefactress, accepted this offer, and refused to return. The good lady, in her distress searching eagerly how she might avoid placing too great blame upon the beloved child of her adoption, attributed her loss to education.

"It was edyecation," she said bitterly, when she had given up all efforts to recover her lost treasure ; "it was edyecation that done it all. I never seed a more biddable child than she was before she went off to school. You may tell me what you please about your edyecation : it's my opinion that the more edyecation people git, the meaner they git."

Woe to the schools and colleges henceforth if she could have had her way with them !

There are, and for a long time there have been many persons in this good State of Georgia who feel like this good woman regarding another great instrument of its civilisation. We all remember (at least those who are old enough) how long a time it required to get the establishment of a Supreme Court for the Correction of Errors. What courts we did have seemed to be such nuisances that men were generally opposed to having any more. At length, being partially convinced that such a tribunal might serve to settle at least some points of law, and thereby lessen some useless litigation, it was established. Yet, notwithstanding the great good that has been accomplished through its instrumentality, there are very many who still regard it as only another addition to the various means of vexing citizens with law-suits; and we yet meet with those who are fond of speaking of the good old times when courts were fewer, and men did not have to carry their cases out of their counties after they had been once settled at home.

Well, those old times were very good in many respects. Beef was cheap, and the temptation to steal it was small. Men did not very often commit malicious mischief, or keep open tippling-houses on forbidden days. Land was not high; men lived more widely apart, and almost every one kept his own whiskey at home. Vagabonds were less numerous than now; mostly because the credit system being not greatly developed, they were wont to carry upon their persons the unmistakable badges of their profession. It is pleasing to an old man like me to recur to those old times. Corn, twenty cents a bushel, except to wagoners, who, being strangers, and considering that their silver might prove to be pewter, were made to pay a quarter of a dollar. Bacon, no price at all, because everybody had a plenty, and because the woods were full of game and the creeks were full of fish. Blessed be the memory of those old times! The most of those who were then my companions and friends are gone, and I am left almost alone. Yet, for the many recollections which they bring to me, I say again, Blessed be the memory of those old times!

But, like all other times, those old ones had their evils and their wants. Men and systems were not perfect, even then. True, they had not many schools, and they had no Supreme Court. Yet, in what schools and courts they had, there were some things which, when men thought of them at all, they thought might have been done differently or left undone. I think that we have improved somewhat in the matter of a few of the institutions of the old times. I speak thus with what I hope is a proper respect for the past. I admit that I see occasionally what seem to be derelictions from the simple habits which prevailed when I was a boy. The young of this generation, it seems to me, are not so respectful to the old as they used to be. Discipline surely has lost some of its ancient control. To take my own case for instance: I am convinced that when I was young I treated men who were as old as I am now with more consideration than that which I receive from the young. I do not like to complain, and a man at my time of life should beware how he complains. Still, I can but notice in the present generation a want of that reverence which, when I was a boy, the young felt for the aged. I know how wont old persons are to find fault with present times, and therefore I try to endure as I would like to be endured. And while I may mistake myself in this regard, nevertheless I do believe that I can fairly compare with one another the various periods in which I have lived. My opinion upon the whole is, that while in some respects there have been deteriorations from the habits of old times, there have been improvements in others. Now, as for the schools in old times, bad as some of them were, they had ways of righting themselves. The things done in them, though seriously inconvenient at the time of their doing, were seldom very serious in their consequences. Boys knew them to be, as they were, institutions, and so learned to get used to them. Or, if a schoolmaster grew to be too bad, or wouldn't give a holiday at Whitsuntide, he got his ducking, and things went on better for a while. The same thing, however, could not be said of the courts and the judges, when, as was sometimes the case, the latter were neither fully educated in all the learning applicable to all cases arising in Law and Equity, nor wholly above the prejudices and other infirmities to which the rest of mankind are subject. The latter generations have surely made advances in the matter of laws and courts of justice. We always had a great Judiciary system, if we had carried it to the point designed by its founders. But we were left with irresponsible judges, and some of them were — what they were.

Let us look back a little into those old times, while men are thinking about them and giving especial praise to them, and reminding one another of how glorious they were. I observe that this habit prevails less with the truly old than with the middle-aged, who have had not enough of old age to obtain its true wisdom. I trust, therefore, it will not be amiss in me, who have lived in both the old times and the new, to describe, as well as my memory will serve, a character or two and a scene or two that figured and were enacted in a court in our neighborhood, long, long ago. And as I have used many introductory words (and those possibly somewhat involved), and as I have mentioned one fact (though it has nothing to do with the narrative except to help in pointing its moral), and as I am a little tired, I will stop for the present where I am, and call what I have already written, a chapter.

CHAPTER II.

A YOUNG man, a native of Virginia, and a graduate of one of the colleges of that State, had come to Georgia for the purpose of seeking a home and practising his profession of the law. One morning, in the beginning of spring, in company with a middle-aged gentleman, whose acquaintance he had newly made, he rode towards the village near which the latter lived, for the purpose of being introduced to some of the members of the Bar residing there. As the two were riding along, after some conversation upon the practice of law and other pursuits in the South, the younger gentleman asked of the elder if there was in the South a Court of Errors.

"I do not remember to have so heard, but I presume that you have such a court."

"Yes, indeed," exclaimed the elder, "many a one. We have no other sort in Georgia. But I know what you mean, sir," he added, seeing the young man's surprise. "I answered your question literally, because what I say is very nearly literally true ; and it is so, doubtless, because we have no court for the correction of errors which our other courts continually commit. I know little of the law myself, although I once studied it and was admitted to the Bar. I never practised, and yet I have seen enough to know that, with our present Judiciary system, the law can never become a science settled upon any ascertained principles."

"There can be very little doubt as to that."

"We have no lack of lawyers of real ability ; but I doubt if there is in the South another State so deficient in its courts as ours. We have, as I said, many able lawyers, but seldom an able judge. The salary is so small that a lawyer of first-rate ability, unless he be a man of property ("and such men," he added, in parenthesis, with a slight touch of dignity which did not escape the other, "rarely enter the professions"), will not go upon the Bench. It is, therefore, generally occupied by men of inferior learning and ability; and as we have no Supreme Court, and every judge is independent in his circuit, there is, of course, no uniformity in their decisions, but many an error, you may be sure. I reside here near the boundaries of two circuits. I and my neighbors of two adjoining counties live under two different systems of laws. I am tolerably well acquainted with that of my own circuit; but I dare not move out of it, as I have known others to do to their sorrow. Even here, whenever a new judge is elected we shall have a new system to learn; for, like every schoolmaster who begins by throwing out of the schoolroom all the text-books which his predecessor employed, he will fear that he will be considered nobody unless he overrules much of what our present judge has decided."

"Does not your constitution provide for a Supreme Court?"

"It does; but, bless you, sir, the people are almost unanimously opposed to its establishment. They say that they are already too much worried by courts to think of making any more of them. The lawyers too, the most of them, are equally opposed to it, because they know — hang them! and who should know so well as they?— that it would lessen litigation by lessening what is to them the glorious uncertainty of the law. A man who would get an office here must not open his mouth in favor of a Supreme Court. He might as well avow himself a disciple of Alexander Hamilton, or a friend of the administration of John Adams."

They had just reached the public square, and alighted, when Mr. Parkinson pointed to a little office on the corner of it, into which two men were entering.

"There go two limbs of the law now. We will go in at once," and leading the way, he walked in and introduced the young man, Mr. Overton, to Mr. Sandidge and Mr. Mobley.

Mr. Sandidge ("Elam Sandidge, Attorney-at-Law," Overton had read upon a shingle as he entered) was about fifty years old, tall, with very long legs, which seemed as if they were ashamed of his rather short body, from the fact that they would never hold it straight up. He had long arms, long hands, and long fingers, which last never looked clean. He wore shabby clothes too, which, if they had been ever so fine, would yet have looked shabby from a habit he had of chewing tobacco all the time when he was not eating or asleep, and spitting on himself. Yet, for all these drawbacks, Mr. Sandidge had, as it seemed, an ambition to appear perfectly and universally agreeable. His countenance, when he looked at another, was invariably clothed in smiles. He never laughed; he only smiled. While nature had given him no very acute sense of the humorous, and while, therefore, he never felt like laughing, he had, apparently from a sense of duty, learned to smile, and he smiled at everything. If one said 'Good morning' to him, he was sure to smile as he returned the salutation. If one, in answer to an inquiry concerning his health, complained of a headache, he smiled the most cordial sympathy. There was no considerable amount of cheer conveyed by his smiles — no more than there was by his shabby coat and hands; but like these, they were a part of him, and one got used to them. But if any one said anything funny where he and others were standing, and no person smiled except the invariable Sandidge, he felt that the joke had been a failure.

When Mr. Parkinson introduced Mr. Overton, Mr. Sandidge arose and extended his hand with a smile, which seemed to say: "Ah! you young dog! You have come at last? I knew you would."

Mr. Mobley was a stout, fine-looking man, about twenty-three years of age, of the middle height, with dark complexion, very black hair and whiskers, and a fine mouth, full of large sound teeth of perfect whiteness. There were an ease and grace in his manner, and an expression upon his face, which marked him at once to Mr. Overton as a man of talent and education. Immediately after the introduction Mr. Sandidge looked at the new-comers and then at Mr. Mobley with a smile, which the latter interpreted at once; and after an exchange of a few words of civility, he rose to go.

"No, do not leave, Mr. Mobley," Mr. Parkinson said. "We have no especial business with Mr. Sandidge, but came to see you both. So please to remain, unless you have business which calls you away."

Mr. Sandidge smiled upon Mr. Mobley as he resumed his seat; and, but that we knew that he was bound to smile at all events, we should have suspected that he was infinitely amused by the idea that Mr. Mobley should have had any business of such pressing importance as to require him to go to it in a hurry. He then turned to Mr. Parkinson and smiled inquiringly; for this was the first time that that gentleman had ever called on him, except upon business.

"Mr. Overton has removed to Georgia with a view of establishing

6

himself somewhere in the State in the practice of the law, and I have brought him here to make him acquainted with you both, knowing that he could obtain from you more of such information as he needs than he could from myself; besides," he added, looking at Mr. Mobley, "I desired to give him an opportunity of extending his acquaintance among those with whom he might spend pleasantly such of his leisure as he will have when he is wearied with the dullness of Chestnut Grove."

Mr. Mobley bowed ; Mr. Parkinson rose, and saying that he would return in an hour, left the office, Mr. Sandidge smiling at him all the while, even at his back as he went out. A conversation was begun at once between the young men, with an occasional but rare contribution from Mr. Sandidge. The latter was no great talker in a social way. It was a wonderful thing to him how many things people could find to say to one another on matters of no business whatever, but only in the way of civility. He could talk forever on business, and in the Court-house often made speeches of two hours' length. He understood such things mighty well ; but it puzzled him to see two persons sitting down together and talking at random and with interest on miscellaneous subjects, sporting from one to another with perfect ease, having no apparent motive except a desire in each to entertain the other. There was Mobley now, he would think, a young man who in the Court-house was as skittish as a girl, whose practice, though he had fine education and ability, after a year's pursuit of it, was barely supporting him, and yet, as soon as he was out of that dread place, and in the society of the most intelligent and able of the profession, would bear his part in the discussion of general subjects, and even of legal questions, with an ease and a fluency which made him the most interesting of them all, and the object of the especial envy of Mr. Sandidge. Being no philosopher, Mr. Sandidge could not, for the life of him, understand how these things could be ; and it seemed to him to be not only strange, but wrong that Mr. Mobley, whom he was accustomed to run over in the Court-house, should not only seem to be, but should actually be above him everywhere else. Yet such things have been before and since, and are to be hereafter, and have excited the surprise of others besides Mr. Sandidge. How many young men of excellent talents and the most finished education have for a year or two striven in vain to begin successfully careers at the Bar, and have at length shrunk from the pursuit, and left its honors and emoluments to be gathered by the Sandidges — the Sandidges whom men laughed at when they saw them enter the profession, and whom they continued to laugh at for half a dozen years, and after half a dozen more years have carried them all their cases, and have at last lived to see them rich and prosperous. Mr. Sandidge would not have thought of exchanging places with Mr. Mobley, or the fine young fellow who had been just now introduced to him; but the more they ran on with each other about law, literature, and what not, the more he wondered at and envied what he thought was their only gift. But he smiled whenever anything was said to him, and when he was expected to say, and did say anything to them. When Mr. Overton inquired if there was much litigation in that circuit, and if money was to be made by the practice, Mr. Mobley slightly blushed, looked at Mr. Sandidge, and answered that there was not a great amount of litigation then originating, and that Mr. Sandidge knew more as to what was to be made by the practice than himself. Regaining instantly his ease of manner, he laughed good-naturedly at himself, who had managed, he said, "thus far to make money to pay my board and store accounts, and not, I think, anything over. I do not, however, despair to do better after a while," he added, looking composedly upon Mr. Sandidge.

Mr. Sandidge being thus appealed to, and looking as if he felt that that was a subject of which he ought to know something, answered that there were some few lawyers in the circuit who were making a living. Law was a mighty hard thing to make a living at. He had been trying it twenty-five years and better, and ought to know how hard it was. There was no business that it was not easier to make money at than law. If he had his time to go over again, he hardly thought he would undertake it. Indeed, he knew he would not if he knew what a young man had to go through with the first five or six years. Now, Mr. Sandidge had commenced the practice of the law without a dollar, and with not even a good suit of clothes. But he economised. He borrowed money at eight per cent., and shaved paper at sixteen and twenty. He went to every Justices' Court in the county; learned the name of every man in it, got acquainted with every man's business, hunted up and set agoing litigation, until here he was in the possession of at least forty thousand dollars. And though many a man would have shrunk from what Mr. Sandidge had to go through with, yet Mr. Sandidge told a story when he said what he did. He would have gone through with it a thousand times over. He was proud of what he had gone through. Like most self-made men, he was fond of exaggerating his early difficulties. Then, next to the money which he had made by the law, he loved the spyings which it gave opportunities to make into the secrets of his neighbors, their silent struggles with sufferings and embarrassments, and he loved yet more the influence which the knowledge thus acquired enabled him to exert over them. But it was not his wont to encourage young lawyers. Nobody encouraged him, he reflected, and let them encourage themselves.

"Yes," he said, "law is a hard thing to get on with. There's a power of books to read, which requires a power of money to buy ; and there are so many contrary decisions on the same p'ints, and the practice and the pleadings are so hard to learn, and then a man, a young man, has so often got to speak before the court, where everybody is watching him, and when he don't know sometimes what to say when a pint is made he didn't expect and aint prepared to meet, and he gets embarrassed, and sometimes even has to give up the case and be non-suited. These things, as I said, and a heap of others I might mention, makes law a hard business to follow. But some men do, by hard labor, make a living by it, by being economical. They say in Augusta and in Savannah it is easier to get along with it, and that some men even make fortunes. There is more litigation there, and not so much competition. But," he ended, smiling quite encouragingly, "it may be worth while to try it even here. The profession is pretty well stocked to be sure, but the more the merrier, you know ;" and he smiled almost audibly, and with such satisfaction at this attempt at pleasantry, that Mr. Mobley laughed at it heartily, and said :

" And, Sandidge, you know it is some consolation to a fellow who is getting along slowly to know that there are others who are at no faster pace than himself ; for apropos to your proverb is the one that misery loves company."

" Just so," answered Mr. Sandidge ; and at this moment Mr. Parkinson returned, and the two took their leave.

When they were on their way home, Mr. Parkinson asked Overton how he liked the *specimens*, as he termed his new acquaintances. The latter answered that he was much pleased with the young man.

" And you are not very much pleased with Sandidge, I suppose ? "

" Why, no, I cannot say that I am greatly prepossessed in his favor ; and I fancy he returns the compliment, as he discourages my notion to practise law."

"He does, does he?" said Mr. Parkinson, laughing. "I knew he would; and though I am much of his opinion in regard to any young man who can do anything else, yet I must say that his example is encouraging. He very well illustrates how a man of little talent and less education can grow rich, and even attain to some eminence at the Bar. Sandidge is certainly a queer genius. Twenty-five years ago everybody laughed at him — the judge, the lawyers, the juries, and the people. But Sandidge laughed too in his way, and worked every day and night; and somehow he got into practice. The judge and lawyers came at last to respect him, the sheriffs to fear him, and the people to be in awe of him; until now he has made a fortune, has more influence with the present judge and is more successful before juries than any lawyer in the circuit. I knew he would attempt to discourage you; he always does. I doubt if it is because he has no feeling, but because it gratifies his vanity to exaggerate those obstacles which he had to overcome, and which nobody thought he would. And Sandidge, though he looks like a fool, is really a pretty good lawyer. There are men infinitely his superiors, but he is untiringly industrious. He prepares his cases so thoroughly, and hangs to them so doggedly, and studies the people so constantly, that he is, I repeat it, the most successful practitioner I know. He loves the law; he glories in it, and knows nothing outside of it."

"But Mr. Mobley; he is certainly a man of real talent and education. Is he not likely to succeed?"

"Mobley has very superior talent and a most finished education. He was educated by an uncle who died in the first year of his collegiate life, leaving in the hands of his executors money to enable him to complete his course and enter his profession. His parents both died when he was a child. But Mobley shines everywhere except in the courtroom. There he does not yet seem to be quite at home. I have heard him speak once or twice, and he certainly speaks well. But Sandidge worries him so with the starting of unexpected issues that he is often put to his wits' end. If he could live without the practice, I am inclined to think that, notwithstanding his pride, he would abandon it. He will succeed though after a while, I doubt not, if he will persevere. He is a fellow of fine wit, and gores Sandidge badly sometimes when he can reach him, which is not often the case, with this weapon. But Sandidge only smiles, and almost always gives things a turn which is sure to give him the best of it at last."

" Do you usually have much business in the courts ? "

" And if so, which of these men do I employ to attend to it, you would ask? Well," continued Mr. Parkinson, somewhat apologetically, " what little I have in that way I usually give to Sandidge. I have known him a long time, and he has always seemed to act an honest part towards me. Besides, a man, you know, does not usually like to change the channel of his business."

Mr. Parkinson did not have the heart, after what he had said of Mr. Sandidge's influence with the presiding judge, to give that as another reason for retaining him.

The young man said nothing; but he thought with himself that, hard as it was on a poor fellow like Mobley, it was natural. And is it the less hard because it is natural, that the world will delay to give help to a man in any business of life until, by long toiling and striving alone, he has at last reached a point where he can live without it ? Yet such is the way of life. You man with many clients, and many more friends, has there not been a time when nineteen of every twenty of those whom you now value the most highly would have forborne to lend you a helping hand, but would have waited until they had seen whether by the aid of the few who did stand by you you were likely to rise or to fall ? Let us not then fall out with what is natural in our fellow-men, and what our very selves would do, and what we actually do, because it is natural to us. We would spare ourselves many an uncomfortable feeling of contempt for the infirmities of human nature as we see them illustrated in the lives of our neighbors, if we would but reflect that, what is more often than otherwise the case with us, we would act in the same circumstances just as they do. Ask yourself, O best of men, how many young men are there in any profession whom you so cordially wish to prosper in it that you would be willing to take any of your business out of its old tried channel — a channel so freighted with yours and other people's business that it would not miss the little you take from it — and risk it in their care until they have proved that the consignment will be a safe one? Or if you sometimes do this, is it not done a little slyly, and do you not feel like apologising, and when discovered, do you not actually apologise to the old channel, and tell how trifling was the freight you have taken from it, and how you sup- posed it would not care to be pestered with such a small matter? Yes, and the old channel says it makes no difference, and that it is all right; but then you feel as if it was not all right, and as if you had injured the old channel, and you go to work straightway and ship a whole boat-load on it at once.

CHAPTER III.

"CAN'T we get through with the docket by Friday night?"

"There's business enough here to occupy the whole week, and more too. You'll have to sit an adjourned term to get through with it."

"I shall do no such thing; and what is more, I shall adjourn the court Friday night."

Mr. Sandidge smiled with wonted complacency. "I don't think we can hardly get to the Appeal before Wednesday dinner; and it looks like a pity but what some of them cases that's been continued so long could be tried. We lawyers aint like judges, to go and draw our salaries every three months, but have to wait until the cases are disposed of, and sometimes a long time getting them then."

This excellent joke put him on a broad grin. The Judge did not seem to appreciate it much, though he smiled in faint commendation.

Let us contemplate this judge a little. He was fifty years old, twenty-five of which had been spent in the practice of the law, in which he had risen to a fourth rank. As a set-off to this professional eminence, he had remained as he had begun, poor in purse. Three years before this an election was held for the office of Judge of the Superior Court of that circuit. Let us remember that at that time the Judge of the Superior Court was the only high judicial officer in the circuit. He was both judge and chancellor. His discretion was uncontrolled and uncontrollable in all cases regarding the security, the property, and reputation of citizens; and even his construction of the Constitution of the State was unalterable by any human power. Three years before, politics had taken one of its turns, and the party to which the fourth-rate lawyer of twenty-five years' practice belonged unexpectedly found itself with a small majority in the legislature. The incumbent of the Bench, being a member of the minority, was of course to share its fate and retire from office. There were two prominent candidates from the party in power; one a retired member of Congress, who was finding it difficult to recover the practice which he had given up fifteen years before, and the other a man of ten years' connection with the profession, of very promising talents, and of a good property, who sought the office for the *éclat* and the power which it would confer upon him. Several ballots had been made without an election. Mr. Elam Sandidge, for certain reasons of his own, had consented to represent his county in the Senate, and was one of the party in minority. A more amused man it was seldom any one's privilege to see than was he, when on the repeated counting out of the votes the presiding officer announced that there had been no election. He looked to this and to that one on either side of the house, and went about whispering to some and winking at others.

"What is that dirty old rascal doing on our side of the aisle?" inquired a majority member of his neighbor.

"I can't tell; but some rascality brings him here, you may swear to that."

While the votes were being counted out for the fifth time, Mr Sandidge walked quickly over to that side. A dozen anxious, pitiful looking members gathered around him.

"Put him up next! put him up next time!" he said, and walked back again, taking in with a sweeping wink the whole of his own party. When the result was announced, and directions given to prepare for another balloting, "Mr. President! Mr. President!" screamed a voice from the majority side, "I announce the name of Littleberry W. Mike, Esq., from the county of ——." This announcement was followed by roars of laughter from the minority, and by hisses and cries of "Who is he?" from the other. Immediately, however, the leaders of both were busy as bees. Threats and criminations were heard among the friends of the two prominent candidates; then entreaties from both to the opposition. "Take him down, for Heaven's sake." "It is a shame by blood." "Don't put him on us, if you please." "Anybody else," etc. All to no purpose. The nominee was elected on the next ballot.

"Why, how did you get elected, Berry?" slyly asked Mr. Sandidge of the judge elect, as on the dispersion of the members he met him, trembling and pale as a corpse, at the foot of the gallery, and shook his cold hand. "It appears like you must have got some votes from our side of the house." The newly elected pressed the hand of his friend, and they went together to the hotel, on the way to which he was forced to hear from among the crowd many a bitter jest of which he was the subject.

This election was an instance of that miserable policy yet adhered to, by which minorities, in order to render majorities odious, do not hesitate to contribute all they can to make them do the greatest amount of harm to public interests. Men may say what they will of caucuses, but until there is a higher standard of public and private virtue amongst us, they will be indispensable.

When a man of inferior parts is raised to an office of great author-ity, he is apt, unless he has great virtue and very amiable dispositions, to exert that authority, as far as is compatible with safety, in enforcing a regard which those parts have been inadequate to secure. Cowardly as this is, it is not more injurious to truth, and justice, and reason, than when such a man is led by such an elevation to look upon himself as having been heretofore depreciated, and to consider the elevation, whatever were the circumstances which effected it, as the decree of infinite justice in his favor, determining at last to give to merit its just reward. Sometimes he is in one, and sometimes in the other of these two states alternately; never being able to determine exactly whether he ought to occupy his position or not, but ever attempting to resolve the doubt by such a vigorous exercise of authority as will at least foreclose all doubts in the minds of others as to his actual possession of it. Of such a character was the newly elected judge. He had long had his heart set upon the Bench. He looked up to it as a mighty eminence — mighty enough to satisfy the most eager ambition. Yet his desires were not actuated wholly by ambition. He wanted the salary. He needed it. He was poor and had a family; and pitiful as the salary was, it was twice as much as he made by his practice. Ashamed as he was to know how the people regarded the notion of his being Judge of the Superior Court, he never, even for one moment, gave up his desire to become so, but kept himself always, yet in a quiet way, in candidacy for it. And though to the leading members of the Bar he had never presumed to speak of the matter, knowing that he would be laughed at if he did, they yet well knew what his thoughts and his hopes were. Nor had he publicly announced his candidacy at the meeting of the Legislature. He knew well that his only chance of election depended upon the fact, whether true or false it made no ma-terial difference with him, that he was considered the weakest and shabbiest of the candidates of his party. While the prominent ones of these were making interest with the leaders of the party in the Leg-islature, he had quietly, and in a way known only to himself and them, and very probably to Mr. Sandidge, obtained the promise of assistance

7

from a few unknown members who should be able by scattering their votes under the direction of him and Mr. Sandidge, to defeat the election of any one until a suitable opportunity should occur for the name to be presented. We have seen with what result this was done.

With the recollection of all the circumstances, Judge Mike thanked two objects for his elevation: first, his own lucky genius, and secondly, Mr. Sandidge. He was, doubtless, quite inclined to indulge in kindly and grateful feeling towards the latter from habit; for he was under a pecuniary indebtedness to him of several hundred dollars, under a writ of *fieri-facias* which Mr. Sandidge three or four years before had been kind enough to "lift," to have transferred to himself, and to forbear enforcing payment thereof, in consideration of sixteen, which he called a living per-centum of interest. What sacrifices the indulgent creditor was always making, when at every renewal of the note for the extra interest he solemnly avowed his need of the money, and of his submission to go without it, for no earthly reason than to oblige his friend! On that friend's accession to the Bench, when first they were alone together, he took the last note of renewal from his pocket-book, and handed it to him without saying a word. The Judge appearing surprised, Mr. Sandidge, with smiling solemnity, protested that he never could exact usurious interest from a Judge of the Superior Court of the State of Georgia. He hoped he had too much respect for the dignity of the office to do any such thing as that. The Judge, after feeble remonstration, took the note, looked at it, sighed, and tearing it slowly to pieces, felt already one of those palpitating and almost painful joys which only men in office have. It was a small matter, but it touched him, and he felt as if henceforth he could live.

But to return to the conversation with which this chapter began, and which took place in the Judge's room at the hotel, on the Sunday night before the sitting of the court.

"How does that smart chap, Mobley, get on?"

"About like he was."

"Knowing everything but law, I suppose, and knowing nothing about that?"

"Just so. The fellow studies like rip; but, Judge, he don't study right. He studies books instead of men."

Mr. Sandidge delivered this sentiment with contemptuous pity.

"He thinks if we had a Supreme Court he would do something grand."

"He's for a Supreme Court, is he?" inquired the Judge, with a frown.

"Warm, warm. Has been from the first."

"It will be some time before he gets it, I'm thinking."

"That's what I tell him."

"Thank God, it's only these book-men that want a Supreme Court. They don't know, Sandidge, they don't know anything outside of books."

"Not the first thing. That's what I tell 'em."

"They think that because such a pint has been decided such a way, by such a judge, that it should be decided so always; and they are forever and eternally talking about settling the law, settling the law — like it was, Sandidge, just like it was so much coffee."

Mr. Sandidge spat all over himself, wiped his mouth with his hand, and came very near laughing outright.

"And I would like to know how, in the name of common sense, it ever could get settled. There aint anything to settle it by. That's the pint; there aint anything to settle it by." He looked inquiringly at Mr. Sandidge, and seemed to wish that gentleman to tell what there was to settle it by if he knew of any such thing. The latter shook his head.

"No sir! there aint nothing to settle it by; and when Mobley is talking about what Lord Mansfield said, and what Lord Hardwick said, or any of them old lords and judges, it's on the end of my tongue to stop him, and tell him that they are all dead, and consequently can't know anything about the case at bar. And, Sandidge, it always struck me as very curious that the laws of England should be the laws of Georgia."

It was a remarkable coincidence that that idea had over and over again struck Mr. Sandidge. He, however, hinted that in some cases (and those were cases in his opinion when the authority happened to be on his own side) the English law was very plain and directly in point, and it ought to be followed.

"Certainly, certainly, in such cases; and I do follow it; but I am the judge of that myself."

Ah, yes, that was right! Now they were exactly agreed! The judge, if he was judge, of course ought to be the judge. If he wasn't, of course he couldn't be, which was absurd; and Mr. Sandidge almost frowned in the effort of elaborating this *reductio ad absurdum.*

"Absurd! so I think; and Mobley and such as he may study

their eyes out for me. When they bring up law that I think is right,
I shall sustain them ; when I don't think so, I shall overrule them.
They may get their Supreme Court if they can. It aint going to be in
my day, thank God ! If it was, I just know that I couldn't and wouldn't
stand it. Before I would have an overseer over me, and I Judge of
the Superior Court, and have to be eternally looking into old books to
find out what them old English lords and judges said a hundred years
ago, when the country wasn't like this, nor the people neither — why,
Sandidge, you know, I havn't got the books, and couldn't afford to buy
them — I say before I would be put to all the trouble and expense of
reading law and nothing else, and then have my decisions brought back
on me, and treated like I was — like I was in fact a nigger — I would
die first ! "

Mr. Sandidge smiled approvingly.

" Why, who would respect me ? "

" Nobody."

" How could I enforce the authority of the Court ? "

" Couldn't be done."

" If I put a fellow in jail, just like as not they would take him out."

" Like as not."

" If I fined one, ten to one it wouldn't stick ! "

" Just so. He wouldn't stay found."

" If I refused to grant a new trial, knowing that I am against them,
they would send a paper ordering me to grant it ! Don't you see they
would, knowing I am against 'em ? "

" Plain as day. Send a paper ordering the Judge of the Superior
Court ! "

" I tell you, Sandidge, before I would stand it I would die first !
In fact, I would RESIGN !! "

This was capping the climax. Dying would be a poor and very inadequate resentment. He would go beyond that. He would volunta-
rily and disgustedly let go his hold upon power. The consequences
might be what they pleased, he would resign. " I tell you, Sandidge,"
he repeated once more, with fearful emphasis, " I should RESIGN !! "

" Oh my conscience, Judge, don't ! don't ! What would become of
the country if you were to resign ? "

Mr. Sandidge, although purposing to appear alarmed, smiled notwithstanding ; and perhaps the more because he thought such a deplor-
able event not very likely to come to pass ; and perhaps yet more,

because it instantly occurred to him that if it ever should, he would console himself in the midst of his own losses and grief as well as he could by replacing the extra interest upon the *fi-fa* not yet paid off and discharged.

"And what will you leading lawyers do when young men, smart young men like Mobley, go before the Supreme Court with books in their hands and turn you down?"

"I shan't live to see it." And it was doubtless the prospect of a far distant organisation of such a tribunal, rather than of his own early decease, which gave the gratified and complacent expression to that smiling countenance.

CHAPTER IV.

A SLY tap at the door.

"Come in."

The door slyly opened, and a short, shaggy individual entered.

"How *do* you *do*, Jedge Mike?" This was uttered in a whining but conciliating tone, and after first a low bow, then a sudden lifting up.

"Why, Sanks, how are you? Take a seat, take a seat."

Mr. Sanks took a seat, after being assured that he was not 'a intrudin'.' "Busy as I war, Sunday night as it air, with a fixin' of all my papers — and — dockiments as it war, I *must*, I *must*, positively I must come by for a minnit, ef jes to tell the Jedge how'd-ye and to ax about *his* health and the likewise health of his family. I also likewise air glad to see Mr. Sandidge a lookin' so well, and as it war ready for the cote."

Mr. John Sanks was the sheriff. Two years ago he had beaten Mr. Triplet, an elderly man and an old inhabitant of Dukesborough, in the race for the sheriffalty. A poor fellow was Sanks; but having got into office by a trick, he had hopes of a long and prosperous official career. Like the Judge, he owed his greatness to Mr. Sandidge, and therefore belonged to him. Such a sheriff as he was a valuable piece of property to such a lawyer. But then Mr. Sandidge was a kind master, and had never put upon his man a service which the latter was not fully willing to perform. Then he got his pay in many ways besides in being elevated to the great office of keeper of the county.

But oh, how glad Mr. Sanks was to see his Honor! and not only so,
but also likewise to see him lookin' so well. Mr. Sanks called Mr.
Sandidge's attention to the glorious fact that the Judge got younger
and younger every court.

"And I am glad to see you too, Sanks. You look, Sanks, you look
right well yourself. All's well, I hope. Everything ready for court —
eh, Sanks?"

"Oh yes, sir. People seems to 'spect a oncommon interestin' cote.
Thar's a power o' business — dockets is right heavy."

"How are you up with your matters, Sanks? No money rules this
term, I hope?"

Mr. Sanks looked a little timidly at Mr. Sandidge, who answered
for him.

"Oh, you are safe in that matter, aint you, Sanks? Oh yes, Judge,
I think so. As a general thing Sanks keeps up with them things."
Mr. S. never wore a prettier smile.

"Ah!" put in Mr. Sanks, reassured. "As long as things is as they
air now, I can git along reasonable well. Tryin' to be 'onest myself,
havin' of a 'onest counsellor, and also likewise havin' of a 'onest judge,
I can git along farly as things is; that is, *ef* they don't git changed."
Mr. Sanks looked suspicious.

"Things get changed? What do you mean?" inquired the Judge.

"Well," continued Mr. Sanks, in a mournful voice, "some people
looks as ef they can't be satisfied with things as they is, and wants 'em
defferent. Some wants defferent lawyers, and also likewise some goes
so fur as to say they wants defferent jedges." And Mr. Sanks did look
so sad in the contemplation of the unreasonableness of the world.

"Wants different judges, eh?" His Honor's expression was one of
contempt, not unmixed with anger and apprehension.

"Well, now, they aint no great numbers of people o' that sort in the
county. It's mostly with them people down about Dukesborough, whar
old Triplet lives. Them Dukesborough people has jest run mad about
Dukesborough, and also likewise thinks it's a bigger place than this
here county-seat. They goes so fur sometimes as to say that the Cote-
house ought to be moved thar. After a while they'll be thinkin' it'll
be as big as Augusty." Mr. Sanks laughed immoderately, but not
loudly; and as Mr. Sandidge smiled, he looked grateful and kept on
laughing. The Judge could not see the joke, and Mr. Sanks grew
serious again.

"Yes, it's the Dukesborough people. Don't you see, Jedge, and also likewise you, Mr. Sandidge, I beat old Triplet for sheriff. John Sanks air known to be for Jedge Mike for jedge at next election above and agin — the multiplied world!" It was terrible to witness the violence with which this defiant conclusion was uttered. The multiplied world might have been there and welcome to hear it.

"Yes, sir, above and agin the multiplied world! And then you see, Jedge, thar's that young fellow, Mobley. The Dukesborough people's proud of him. He was raised thar, you know; and also likewise they goes on to say that he air a bigger man than what even Mr. Sandidge air, or leastways he air goin' to be, and that in short. Then agin, this fellow have been puttin' in their heads that we ought to have a new jedge, and he also likewise air been talkin' about another sort of a cote that can *sas sarire* proceedances and carry cases yit higher. But I tells 'em they better be satisfied with things as they air; and so likewise they're agin me at my next election, and swear they intend to beat me with old Triplet yit. I don't keer about thar threats about what they can do to me. Yit I hates to lose my office jest for bein' of a friend to things as they is. It war no longer than last night I told my wife, says I, Sylvy, says I, I don't keer so much about the office myself, says I, but because also likewise I know it air mostly aimed and pinted, says I, at Jedge Mike and Mr. Sandidge, says I, which is my friends, and which I would go fur all things above and agin, says I, the multiplied world, says I. Them's the very words I said to Sylvy, no longer than last night."

The artful fellow knew well how to strengthen both himself and Sandidge with the Judge. The lawyer smiled with sincere pleasure at the sight of the increased prejudice of Judge Mike against Mr. Mobley, whom, as we shall see, he had some reason to respect more highly than he pretended. Mr. Sandidge admitted that the pernicious ideas of Mr. Mobley had somewhat infected the Dukesborough people; that is, not all — some of them; he, Mr. Sandidge, had some clients among the Dukesborough people, and he was pretty sure that they were right on the judge question. Still, there was a considerable *sprinkling* (as he expressed it) of Dukesborough people in favor of some changes.

When the visitors had retired, the Judge sat for a long time looking gloomily into the fire. "That's the way," he muttered at length. "They go to their colleges, learn their Latin and their Greek and their Algebry, and then git above their sizes, and come home and git impudent to old people, and even want to be so to — to *me*. But they *shan't* do it. I mean to — sq-uelch 'em." And then his Honor went to bed.

Thereupon Messrs. Sandidge and Sanks had some confidential chat before separating for the night. Among other things the sheriff ascertained that the lawyer would like to avoid the trial of the Rickles case at this term of the court. Mr. Sandidge on the other hand was made acquainted with the fact that that young fellow, Mobley, would probably apply for a money rule against Mr. Sanks, for which the latter feared he could not make a satisfactory showing, and which also likewise he would probably need — leastways — oh, cert'inly, cert'inly — providin' — *ahem!* Mr. Sanks never had communicated important information more delicately.

The night was cloudy, though it was the season of the full moon. The latter shone suddenly as they stopped at the corner where they were to separate. The lawyer looked down for a moment upon the sheriff, and the sheriff looked up to the lawyer, and the white moon looked upon both. It seemed a poor sight for all ; so the moon retired, and each of the other two slunk away to his home.

CHAPTER V.

MR. OVERTON attended the court, and by the assistance of Mr. Mobley, obtained a seat within the bar. He had been introduced to several lawyers from different counties, and to the Judge. He could but remark the immense distance between the latter and several of the former, who were men of decided ability. A certain becoming respect was paid by them to the dignitary, not only in the Court-house, but at the hotel, where the best seat, both in the lawyers' room and at the dinner-table, was reserved for him always. This treatment was received in a way which denoted both pleasure that it could not be avoided, as he thought, and a sullenness from the reflection that it was rendered entirely to his office and not to himself. Upon the introduction of the young man to him, after scanning him closely and rudely for a moment, he made an ungainly attempt to congratulate him upon his expected accession to the Bar. Mr. Mobley was heard to speak of his new acquaintance as a youth of talent and education. Then Mr. Sandidge, who sat by the Judge (it was at the hotel), whispered :

"Them's the sort that always wants the Supreme Court."

Judge Mike scowled at the new-comer, and afterwards took no further notice of him.

During the week one could not avoid noticing how much of an art it was to conciliate and control the Court. Mr. Sandidge was the favorite. Everybody knew that; none better than Mr. Sandidge himself, who had foreseen and foreordained it. Now of all positions in a free government, the one where favoritism was most worth having, was that of a pet of a Circuit Judge in those times. When the fortunes of men, their security, and even their lives were dependent upon the will of an individual, and he amenable to no earthly tribunal for whatever errors he might commit, or even for wilful injustice, except upon principles the most vague and uncertain, it was an art ranking almost as high as the science of the law itself, and attainable by greater cost and sacrifice, to obtain an easy access to the ear of that most important depositary of power. It was the fortunate accident of our ancient judiciary system that there was a goodly number of virtuous and able men upon the Bench: for neither virtue nor a very considerable amount of talent seemed to be essential qualifications. If the incumbent for the time possessed them, very well: if not, then not so well, but well enough.

Judge Mike in the matter of virtue was neither good nor very bad. If he was below the capacity to feel or to understand a noble impulse, he was probably above the perpetration of an act of plain judicial dishonesty. He was a considerably better man than Sandidge. Indeed he might be said to maintain in this respect a sort of middle place between high and low, but tending downwards. Fortunately for some, unfortunately for others, he was not brave. Now, of all official personages, cowards are the most troublesome and oppressive. They are troublesome to those of whom they are afraid, and oppressive to those who are afraid of them: troublesome to the former by inflicting petty annoyances in the use of small advantages and the punishment of unimportant lapses, on account of the remembrance and the resentment they feel towards them; and oppressive to the latter in order to preserve the equilibrium between the feeling and the excitement of fear. These infirmities are not peculiar to official, nor even to human cowards. For indeed, I remember well to have been much amused, many years ago, by a cur who had been badly bitten and conquered by another. As soon as he was disengaged from his adversary, and, with his tail bent between his hind legs, was making his way home with

8

what speed he could employ, he spied one of those little dogs commonly designated amongst the Southern people as *fice.* The little fellow came trotting down the street in innocent gayety, and I thought then and think now that I had never seen an individual of his species less expectant both of doing and especially of suffering wrong. Yet so it was, that the cur rushed furiously upon him without any known justifiable cause, and even, as I suspected, without any previous acquaintance ; and then he shook him until he was beaten off with rods. After he had gotten out of the reach of these he went on his way leisurely, apparently satisfied that he was again even with the world. And then, notwithstanding the little beast made, as I considered, rather more ado and for a longer time than was at all necessary, and notwithstanding he was a very useless creature, yet I could but pity him and at the same time be amused, because he seemed to have so thorough a sense of having been made to suffer without the slightest provocation.

But to return to the Judge. Mr. Sandidge was the favorite. Judge Mike liked Mr. Sandidge ; not only for past favors of the kind we know of, but for another reason. He considered Mr. Sandidge as a man like himself, and about of his quality. He liked to see such a man succeed if anybody must succeed. He felt that he did honor to himself in thus honoring his image, as it were. Mr. Sandidge made no great pretension to a knowledge of books, and he thanked him for that. Mr. Sandidge never so much as hinted about a Supreme Court, but seemed to be, as in fact he was, satisfied with the present ways of administering justice. Such being the relations between them, Mr. Sandidge was lucky in getting rulings in his favor. He was, indeed, a much better lawyer than the Judge, and shrewd enough to beguile him of many a wrong decision, even had the latter been indifferent to him.

But notwithstanding this favoritism, there were two or three lawyers of real, and even of first-rate ability, who, in spite of their contempt for him and his dislike of them, exerted over him that influence which a strong and bold intellect must always have over a weak and timid one. Above flattering him, they often, and even against Sandidge, obtained rulings of doubtful right, when he was unable, both from his dread of them, and from his confused senses, to resist them. But to compensate Mr. Sandidge for this, and as if to preserve his own regard for himself, he eagerly sought for opportunities to help him in taking advantage of oversights in pleadings and in proof; oversights which Mr. Sandidge himself never committed, and never failed to observe when committed by others. Then he was graciously allowed to domineer to any extent over the younger lawyers. These stood in great awe of the Bench. They could neither cajole nor browbeat. Even a respectful remonstrance from them was usually followed by a fine, or a threat of it. They therefore timidly went about their business in the Court, hoping for the advent of the time when they could be browbeaters or Sandidges.

Like most small-minded men who go upon the Bench, Judge Mike set himself up as a great reformer of abuses. He was a terror to evil-doers, especially to those who did it on a small scale. Before great criminals, who had the great lawyers for their advocates, he was wont sometimes to be quite moderate; but whenever he got a chance at petty offenders, he would stick the law on to them (to use his own phrase) up to the very hub. There were two vices in particular which he hated cordially. These were fighting and usury. Whenever he could get a blow at either of these, he struck with all his official might. On the third day of the term, when a man was tried and convicted of giving a moderate drubbing to a scoundrel who had used insulting language to his wife, he imposed a fine so heavy that the defendant, not being able to raise the money, was forced to lie in jail for many weeks. It was a great recommendation to the prosecutor that he was known to be one who had been whipped several times for sundry rascalities.

Mr. Sandidge well knew the Judge's weakness on the subject of usury, and ever since his elevation had been confining his financial operations to shaving paper, or so wording usurious contracts as to render their proof exceedingly difficult. Then he was lucky enough to make more money from such transactions than ever before; for now, almost by the invitation of the presiding Judge, the pleading of usury became frequent, and there was no lawyer to be compared with Mr. Sandidge in ferreting testimony in its proof.

Of the younger lawyers, Mr. Mobley was an exception to being in fear of the Judge. He was usually much embarrassed in the conduct of cases merely from his want of familiarity with precedents and forms. Here was Mr. Sandidge's forte. He understood pleadings thoroughly, and it was his delight to pick flaws in his adversary's papers and drive him out of Court. Mr. Mobley dreaded both the Court and its favorite on this ground; but otherwise he was insensible to fear.

But the people : they felt the weight of this power, and they should feel it. All absences of witnesses and jurors, all noises in the Court-room and Court-yard, all misdemeanors of all sorts, met with ready and condign punishment ; always more condign when their convictions came on shortly after a series of browbeatings from those whom he could not frighten. These had been more frequent than usual during the week from one and another cause. He had reached to Thursday afternoon, and was engaged in a peculiarly perplexing case, when an incident occurred which would seem to be rather singular for a Court of Justice.

A man in the crowd outside of the bar having a cold, blew his noise — an action natural and even frequently necessary to a man with that ailment. The action in this case was accompanied by the usual loudness of sound produced by those who have uncommonly good lungs; so loud indeed that several members of the Bar, with amused countenances, looked in the direction from which it proceeded. The Judge became thoroughly fierce in an instant ; and he needed a diversion from the lawyer who had been goading him, to a less formidable adversary.

"Stop this case a minute. Mr. Sheriff, bring that nose-blower inside of this bar."

Mr. Sanks obeyed with alacrity, and went to the culprit, laying his hand rudely upon him.

"Look ye here, John Sanks, what do you want with me?" the man said, in a subdued tone, for he had not heard the Judge's order.

"Well, now," answered Sanks, loudly, "you jest better come along, and also likewise you better come quick!"

"I have *yit* to see the man," began the gentleman with the cold. But a bystander having whispered to him that the Judge had sent for him, he went in at once. Perhaps it was fortunate that his words had not reached the Bench.

"I wish to know, sir, if this Court-house is a stable, sir, that you must bray in it like a jackass." The man seemed greatly surprised by the question, but answered it respectfully and candidly in the negative.

"What do you bray in it for then, sir?"

The poor fellow was now becoming confused and alarmed. He said nothing at first, but looked around and seemed to be trying to make out how it was that he should be there.

"Do you hear, sir?" roared the Judge ; "what are you braying here for, sir?"

"Why, Jedge, I aint been a brayin'."

"What, sir?"

"I said I didn't br — Oh! — leastways I didn't *know* that I was a brayin'. I jest blowed — Oh! — leastways I *thought* I jest blowed my nose, havin' of a bad cold."

"What are you doing here anyway, sir?"

"Why, Jedge, I jest come to Cote."

"Got any business here?"

"No, sir. Leastways I haint got no particklar business."

"What did you come here for then, sir?"

"Why, I thought, Jedge, that everybody was liable to come to Cote."

"*Liable!* LIABLE! Yes, and so they are. And you will find that they are liable to behave themselves; and if they don't, that they are *liable* to be fined. What is your name, sir?"

"Allen Thigpen, sir."

"Thigpen! THIGPEN! I might have known that anybody with that name couldn't tell a Court-room from a stable. And whereabouts do you live?"

This question seemed to relieve Allen of a portion of his apprehension; for he was proud of the location of his home. So he answered, almost with dignity:

"Why, Jedge, I live mighty nigh too Dukesborough, on the big, plain, straightforrard road from Dukesborough to Augusty. Yes, sir, that's right whar I live, shore." And Allen looked as if he thought that if any fact could save him, it was that of his residence.

"Dukesborough, eh? De-ukesborough! A big place is Dukesborough. But I must let the Dukesborough people know that it aint quite big enough for them to run over me. Mr. Thigpen, you of the great town of Dukesborough, you are fined in the sum of two dollars." The Judge turned from him, and ordered the parties to proceed with the cause. Allen in the meanwhile ran his hand into his pocket, and withdrawing an old buckskin purse, emptied its contents into the other hand, and counting the pieces with a rueful face, walked up two or three steps and extended them to the Judge.

"Jedge," said he, "dollar one and nine is the highth of my ambition, ef I was goin' to be hung. But, Jedge, ef you will trust me, I'll pay you the other half and seven-pence as shore as my name is Thig — that is as — ah! — oh!"—

But Allen could not finish it. Whether from looking upward at so resplendent a luminary, or from the violence of his cold, we could not say ; but as his Honor was gazing upon the extended hand in ludicrous surprise and wrath, Allen felt a sudden impulse to sneeze — an impulse which, whenever it comes, in court-rooms or elsewhere, must be obeyed. No human being ever could have made greater efforts to suppress it ; and as is usual in such cases, its victory was only the more triumphant, and violent, and disastrous.

"Oh, Jedge ! Lord 'a mercy ! "—

In his terror, and endeavoring to assure the Judge that he was doing his best, he could not avert his eyes from him. His face assumed the agonized contortions of a maniac, his great chest heaved like a mountain in labor, and he uttered a shriek which, in any circumstances but those that plainly showed that nothing uncommonly serious was the matter, would have filled all within a circle of two hundred yards diameter with consternation. In the violence of the paroxysm the coin flew up from his hand as if they had been discharged from a catapult, and coming down, several of them fell upon the Judge's head and rolled into his lap. An .instantaneous roar of laughter followed this explosion, but was as instantly hushed. No words could depict the expressions upon the faces of the two prominent actors. The Judge had been lifted out of his chair, and there the two stood glaring at each other, speechless. His Honor snatched up the docket with the evident intention of knocking Mr. Thigpen down. Mr. Thigpen looked at it beseechingly, as much as to say, " Knock me down in welcome, but please don't hang me." Thus they were for a quarter of a minute; then the Judge, feeling doubtless that neither the penal code nor the Court's discretion was adequate to punish the outrage as it deserved, said almost in a whisper, as the offender stood now with both hands extended and his face yet contorted and unwiped :

" For God's sake, be off from here, you cussed fool, and never let me see you again in this world ! "

Allen picked up his hat.

" I'm mighty much obleeged to you, Jedge. Far you well, Jedge," and then he hurried away. It was well that he did ; for the Judge was well-nigh committing him for what he would have considered a contempt, his thus bidding him adieu.

A crowd followed him, and were roaring with laughter as soon as they had gotten fairly without hearing of the Court.

" How did you feel, Allen ? "

"Feel?" replied Allen; "I didn't have no feelins to feel with. They was all scared out o' me. Je-rusalem! wan't the old man hot, and aint he brash with people that's got colds?"

"He called you names, eh, Allen?"

"He did that, and when he looked so vi-grous at me, and called me a jackass, ding my skin ef I war exactly certin whether I war one or not."

"But what made you carry him the money?"

"Carry him the money? Why, wan't that right? He found me. I thought the money was his'n. I 'lowed that was the way he got his livin'."

They whooped.

"But what made you tell him farwell? If you hadn't come out so quick after that, he would have had you again."

"What? Why he told me to be off, and I war off, and as I spozened that I mout never see him no more, I thought I ought to bid him farwell. Well, it doo beat! It did look like I ought to be perlite; but sich it is. Tryin' to brace myself agin onpoliteness, it seem like I were mighty nigh bustin' on tother."

"Well, gentle-men," he continued, after they had somewhat subsided, "I say, gentle-men! Thar's two things in this country that I am agin: and them's schools and cote-houses. When I war standin' thar before him, and he war talkin' about jackasses, and brayin' and all sich, ef my feelins hadn't been all skeerd out o' me, and ef I had of had my jedgment about me, I should a felt like little Asa Boatright and Sam Pate used to look like they felt when Iserl Meadows told 'em to go to horsin': and I did hope and did cal'clate never to have them feelins endurin' o' my nat'ral life. Howbesomever, that aint neither here nor thar now. Gentlemen, I never seed a man before that I was afeerd of. I thought everybody was liable to come to Cote: but I comes no more without I'm fotch. It 'pears like, as the old sayin' goes, that he neither likes my name nor my nation. When I sneezed — and I tell you, gentle-men, I couldn't a helped it ef the gallis had been right afore me — when I sneezed, says I to myself — *gone!* But ding my skin, ef I don't believe that's what saved me. I tell you, gentle-men, I'm agin 'em; and now I goes home. So far you well."

So Mr. Thigpen ·left. Many, many times after that day, yea even down to old age, he was heard to say that he had "never seed but one man that he was afeerd of, and that was the Jedge — old Jedge Mike as used to be."

CHAPTER VI.

"Strain *vs*. Rickles."

It was now Friday morning. Judge Mike was weary with the session, and fretful from repeated wranglings with several leading lawyers. These had now all gone, the great cases having been either tried or continued. He had announced his determination to adjourn early that afternoon, whether the dockets were finished or not. The Court had not seen its family in two weeks, and it must and would see its family by to-morrow night. Mr. Sandidge was in the enjoyment of mild happiness; not only from the remembrance of having had a good run of luck during the week, but because the Judge was in a hurry, and the case of Strain *vs*. Rickles was yet untried. He wished it continued; for he was of counsel for the defendant, and they had no just defence. Mr. Mobley, though he had appeared but few times, was sore from more than one insult from the Bench.

"Strain *vs*. Rickles," called the Judge, rapidly and fretfully, with pen in hand, as if to say that this case was expected to follow the fate of the half-dozen preceding, and be disposed of summarily.

"Ready for the plaintiff," announced Mr. Mobley.

The Judge dropped his pen, leaned back in his chair, and cast a threatening look at the counsel. It did not seem to produce the effect desired. Mr. Mobley looked at him steadily.

Mr. Sandidge would remark that that was a case in which some pints of law were involved; and as the Court had not seen its family in two weeks, and as it was anxious to adjourn itself, and to go home and to see its family, he therefore would suggest that, if the counsel was willing, it might be continued generally until the next term. Mr. Mobley, objecting to this disposition, Mr. Sandidge, after having a witness called and receiving no answer, proceeded to make a showing for a continuance by the defendant. This was the absence of a witness who, as he had been informed, knew all about the case from beginning to end. Mr. Mobley had begun to argue the insufficiency of the showing for its indefiniteness, when his client, Strain, informed him that he had just seen the witness, who had heard the sheriff's call, and had answered to a bystander, who asked him why he did not obey it, "It's nobody but Mr. Sandidge, and I know what he wants." Mr. Mobley made this fact known to the Court. Mr. Sandidge seemed a little confused by this accident, until Sanks whispered in his ear:

" You needn't be afeerd o' that jury. There's two men on it which they knows me, and which also likewise I knows them."

The Judge hesitated. Mr. Sandidge, foreseeing the effect upon both of an exposure of what was the fact, that he had instructed the witness not to obey the call, withdrew his motion.

" I do this, may it please your Honor, not from anything my brother Mobley has said in his argument, nor from his insinuations, and so forth, and so forth. The showing is a sufficient one ; but I'll waive it, I'll waive it, sir."

And Mr. Sandidge gave such a mighty sweep with his long arm that Mr. Sanks had to dodge in order to prevent his hat being knocked off. Yet that official seemed greatly to admire the action, and also likewise sat down in a chair and giggled.

" Yes, sir," continued Mr. Sandidge, " I'll waive it, and I think I am prepared — I say, I think I'm prepared " (noticing the dissatisfaction of the Court with the direction the matter was taking) " to end this case in short order. The defendant is ready."

The jury were in the box. Mr. Mobley proceeded with his case. It was a simple action upon a promissory note given by the defendant to the plaintiff, who was a merchant from Augusta. He read the declaration, exhibited the note, and closed.

Mr. Sandidge rose, and with a smile which was meant to assure all present that he was expecting a speedy triumph, remarked that this was a case which he apprehended would not long be occupying the time of the Court and time of the country. He then announced to Mr. Mobley, that upon consulting with his client he had just discovered that the consideration of the note sued on was usurious, and that his conclusion being to rely on that defence solely, he should be compelled to ask for time in order to make out the plea, unless counsel would agree to consider it in already. Mr. Mobley, turning to his client, who assured him that it was false, allowed him to proceed.

A witness, the same who had been called, and who was sent for privately by Mr. Sandidge, went to the stand. After the usual preliminary that he did not in particular charge his mind, not expecting to be called on, he did testify that he was present at the giving of the note, and that he heard the parties say that it was in settlement of accounts of three or four years' standing, which the plaintiff held against the defendant. In answer to a question from Mr. Mobley if anything was said about extra interest, the witness declared that he did

9

not in particlar charge his mind, not expecting to be called on.
None but Mr. Sandidge would have seen any advantage to be obtained
from such testimony.   But he looked most gratefully at the witness,
expressed himself fully satisfied, dismissed him, smiled benignly on
the jury, compassionately on Mr. Mobley, then sat down with the air
of a man who had satisfactorily finished one piece of business and
after a little rest would be ready for another.

Plaintiff's counsel looked at the Judge with an expression which
seemed to say, "Surely no fool, not even you, would admit such testimony."   The Judge looked at him, and his expression seemed to ask,
"What do you say to that, Mr. Mobley?"   The latter avowed his
belief that in all judicial history a thing so absurd had never been
proposed, and he moved to be allowed to take his verdict.   Mr. Sandidge began at once to argue the law point, and was proceeding to say
that in all his recollection, in a practice of twenty-five years and better,
he had never seen a case where interest could be collected on open
accounts.   "But, may it please your Honor, the plaintiff in this case —
and these Augusty merchants"—

"Go on to the jury!" thundered the Judge.

Mr. Sandidge bowed, and turned to the panel.   "Gentlemen of the
jury, these Augusty merchants as a general thing always know what
they are about.   I say always — not a single exception;" and he
bestowed on the plaintiff a look fully significant of his admission that
he was entitled to his share of the encomium thus passed upon the
class of which he was an individual.

"These Augusty merchants know more in an hour about some things
than we plain country-people know in a week.   And it is reasonable to suppose that they do, and that's because they are Augusty
merchants."   Then Mr. Sandidge took a big smile and a small drink
of water, and oh how cunning he did look as his eyes peered over the
tumbler at the jury.

"Why, gentlemen, what chance have we got, away off here in the
country, to keep up along with them Augusty merchants?   We don't
have the boats, and the power of the wagons, and the thousands of
cotton-bags, and tobacco-hogsheads, and the fine brick war-houses,
and the hardwar-stores, and the other stores that always keeps full of
one particlar kind of goods, and sometimes more in one of 'em there
than there is in every store in this here town — yes, and them in Dukesborough put together.   Why, gentlemen, if Tommy Rickles was to go

to Augusty — you aint never been there, have you, Tommy? No —
you may tell from Tommy Rickles' looks and from this case that *he's*
never been to Augusty. But if he was to go there, and was to want
to buy a dog-knife for his little boy, Tommy Rickles would just as apt
to go into a store that had nothing but calico and dry-goods ; and
when they laughed and told him they was jest out of knives, he might
go to a hat-store, and then into a shoe-store, and then into a candy-
store — yes, gentlemen, into a store that the shelves was farly linded
with jars of candy and nothing but candy. And so it might be an
hour before he got to a hardwar-store and found a dog-knife for his
little boy ; and then ten to one Tommy Rickles couldn't find his way
back to his wagon."

Oh how Mr. John Sanks did laugh at Tommy during this harangue !
not loudly, but heartily and good-humoredly. And then how innocent
and pitiful Tommy did look, and how ashamed of his ignorance ! The
jury smiled approvingly with Mr. Sanks ; but Tommy looked so bashful
and bad that they got sorry for him and quit smiling.

"I say, gentlemen of the jury," continued Mr. Sandidge, "we don't
know anything at all to compare with these Augusty merchants. But
still there are some things that we do know, if we do live here in the
country where there aint any boats, and hat-stores and candy-stores
and hardwar-stores ; and one of them things is that you ce-ant collect
interest on open accounts. We all know that — that is, all except
Tommy Rickles."

General laughter, notwithstanding that Tommy looked still more
pitiful. Mr. Sanks winked at the two jurymen which he knew and
which also likewise knew him. Mr. Mobley noticed this action, but
perhaps he did not mind it.

"And, gentlemen, Tommy Rickles knew it too, if he had thought
about it and hadn't been with a Augusty merchant, and hadn't been
thinking of the boats, and the power of the wagons, and the hat-stores
and the shoe-stores and the candy-stores and the hardwar-stores, and
got his senses all mixed up, and confused up, and muddled up together,
as it war."

Continued laughter, several of the jury appearing to be fully satisfied.
The Judge waxing stern at the disorder, Mr. Sandidge had to moderate
his humor, and concluded by arguing, as heatedly and seriously as he
could, that interest not being collectible on open accounts, even the
defendant ought not to have included it in the note, and that therefore

the whole transaction was usurious. With another avowal of his desire not to take up the time of the Court and the time of the country by arguing so plain a case, he sat down, his countenance expressing both a virtuous indignation at a great wrong which was attempted, and a proud satisfaction that it could not be done over his shoulders.

Mr. Mobley felt, that with all the prejudices of the Judge against himself and his weakness on the subject of usury, he was in some danger of losing his case. He spoke with great energy on the absurdity of the defendant's plea, and of its plain dishonesty. In the midst of his argument, Mr. Sandidge flippantly asked him for his authorities. This was done of course to embarrass him, as he would have been forced to admit that there was no authority on such a point. But he had now gotten too high to be reached by Mr. Sandidge.

"I am asked," he said, "for the production of authority that the giving a promissory note in liquidation of a just debt is not usurious. I am thus asked by a lawyer of twenty-five years' practice — a lawyer who is old enough and prominent enough to be what it behooves every lawyer to be, a conservator of public tranquillity and private integrity — one who, with all his boasted contempt of legal precedents and his real ignorance of them, yet knows full well that in no Court of Justice, even the most insignificant, was this question, or any other one so absurd as this, ever raised ; and whose only reason for raising it at this time was his knowledge of the existence of dishonest habits and unreasonable prejudices which, as a leading citizen, he ought to be one of the last to encourage. Violent as the presumption often is, and far from the very semblance of truth, it is nevertheless a presumption that Judges know the laws ; and it ought to be the habit of attorneys and solicitors, especially those of experience and influence, to refrain from raising questions, a moment's entertainment of which by any Court is sufficient to deprive it of the respect of all men. But it has remained for this day to witness that the highest Court in one of the sovereign States of this Confederacy shall be insulted in its dignity and majesty by a course of conduct which seems to have been designedly pursued in order to test the sanity of that Court's presiding officer. Assuredly to no other mind than to that of the counsel had it been possible to fail to occur, that an insignificant advantage in a suit at law was scarcely worth the having when it was to be gained in a way which, to say nothing of its influence upon his client, would establish either the stultification of the Court, or " (and he looked fixedly and

fearlessly into the Judge's face) "raise the suspicion of a yet greater
infirmity. Even if he should consider himself as so great a friend to
the Court, whether from past favors or present adulation, or from any
other cause, as to think himself entitled to the exalted privilege of
being its favorite, one would have supposed that, if for no other
reason, at least from motives of prudence and decency, he would have
confined his conduct within that sphere where there would have been
left at least a doubt as to what judgment that conduct ought to receive.
It is a duty which we owe even to our private friends not to demand
a service of which there can be found no reason but friendship to
justify the rendering, while every other reason but friendship would
demand its refusal. There are some services which no ardor of
friendship is adequate to procure — some indeed which a proper and
worthy friendship would be the last to exact."

A large crowd had gathered into the Court-room, attracted by the
vehemence of the young lawyer's declamation. He was an eloquent
speaker, and his speech was telling upon the bystanders. He saw it,
and it stimulated him to continually increasing endeavor.

"There is a vulgar maxim that there is nothing to be lost by the
asking of favors. The counsel has long and well learned how to
profit by it. His successful experience in this respect, while it reflects
no great honor upon his sincerity, or even upon his ingenuity, pays a
consideration to the source from which these favors flow, which it is
impossible to be considered as in the smallest degree respectful. I
warn him this day of the necessity to beware how he abuses an influence which his every action shows that he is conscious of exerting.

"There is a decorum which men, even of the greatest ability, when
in the enjoyment of honors, even those the most fairly won, cannot
neglect with impunity. Let him, then, especially beware, the success
of whose career is mainly dependent upon favor. For granting that
the power which, strange as it is, he may truly think that he has im-
measurably above others succeeded in conciliating and controlling, is
absolute and unlimited, yet when it shall at last of all others become
convinced that such a control is no longer compatible, not only with
the appearance of respectability, but even with its own security, and
shall, as it assuredly will, withdraw from him the favor in which he
seems to live, and move, and have his being, he must then know how
vain will be the late pursuit of those other and higher means of success
which it has been his constant habit to neglect. And even if this

should come to pass, if dullness shall never be able to be conscious of and to resist a control which binds it like the spell of the charmer, surely, in a country so free and so humane in all its institutions except its Courts of Justice, in a country where there are so many good and brave men — men who have been good enough and brave enough to resist and to destroy every other form of tyranny, it is not too much to expect that the time must come, and come soon, when this last form must yield to the necessities of an advancing civilisation, and follow the fate of those which have gone before it. Surely, surely, it cannot long remain that a free people, who have broken the last shackle of political despotism, must continue to bow in abject submission before another which is the more odious because their own hands have created it, and because their own hands may peaceably destroy it."

Mr. Mobley spoke for half-an-hour in this strain, during many parts of which, Mr. Sandidge, smiling as he was, was rather piteous to be seen ; and when he spoke of the merits of the plea itself, Tommy Rickles, but that he had the great Mr. Sandidge for his friend, would have felt as if he ought to be in the Penitentiary.

In the midst of this harangue, one of the jury, a Sanks and Sandidge man, rose up and hastily rushed out of the box. Upon being caught and brought back, he was asked by the Judge why he had left his seat. The man, looking timidly at Mr. Sanks, answered :

"Ef it mout please the Cote, I had heerd Mr. Sandidge speak and made up my mind, and when that youngster was a speakin' I didn't like the way the argiment was a gwine, and my idees got confusid, and so I thought I better leave."

The Judge sternly informed him that his ideas must be controlled by the Court, and that in future he would do well to remain in the box. Mr. Sanks also gave him a look which seemed to nail him to his seat.

Mr. Mobley caught up his Honor at this juncture, and had much to say about the rights both of juries and counsel. Besides, he cut Mr. Sanks without mercy, whose secret meddling with the jury he had noticed. The Judge, although he saw that Mobley was quite superior to what he supposed, yet felt that he must do something in order to restrain him. Several times he had been upon the point of fining him ; but he seemed to be waiting for the most favorable opportunity. Mr. Mobley called for the Digest of the laws of the State, and was proceeding to read upon the subject of Usury. Judge Mike, who had now lost all patience, ordered him to put down the book, and declared that he should pay no regard to whatever he might read.

The young man shut the book at once, and abandoning himself to his rage, exclaimed:

"Then must the laws of Georgia lie prostrate at the feet of a *Nisi-Prius* Judge, because there is no higher tribunal to correct his follies or restrain his audacity!" And lifting the book with both hands high above his head, he brought it down upon the clerk's desk with a vehemence which made that official rise suddenly from his seat and retreat to the farthest corner of the bar.

"Mr. Sheriff, arrest that man!" roared Judge Mike, and he seized his pen to make out the order. Mr. Sanks arose and approached the counsel. The latter raised his left hand and turned the palm towards him with a warning gesture, when the sheriff hesitated a moment and then retreated behind Mr. Sandidge. Then turning to the Judge, Mr. Mobley said, almost in a whisper:

"Behold!"

The Judge paused in his writing and looked at him. His hair stood almost upright; his color was that of the dead; and looking alternately at the Judge and the sheriff, his eyes rolled and burned like the chafed lion's, as lifting his right arm above his head, he said:

"There are some things which, in so far as I am concerned, even a Judge of the Superior Court and his most servile minister would do well to hesitate before they attempt to perform."

The poor creature sank back in his chair, and bowed his head in the unutterable anguish of feeling that a mere boy, whom he had unjustly assaulted, had turned upon him and vanquished him in his own castle.

Mr. Mobley sat down. His Honor had determined to charge the jury in favor of the defendant. For he desired to uproot in his circuit not only usury, but everything that looked at all like it. Indeed, all rates of interest in his eyes seemed criminal, and therefore usurious. He honestly believed that there was no evil under the sun to be compared with it. Some wag had told him that it was interest that had overthrown the great Roman Empire, and that it was once sold under execution by the sheriff. So a transaction had but to look in the slightest degree usurious, and it would have his condemnation. He intended so to charge in this case; but now he was so subdued that he dismissed the jury to their room without a word, and proceeded with taking the rules usual at the end of the term. Half-an-hour afterwards, the jury having obtained leave to return to the box, upon inquiry as to whether they had agreed upon a verdict, their foreman, a little dark man with short straight-up hair and a sharp voice, answered :

"May it please the Cote, we has not. We desires to ask the Cote ef upon the provoso — you mind, Jedge — ef upon the provoso "—

" I don't want to hear any more about your provosoes," screamed the Judge, feeling that he must reassert himself after his late defeat ; " I have no instructions to give on your provosoes. Go back to your room, and, mark me, I am going to adjourn this Court at three o'clock. Mr. Sanks, if this jury have not agreed upon a verdict by that time, do you have ready a wagon and a six-horse team. Hire it at the county's expense. If you jury don't agree upon a verdict by that time, I'll have you hauled around this circuit with me until you do agree. Now go to your room."

The little man dodged, turned quickly, and pocketing his *provosoes*, led his followers back. But Mr. Sanks spoke the truth when he said, " There's two men on that jury which they knows me, and which I also likewise knows them." And so after another hour both counsel agreed to a mis-trial.

And now the sun was fast declining. Unless the Court could get fifteen or twenty miles on its way home to-day, it would not reach it and see its family by to-morrow night. Business had to be dispatched in a hurry, as everybody knew that that Court was bent on seeing its family at all cost.

Mr. Mobley was writing rapidly. Mr. Sanks peeped over his shoulder, and then went to Mr. Sandidge and whispered in his ear.

" What are you so skeerd about ? " asked the lawyer.

"Yes, but I aint ready ; and ah — and also likewise I let the money go," answered the sheriff.

" How much do you happen to have about you at this particlar time ? "

" Twenty dollars."

" Hand 'em to me. That'll do. Don't you see he's bent on home ? "

The last docket was cleared, the juries discharged, and the Judge took out his watch.

" May it please your Honor," said Mr. Mobley, " I desire to take a rule against the sheriff."

" Will it be resisted ? " asked the Judge, with a sullen look.

" It will, may it please your Honor," blandly but firmly answered Mr. Sandidge.

" Mr. Sheriff, go to my office and get me the Acts of the last Legis-

lature. Bring those of the two last, if you please, Mr. Sheriff; I dis-
remember which it is that contains the law I wish to refer to. I ask
the indulgence of the Court for a few, only a very few minutes, until I
can make out the showing," and Mr. Sandidge looked as if he would
indeed like to be in a hurry, if such a thing were possible.

"Will there be any other rules?" asked the Judge.

"I have several," Mr. Sandidge answered. "But unless your Honor
could hold over until to-morrow, I shall be obliged to postpone them
until the next term, as this rule will take up all, or pretty much all of
the balance of to-day — leastways, probably"—

Mr. Mobley, knowing his adversary's intention, rose and exclaimed :

"It is a most base subterfuge with both client and counsel! Within
my certain knowledge this money was collected more than a month
ago. I think that knave has had indulgence enough for his rascalities."

The sheriff was going slowly towards the door, and was looking
back beseechingly to the Judge.

"Come back here, sir!" cried the latter, rising in his chair. "This
Court has got powers ; it has got rights ; it may be insulted, but it
has got privileges. Mr. Sheriff, adjourn this Court till the Court in
course !"

"I protest against this disgraceful"—began Mr. Mobley ; but the
sheriff was shrieking the announcement at the door ; and as his Honor,
pale and haggard, rushed rapidly past him, "God save the State !" he
cried in thankful glee, "and the onerble Cote." Mr. Mobley was too
full of indignation to trust himself with many words.

"You two, and he, form a beautiful trio in the dispensation of
human justice," he said bitterly to the lawyer and the sheriff. "It
was well that you" (to Mr. Sanks) "kept your dirty hands off me to-
day. As for you, Sandidge, mark me, your day is passing ; mine is
coming ; ay, it is already here !"

"I think he'll have to wait for his big Cote, eh, Mr. Sandidge?" Mr.
Sanks remarked as Mobley left. Mr. Sandidge made no answer,
but taking a big chew, smiled seriously. In twenty minutes from that
time, the two rascals compelled the plaintiff in execution who had
sought the rule to settle his debt by taking off twenty per cent., and
deducting also the twenty dollars paid Mr. Sandidge for his fee ;
"which war but jestice," claimed Mr. Sanks, "because, and so forth,
and also likewise because of them disgraceful proceedances."

"Rather lively times in Court to-day," said the young lawyer to
Overton, after they had reached the former's office.

10

"Surely such scenes must happen seldom?"

"Exactly, such do happen seldom indeed ; but something like them occurs often."

"In all the circuits?"

"No, thank Heaven! We do have some Judges who are neither fools nor rascals. Indeed, we have some who are eminently able and honest. Our judiciary system is the best in the world, I believe, except that it has no Court of Appeals — in fact, no head. When, therefore, a fellow like Mike gets upon the Bench, there is no counting what folly or what rascality he may commit. The miserable creature used to crowd me until I felt that I must resist, or become as vile as a collared slave. He knows now, I think, that I am not afraid of him."

"He is now evidently afraid of you."

"I do not know as to that." Mr. Mobley brushed the hair from his forehead, and looked as if he did know as to that.

"Well, well," he continued, "let it be so, if it be so. For humiliating as it is to a gentleman's sense of propriety and decency, he must either become a favorite of the Court or make the Court afraid of him. Between the two, unhappy as is the choice of either, he cannot hesitate."

The student made no answer, but parting from him, ordered his horse, and rode slowly back to Mr. Parkinson's.

And now as I look back to the scenes of this week, they seem long, oh! so long ago.

HOW MR. BILL WILLIAMS TOOK THE RESPONSIBILITY.

"Our honor teacheth us
That we be bold in every enterprise."

CHAPTER I.

WHEN Josiah Lorriby came into our neighborhood to keep a
school I was too young to go to it alone. Having no older
brother or sister to go along with me, my parents, although they were
desirous for me to begin, were about to give it up, when fortunately it
was ascertained that William Williams, a big fellow whose widowed
mother resided near to us, intended to go for one term and complete
his education preparatory to being better fitted for an object of vast
ambition which he had in view. His way lay by our door, and as he
was one of the most accommodating persons in the world, he proffered
to take charge of me. Without hesitation and with much gratitude
this was accepted, and I was delivered over into his keeping.

William Williams was so near being a man that the little boys used
to call him Mr. Bill. I never can forget the stout homespun dress-
coat which he used to wear, with the big pockets opening horizontally
across the outer side of the skirts. Many a time, when I was fatigued
by walking or the road was wet with rains, have I ridden upon his
back, my hands resting upon his shoulders and my feet standing in
those capacious pockets. Persons who have never tried that way of
travelling have no just idea, I will venture to say, how sweet it is.
Mr. Bill had promised to take care of me, and he kept his word.

On the first morning when the school was opened, we went together to it. About one mile and a half distant stood the school-house. Eighteen by twenty feet were its dimensions. It was built of logs and covered with clap-boards. It had one door, and opposite to that a hole in the wall two feet square, which was called the window. It stood in the corner of one of our fields (having formerly been used as a fodder-house), and on the brow of a hill, at the foot of which, over-shadowed by oak trees, was a noble spring of fresh water. Our way led us by this spring. Just as we reached it, Mr. Bill pointed to the summit and said :

"Yonder it is, Squire."

Mr. Bill frequently called me Squire, partly from mere facetious-ness, and partly from his respect for my father, who was a Justice of the Peace.

I did not answer. We ascended the hill, and Mr. Bill led me into the presence of the genius of the place.

Mr. Josiah Lorriby was a remarkable man, at least in appearance. He was below the middle height, but squarely built. His body was good enough, but his other parts were defective. He had a low flat head, with very short hair and very long ears. His arms were reason-ably long, but his hands and legs were disproportionately short. Many tales were told of his feet, on which he wore shoes with iron soles. He was sitting on a split-bottom chair, on one side of the fire-place. Under him, with his head peering out between the rounds, sitting on his hind legs and standing on his fore legs, was a small yellow dog, without tail or ears. This dog's name was Rum. On the side of the hearth, in another split-bottom, sat a tall raw-boned woman with the reddest eyes that I have ever seen. This was Mrs. Mehitable, Mr. Lorriby's wife. She had ridden to the school on a small aged mare, perfectly white and totally blind. Her name was Kate.

When I had surveyed these four personages,— this satyr of a man, this tailless dog, this red-eyed woman, and this blind old mare, a sense of fear and helplessness came over me, such as I had never felt before, and have never felt since. I looked at Mr. Bill Williams, but he was observing somebody else, and did not notice me. The other pupils, eighteen or twenty in number, seemed to be in deep meditation. My eyes passed from one to another of the objects of my dread ; but they became finally fastened upon the dog. His eyes also had wandered, but only with vague curiosity, around upon all the pupils, until they became fixed upon me. We gazed at each other several moments. Though he sat still, and I sat still, it seemed to me that we were drawing continually nearer to each other. Suddenly I lifted up my voice and screamed with all my might. It was so sudden and sharp that everybody except the woman jumped. She indifferently pointed to the dog. Her husband arose, came to me, and in soothing tones asked what was the matter.

"I am scared!" I answered, as loud as I could speak.

"Scared of what, my little man? of the dog?"

"I am scared of ALL of you!"

He laughed with good humor, bade me not be afraid, called up Rum, talked to us both, enjoined upon us to be friends, and prophesied that we would be such — the best that had ever been in the world. The little creature became cordial at once, reared his fore feet upon his master, took them down, reared them upon me, and in the absence of a tail to wag, twisted his whole hinder-parts in most violent assurance that if I should say the word we were friends already. Such kindness, and so unexpected, dissolved my apprehensions. I was in a condition to accept terms far less liberal. So I acceded, and went to laughing outright. Everybody laughed, and Rum, who could do nothing better in that line, ran about and barked as joyously as any dog with a tail could have done. In the afternoon when school was dismissed, I invited Rum to go home with me; but he, waiting as I supposed for a more intimate acquaintance, declined.

CHAPTER II.

It was delightful to consider how auspicious a beginning I had made. Other little boys profited by it. Mr. Lorriby had no desire to lose any of his scholars, and we all were disposed to take as much advantage as possible of his apprehension, however unfounded, that on account of our excessive timidity our parents might remove us from the school. Besides, we knew that we were to lose nothing by being on friendly terms with Rum. The dread of the teacher's wife soon passed away. She had but little to say, and less to do. Nobody had any notion of any reason which she had for coming to the school. At first she occasionally heard a spelling-class recite. After a little time she began to come much less often, and in a few weeks her visits had decreased to one in several days. Mrs. Lorriby seemed a very proud woman ; for she not only had little to say to anybody, but although she resided only a mile and a half from the school-house, she never walked, but invariably rode old Kate. These were small things, yet we noticed them.

Mr. Lorriby was not of the sort of schoolmasters whom men use to denominate by the title of *knock-down and drag out.* He was not such a man as Israel Meadows. But although he was good-hearted enough, he was somewhat politic also. Being a new-comer, and being poor, he determined to manage his business with due regard to the tastes, the wishes, and the prejudices of the community in which he labored. He decidedly preferred a mild reign ; but it was said he could easily accommodate himself to those who required a more vigorous policy. He soon learned that the latter was the favorite here. People complained that there was little or no whipping. Some who had read the fable of the frogs who desired a sovereign, were heard to declare that Josiah Lorriby was no better than "Old King Log." One patron spoke of taking his children home, placing the boy at the plough and the girl at the spinning-wheel.

Persons in those days loved their children, doubtless, as well as now ; but they had some strange ways of showing their love. The strangest of all was the evident gratification which the former felt when the latter were whipped at school. While they all had a notion that education was something which it was desirable to get, it was believed that the impartation of it needed to be conducted in most mysterious ways. The school-house of that day was, in a manner, a cave of Trophonius, into which urchins of both sexes entered amid certain incomprehensible ceremonies, and were everlastingly subject and used to be whirled about, body and soul, in a vortex of confusion. I might pursue the analogy and say that, like the votaries of Trophonius, they were not wont to smile until long after this violent and rotatory indoctrination ; but rather to weep and lament, unless they were brave like Apollonius, or big like Allen Thigpen, and so could bully the priest far enough to have the bodily rotation dispensed with. According to these notions, the principles of the education of books were not to be addressed to the mind and to the heart ; but, if they were expected to stick, they must be beaten with rods into the back. Through this ordeal of painful ceremonies had the risen generation gone, and through the same ordeal they honestly believed that the present generation ought to go, and must go. No exception was made in favor of genius. Its back was to be kept as sore as stupidity's; for, being yoked with the latter, it must take the blows, the oaths, and the imprecations. I can account for these things in no other way than by supposing that the old set of persons had come out of the old system with minds so bewildered as to be ever afterwards incapable of thinking upon it in a reasonable manner. [In one respect there is a considerable likeness between mankind and some individuals of the brute creation. The dog seems to love best that master who beats him before giving him a bone. I have heard persons say (those who had carefully studied the nature and habits of that animal) that the mule is wont to evince a gratitude somewhat touching when a bundle of fodder is thrown to him at the close of a day on which he has been driven within an inch of his life. So with the good people of former times.] They had been beaten so constantly and so mysteriously at school, that they seemed to entertain a grateful affection for it ever afterwards. It was, therefore, with feelings of benign satisfaction, sometimes not unmixed with an innocent gaiety of mind, that they were wont to listen to their children when they complained of the thrashings they daily received, some of which would be wholly unaccountable. Indeed the latter sort seemed to be considered, of all others, the most salutary. When the punishment was graduated by the offence, it was supporting too great a likeness to the affairs of every-day life, and therefore wanting in solemn impressiveness. But when a schoolmaster for no accountable reason whipped a boy, and so set his mind in a state of utter bewilderment as to what could be the matter, and the most vague speculations upon what was to become of him in this world, to say nothing of the next, ah! then it was that the experienced felt a happiness that was gently ecstatic. They recurred in their minds to their own school time, and they concluded that, as these things had not killed them, they must have done them good. So some of our good mothers in Israel, on occasions of great religious excitement, as they bend over a shrieking sinner, smile in serene happiness as they fan his throbbing temples, and fondly encourage him to shriek on; thinking of the pit from which they were digged, and of the rock upon which they now are standing, they shout, and sing, and fan, and fanning ever, continue to sing and shout.

CHAPTER III.

WHEN Mr. Lorriby had sounded the depths of public sentiment, he became a new man. One Monday morning he announced that he was going to turn over a new leaf, and he went straightway to turning it over. Before night several boys, from small to medium, had been flogged. He had not begun on the girls, except in one instance. In that I well remember the surprise I felt at the manner in which her case was disposed of. Her name was Susan Potter. She was about twelve years old, and well grown. When she was called up, inquiry was made by the master if any boy present was willing to take upon himself the punishment which must otherwise fall upon her. After a moment's silence, Seaborn Byne, a boy of fourteen, rose and presented himself. He was good-tempered and fat, and his pants and round jacket fitted him closely. He advanced with the air of a man who was going to do what was right, with no thought of consequences. Miss Potter unconcernedly went to her seat.

But Seaborn soon evinced that he was dissatisfied with a bargain that was so wholly without consideration. I believed then, and I believe to this day, that but for his being so good a mark he would have received fewer stripes. But his round fat body and legs stood so temptingly before the rod, and the latter fell upon good flesh so entirely through its whole length, that it was really hard to stop. He roared with pain so unexpectedly severe, and violently rubbed each spot of recent infliction. When it was over, he came to his seat and looked at Susan Potter. She seemed to feel like laughing. Seaborn got no sympathy, except from a source which he despised; that was his younger brother, Joel. Joel was weeping in secret.

"Shut up your mouth," whispered Seaborn, threateningly, and Joel shut up.

Then I distinctly heard Seaborn mutter the following words:

"Ef I ever takes another for her, or any of 'em, may I be dinged, and then dug up and dinged over again."

I have no doubt that he kept his oath, for I continued to know Seaborn Byne until he was an old man, and I never knew a person who persistently held that vicarious system of school punishment in deeper disgust. What his ideas were about being "dinged," and about that operation being repeated, I did not know; but I supposed it was something that, if possible, would better be avoided.

Such doings as these made a great change in the feelings of us little ones. Yet I continued to run the crying schedule. It failed at last, and I went under.

Mr. Lorriby laid it upon me remorselessly. I had never dreamed that he would give me such a flogging — I who considered myself, as everybody else considered me, a favorite. Now the charm was gone ; the charm of security. It made me very sad. I lost my love for the teacher. I even grew cold towards Rum, and Rum in his turn grew cold towards me. Not that we got into open hostilities. For saving an occasional fretfulness, Rum was a good fellow and personally I had liked him. But then he was from principle a thorough Lorriby, and therefore our intimacy must stop, and did stop.

In a short time Mr. Lorriby had gone as nearly all round the school as it was prudent to go. Every boy but two had received his portion, some once, some several times. These two were Mr. Bill Williams, and another big boy named Jeremiah Hobbes. These were, of course, as secure against harm from Mr. Lorriby as they would have been had he been in Guinea. Every girl also had been flogged, or had had a boy flogged for her, except Betsy Ann Acry, the belle of the school. She was a light-haired, blue-eyed, plump, delicious-looking girl, fourteen years old. Now for Miss Betsy Ann Acry, as it was known to everybody about the school-house, Mr. Bill Williams had a partiality which, though not avowed, was decided. He had never courted her in set words, but he had observed her from day to day, and noticed her ripening into womanhood with constantly increasing admiration. He was scarcely a match for her even if they both had been in condition to marry. He knew this very well. But considerations of this sort seldom do a young man any good. More often than otherwise they make him worse. At least such was their effect upon Mr. Bill. The greater the distance between him and Miss Betsy Ann, the more he yearned across it. He sat in school where he could always see her, and oh, how he eyed her ! Often, often have I noticed Mr. Bill, leaning the side of his head upon his arms, extended on the desk in front of him, and looking at her with a countenance which, it seemed to me, ought to make some impression. Betsy Ann received it all as if it was no more than she was entitled to, but showed no sign whether she set any value upon the possession or not. Mr. Bill hoped she did ; the rest of us believed she did not.

Mr. Bill had another ambition, which was, if possible, even higher

11

than the winning of Miss Acry. Having almost extravagant notions of the greatness of Dukesborough, and the distinction of being a resident within it, he had long desired to go there as a clerk in a store. He had made repeated applications to be taken in by Messrs. Bland & Jones, and it was in obedience to a hint from these gentlemen that he had determined to take a term of finishing off at the school of Mr. Lorriby. This project was never out of his mind, even in moments of his fondest imaginings about Miss Betsy Ann. It would have been not easy to say which he loved the best. The clerkship seemed to become nearer and nearer after each Saturday's visit to town, until at last he had a distinct offer of the place. The salary was small, but at he waived that consideration in view of the exaltation of the office and the greatness of living in Dukesborough. He accepted, to enter upon his duties in four weeks, when the quarter session of the school would expire.

The dignified ways of Mr. Bill after this made considerable impression upon all the school. Even Betsy Ann condescended to turn her eyes oftener in the direction where he happened to be, and he was almost inclined to glory in the hope that the possession of one dear object would draw the other along with it. At least he felt that if he should lose the latter, the former would be the highest consolation which he could ask. The news of the distinguished honor that had been conferred upon him reached the heads of the school early on the Monday following the eventful Saturday when the business was done. I say heads, for of late Mrs. Mehitable and old Kate came almost every day. Mrs. Lorriby received the announcement without emotion. Mr. Lorriby, on the other hand, in spite of the prospect of losing a scholar, was almost extravagant in his congratulations.

"It was a honor to the whole school," he said. "I feels it myself. Sich it war under all the circumstances. It was obleeged to be, and sich it war, and as it war sich, I feels it myself."

Seaborn Byne heard this speech. Immediately afterwards he turned to me and whispered the following comment:

"He be dinged! the decateful old son-of-a-gun!"

CHAPTER IV.

IT was the unanimous opinion amongst Mr. Lorriby's pupils that he was grossly inconsistent with himself: that he ought to have begun with the rigid policy at first, or have held to the mild. Having once enjoyed the sweets of the latter, thoughts would occasionally rise and questions would be asked. Seaborn Byne was not exactly the head, but he was certainly the orator of a revolutionary party. Not on his own account ; for he had never yet, except as the voluntary substitute of Miss Susan Potter, felt upon his own body the effects of the change of discipline. Nor did he seem to have any apprehensions on that score. He even went so far as to say to Mr. Bill Williams, who had playfully suggested the bare idea of such a thing, that "ef old Jo Lorriby raised his old pole on him, he would put his lizzard" (as Seaborn facetiously called his knife) "into his paunch." He always carried a very big knife, with which he would frequently stab imaginary Lorribys in the persons of saplings and pumpkins, and even the air itself. This threat had made his brother Joel extremely unhappy. His little heart was bowed down with the never-resting fear and belief that Seaborn was destined to commit the crime of murder upon the body of Mr. Lorriby. On the other hand Seaborn was constantly vexed by the sight of the scores of floggings which Joel received. Poor Joel had somehow in the beginning of his studies gotten upon the wrong road, and as nobody ever brought him back to the starting point, he was destined, it seemed, to wander about lost evermore. The more floggings he got, the more hopeless and wild were his efforts at extrication. It was unfortunate for him that his brother took any interest in his condition. Seaborn had great contempt for him, but yet he remembered that he was his brother, and his brother's heart would not allow itself to feel no concern. That concern manifested itself in endeavoring to teach Joel himself out of school, and in flogging him himself by way of preventing Joel's having to submit to that disgrace at the hands of old Joe. So eager was Seaborn in this brotherly design, and so indocile was Joel, that for every flogging which the latter received from the master he got from two to three from Seaborn.

However, the inflictions which Seaborn made, strictly speaking, could not be called floggings. Joel, among his other infirmities, had that of being unable to take care of his spelling-books. He had torn to pieces so many that his mother had obtained a paddle and pasted on both sides of it as many words as could be crowded there. Mrs. Byne, who was a woman of decision, had been heard to say that she meant to head him at this destructive business, and now she believed that she had done it. But this instrument was made to subserve a double purpose with Joel. It was at once the object, and in his brother's hands was the stimulus, of his little ambition. Among all these evils, floggings from Mr. Lorriby and paddlings from Seaborn, and the abiding apprehension that the former was destined to be murdered by the latter, Joel Byne's was a case to be pitied.

"It ar a disgrace," said Mr. Bill to me one morning as we were going to school, "and I wish Mr. Larrabee knowed it. Between him and Sebe, that little innocent individiel ar bent on bein' useded up bodaciously. Whippins from Mr. Larrabee and paddlins from Sebe! The case ar wusser than ef thar was two Larrabees. That ar the ontimeliest paddle that ever *I* seen. He have to try to larn his paddle, and when he can't larn it, Sebe, he take his paddle, fling down Joel, and paddle him *with* his paddle. In all my experience, I has not seed jest sich a case. It ar beyant hope."

Mr. Bill's sympathy made him serious, and indeed gloomy. The road on which the Bynes came to school met ours a few rods from the spring. We were now there, and Mr. Bill had scarcely finished this speech when we heard behind us the screams of a child.

"Thar it is agin," said Mr. Bill. "At it good and soon. It do beat everything in this blessed and ontimely world. Ef it don't, ding me!"

We looked beind us. Here came Joel at full speed, screaming with all his might, hatless, with his paddle in one hand and his dinner-bucket, without cover, hanging from the other. Twenty yards behind him ran Seaborn, who had been delayed by having to stop in order to pick up Joel's hat and the bucket-cover. Just before reaching the spring, the fugitive was overtaken and knocked down. Seaborn then getting upon him and fastening his arms with his own knees, seized the paddle and exclaimed:

"Now, you rascal! spell that word agin, sir. Ef you don't, I'll paddle you into a pancake. Spell ' *Crucifix*,' sir."

Joel attempted to obey.

"*S* agin, you little devil! *S-i, si!* Ding my skin ef you shan't larn it, or I'll paddle you as long as thar's poplars to make paddles outen."

And he turned Joel over and made him ready.

"Look a here, Sebe!" interposed Mr. Bill; "fun's fun, but too much is too much."

Now what these words were intended to be preliminary to, there was no opportunity of ascertaining; for just then Mr. Josiah Lorriby, who had diverged from his own way in order to drink at the spring, presented himself.

"What air you about thar, Sebion Byne?"

Seaborn arose, and though he considered his conduct not only justifiable, but praiseworthy, he looked a little crest-fallen.

"Ah, indeed! You're the assistant teacher, air you? Interfering with *my* business, and *my* rights, and *my* duties, and *my* — hem! Let us all go to the school-house now. Mr. Byne will manage business hereafter. I — as for me, I aint nowhar now. Come, Mr. Byne, le's go to school."

Mr. Lorriby and Seaborn went on, side by side. Mr. Bill looked as if he were highly gratified. "Ef he don't get it now, he never will."

Alas for Joel! Delivered from Seaborn, he was yet more miserable than before, and he forgot his own griefs in his pity for the impending fate of Mr. Lorriby, and his apprehension for the ultimate consequence of this day's work to his brother. He pulled me a little behind Mr. Bill, and tremblingly whispered:

"Poor Mr. Larrabee! Do you reckon they will hang Seaby, Phil?"

"What for?" I asked.

"For killing Mr. Larrabee."

I answered that I hoped not.

"Oh, Phil! Seaby have sich a big knife! An' he have stob more saplins! and more punkins! and more watermillions! and more mush-millions! And he have even stob our old big yaller cat! And he have call every one of 'em Larrabee. And it's my pinion that ef it warn't for my paddle, he would a stob me befo' now. You see, Phil, paddlin me sorter cools and swages him down a leetle bit. Oh, Seaby ar a tremenduous boy, and he ar *goin* to stob Mr. Larrabee this blessed day."

As we neared the school-house we saw old Kate at the usual stand, and we knew that Mrs. Lorriby was at hand. She met her husband at the door, and they had some whispering together, of which the case of Seaborn was evidently the subject. Joel begged me to stay with him outside until the horrible thing was over. So we stopped and peeped in between the logs. We had not to wait long. Mr. Lorriby, his mate standing by his side, at once began to lay on, and Seaborn roared. The laying on and the roaring continued until the master was satisfied. When all was over, I looked into Joel's face. It was radiant with smiles. I never have seen greater happiness upon the countenance of childhood.   Happy little fellow!   Seaborn would not be hung.   That illusion was gone forever.   He actually hugged his paddle to his breast, and with a gait even approaching the triumphant, walked into the house.

CHAPTER V.

HAVING broken the ice upon Seaborn, Mr. Lorriby went into the sport of flogging him whenever he felt like it.   Seaborn's revolutionary sentiments grew deeper and stronger constantly.   But he was now, of course, hopeless of accomplishing any results himself, and he knew that the only chance was to enlist Jeremiah Hobbes, or Mr. Bill Williams, and make him the leader in the enterprise.   Very soon, however, one of these chances was lost.   Hobbes received and accepted an offer to become an overseer on a plantation, and Seaborn's hopes were now fixed upon Mr. Bill alone.   That also was destined soon to be lost by the latter's prospective clerkship.   Besides, Mr. Bill, being even-tempered, and never having received and being never likely to receive any provocation from Mr. Lorriby, the prospect of making anything out of him was gloomy enough.   In vain Seaborn raised innuendoes concerning his pluck.   In vain he tried every other expedient, even to secretly drawing on Mr. Bill's slate a picture of a very little man flogging a very big boy, and writing as well as he could the name of Mr. Lorriby near the former and that of Mr. Bill near the latter. Seaborn could not disguise himself; and Mr. Bill when he saw the pictures informed the artist that if he did not mind what he was about he would get a worse beating than ever Joe Larrabee gave him. Seaborn had but one hope left, but that involved some little delicacy, and could be managed only by its own circumstances.   It might do, and it might not do.   If Seaborn had been accustomed to asking special Divine interpositions, he would have prayed that if anything was to be made out of this, it might be made before Mr. Bill should leave.   Sure enough it did come.   Just one week before the quarter was out it came.   But I must premise the narration of this great event with a few words.

Between Mrs. Lorriby and Miss Betsy Ann Acry the relations were not very agreeable.   Among other things which were the cause of this were the unwarrantable liberties which Miss Acry sometimes took with

Kate, Mrs. Lorriby's mare. Betsy Ann, in spite of all dangers (not the least of which was that of breaking her own neck), would treat herself to an occasional ride whenever circumstances allowed. One day at play-time, when Mrs. Lorriby was out upon one of her walks, which she sometimes took at that hour, Betsy Ann hopped upon the mare, and bantered me for a race to the spring and back. I accepted. We set out. I beat old Kate on the return, because she stumbled and fell. A great laugh was raised, and we were detected by Mrs. Lorriby. Passing me, she went up to Betsy Ann, and thus spoke :

"Betsy Ann Acree, libities is libities, and horses is horses, which is mars is mars. I have ast you not to ride this mar, which she was give to me by my parrent father, and which she have not been rid, no, not by Josiah Lorribee hisself, and which I have said I do not desires she shall be spilt in her gaits, and which I wants and desires you will not git upon the back of that mar nary nother time."

After this event these two ladies seemed to regard each other with even increased dislike.

Miss Betsy Ann Acry had heretofore escaped correction for any of her shortcomings, although they were not few. She was fond of mischief, and no more afraid of Mr. Lorriby than Mr. Bill Williams was. Indeed, Miss Betsy Ann considered herself to be a woman, and she had been heard to say that a whipping was something which she would take from nobody. Mr. Lorriby smiled at her mischievous tricks, but Mrs. Lorriby frowned. These ladies came to dislike each other more and more. The younger, when in her frolics, frequently noticed the elder give her husband a look which was expressive of much meaning. Seaborn had also noticed this, and the worse Miss Acry grew, the oftener Mrs. Lorriby came to the school. The truth is that Seaborn had pondered so much that he at last made a profound discovery. He had come to believe fully, and in this he was right, that the object which the female Lorriby had in coming at all was to protect the male. A bright thought! He communicated it to Miss Acry, and slyly hinted several times that he believed she was afraid of Old Red Eye, as he denominated the master's wife. Miss Acry indignantly repelled every such insinuation, and became only the bolder in what she said and what she did. Seaborn knew that the Lorribys were well aware of Mr. Bill's preference for the girl, and he intensely enjoyed her temerity. But it was hard to satisfy him that she was not afraid of Old Red Eye. If Old Red Eye had not been there, Betsy Ann would have done so and so. The reason why she did not do so and so, was because Old Red Eye was about. Alas for human nature! — male and female. Betsy Ann went on and on, until she was brought to a halt. The occasion was thus.

There was in the school a boy of about my own size, and a year or two older, whose name was Martin Granger. He was somewhat of a pitiful-looking creature — whined when he spoke, and was frequently in quarrels, not only with the boys, but with the girls. He was suspected of sometimes playing the part of spy and informer to the Lorribys, both of whom treated him with more consideration than any other pupil, except Mr. Bill Williams. Miss Betsy Ann cordially disliked him, and she honored myself by calling me her favorite in the whole school.

Now Martin and I got ourselves very unexpectedly into a fight. I had divided my molasses with him at dinner-time for weeks and weeks. A few of the pupils whose parents could afford to have that luxury, were accustomed to carry it to school in phials. I usually ate my part after boring a hole in my biscuit and then filling it up. I have often wished since I have been grown that I could relish that preparation as I relished it when a boy. But as we grow older our tastes change. Martin Granger relished the juice even more than I. In all my observations I have never known a person of any description who was as fond of molasses as he was. It did me good to see him eat it. He never brought any himself, but he used to hint, in his whining way, that the time was not distant when his father would have a whole kegful, and when he should bring it to school in his mother's big snuffbottle, which was well known to us all. Although I was not so sanguine of the realisation of this prospect as he seemed to be, yet I had not on that account become tired of furnishing him. I only grew tired of his presence while at my dinner, and I availed myself of a trifling dispute one day to shut down upon him. I not only did not invite him to partake of my molasses, but I rejected his spontaneous proposition to that effect. He had been dividing it with me so long that I believe he thought my right to cut him off now was estopped. He watched me as I bored my holes and poured in and ate, and even wasted the precious fluid. I could not consume it all. When I had finished eating, I poured water into the phial and made what we called "beverage." I would drink a little, then shake it and hold it up before me. The golden bubbles shone gloriously in the sun-light. I had not said a word to Martin during these interesting operations, nor even looked towards him. But I knew that his eyes were upon me and the phial. Just as I swallowed the last drop, his full heart could bear no more, and he uttered a cry of pain. I turned to him and asked him what was the matter. The question seemed to be considered as adding insult to injustice.

"Corn deternally trive your devilish hide," he answered, and gave me the full benefit of his clenched fist upon my stomach. He was afterwards heard to say that "thar was the place whar he wanted to hit fust." We closed, scratched, pulled hair, and otherwise struggled until we were separated. Martin went immediately to Mr. Lorriby, gave his version of the brawl, and just as the school was to be dismissed for the day, I was called up and flogged without inquiry and without explanation.

Miss Betsy Ann Acry had seen the fight. When I came to my seat, crying bitterly, her indignation could not contain itself.

"Mr. Larribee," she said, her cheeks growing redder, "you have whipped that boy for nothing."

Betsy Ann, with all her pluck, had never gone so far as this. Mr. Lorriby turned pale and looked at his wife. Her red eyes fairly glistened with fire. He understood it, and said to Betsy Ann in a hesitating tone,—

"You had better keep your advice to yourself."

"I did not give you any advice. I just said you whipped that boy for nothing, and I said the truth."

"Aint that advice, madam?"

"I am no madam, I thank you, sir; and if that's advice —"

"Shet up your mouth, Betsy Ann Acry."

"Yes, sir," said Betsy Ann, very loud, and she fastened her pretty pouting lips together, elevated her head, inclined a little to one side, and seemed amusedly awaiting further orders.

The female Lorriby here rose, went to her husband, and whispered earnestly to him. He hesitated, and then resolved.

"Come here to me, Betsy Ann Acry."

She went up as gaily as if she expected a present.

"I am going to whip Betsy Ann Acry. Ef any boy here wants to take it for her, he can now step forrards."

Betsy Ann patted her foot, and looked neither to the right nor to the left, nor yet behind her.

12

When a substitute was invited to appear, the house was still as a graveyard. I rubbed my legs apologetically, and looked up at Seaborn, who sat by me.

"No, sir ; if I do may I be dinged, and then dug up and — " I did not listen to the remainder ; and as no one else seemed disposed to volunteer, and as the difficulty was brought about upon my own account, and as Betsy Ann liked me and I liked Betsy Ann, I made a desperate resolution, and rose and presented myself. Betsy Ann appeared to be disgusted.

"I don't think I would whip that child any more to-day, if I was in your place, especially for other folk's doings."

"That's jest as you say."

"Well, I say go back to your seat, Phil."

I obeyed, and felt relieved and proud of myself. Mr. Lorriby began to straighten his switch. Then I and all the other pupils looked at Mr. Bill Williams.

CHAPTER VI.

OH! what an argument was going on in Mr. Bill's breast. Vain had been all efforts heretofore made to bring him in any way into collision with the Lorribys. He had even kept himself out of all combinations to get a little holiday by an innocent ducking, and useless had been all appeals heretofore to his sympathies; for he was like the rest who had been through the ordeal of the schools, and had grown to believe that it did more good than harm. If it had been anybody but Betsy Ann Acry, he would have been unmoved. But it *was* Betsy Ann Acry, and he had been often heard to say that if Betsy Ann Acry should have to be whipped, he should take upon himself the responsibility of seeing that that must not be done. And now that contingency had come. What ought to be done? How was this responsibility to be discharged? Mr. Bill wished that the female Lorriby had stayed away that day. He did not know exactly why he wished it, but he wished it. To add to his other difficulties, Miss Betsy Ann had never given any token of her reciprocation of his regard ; for now that the novelty of the future clerkship had worn away, she had returned to her old habit of never seeming to notice that there was such a person as himself. But the idea of a switch falling upon her whose body from the crown of her head to the soles of her feet was so precious to him, outweighed every other consideration, and he made up his mind to be as good as his word, and *take the responsibility.* Just as the male Lorriby (the female by his side) was about to raise the switch —

"Stop a minute, Mr. Larrabee!" he exclaimed, advancing in a highly excited manner.

The teacher lowered his arm and retreated one step, looking a little irresolute. His wife advanced one step, and looking straight at Mr. Bill, her robust frame rose at least an inch higher.

"Mr. Larrabee! I — ah — don't exactly consider myself — ah — as a scholar here now; because — ah — I expect to move to Dukesborough in a few days, and keep store thar for Mr. Bland & Jones."

To his astonishment, this announcement, so impressive heretofore, failed of the slightest effect now, when, of all times, an effect was desired. Mr. Lorriby, in answer to a sign from his wife, had recovered his lost ground, and looked placidly upon him, but answered nothing.

"I say," repeated Mr. Bill distinctly, as if he supposed he had not been heard, "I say that I expect in a few days to move to Dukesborough; to live thar; to keep store thar for Mr. Bland & Jones."

"Well, William, I think I have heard that before. I want to hear you talk about it some time when it aint school time, and when we aint so busy as we air now at the present."

"Well, but —" persisted Mr. Bill.

"Well, but?" inquired Mr. Lorriby.

"Yes, sir," answered the former, insistingly.

"Well, but what? Is this case got anything to do with it? Is *she* got anything to do with it?"

"In cose it have not," answered Mr. Bill, sadly.

"Well, what makes you tell us of it now, at the present?" Oh! what a big word was that *us*, then, to Josiah Lorriby.

"Mr. Larrabee," urged Mr. Bill, in as persuasive accents as he could employ; "no, sir, Mr. Larrabee, it have not got anything to do with it; but yit —"

"Well, yit what, William?"

"Well, Mr. Larrabee, I thought as I *was* a-goin to quit school soon, and as I *was* a-goin to move to Dukesborough — as I *was* a-goin *right outen* your school intoo Dukesborough as it war, to keep store thar, may be you mout, as a favor, do me a favor before I left."

"Well! may I be dinged, and then dug up and dinged over agin!" This was said in a suppressed whisper by a person at my side. "Beggin! beggin! ding his white-livered hide — beg-gin!"

"Why, William," replied Mr. Lorriby, "ef it war convenant, and the favor war not too much, it mout be that I mout grant it."

"I thought you would, Mr. Larrabee. The favor aint a big one — leastways, it aint a big one to you. It would be a mighty — " But Mr. Bill thought he could hardly trust himself to say how big a one it would be to himself.

"Well, what is it, William?"

"Mr. Larrabee! — sir, Mr. Larrabee, I ax it as a favor of you, not to whip Betsy Ann — which is Miss Betsy Ann Acry."

"Thar now!" groaned Seaborn, and bowed his head in despair.

The male Lorriby looked upon the female. Her face had relaxed somewhat from its stern expression. She answered his glance by one which implied a conditional affirmative.

"Ef Betsy Ann Acry will behave herself, and keep her impudence to herself, I will let her off this time."

All eyes turned to Betsy Ann. I never saw her look so fine as she raised up her head, tossed her yellow ringlets back, and said in a tone increasing in loudness from beginning to end:

"But Betsy Ann Acry won't *do it.*"

"Hello agin thar!" whispered Seaborn, and raised his head. His dying hopes of a big row were revived. This was the last opportunity, and he was as eager as if the last dollar he ever expected to make had been pledged upon the event. I have never forgotten his appearance, as with his legs wide apart, his hands upon his knees, his lips apart, but his teeth firmly closed, he gazed upon that scene.

Lorriby, the male, was considerably disconcerted, and would have compromised ; but Lorriby, the female, again in an instant resumed her hostile attitude, and this time her great eyes looked like two balls of fire. She concentrated their gaze upon Betsy Ann with a ferocity which was appalling. Betsy Ann tried to meet them, and did for one moment ; but in another she found she could not hold out longer ; so she buried her face in her hands and sobbed. Mr. Bill could endure no more. Both arms fairly flew out at full length.

"The fact ar," he cried, "that I am goin to *take the responsibility !* Conshequenches may be conshequenches, but I shall take the responsibility." His countenance was that of a man who had made up his mind. It had come at last, and we were perfectly happy.

The female Lorriby turned her eyes from Betsy Ann and fixed them steadily on Mr. Bill. She advanced a step forward, and raised her arms and placed them on her sides. The male Lorriby placed himself immediately behind his mate's right arm, while Rum, who seemed to understand what was going on, came up, and standing on his mistress's left, looked curiously up at Mr. Bill.

Seaborn Byne noticed this last movement. "Well, ef that don't beat creation! You in it too, is you?" he muttered through his teeth. "Well, never do you mind. Ef I don't fix you and put you whar you'll never know no more but what you've got a tail, may I be dinged, and then," etc.

It is true that Seaborn had been counted upon for a more important work than the neutralising of Rum's forces; still, I knew that Mr. Bill wanted and needed no assistance. We were all ready, however — that is, I should say, all but Martin. He had no griefs, and therefore no desires.

Such was the height of Mr. Bill's excitement that he did not even seem to notice the hostile demonstrations of these numerous and various foes. His mind was made up, and he was going right on to his purpose.

"Mr. Larrabee," he said firmly, "I am goin to take the responsibility. I axed you as a favor to do me a favor before I left. I aint much used to axin favors; but sich it war now. It seem as ef that favor cannot be grant. Yea, sich is the circumstances. But it must be so. Sense I have been here they aint been no difficulties betwixt you and me, nor betwixt me and Miss Larrabee; and no nothin of the sort, not even betwixt me and Rum. That dog have sometimes snap at my legs; but I have bore it for peace, and wanted no fuss. Sich, therefore, it was why I axed the favor *as* a favor. But it can't be hoped, and so I takes the responsibility. Mr. Larrabee, sir, and you, Miss Larrabee, I am goin from this school right intoo Dukesborough, straight intoo Mr. Bland's store, to clerk thar. Sich bein all the circumstances, I hates to do what I tells you I'm goin to do. But it can't be hoped, it seem, and I ar goin to do it."

Mr. Bill announced this conclusion in a very highly elevated tone.

"Oh, yes, ding your old hides of you!" I heard at my side.

"Mr. Larrabee, and you, Miss Larrabee," continued the speaker, "I does not desires that Betsy Ann Acry shall be whipped. I goes on to say that as sich it ar, and as sich the circumstances, Betsy Ann Acry can't be whipped whar I ar ef I can keep it from bein done."

"You heerd that, didn't you?" asked Seaborn, low, but cruelly triumphant; and Seaborn looked at Rum as if considering how he should begin the battle with him.

Mrs. Lorriby seldom spoke. Whenever she did, it was to the point.

"Yes, but Weelliam Weelliams, you can't keep it from bein done." And she straightened herself yet taller, and raising her hands yet higher upon her sides, changed the angle of elbows from obtuse to acute.

"Yes, but I kin," persisted Mr. Bill. "Mr. Larrabee! Mr. Larrabee!"

This gentleman had lowered his head, and was peering at Mr. Bill through the triangular opening formed by his mate's side and arm. The reason why Mr. Bill addressed him twice, was because he had missed him when he threw the first address over her shoulder. The last was sent through the triangle.

"Mr. Larrabee! I say it kin be done, and I'm goin to do it. Sir, little as I counted on sich a case, yit still it ar so. Let the conshequenches be what they be, both now and some futur day. Mr. Larrabee, sir, that whippin that you was a-goin to give to Betsy Ann Acry cannot fall upon her shoulders, and — that is, upon her shoulders, and before my face. Instid of sich, sir, you may jest — instid of whippin her, sir, you may — instid of her, give it, sir — notwithstandin and nevertheless — you may give it to ME."

CHAPTER VII.

"Oh! what a fall was there, my countrymen!
Then you and I and all of us fell down!"

IF the pupils of Josiah Lorriby's school had had the knowledge of all tongues; if they had been familiar with the histories of all the base men of all the ages, they could have found no words in which to characterise, and no person with whom to compare, Mr. Bill Williams. If they had known what it was to be a traitor, they might have admitted that he was more like this, the most despicable of all characters, than any other. But they would have argued that he was baser than all other traitors, because he had betrayed, not only others, but himself. Mr. Bill Williams, the big boy, the future resident of Dukesborough, the expectant clerk, the vindicator of persecuted girlhood in the person of the girl he loved, the pledge-taker of responsibilities,— that he should have taken the pains, just before he was going away, to degrade himself by proposing to take upon his own shoulders the rod that had never before descended but upon the backs and legs of children! Poor Seaborn Byne! If I ever saw expressed in a human being's countenance, disgust, anger and abject hopelessness, I saw them as I turned to look at him. He spoke not one word, not even in whispers, but he looked as if he could never more place confidence in mortal flesh.

When Mr. Bill had concluded his ultimatum, the female Lorriby's arms came down, and the male Lorriby's head went up. They sent each the other a smile. Both were smart enough to be satisfied. The latter was more than satisfied.

"I am proud this day of William Williams. It air so, and I can but say I air proud of him. William Williams were now in a position to stand up and shine in his new spere of action. If he went to Dukesborough to keep store thar, he mout now go sayin that as he had been a good scholar, so he mout expect to be a good clerk, and fit to be trusted, yea, with thousands upon thousands, ef sich mout be the case. But as it was so, and as he have been to us all as it war, and no difficulties, and no nothin of the sort, and he war goin, and it mout be soon, yea, it mout be to-morrow, from this school straight intoo a store, I cannot, nor I cannot. No, far be it. This were a skene too solemn and too lovely for sich. I cannot, nor I cannot. William Williams may now take his seat."

Mr. Bill obeyed. I was glad that he did not look at Betsy Ann as she turned to go to hers. But she looked at him. I saw her, and little as I was, I saw also that if he ever had had any chance of winning her, it was gone from him forever. It was now late in the afternoon, and we were dismissed. Without saying a word to any one, Mr. Bill took his arithmetic and slate (for ciphering, as it was called then, was his only study). We knew what it meant, for we felt, as well as he, that this was his last day at school. As my getting to school depended upon his continuance, I did not doubt that it was my last also.

On the way home, but not until separating from all the other boys, Mr. Bill showed some disposition to boast.

"You all little fellows was monstous badly skeerd this evening, Squire."

"Wasn't you scared too?" I asked.

"Skeerd? I'd like to see the schoolmaster that could skeer me. I skeerd of Joe Larrabee?"

"I did not think you were scared of him."

"Skeerd of who then? Miss Larrabee? [Old Red Eye?] She mout be redder-eyed than what she ar, and then not skeer me." Why look here, Squire, how would I look goin into Dukesborough, into Mr. Bland and Jones' store, right from bein skeerd of old Miss Larrabee; to be runnin right intoo Mr. Bland and Jones' store, and old Mehetibilly Larrabee right arter me, or old Joe nuther. It wur well for him that he never struck Betsy Ann Acry. [Ef he had a struck her, Joe Larrabee's strikin days would be over."]

"But wasn't you goin to take her whippin for her?"

"Lookee here, Squire, I didn't take it, did I?"

"No, but you said you was ready to take it."

"Poor little fellow!" he said, compassionately. "Squire, you are yit young in the ways of this sorrowful and ontimely world. Joe Larrabee knows me, and I knows Joe Larrabee, and as the feller said, that ar sufficient."

We were now at our gate. Mr. Bill bade me good evening, and passed on; and thus ended his pupilage and mine at the school of Josiah Lorriby.

THE PURSUIT OF MR. ADIEL SLACK.

CHAPTER I.

" Companions
That do converse, and waste the time together,
Whose souls do bear an equal yoke of love."
MERCHANT OF VENICE.

MR. BENJAMIN (but as everybody called him, Uncle Ben) Pea resided two miles out of Dukesborough. He was a small farmer — not small in person, but a farmer on a small scale. He raised a fair crop of corn, a trifle of cotton, great quantities of potatoes, and some pinders. It was said that in his younger days he used to be brisk in his business, and to make something by hauling wood to town. He spent as little as he could and saved as much as he could ; but for a certain purpose he kept as good an establishment as he could. His little wagon used to be good enough to carry him and the old woman to town ; yet he bought a second-hand gig, and did other things in proportion. It was extravagant, and he knew it, but he had a purpose. That purpose was to marry off his daughter Georgiana. Now, Georgiana had told him for years and years, even before the old woman died, that if he wanted to marry her off (a thing she cared nothing about herself), the only way to do that was for the family to go in a decent way. And now that the old woman had died and her father had grown old, she had her own way, and that was as decent as could be afforded, and no more.

Miss Georgiana Pea was heavy — heavy of being married off, and heavy of body. Her weight for fifteen years at the least had not been

13

probably less than one hundred and seventy pounds.   In her seasons .
of highest health, which were probably oftener in the latter part of the
Fall than at any other period of the year, people used to guess that
it might be even more ; but there was no getting at it at any time,
because she always stoutly refused to be weighed.   True, she laced ;
but that did not seem to diminish her materially ; for what was pressed
down in one region re-appeared in another.   She had a magnificent
bust.   This bust was her pride, that was evident.   Indeed, she as
good as confessed as much to me one day.   I knew the family well ;
she didn't mind me, I was a very small boy, and she was aware that I
considered that bust a wonderful work of nature.   I have often been
amused, since I have grown old and less impressible by such things,
to remember how tremendously magnificent I used to regard the bust
of Georgiana Pea.

Yet she didn't marry.   The old gentleman had been so anxious
about it that he had long ago rather given it out in a public way, that
upon her marriage with his consent (she was the only child — Peterson
died when a boy, of measles) he should give up everything, houses,
lands, furniture, and money, and live upon the bounty of his son-in-
law.   These several items of property had been often appraised by the
neighbors as accurately as could be done (considering that the exact
amount of money could not be verified), in view of ascertaining for
their own satisfaction what her dowry might be.   The appraisement
had gone through many gradations of figures while the bridegroom
delayed his coming.   At the period of which I am now telling, there
were those who maintained that Uncle Ben was worth four thousand
dollars ; others shook their heads and said thirty-five hundred ; while
others yet, who professed to know more about it than anybody else,
they didn't care who it was, insisted that three thousand was the outside.
Many a man, it seemed to me, and some that would have been worth
having, might have been caught by that bust and that prospective
fortune.   But they were not ; and now, at thirty, or thereabout, she was
evidently of the opinion that even if she had many desires to enter
into the estate of marriage, their chances of gratification were few.
Indeed, Miss Pea was at that stage when she was beginning to speak
at times of the other sex with disgust.

Mr. Jacob Spouter resided in the very heart of Dukesborough, and
kept a hotel.   The town being small, his business was small.   He was
a small man, but looked bright, capable, and business-like.   He dressed

pretty well. But this was for effect, and was both a delusion and a snare. It was for a sign for his hotel. To look at him, you would have supposed that he kept a good hotel; but he did not. It is surprising, indeed, to consider how few men there are who do. But this is a great theme, and entirely independent of what I wish to tell, except so far as it may relate to the fact that Mr. Spouter had yet living with him an only child, a daughter, whose name was Angeline. Miss Angeline, instead of taking after the Spouters, who were short, took after the Fanigans, who were long. She was a very thin young lady, almost too thin to look well, and her hair and complexion were rather sallow. But then that hair curled — every hair curled.

Who has not a weakness? Miss Pea had hers, as we have seen; and now we shall see, as everybody for years had seen, that Miss Spouter had hers also. It was an innocent one: it was her curls. In the memory of man that hair had never been done up; but through all changes of circumstances and weather it had hung in curls, just as it hung on the day when this story begins. They had been complimented thousands of times, and by hundreds of persons; the guests of years had noticed them, and had uttered and smiled their approbation; and there had been times when Miss Spouter hoped, in spite of the want of other as striking charms, and in spite of the universally known fact that her father had always been insolvent and always would be, that those curls would eventually entangle the person without whom she felt that she could never be fully blest. While this person was a man, it was not any particular individual of the species. Many a time had she seen one who, she thought, would answer. She was not very fastidious, but she positively believed (and this belief made her appear to be anxious) that in view of all the circumstances of her life, the best thing that she could do for herself would be to marry. Yet Miss Spouter did not regard herself as wholly selfish in this wish; for there was something in her, she thought, which she constantly understood to be telling her that if she had the opportunity she could make some man extremely happy.

But though those curls had been so often praised — yea, though they had been sometimes handled — to such a degree did people's admiration of them extend, that Miss Spouter, like her contemporary in the country, was unmarried, and beginning to try to feel as if she despised the vain and foolish world of man.

These young ladies were friends, and always had been. They were so much attached that each seemed, to a superficial observer, to believe that she had been born for but one special purpose, and that was to help the other to get married; for Miss Spouter believed and Miss Pea knew that marriage was a subject which, without intermission, occupied the mind of her friend. It was pleasant to hear Miss Pea extol Miss Spouter's curls; then it was pleasant to hear Miss Spouter, who was more sentimental and the better talker of the two, praise Miss Pea's "figger," by which term she meant only her bust. No one ever dreamed that it was possible for any jealousy to rise between them; for Miss Spouter had no figure worth mentioning, and not a hair of Miss Pea's head could be curled. Not only so, but the fact was, that in her heart of hearts (so curious a thing is even the most constant friendship) neither thought much of the other's special accomplishment; rather, each thought that there was entirely too much of it, especially Miss Spouter touching the "figger." If Miss Pea considered the property qualification in her favor, Miss Spouter did not forget that she resided right in the very heart of Dukesborough, and that her father kept a hotel. Now, as long as the world stands, persons of their condition who live in town will feel a little ahead of those who live in the country; while the latter, though never exactly knowing why, will admit that it is so. Miss Pea was generally very much liked by the neighbors; Miss Spouter had not made a great number of friends. Probably town airs had something to do in the matter. Miss Pea was considered the superior character of the two, but neither of them thought so; Miss Spouter, especially, who knew the meaning of many more words in the dictionary than her friend, and who had read Alonzo and Melissa, and the Three Spaniards, until she had the run of them fully, never dreamed of such a thing.

Miss Spouter was fond of visiting Miss Pea, especially in water-melon time. Miss Pea valued the friendship of Miss Spouter because it afforded her frequent opportunities of staying at a hotel, a privilege which she well knew not many country girls enjoyed. To stay there, not as a boarder, but as a friend of the family, to eat there and sleep there, and not to pay for either of these distinctions as other people did, but to do these things on invitation. Now, while Miss Pea got much better eating and sleeping at home, yet she could but consider the former as privileges. She never would forget that once when there was a show in Dukesborough, given by a ventriloquist who was also a juggler, she had been at Mr. J. Spouter's, and had been introduced to the wonderful man, and his wife too, and had heard them talk about general matters just as other people did.

But time was waxing old. The bust had about ceased to be ambitious, and the curls, though wishful yet, were falling into the habit of giving only despondent shakes.

CHAPTER II.

MISS SPOUTER sat in the hotel parlor; it was on the first floor and opened upon the street. In it were two wooden rocking-chairs, six split-bottoms, and a half-round. I shall not undertake to describe the window-curtains. She was pensive and silent; the still summer evening disposed her to meditation. She sat silent and pensive, but not gloomy. Looking out from the window, she espied on the further side of the square, Miss Pea, who was in the act of turning towards her. Here she came, in yellow calico and a green calash. As she walked, her arms were crossed peacefully upon her chest.

" Howdye, stranger !" saluted Miss Spouter. They had not met in a fortnight.

" Stranger yourself," answered Miss Pea, with a smile and a sigh. They embraced; the curls fell upon the bust and the bust fostered the curls, as only long tried friends can fall upon and foster. Miss Pea came to stay all night; never had they slept in the same house without sleeping together.

" Well, Georgy," Miss Spouter remarked, sweetly, but almost invidiously, as they were getting into bed, " figger is figger."

" It's no sich a thing," answered Miss Pea, with firm self-denial ; " it's curls, you know it's curls."

" No, George, its figger."

" Angeline Spouter, you know it aint; it's curls, and you know it's curls."

They blew out the candle, and for a short time continued this friendly discussion ; but soon Miss Pea got the best of it, as usual, and Miss Spouter, by silence and other signs, admitted that it was curls.

" We've been sleeping a long time together, George."

" We have that."

"Ten years."

"Yes, fifteen of 'em."

"Gracious me! fifteen?"

"Yes, indeed."

"Well, but I was but a child then."

Miss Pea coughed.   She was the elder by exactly six months.

"Did we think ten years ago that you would now be a Pea and I a Spouter?"

"I didn't think much about myself, but I had no idea you would."

"Yet so it is; you with your figger and yet a Pea."

"And what is worse, you with your curls and yet a Spouter."

"No, not worse.   You ought to have been married years ago, Georgiana Pea."

"If I had had your curls and had wanted to marry, *I should* a been married and forgot it."

"No, George, I never had the requisite figger."

"Angeline Spouter, do hush."

"Suppose we had married, George?"

"Well."

"I think I could have made my husband love me, as few men have ever loved, be they whomsoever they might."

"Ah! everybody knows that."

"No, alas! none but thee, George."

"Yes, but I know better."

Miss Spouter again gave it up.

Miss Pea would fain have gone to sleep.   Her hour for that purpose had come.   But there was yet no slumber upon the eyelids of Miss Spouter.   She talked away.   She made hypothetical cases; supposing for instance they were married.   Miss Spouter ventured to look far into such a possible future, and made some speculations upon the best and properest ways of bringing up families.   It appeared during the conversation that Miss Spouter, as a general thing, liked girls in families better than boys, while Miss Pea's preference for boys was bold and decided.   She admitted Miss Pea's argument to be true, that girls are prettier, especially if they have curls; but, La me! they *are* such a trouble!   Besides, boys were bad.   She must admit that too.   But then they could be whipped and made to mind.

"Oh, you cruel creature!" right there exclaimed the merciful Miss Spouter.

"No, Angeline," remonstrated her companion, "no, I am not cruel; but I believe in makin children mind and behave theirselves." Miss Pea was as firm as a rock.

"So do I," replied Miss Spouter; "but I can't understand how a woman, a good woman, and a kind woman, and an affectionate woman, and a woman that had — La, bless me! how *could* such a woman beat her own family to death, when in the wide, wide world there was none others to stand by them in the solemn hour, and — "

"No! no! no!" interposed Miss Pea, "I don't *mean* that. What I *do* mean — La! Angeline Spouter, what *are* you and me a talkin about? It's redickerlous. I'm done."

Miss Pea laughed outright.. But Miss Spouter sighed, and remarked that it wasn't in people to say neither what was to be, nor what wasn't to be.

"George, I do believe you are going to sleep."

Miss Pea declared that she wasn't, and like all persons of her size, she thought she was telling the truth. Miss Spouter had one or two other remarks which she always made on such occasions, and which she wanted to make now.

"Georgiana Pea, do you or do you not ever expect to marry? I ask you candidly."

"No, Angeline, I don't. I may have had thoughts, I may have had expectations; pap looks as if he would go distracted if I don't marry; but to tell you the truth, I have about come to the conclusion that there's more marries now than ever does well. Pap declares that he means to marry me off to somebody before he dies. He thinks that I couldn't take care of myself if he was to die, and that he takes care of me now himself. I think I'm the one that takes care of *him*, and I think I could take as good care of myself then as I do now. He says I shall marry though, and I'm waitin to see how it'll be. But I tell you, Angeline Spouter, that there's more marries now than *ever* does well."

"And — well," answered Miss Spouter, "and so have I concluded about it. It is the honest expression of the genuine sentiments of my innermost heart. What is man? A deceitful, vain and foolish creature, who will to-day talk his honey words and praise a girl's curls, and to-morrow he is further off than when we first laid our eyes on him. What is your opinion of man, George? What now is your opinion of Tom Dyson, who used to melt before the sight of you like summer clouds ere the sun had set?"

"I think of Tom Dyson like I think of Barney Bolton who used to praise your curls just like they were so much gold, and like I think of all of 'em, and that's about as much as I think of an old dead pine tree or post-oak."

Miss Pea had not read many books like Miss Spouter, and must necessarily, therefore, borrow her comparisons from objects familiar to her country life. Miss Spouter noticed the difference, but refrained from remarking on it.

"And yet, Georgiana, there is something in me; I feel it. It tells me that I could have made Barney Bolton much happier than Malinda Jones has. Barney Bolton is not happy, Georgiana Pea."

Miss Pea only coughed.

"Yes, indeed! Alas! I see it in his eye; I see it in his walk; I see it in his every action. The image of Angeline Spouter is in his breast, and it will stay there forever."

Miss Pea was always perfectly silent, and endeavored to feel solemn when this last speech was said.

"If you were to marry, George, I should be the *lonesomest* creature in the wide, wide world."

"Ah, well! when I marry, which is never going to.be the case (that is exceptin pap do go distracted and hunt me up a good chance), you'll be married and forgot it, and that little curly-headed girl will be readin, ritin and cypherin." Miss Pea yawned and laughed slightly.

"Never, never! But won't you let your little boy come sometimes in a passing hour to see a lonesome girl, who once was your friend, but now, alas! abandoned?"

"Angeline Spouter, do hush."

"George, it is very warm to-night. Is it late?"

"I should — think — it was," answered Miss Pea, and snored.

Miss Spouter lay for some time awake, but silent. She then lifted the curtain from the window, through which the moon, high in heaven, shone upon the bed, withdrew from her cap five or six curls, extended them upon her snowy breast, smiled dismally, put them up again, looked

a moment at her companion, then abruptly turned her back to her and
went to sleep.

CHAPTER III.

"Is all the counsel that we too have shared,
The sisters' vows, the hours that we have spent
When we have chid the hasty-footed time
For parting us — O, and is all forgot?"

MIDSUMMER-NIGHT'S DREAM.

BUT friendship, like other good things, has enemies. One of the most
dangerous of these is a third person. These beings are among the most
inconvenient and troublesome upon earth. Not often do confidential
conversations take place in a company of three, especially conversations appertaining to friendship or love. When sentiment, hot from
the heart, has to move in triangles, it must often meet with hindrances
and cool itself before it has reached its destination. As in mathe-
matics, between two points, so in social life between two hearts, the
shortest way is a straight line. A third person makes a divergence
and a delay. Third persons have done more to separate very friends
and lovers than all the world besides. They had gotten between
other persons before, and now one of them had come to get between
Miss Spouter and Miss Pea.

Adiel Slack had left his native Massachusetts, and from going to
and fro upon the earth, came in an evil day and put up at the inn of
Jacob Spouter. He was tall, deep-voiced, big-footed, and the most
deliberate-looking man that had ever been in Dukesborough. He was
one of those imperturbable Yankees that could fool you when you were
watching him just as well as when you were not. When he said that
he was twenty-eight his last birth-day, his fresh-looking hair, his un-
wrinkled and unblushing cheek, and his entire freedom from all signs
of wear and care, made one believe that it must be so. If he had said
that he was forty-five, the gravity of his countenance, the deliberation
of his gait, and the deep worldly wisdom of his eye would have made
one believe that he spoke truly.

The mere arrival of such a person in that small community must
necessarily create some stir. He was decidedly the most remarkable
of all the passengers who came by that morning's stage. While they

. 14

ate their breakfast with that haste which is peculiar to the travelling public, he took his time. The stage went away and left him at the table eating his fifth biscuit, while Mrs. Spouter's eyes were fixed upon him with that steadfast look with which she was wont to regard all persons who ate at her table more than she thought was fair. He took another biscuit, looked about for more butter, and attempted to open a conversation with that lady; but she was not in the mood to be communicative, so he set to the work of studying her. He made her out to be a woman of a serious turn of mind, less attentive to dress than her husband, but at the same time aspiring, and possibly with propriety and with success, to be the head of the family. After breakfast, he stood about, sat about, picked his teeth ("with a ivory lancet, blamed if it weren't," Mr. Spouter said), then took his hat and strolled about the village all the forenoon. He went into both the stores, got acquainted with the doctor, and the blacksmith, and the shoemaker, found and bargained for the rent of a room, and at dinner announced himself a citizen of Georgia and a merchant of Dukesborough. In less than a week a small stock of goods had arrived, and were neatly arranged in the room, over the door of which hung a sign-board, painted by himself, which made Mr. Boggs and Messrs. Bland & Jones wish either that they had never had sign-boards, or that Adiel Slack, dry-goods merchant, had never come there.

Being a single man, Mr. Slack boarded at the hotel of J. Spouter. Now, no sooner was it settled that he was to become a citizen, than Miss Spouter, according to ancient usage in such cases, felt herself to be yielding to the insidious influences of yet another love. Who knew, she thought, that the fond dream of her life was not destined now to become a blissful realisation? The fact that Mr. Slack had come from afar, made her sentimental soul only the more hopeful. How this was so she could not tell; but it was so, and the good girl began at once to bestow the most assiduous cultivation upon every charm which she thought she possessed. Mr. Slack soon began to be treated with more consideration than any of the boarders. He had within a week moved from Mr. Spouter's end of the table up to Mrs. Spouter's, and become, as it were, that lady's left bower, Miss Angeline being, of course, her right. The hot biscuit were always handed first to him, and if anybody got a hot waffle, it was he. People used to look up towards Mrs. Spouter and get occasional glimpses of little plates of fresh butter and preserves that tried to hide behind the castors or the candlestick. When there was pie, Mr. Slack was helped first; because, among other things, he was the more sure of getting another piece, if the pie, as it sometimes would happen, in spite of precaution, should not go around the second time.

The servants did not like him because he never gave them a kind word nor a cent of money. But let any one of them omit to hand the best things to him first. Oh, the partiality that was shown as plain as day to that man! Everybody saw it, and spoke of it among confidential friends. Some said it was a sin; some said it was a shame; and some went so far as to say it was both.

Among the boarders was one whom we have seen before. For Mr. Bill Williams had now been installed in his office, and had already begun to take new responsibilities. When this conduct towards the new-comer had become notorious, he was heard by many persons even to swear that he'd "be dinged ef he had had a hot waffle, even when thar was waffles, sense that dadblasted Yankee had moved up to old Miss Spouter's eend. As for the second piece of pie, he had done gin out ever hearin of the like any more, thro'out the ages of a sorrowful and ontimely world." He spoke with feeling, it is true; but he was a clerk in Mr. Bland's store, and he thought that if he could not take some responsibility, the question was who could. "Consequenches mout be consequenches," said Mr. Bill, "be they now or at some futer day. I takes the responsibility to say that the case ar a onfair, and a imposition on the boarders and on the transhent people, and it war also a shame on Dukesborough, and also — " Mr. Bill shook his head for the conclusion.

But in spite of everybody and everything, Mr. Slack kept his place. He soon discovered Miss Spouter's weakness and her passion. Flattering as it might be to find himself the favored object of her pursuit, yet the reflection that her only capital was a head of curls which in time would fade, caused him to determine, after making his calculations, that no profit was to be netted in being caught. It was not to be overlooked, however, that there would be, if not an entire saving of expense, at least a postponement of its payment in keeping his thoughts to himself and in seeming to be drawing nearer and nearer the vortex which was ready to swallow him up. The terms of board at Mr. Spouter's included monthly payments. These did not suit calculations which were made upon the principle of collecting his own dues at once and postponing his payments as long as possible, and if possible, to the end of time.   Now, he guessed that great as were Mr. Spouter's needs, that affectionate father would not be the man to run the risk of driving off his daughter's suitor by worrying him with dues for a little item of board, which might all come back again into the family.   In addition to this, he was not insensible to the advantage of maintaining his seat at the dinner table, where biscuits, waffles and pies, when they came at all, were wont to make their first appearance.   These several matters, being actual money to him, were not to be overlooked by a man who did nothing without deliberation.   After deliberating, therefore, he determined to so conduct himself before the Spouters as to create the hope that the time would come when he would solicit the hand of her who long had been willing to bestow it upon somebody. But he was careful to keep his own advances and his meetings of advances without the pale of such contingencies as he had learned were accustomed in the South to follow breaches of marriage contracts. If there was anything that Mr. Slack was afraid of, it was a cane, or perhaps a cowhide.   He maintained his place at the table, therefore, and took what it afforded in the manner of a man who was very near to being one of the family.   He chatted in a very familiar manner with Mrs. Spouter, and sympathised with her and Mr. Spouter's complaints of the high price of everything except board.   He lounged in the parlor, where he told to Miss Angeline touching stories of his boyhood's home. He bestowed due admiration upon those curls which, every time he saw them, reminded him of a portrait of his mother (now a saint in heaven), taken when she was a girl eighteen years old.   Then he spoke feelingly of how he had been a wanderer, and how he began to think it was time he had settled himself for good ; how he had never felt exactly ready for that until since he had come to Dukesborough ; and how — and how — and how —— embarrassment would prevent him from saying more.   But whenever he got to this point, and Miss Angeline's heart would be about to burst, and she would be getting ready to cast herself upon his faithful bosom, he would change abruptly, become frightened, and go away and stay away for a week.

At their first meeting at the breakfast table after such scenes, Miss Spouter would appear quite conscious, hold herself yet straighter, and endeavor to show that she had spirit.   But before she had carried it far, she would conclude to stop where she was, go back and begin again.

CHAPTER IV.

BUT while these things were going on among the Spouters, what had become of the Peas? Whoever supposes that Miss Georgiana was buried in the country dead or alive, is simply mistaken. When she heard that there was a new store in town she wanted to see it; and when Uncle Ben heard that it was kept by a bachelor, he was determined that he should see his daughter; for as he grew older, his anxiety became more intense for Georgiana to find somebody, as he expressed it, "to take keer of her when my head gits cold." He begged her several times to go before she was ready.

"Georgy, put on your yaller calliker, and go long."

"Pap, do wait till I get ready. I do believe you will go distracted."

Georgiana waited until she got ready, and when she did get ready she went. Her plan was to go and spend the night with Miss Spouter, and in company with her visit the new store the next morning.

Some persons believe in presentiments, and some do not. I hardly know what to think of such things, and have never yet made up my mind whether they are reliable or not. Sometimes they seem to fore-shadow coming events, and sometimes they are clearly at fault. I have occasionally had dreams, and subsequent events were in such exact sequence with them that I have been inclined to accord to them much of the importance that by some persons it is maintained they have. Then again, the dreams I have had (for I have always been a dreamer) have been so entirely unreasonable, nay, absurd, and even ridiculous, as to be impossible of fulfilment. For instance, I have more than once dreamed that I was a woman; and I have since been much amused by the recollection of some of the strange things that I did and said while in that estate. I do not consider this an opportune place to mention them, even if they were worthy of mention on any occasion, and I allude to them for the purpose of saying that after such dreams I have been disposed to reject the whole of the theory of dreams.

But all this is neither here nor there. The divergence from my story, though natural, cannot with propriety be farther extended; and I will return at once to my two heroines, in whose deportment will be found the reason why such divergence was made.

No sooner had Miss Spouter determined fully in her mind that she would catch Mr. Slack if she could, than she was conscious of a wavering in her friendship for Miss Pea; for she felt that that person was destined to be the greatest, if not the only barrier between her and the object of her pursuit. She, Miss Spouter, had seen him first, she thought. She had, as it were, found him, and when George was not even looking for any such property. George did not have even a shadow of the remotest claim to him. It was wrong and unkind in George to interfere. She, Miss Spouter, wouldn't have treated her so. Now all this was before Miss Pea had ever laid eyes on Mr. Slack, and Miss Spouter knew it. That made no difference, she said to herself. If anything, it made it worse. She was hurt, and she could not help it.

Miss Pea might have had a presentiment of this state of things, and she might not. But at all events, when she went upon her visit she carried a bucket of butter as a present to Mrs. Spouter. It was just before supper-time, and consequently too late for her to return that evening. If it had not been, as she afterwards declared upon her word and honor, she would have done so. The Spouters were as cold as ice. Not even the bucket of butter could warm Mrs. Spouter a single degree. Strange conduct for her! Miss Angeline at first thought that she would not go in to the supper table. But then that would be too plain, and upon reflection she thought she preferred to be there.

Miss Pea and Mr. Slack, of course, had to be introduced. He found her disposed to be chatty. Miss Spouter looked very grave, and raised her pocket handkerchief to her mouth as an occasional provincialism fell from the lips of her country visitress, while her dear mother, taking the cue, would glance slyly at Mr. Slack and snicker.

"This is oncommon good butter, Mrs. Spouter," he remarked to the lady of the house; and oh, the quantities of butter that man did consume!

Now, it was from Miss Pea's bucket; they did not like to confess it, but they had it to do.

"Want' know! Wal, Miss Pea's mother must be a noble housekeeper."

Mrs. Pea had been dead several years.

"Dew tell! You, then?"

Miss Georgiana would have told a lie if she had not acknowledged that it was.

Mr. Slack bestowed a look of intense admiration upon her, which made Miss Spouter become quite grave, and her mother somewhat angry.

After supper the gentleman followed the ladies into the parlor. Miss Spouter was pensive, and complained of headache. Miss Pea did not believe she had it, and therefore she spoke freely of her father's plantation, of what he was to her and she to him, and of how he was always urging her to get married, a thing which she had made up her mind never to do. When they retired for the night, Miss Spouter being no better, but rather worse, they did what they had never done in their lives before, whenever there had been an opportunity of doing differently — they slept apart. This was capping the climax, and Miss Pea went home the next morning, asking herself many times on the way if friendship was anything but a name.

It seemed to be a sad thing that these young ladies should part. Hand in hand they had traveled the broad road of life, and never jostled each other when men were plentiful. But these animals had broken from them like so many wild cattle, some dodging and darting between them, some taking to by-paths, and some wildly leaping over precipices, until now they were drawing nigh to the road of young womanhood, and there was but one left for them both. If they could have divided him it might have been well; but he was indivisible. The fact is, Mr. Slack ought never to have come there, or he ought to have brought his twin-brother with him.

"Wal, where's your friend?" he inquired at breakfast.

"She's gone to look after what she calls her father's plantation, I reckon," answered Mrs. Spouter, sharply.

"Be n't her father got no plantation, then?"

"He's got a little bit of two hundred acres of tolerble poor land. That's all the plantation he's got."

"Oh, Ma!" interceded Miss Angeline, "Georgiana is a very good girl."

"She may be good, but if you call her a girl I don't know what you would call them that's fifteen or twenty years younger; and if she is young that wouldn't make her daddy rich."

"Oh, no! But, oh, Ma!" Miss Spouter persisted in a general way, for she seemed to think that this was all that could be said in her favor. Upon reflection she asked Mr. Slack if he did not think Miss Pea had a good figger. Then she took a very small sip of water, wiped her mouth carefully and coughed slightly.

"Wal, I — ah," began Mr. Slack, but Ma laughed so immoderately that he laughed too, and did not finish giving his opinion in words. Alas, for Miss Pea! Big as she was, she was cut all to pieces and salted away by Mrs. Spouter, while Miss Angeline could only look a little reproachfully now and then, and say "Oh, Ma!"

"Two hundred acres," mused Mr. Slack on his bed that night. "In Maas'chewsetts that is a considerable farm; other property in proportion. What would it bring in ready money if the old man (I cal'late he's old) should take a notion tew give it up *neow?* Already some money. He brought me a watermelon this morning, and asked me to go out and see them all. I'm a going. Quick work, Adiel, quick work."

Mr. Slack was a hard man to catch; it had been tried before and had failed. Nevertheless, Mrs. Spouter and Miss Spouter, about six weeks later, actually caught him in the act of coming away from Mr. Pea's. What made it worse, he had a bunch of pinks in his hand. The next time Miss Spouter met Miss Pea she did not speak to her. She only shook her curls and said to herself in words which were audible, "Such is life!" Georgiana folded her hands over her bosom and asked, if friendship was anything but a name, what was it?

But the man maintained his place at the table, to which he marched with unusual confidence and good humor at the first meal after his detection; what is more, the little plates maintained their places. In spite of all his goings to the Peas and his returning with bunches of pinks in his hands, his deportment in any other respect had not, at least for the worst, changed. Indeed, he looked oftener and more fondly at the curls. Yes, thought Miss Spouter, he may marry her, but the image of Angeline Spouter is in his breast, and it will stay there forever. But for her entreaties her Ma would have removed the little plates and sent him back to the other end of the table, where he came from.

"I'm jest the woman to do it," she said. "That long-legged Yankee has eat more than his worth in butter alone. The house'll break or be eat up, it makes no difference which, and nary cent of money has he paid yit. Settle hisself, indeed! He'll never settle his nasty self except whar thar's money, or everlastin butter, and he not to pay for it neither. And I'll move them plates to-morrow mornin. If I don't you may — "

"Oh, Ma! he DON'T love her, I know he don't. Let them stay a while longer."

And the next morning the little plates would come in, take their places and look as cheerful as if nothing had happened.

Mr. Slack did a cash business. Time rolled on; the faster it rolled the cheaper he sold. His stock dwindled, and everybody asked why it was not being replenished. It began to be rumored that he was going to buy a plantation and settle himself. The rumor was traced to Uncle Ben Pea. Miss Georgiana was asked about it and became confused.

"She jest as well a give it up," said Mr. Bill Williams, at Mr. Spouter's table. Mr. Bill was gradually edging up towards "quality eend," as he termed the head. "In fac, she did give it up farly. I axed her a plain question; she couldn't say nothin, and she didn't. She merrily hung her head upon her bres, and she seemed monsous comfortubble. She ar evidently scogitatin on the blessed joys of a futur state."

The next morning the little plates were absent, and Mr. Slack, without seeming to notice that Mr. Bill Williams had usurped his place, took his seat by Mr. Spouter and talked with him in the manner of a man who had been on a journey of some weeks and had now returned. That gentleman did not seem to be at all congratulatory on the occasion, but immediately after breakfast brought within view of his guest an account for three months' board. The latter looked over it carefully, remarked that he thought it was correct, begged that it might be considered as cash, and walked away. This was an eventful day to Mr. Slack, for besides the aforementioned incident, he sold out the remainder of his stock to Messrs. Bland & Jones, went without his dinner, borrowed a gig from the Justice of the Peace, took him along with him to Mr. Pea's, where, at three o'clock P. M. he was married to Miss Georgiana.

"Wretched creature!" exclaimed Angelina, the forsaken, when her mother informed her of the news at night. At first she thought she would faint; but she did not. She retired to her room, undressed, looked at her curls in the glass even longer than was her wont, put them away tenderly, got into bed, apostrophised property and the other sordid things of this world, and went to sleep with this thought upon her mind: "Georgiana Pea may be by his side; but the image of Angeline Spouter is in his breast, and it will stay there forever."

15

CHAPTER V.

"Are we not one? are we not joined by Heaven?"

FAIR PENITENT.

GEORGIANA was married, and her father was glad of it. It was what he had wanted long to see. The danger of going distracted was over. He was happy; indeed, jubilant. For the truth is, he had made the match. He and Mr. Slack had persuaded and begged, and made such fair promises, that she had been won rather against her judgment. Uncle Ben at one time would have preferred a Southern man; but all of that class had shown such a want of sense to appreciate his Georgy that he persuaded himself that she had made a narrow escape in not marrying one of them. Then Mr. Slack had come from such an immense distance, and knew so much, and talked so much, that Uncle Ben, as he admitted, was actually proud of him. He maintained upon the day of the marriage that *Mas-sa-chu-setts* was the biggest word in the English language. But Georgiana, who was as honest and as truthful a woman as was in the world, insisted that her " Pap " went too far, or rather that he did not go far enough, and that *Con-stan-ti-no-ple* was a bigger. Uncle Ben didn't like to have to give it up; but when he found out from Mr. Slack that the place bearing that name was not in this country, and not even in America, he and Mr. Slack together got Georgy so badly, and wound her up so completely that — oh, how they all did laugh and go on! The truth is that Uncle Ben was rapidly lapsing into a state where he could scarcely be considered faithful to his native section.

Yet in spite of all this, his son-in-law had some ways of doing and talking that he did not quite understand; but he trusted that they would wear off. Georgy now had a husband to take care of her when his head got cold; by which he meant to signify the time when he should be a dead man. She did not seem to be perfectly happy, but, on the contrary, somewhat ill at ease. But then she wasn't any young thing to let getting married run her raving distracted. He liked Mr. Slack upon the whole; he suited *him* well enough, and that is what parents generally care most for. He was a *business* man, that's what he was. He talked upon business even on the afternoon of his marriage, and renewed the subject after supper and the next morning.

One would have thought, to hear him talk about business, that the honeymoon had shone out and gone down long ago. It did not look exactly right ; but now that Mr. Slack was a married man, he was for making something. If *he* owned the farm, he should do this thing and that thing ; sell this piece of property and convert it into cash ; in short, he should sell out the whole concern and go where land was cheaper and better. If it were left to him, he should turn it over so that in twelve months it should be worth at least twice as much as it was now. It was very clear to Uncle Ben that his son-in-law was a business man. Still he did not make out the title-deeds. Notwithstanding his hints to that effect heretofore, he had never entertained the slightest notion of such a thing. When Mr. Slack persisted in saying what he should do if he were the owner, the old gentleman took occasion to say, but in a some-what jocose way, that he and Georgy would have to wait for that until his head got cold ; which, he said by way of consoling for the disap-pointment, wouldn't be much longer. Mr. Slack seemed to be some-what hurt, but he merely remarked that he had a plenty to live on, and that all *he* wanted with property was for Georgiana to enjoy it. He had money enough to buy a tract of land adjoining Mr. Pea's, and two or three " fellows." If Georgiana had a good house-woman it would save her from a good deal of work which now, since she was his wife, he would rather she didn't have to do ; but — ah — he supposed he should have to wait for that.

Yes, but he needn't do any such thing, Mr. Pea stoutly maintained. Those being Mr. Slack's intentions, the 'oman should be bought. The money was there in that side-board drawer whenever they found one to suit them. He should buy the 'oman himself. The son-in-law's countenance brightened a little. He might have to go to Augusta in a few days ; the likeliest gangs were there generally ; and it might suit just as well to take the money along with him and buy the woman there. Georgiana didn't say anything ; but, La me ! what did she know about business ?

Mr. Slack sent into the village every day for the mail, for Dukes-borough being immediately on the great line of travel, had its daily mail. He had been married just two days, when one morning a letter was brought to him which made him turn a little pale. Upon his father-in-law's inquiry from whence it came, he answered after a moment's hesitation that it was from a man who owed him some money, and who had written to say that if he would meet him the next day in Augusta, he would pay him a hundred dollars and renew the note. A hundred dollars, indeed! The rascal had promised to pay half the note, and now as he was about settling himself he was· to be put off with a hundred dollars! He had a good mind not to go, and would not but for the importance of having the note renewed. But *could* he get there in time? How was that, Mr. Pea? Why, it was easy enough; the stage would pass in a couple of hours, and as it travelled all night, he could reach Augusta by nine o'clock the next morning. Mr. Slack hesitated. He was loth to go so soon after being married; but as he had expected to go in a few days anyhow, he guessed he had as well go on at once, especially as negroes seemed to be rising in price, and it was important to get the woman as soon as possible. Certainly; business was business, if people *were* married. Mr. Slack ought to go at once; *he* should, if it was him.

Uncle Ben took out the money, and Georgiana ordered lunch. Mr. Slack had so often complained of the old gentleman's time-piece that the latter, upon his entreaties to be allowed to take it with him for repairs (at no expense to the owner, of course), consented. The man of business then went to packing his trunk and satchel. Although he was to stay but three days at furthest, yet, not knowing but that he might need them, he packed in all his clothes, looking about all over the house to be sure that he had not mislaid anything.

It was a nice lunch. It ought to have been, for it took a long time in getting ready. Mr. Slack was not sure that he was going to get his supper, and he therefore determined to put away enough to last him to the end of his journey. He had barely finished when the servant, who had been stationed to watch for the stage, announced that it was coming. He bade both an affectionate adieu, looked into the stage to see if there was any person in it whom he knew, didn't seem to be disappointed that there was not, hopped in, and off he went.

Far from pining on account of the absence of her mate, Georgiana, sensible woman that she was, went about her work as cheerfully as if nothing had happened. She had been so taken up with Mr. Slack that several small domestic matters needed to be put to rights again, and she seemed to be even glad of the opportunity to look after them. She actually sang at her work; she was a good singer, too. The Peas always had been: I knew the family well. Georgiana wasn't going to fret herself to death; so she resumed her old tasks and habits, moved things back to their old places, and in every respect did as if she had forgotten that she had ever been married.

Uncle Ben was glad to see her in such gay spirits. He knew what it was all for, and he laughed inwardly and became gay himself. It was that nigger 'oman. The old man counted the days and nights. As much as he wanted to see Mr. Slack, he wanted yet more to see his watch; without it he felt like a man without a newly-amputated leg; but he would not allow it to trouble him very much. He talked a great deal, especially at meal times, about his Georgy's prospects, joked her about many things, talked of the prospects again, and what he and Mr. Slack were going to do to make her the happiest woman in the world. Georgiana never suggested any change of their plans, and looked as if she intended to be but clay in their hands.

Three days passed. Mr. Slack's very longest time was out. The stage hove in view ; Mr. Pea was at his gate ; his hat was in his hand.

"Good mornin, Uncle Ben," said the driver, and was passing on.

"Hello! hello, Thompson!" shouted the old man. Thompson drew up.

"Haint you got Mr. Slack aboard?"

"No, SIR!"

"Haint you got a nigger 'oman?"

"No, Sir."

"Whar's Mr. Slack?"

"I don't know."

"Haint you seed him?"

"No, Sir."

"Haint you heern of him?"

"No, Sir."

"Why, what upon yearth does it mean?"

"Mr. Slack didn't go to nary tavern, but got off at a privit 'ouse way up town. I haint seed him nor heern from him sence. Was he to get back to-night?"

"Why, yes, certain and shore, without fail."

"Well, he aint here, certin. Good evenin."

"He haint come, Georgy," said Uncle Ben as he went into the house.

"Hasn't he?"

"Why, no, he haint."

"Well, we must try and wait till he does come."

Uncle Ben was too much occupied with his own disappointment to observe the equanimity with which Georgy bore hers. It was now bed-time ; the daughter went to her room: the father sat up at least half an hour longer than usual. He was disappointed, certain and sure. When people told people they were coming at a certain time, people wanted 'em to come ; especially when they had people's watches. Oh, how he had missed it ! If he had missed it by day, he had missed it as much by night. It used to hang by a nail over his bed, and he longed for the gentle lullaby of its tickings. He had to go to bed, of course, but he lay awake another half hour. A dreadful thought came : What if Mr. Slack, after all, was an IMPOSTERER ! Oh, he couldn't bear it ! So he turned over and went to sleep; but it wouldn't stay behind, it crawled over and came close to him in his sleep, and he dreamed that he was the owner of a jeweller's shop, and that while he had no power to move, thieves were breaking through and stealing.

The next morning, immediately after breakfast, Uncle Ben stood at his gate. He had a notion that Mr. Slack was coming in a private conveyance. Sure enough, yonder came a gig with a man in it, and a horse behind with something on the horse. Uncle Ben's eyes were dim, and he couldn't make it out ; but he hoped and believed that it was a nigger 'oman. Vain hope and vain belief! The gig carried Mr. Triplet, the sheriff, and the horse bore Mr. Pucket, a young lawyer from town. Uncle Ben had no business with them ; so he bade them a good-morning as they came up, and again turned his eyes up the road. But the gentlemen stopped and inquired if Mr. Slack was at home. No, but Mr. Pea looked for him every instant. He had been gone to Augusty three days, and was to a been back last night, but he didn't.

Mr. Triplet looked upon Mr. Pucket and smiled. We must observe that a new election had come on, and Mr. Triplet had beaten Mr. Sanks. Mr. Pucket looked upon Mr. Triplet, but did not smile.

"You must follow him."

"Them must some foller him that kin run faster than I kin," answered Mr. Triplet.

"Foller who?" asked Mr. Pea.

"Mr. Slack."

"Why, he'll be here to-night. Or I'll be bound he's in a private conveyance, and'll be here this mornin. In cose he's comin back, becase he's got four hundred dollars of my money to buy a nigger oman with, and my watch besides. *In cose* he's coming back."

Mr. Triplet looked upon Mr. Pea and smiled compassionately.   Mr. Pea looked upon Mr. Triplet and frowned threateningly.

"What's the matter, Jim Triplet?"

"The matter ar, that you won't see your four hundred dollars agin, nor your watch, nor the gentleman what carried 'em off."

"Why, what upon yearth is you talkin about?"

"I ar talkin about the business of my office; which ar to arress Mr. Adiel Slack, or Mr. Elishay Lovejoy, or Mr. Ephraim Hamlin, or what mout be the name of the gentleman that carried off your four hundred dollars and your watch."

"Don't kick before you're spurred, Triplet; becase nobody aint accused him of takin the money and watch—leastways of stealin it. Mr. Slack is a honest man and my son-in-law; and I tell you he'll be back to-night, and I look for him every minnit of the day."

"So much the better for us if he do come.   I has not come to arress him for taking of the money and the watch, which is misdemeanors that I didn't know tell now.   But he is charge of obtainin credit by false pretensions, of stealin divers money, of tradin with niggers, and finually, with marryin three wimming, and not waitin for nary one of 'em to die fust."

"Oh, Lordy!" exclaimed Mr. Pea.   He then approached the sheriff, and in a tone which invited candor and confidence, and even hinted at gratitude, said, "Jeems Triplet, I voted for you: you know I did; I always has.   Ar what you say a fac?"

"I know you did, Uncle Ben, and I tell you the plain truth—it ar a fac.   Thay aint no doubt about it.   Mr. Pucket here can tell you all about it."

Mr. Pea, without waiting to hear further, turned and got into the house as fast as he could.   He went into a shed-room with uncommon desperation for a man of his years, and raised his hands in order to take down a shot-gun from two forks on which it used to hang.   The forks were there, but the gun was gone.   He looked at the forks with the most resentful astonishment, and with a voice towering with passion asked them what in the name of thunder had become of his gun?   Not receiving any answer, he put the same interrogatory to the corner behind the door, to the space under the bed, and even to two small glass drawers, after opening and shutting them with great violence. He then ran back to the front door and questioned the whole universe on the subject.

"ROBBED! ROBBED!!" roared the old man. "Gen-tul-men, ef I aint robbed —" Mr. Pea had not "cussed" before (as he afterwards declared upon his word and honor) "in twenty year."

"Georgy! Where's Georgy?" It just now occurred to him that it was possible Georgy might not like the state of things herself.

Georgiana had been at the dairy, superintending her butter. She had seen the men as they came, had gone into the house as quietly as she could, and was peeping and listening through the window of her own room.

"Pap," she said, not loudly, but earnestly, "do come here, if you please."

He went into her room.

"I reckon now you're satisfied. He's got what he came here for; he's stole from you, and he's stole from me; I haint got a pocket-handkerchief to my name. But do, for goodness' sake, go and send them men away."

"Oh, Lordy!" reiterated Mr. Pea, retiring. "Gen-tul-men, it's no use : we are cotcht ; Georgy and me has both been cotcht — I acknowledge the corn ; and what is worser, it seem that I am the cause of it all. He have took my money ; he have took my watch ; he have took my gun ; he have took my rumberiller ; and da-ing his low-life skin, he have even took Georgy's pocket-handkerchers. It seem like he jest picked me and Georgy out for all his rascalities. And to think that I should be 'cused of it all. I *did* want her to marry. It look like a pity for her not to git married. And now she is married, and what have she married? A nasty, dad-blasted, thievious Yankee ; and aint even married at that! She is married, and she aint married ; and she's a orphlin ; and she's a widder ; and nobody can't tell what she ar and what she aint ; and I don't understand it ; and Georgy's name will go *down* to posterity, and the Peas wont be nobody any more ; and — oh, Lordy!"

"Pap, do for goodness gracious' sake hush and come in the house!" said Georgiana, advancing to the front door. "The Lord knows, I'm glad I aint married ; and if them other women don't grieve after him any more than *I* grieve after him, they've done forgot him, that's all. Pap, do come in the house."

Mr. Pea subsided, and the men rode away. Mr. Pucket begged Mr. Triplet to hasten ; but the latter, who was too old to be running for nothing, declared in round terms that he'd be dinged ef he did.

" I wouldn't a made myself ridicerlous, Pap, before company, if I'd a been in your place. That was pretty talk to have before men, and I in the house hearin every word."

Mr. Pea, hearing himself accused of a new crime, couldn't stand it.

" I do believe that if old Saton was to come, it would be me that fotch him; or leastways sent for him; and I'd leave he had a come as that d-adblasted Yankee. Yes, it's me: in cose it's me. Anything wrong, I done it; oh yes, in cose: certing. Whar's my hat?" And the good man sallied forth to his field, where he remained until dinner-time. There were so many contending emotions in his breast that he ate in silence. Georgiana had a good appetite; she ate away with a gusto and eyed her father amusedly.

" Pap, if I'll tell you something will you swear you'll keep it?"

Uncle Ben laid down his knife and fork and gazed at her in amazement.

" Wipe your mouth, Pap, and tell me if you'll swear."

" What is it?" he demanded authoritatively.

" Will you swear, I asked you?"

" That's a mighty pooty question for a child to ask its parrent."

" Oh, very well." And she helped herself again from her favorite dish. " Won't you have some more, Pap?"

" Georgy, what *does* you mean?"

" Will you swear?"

" No, I won't."

" Oh, very well then." And she peppered and salted.

" Well, I never 'spected to come to this while my head was hot. My own child: that I've raised: and raised respectable: to be settin thar, at my own table: a axin her own parrent to swar: jest the same as ef I was gwine into a Free Mason's lodge: which she knows I don't hold with no sich."

" Pap, I've heard you often talking against the Free Masons. I never thought they were so mighty bad. What do they do that is so awful bad?"

" You don't, do you? No, I suppose you don't; in cose you don't: takin arter them as you do: in cose you don't. I sposen you'll be a jinin 'em yourself befo long. For they tells me they takes in wimming too; and swars *them;* and they rips and rears round jest like the men, and car's on ginnilly. Oh no: in cose you don't: takin arter 'em as you do."

16

"I don't know what I might do after what I've done already. But how do I take after 'em?"

"In havin o' secrets that's a sin to keep; and in trying to make people swar that they won't tell 'em; and not even to their own parrents. That's how you are takin arter 'em."

"Oh, yes, I see now," she said, appearing to muse. "Still, this is something that I couldn't tell without your swearing not to mention to a blessed soul. It's worth swearin for, Pap."

The old man was silent for a moment.

"Arit anything concernin that mean runaway Yankee?"

"If it is, will you swear?"

"Yes, I WILL, and cuss too, if you want me. I've been a cussin to myself all day anyhow."

"You've cursed to other people besides yourself: but I only want you to swear."

She brought the family Bible.

"La, Georgy! is you in yearnest, sure enough? Why, what do you mean? You aint no Jestice."

It made no difference; she made him place his hand on the book and swear that he would never reveal what she was going to tell him without her consent. Uncle Ben was very solemn while the oath was being administered. It required several minutes to impart the secret. When it was over the old man's joy was boundless. He jumped up and ran into his own room, where he cut up more capers than any one could have believed that he could cut up; he ran back again, made Georgiana rise from the table, hugged her, and made her sit down again; he rushed to the front door and huzzaed to the outer world; he rushed back again and hugged Georgy as she sat. Then he took his seat again and looked upon her with ineffable admiration. Suddenly he grew serious.

"Oh, Georgy, now if I only had —"

Before he could speak further she had taken something from her bosom, and handed it to him. He seized it with both hands, gazed at it, held it at arm's length and gazed at it, opened and looked into it, shut it up again, held it for a moment to his ear, patted it gently, laid it on the table, then lifted up his voice and wept.

CHAPTER VI.

'I grant I am a woman.'

JULIUS CÆSAR.

WHEN the news of Mr. Slack's escapade reached Dukesborough, there was running to and fro. Business was suspended. Some asked if the like had ever been heard of; others asked everybody if they hadn't told him so. J. Spouter was among the former, and Mr. Bill Williams among the latter. He got leave of absence from the store, in order to roam up and down all the forenoon for the purpose of proving that he had prophesied what had taken place, or its equivalent. He was delighted : my observation is that almost everybody is, by the verification of a prophecy which he has made, or which he thinks he has made. Miss Spouter tried to laugh, but she didn't make much out of it. Mrs. Spouter didn't laugh at all. How could she when she remembered the plates of butter that had been consumed, not only without thanks but without pay? She did all the talking in the domestic circle. Mr. Spouter seemed inclined to be taciturn. . He merely remarked that he had never been so outed in his born days, and then shut up. But then Mr. Spouter never had much to say when Mrs. Spouter had the floor ; if, however, he had had the floor now, there was nothing for him to say. He had not sued his debtor, but for reasons other than the being a merciful creditor. He was not used to such things. Indeed, the very word SUIT was, and had long been, disagreeable to his ear ; so much so that he had never gone into court of his own accord. It was one of his boasts, in comparing himself with some others, that he had never been plaintiff in an action, and never expected to be. He always discouraged people from going to law, maintaining that people never got much by going there : a remark that was true when confined in its application to those who had gone there carrying him with them. Yet, Mr. Spouter seldom lost a bill. It was always a wonder to me how rapidly persons in his condition could collect their bills. But this time Mr. Spouter, as he said, was "outed." As he didn't relish Mr. Bill Williams' jokes ; and as Mrs. Spouter didn't, and at last as Miss Spouter didn't, Mr. B. W. had to suspend.

Poor Mr. Pucket! his mind had been set upon a fee ; but as no one

could be found who could run faster than Mr. Triplet, and as the
fugitive had three days' start, there was no pursuit.   None but a brief-
less lawyer can imagine how badly Mr. Pucket felt.

"And so she isn't married after all!" said Miss Spouter to herself,
when she was alone in her chamber that night.   "Not married after
all ; no more than I am.   Yes, I suppose more than I am ; because
she *thought* she was married, and I KNEW I wasn't.   That makes some
difference ; and then — and then—"   But it was too wonderful for
Miss Spouter : she couldn't make it out.   So she only said, "Oh, I
wonder how she feels!"

Now, there was but one way to get the desired information, and
that was to see her and hear it from her own mouth.   To most persons
that way would seem to be barred, because the last time the two ladies
met, Miss Spouter had refused to speak.   But it did not seem so to
her ; she would herself remove all obstacles.   SHE WOULD FORGIVE
GEORGE !   Yes, that she would.   Wasn't it noble to forgive?   Didn't
the Bible teach us to forgive?   Yes, she would forgive.   What a glory
overspread the heart of the injured when, in that tender moment, she
found she could forgive.   She wished now that she had gone to
Georgiana to-day ; she would go to-morrow.   Malice should never
have an abiding place in that heart.   It might have it in other people's
hearts, but it should never have it in that one.   Never, no never,
while memory remains.   She laid herself calmly and sweetly upon her
bed, and was forcibly reminded, as she thought of herself and her
conduct, of the beauty and the serenity of a summer's evening.

CHAPTER VII.

"In that same place thou hast appointed me,
To-morrow truly will I meet with thee."

MIDSUMMER-NIGHT'S DREAM.

MR. PEA writhed and chafed under his oath.   He begged his Georgy
to let him tell somebody.   He swore another oath — that he should
die if he didn't.   He did tell it there in the house several times to
imaginary auditors, after looking out of the doors and windows to see
if no real ones were near.   Even when he was out of doors, he went

all about whispering excitedly to himself, occasionally laughing most tumultuously. Georgiana became uneasy.

"Pap, are you going to run distracted again?"

"Georgy, ef I don't believe I am, I'll — you may kill me!"

Georgiana had to yield. She wished to see Mr. Spouter upon a little matter of business connected with Mr. Slack, and she concluded to consent for him to be sent for and her father to inform him of what she saw he must inevitably tell somebody. The old man was extremely thankful, but he wanted to make a request.

"Georgy, you must let me send for Triplet. I've got a good joke on Triplet: a powerful joke on him. And he's a officer, Georgy, too," he added, seriously. "Things like them, when they ar told, ought to be told befo a officer, Georgy. Triplet is a officer. This case, an a leetle more, an it would a got into cote ; an as Triplet ar a officer, he ought to be here, in cose." •

Georgiana consented on hearing this last argument. But she expressly enjoined upon her father, that at any period of his disclosures, when she called upon him to stop, he would have to do it. He promised to obey ; and the servant was sent into Dukesborough with the request that Messrs. Spouter and Triplet should come out the next morning on particular business. Georgiana knew fully what she, who was her friend, but now, alas! abandoned, was thinking about, and therefore she was included in the summons.

Early the next morning the party arrived. Miss Spouter alighted in great agitation, rushed through the front room into Georgiana's, who was there waiting for what she knew was to happen, looked all around as if she was expecting to find somebody besides Georgiana, fell upon her in the old way, pronounced her pardon, and then demanded to be told all about it. Oh, my! Dreadful! Did ever! Vain and foolish man! How did Georgiana feel?

Georgiana led her into her father's room, which also served for the parlor. She was surprised and annoyed to find Mr. Pucket there with the other gentlemen. Mr. Pucket had, somehow, gotten the wind of it, and said to himself that he didn't know what might happen. He had been told by an old lawyer that the only way for a young man to succeed at the bar was to push himself forward. So he determined to go, and he went. Uncle Ben was glad of it. He was going, for the first time in his life, to make a speech ; and he wished as large an audience as possible. No, no ; in cose there wern't no intrusion, and no nothin of the sort, nor nothin else.

Georgiana sat very near her father.

Then Uncle Ben opened his mouth, and began :—

"You see, gentul-men, it was all my fault, from the fust. After Georgy seed him she didn't think much of him. She said she didn't keer about marryin nohow, and ef she did, she wanted it to be to a Southering man. But I and him too, we overpersuaded her. He seemed to think so much of me and her too ; and he had a store, and 'peared like a man well to do. And I did want to see my only daughter settle herself. The feelin is nat'ral, as you know yourself, Mr. Spouter ; all parrents that has daughters, has 'em : aint it so, Mr. Spouter ?"

Mr. Spouter answered rather by his manner than in words. Miss Spouter became confused, and didn't look at Mr. Pucket when he coughed. Mr. Triplet had seen something of life in his time : still he took a chew of tobacco.

"Go on, Pap," said Georgiana.

"Yes. Well, you see, gentulmen, sich it war — anyhow they got married. Georgy said when she gin her consent she gin it to keep me from runnin distracted, as it did 'pear like I war. Howbeever, I ar clean out o' that now. Circumances is altered powerful. Well, as I said, anyhow they got married — that is, they didn't git married ; because he were already married, and thay warn't no law for it, as you know yourself, Mr. Pucket, thay warn't. But — ah — leastways they went throo the — ah — the motions, and the — ah — gittin out lisens, and the — ah — stannin up in the floor and jinin o' hands ; and he come here to live. Well, now, don't you b'leeve that Georgy, she spishuned him from the very fust day : for no sooner were he married hardly, than he begun to sarch behind every nuke and corner about here, and before night, bless your soul, he knowed more about whar things was in this house than I did. Leastways, Georgy says so, and it's obleeged to be so ; for there's things, many of 'em in this house, that I don't know whar they are." And Mr. Pea looked around and above, taking as big a view as if he were surveying the whole universe.

"Well, Georgy, she and he tuk a walk that fust evenin. Instid of talkin along like tother folks that's jest got married, he went right straight to talkin about settlin hisself, and put at her to begin right away to git all she could out'n me ; which Georgy she didn't like no sich, and nobody wouldn't a liked it that thought anything of herself. You wouldn't, Angeline Spouter, you know you wouldn't, the very fust day you was married."

"Go on, Pap, please."

"Yes. Well, Georgy spishuned him again at supper, from the way he looked at the spoons on the table; which ef they had a been the ginuine silver, they wouldn't a been in this house now, to my opinion; probly; leastways, ef—" Uncle Ben smiled, and concluded to postpone the balance of this sentence.

"Well, you see, Georgy Ann, arter supper, she got sick, she did, and she hilt on to her head powerful. In cose, bed-time, hit had to come arter a while. When hit did come, she were wusser, and she give that feller a candle to go long to bed. When Georgy goes to bed, she goes on throo into the little jinin back room and she locked the door arter her. I never knowed one word o' this untel arter he went off. Well, arter he went to sleep, Georgy she heerd a mighty groanin. So she ups, she does, an onlocks the door, and creeps in mighty sly. It seem like he were dreamin and talkin in his sleep powerful. He called names, sich as Jemimy, Susan Jane, Betsy Ann, and — what was all them names, Georgy?"

"It makes no difference, Pap; go on."

"And a heap more of 'em. Georgy can tell you, cose she heard 'em over and ofting. Well, he seemed to be powerful shamed of all of 'em, and he swore he wern't married, and them that said so was a liar, and all sich. Well, sich carrin on made Georgy b'leeve that he was a married man befo, and had two or three wives already, or probable four or five. And so Georgy seed rightaway that she wasn't no wife o' his'n, and didn't have no intrust in no sich a d-evil. And she war right, Triplet. Triplet, warn't she right?"

"In cose," answered Mr. Triplet.

"Do go on, Pap."

"Well, yes. Yit still she didn't let on. She kept up tolerble well in the day-time, but when night come agin, Georgy she gits sick agin and goes into the jinin little room agin. I never seed sich carrin on befo."

Uncle Ben had to stop and laugh a while. Georgy begged him to go on.

"Well, she kep on hearin him a goin on, and you think she would tell me the fust thing o' all this? Ef she had a told me — howbeever, that aint neither here nor thar. Well, it seem he talked in his sleep about other people besides wimming, about men and about money, and declared on his soul that he never stole it, which goes to show Georgy that he war a rogue, as well as a rascal about wimming. Yit in this

time he begin to hint even around *me* about property, and even insini-
vated that he would like to have the whole plantation and all that's on
it!" Mr. Pea showed plainly by his manner, after making this last
remark, that no man had ever had an ambition more boundless than
the late Mr. Slack. "But I mighty soon give him to understand that
he war barkin up the wrong tree ef he thought I was gwine to give
up *this* plantation and *my* property before my head got cold. Them's
always fools that does it. Howbeever, he talked so much about settlin
hisself, and so easy and good about Georgy, and how that all he keered
about property was for her, and I knowed that was all *I* keered about it
for, that I told him I'd pay for a nigger 'oman for 'em. Well, you see,
I no sooner says that than he ups with a lie about havin to go to Augusty.
But shore enuff, arter he had been here two days, he *had* to go too
Augusty, or somewhar else. Becase he got a letter which skeered him
powerful, and he said he war goin right off. I didn't spishun nothin
agin the man, and I lets him have the money to buy the nigger 'oman. I
had no more spishun of him, Jeems Triplet, than I have of you, only
knowin that he was monstrous fond of money, which is all right enough
ef a man comes by it honest. Well, Georgy she was tuk back tremenduous by his gittin the money so all on a suddin. Yit she didn't let on,
but makes out like she's mighty sorry he war goin so soon, but mighty
glad he's goin to fetch her a nigger 'oman when he come back. She has
him got a mighty good snack of vittles, and what ain't common for
dinner, she puts on the table a plate of nice fresh butter and a plenty
of biscuit, Triplet." Mr. Pea now looked as sly and as good-humored
as it was possible for him to be. "Triplet, I've got a good joke on
you."

Mr. Triplet seemed to guess what it was, and smiled subduedly.

"You know what you said about my never seein certing people and
certing things — certing property no more?"

Mr. Triplet acknowledged that he did.

"Well, Triplet, part of it was so and part of it were not so; all which
both is jest as I wants it to be. Triplet, that butter and them biscuit
is what saved me. He never expected to eat no more tell he got to
Augusty, and I tell you he hung to that butter and them biscuit. While
he was at 'em, and Georgy she made 'em late a comin in a purpose,
she takes some old keys which she had picked up, and finds one that
could onlock his peleese whar she seed him put the money, and whar
she knowed he kep all he had."

Uncle Ben intended to laugh mercilessly at Triplet, but he was stopped by the sight of Mr. Pucket, who did look as if he was trying to swallow something that was too big for his throat.

"Ar anything the matter with you, Mr. Pucket? Is you got a cold? Ar your thoat so'?" asked the old gentleman, with undisguised interest.

Triplet snickered as Mr. Pucket denied being sick.

Uncle Ben proceeded:

"So she jest opened it sly as a mice and tuk out my money — "

"And what else?" eagerly asked Mr. Pucket.

"My watch, that the villion beg me to let him take with him to have it worked on, which I didn't like no — "

"What else?" asked Mr. Pucket again.

"That's the last pint I'm a comin too, and that's why Georgy sent arter Mr. Spouter. She knowed that he owed Mr. Spouter thirty dollars, and she made up her mind to pay the debt as now she seed his money, and she tuk out thirty dollars o' his money, which here it ar for you, Mr. Spouter."

"I garnishee the thirty dollars!" interposed Mr. Pucket, holding out his hands.

"You are too late," answered Mr. Spouter, taking the money, putting it into his pocket, and looking as if he had gotten in again after being outed by Mr. Slack.

"Can't I garnishee, Triplet?"

"Garnishee for what?"

"For my fee?"

"Fee for what?"

"Why, for my services in — ah — coming out here on two occasions."

"Well, you can't garnishee."

Mr. Triplet looked as if he was ashamed of Mr. Pucket. Uncle Ben hoped there was goin to be no bad feelins, and no difficulties.

"Certainly not," answered Mr. Triplet. "Mr. Pucket ar a young lawyer, and forgot at the minnit that it war other people that owed him for his services instid of Mr. Slack. Besides, furthermo, Mr. Pucket ought to know that you can't garnishee jest dry so, without fust gittin out some sort o' paper from the cote. That would take so much time that Spouter here mout spend his thirty dollars befo he got it, that is ef Spouter wanted too." Mr. Triplet looked interrogatively at the other gentleman.

"Yes, ef I wanted too," answered Mr. S., oracularly.

17

"But," persisted Mr. Pucket, "there was other moneys."

"Whar?" asked Mr. Triplet.

"In Mr. Slack's trunk."

"No thay wan't," answered Mr. Pea, who thought he ought to keep Mr. Pucket to the true word. "They was in his pelcese."

"Well, in his pelcese. That makes no difference," and Mr. Pucket looked as if he thought he had them on that point.

"Pucket," said Triplet, "it won't make no difference. You are right. It don't make nary bit o' difference with nobody, ner with your fee neither. That fee ar a lost ball. Thay aint no money here to pay it with, an ef there was, it would be Mr. Slack's lawyer and not you that would git it. Well, gin it up, and another time try to have better luck."

Mr. Pucket *was* a young lawyer, and was, in part, owned by Mr. Triplet. So he subsided. Uncle Ben looked troubled, until the sheriff assured him that there could be no difficulties. "Go on, Uncle Ben. You got your gun, of course?"

"Triplet, you rascal! You may laugh; but I don't want the gun. He may keep it, and do what he pleases with it, even to blowin out his own thievious brains with it for what I keer. He's welcome to the gun. You, Triplet!"

"Don't mind me, Uncle Ben. Go on."

"Well, thar's lots more to tell, ef Georgy would only let me; and some things as would make you laugh powerful, Triplet, ef you was to hear 'em. But she's made me swar, actilly swar, that I won't tell without her leave. Maybe she'll tell your ole 'oman some o' these days. Well, I felt mighty glad when I got my money back, and, ef anything, a leetle gladder when I got back my watch agin. Triplet, when I seed her" (and the old man drew out a watch as big and as round as a turnip), "when I seed her agin, ef I didn't cry you may kill me. I've had her thirty year, and none o' your new-fangled ones can beat her runnin when you clean her out and keep her sot right with the sun. Ah, well," he continued, putting it back and shaking his foot in mild satisfaction, "the thing is over, and the best of it all ar that—"

"Hush, Pap," said Georgiana, raising her finger.

The old man smiled, and hushed.

After hearing parts of the story over several times, the party rose to go. Mr. Triplet rising, said that in cose it war not any of his bisiness, but he would like to ax Miss Georgy one question, ef he wouldn't be considered as meddlin with what didn't belong to him; and that was, why she didn't tell on the villion as soon as she found him out? Georgiana answered:

"Well, Mr. Triplet, I many times thought I would; but you see I didn't know for certain that he had done all the things that I was afraid he had. Besides, Mr. Triplet, even if he wasn't my husband, I one time thought he was, and before God and man I had promised to be faithful to him. And then he had stayed in this house: and eat at our table: and — and called Pap father, and — and — and — Well, Mr. Triplet, somehow it didn't look right for me to be the first one to turn against him; and — and when I did think of telling on him, something would rise up and tell me that I ought not."

"Wimming aint like men nohow, Uncle Ben," said Triplet, wiping his eye as he bade him good-bye.

"No they aint, Triplet," and he laid his hand fondly on his daughter's shoulder while the tears ran down his cheeks.

The visitors now left, all except Miss Spouter. She wished to get behind the scenes and know more. How much more she learned I cannot say. They went to bed early when the day ended, and to sleep late. There was something which made them easily reunite. It was pity. Miss Spouter imagined that she pitied her friend because she had been deceived by a man, even more than herself had ever been, and because of the hurtful influence which that deception would probably exert upon any future expectations of marriage. Miss Pea, who, instead of having any regrets, felt relief in the thought that henceforth her father would be satisfied to allow her to manage such matters for herself, and that she should be satisfied to have none to manage, really pitied her friend because she yet yearned for an impossible estate. When the time came for them to go to sleep (and Georgiana thought it long coming), she did not wait a moment. Miss Spouter lay awake some time further. She pondered long on what she had heard. It was strange. It was almost like a novel. How could George be still the same Georgiana Pea? She had been Mrs. Slack. Wasn't she Mrs. Slack now? And how, oh! how exciting everything must have been. Her thoughts followed Mr. Slack a while; but he was so far away that they came back and went looking after Mr. Bill Williams. He was not much; but he was something. He had never exhibited any regard for her yet, but it was possible that he would some day. He was at least ten years younger than herself. But her curls were the same as ever ; and besides, were not marriages made in heaven? or were they not a lottery, or something of the sort? Mr. Bill Williams, after all, might be the very one to whom the something in her alluded when it had so repeatedly told her that she was destined to make some man so happy ; who knows? Then her mind turned again, and notwithstanding Mr. Slack's great distance ahead, it started forth in the direction he had taken. She dwelt upon his strange conduct and his running away, and although it was plain that he had done the like before, and when he had never seen her nor heard of her, yet she half persuaded herself that she was the cause, though the perfectly innocent cause of it all. "Yes, yes!" she was saying to herself, as sleep stole upon her at last, "he is gone ; but the image of Angeline Spouter is in his breast, and it will stay there forever!"

THE EARLY MAJORITY OF MR. THOMAS WATTS.

"O 'tis a parlous boy."

RICHARD III.

LITTLE TOM WATTS, as he used to be called before the unexpected developments which I propose briefly to narrate, was the
second in a family of eight children, his sister Susan being the eldest.
His parents dwelt in a small house situate on the edge of Dukesborough. Mr. Simon Watts, though of extremely limited means, had
some ambition. He held the office of constable in that militia district,
and in seasons favorable to law business, made about fifty dollars a
year. The outside world seemed to think it was a pity that the head
of a family so large and continually increasing should so persistently
prefer mere fame to the competency which would have followed upon
his staying at home and working his little field of very good ground.
But he used to contend that a man could not be expected to live
always, and therefore he ought to try to live in such a way as to leave
to his family, if nothing else, a name that they wouldn't be ashamed
ever to hear mentioned after he was gone.

Yet Mr. Watts was not a cheerful man. Proud as he might justly
feel in his official position, it went hard with him to be compelled to live
in a way more and more pinched as his family continued to multiply
with astonishing rapidity. His spirits, naturally saturnine, grew worse
and worse with every fresh arrival in the person of a baby, until the
eighth. Being yet a young man, comparatively speaking, and being
used to make calculations, the figures seemed too large as he looked
to the future. I would not go so far as to say that this prospect

actually killed him ; but at any rate he took a sickness which the doctor could not manage, and then Mr. Watts gave up his office and everything else that he had in this world.

But Mrs. Watts, his widow, had as good a resolution as any other woman in her circumstances ever had. She had no notion of giving up in that way. She gave up her husband, it is true ; but that could not be helped ; and without making much ado about even that, she kept going at all sorts of work, and somehow she got along at least as well after as before the death of Mr. Simon.

A person not well acquainted with the brood of little Wattses often found difficulty in discriminating among them. I used to observe them with considerable interest as I went into Dukesborough occasionally with one, or the other, or both of my parents. They all had white hair, and red chubby faces. It was long a matter of doubt what was their sex. Such was the rapidity of their succession, and so graduated the declivity from Susan downwards, that the mother used to cut all their garments after a fashion that was very general, in order that they might descend during the process of decay to as many of them as possible. Now, although I saw them right often, I had believed for several months, for instance, that little Jack was a girl, from a yellow frock that had belonged to his sister Mary Jane, but which little Jack wore until his legs became subjected to such exposure that it had to descend to Polly Ann, his next younger sister. Then I made a similar mistake about Polly Ann ; who, during this time, had worn little Jack's breeches, out of which he had gone into Mary Jane's frock ; and I thought on my soul that Polly Ann was a boy.

In regard to little Tommy, not only I, but the whole public had been in a state of uncertainty in this behalf for a great length of time. Having no older brother, and Susan's outgrown dresses being alone available, his male wardrobe was inevitably only half as extensive and various as by good rights, generally speaking, it ought to have been. Therefore little Tommy had to make his appearance alternately in frock and breeches, according to the varying conditions of these garments, for a period that annoyed him the more the longer it extended, and finally began to disgust. Tom eagerly wished that he could outgrow Susan, and thus get into breeches out and out. But Susan, in this respect, as indeed in almost all others, kept her distance in the lead.

There was a difference, easily noticeable, in Tom's deportment in these seasons. While in frocks it was subdued, retiring, and, if not melancholy, at least fretful. Curiosity, perhaps, or some other motive equally powerful, might, and indeed sometimes did, lead him outside of the gate ; but never to linger there for any great length of time. If he had to go upon an errand during that season (a necessity which that resolute woman, his mother, enforced without the slightest hesitation), he went and returned with speed. Yet, before starting out on such occasions, he was wont to be careful to give his hair such a turn that his manly head might refute the lie which Susan's frock had told. For it is probable that there have been few, if indeed any boys who were more unwilling either to be, or to be considered of the opposite sex than that same Tom Watts. I do not remember ever to have seen a boy whose hair had so high and peculiar a roach as his exhibited, especially when he wore his sister Susan's frocks. Instead of being parted in the middle, it was divided into three parts. It was combed perfectly straight down on the sides of his head, and perfectly straight up from the top. An immense distance was thus established between the extremities of any two hairs which receded contiguously to each other on the border lines.

All this was an artful attempt to divert public attention from the frock which intimated the female, to the head which asserted and which was supposed to establish the male. He once said to Susan :

"When they sees your old frock, they makes out like that they 'spicions me a gal ; but when they looks at my har all roached up, then they knows who I air."

"Yes, indeed," answered Susan, "and a sight you air. Goodness knows, I'd rather be a girl, and rather look like one if I weren't, than to look like you do in that fix."

But it was during the other season, that which he called his breeches week, that Tommy Watts was most himself. In this period he was cheerful, bold, and notorious. He was as often upon the street as he could find opportunities to steal away from home ; and while there, he was as evidently a boy as was to be found in Dukesborough or any other place of its size. In this happy season he seemed to be disposed to make up as far as possible for the confinements and the gloominesses of the other. So much so, indeed, that he had to be whipped time and time again for his unlicensed wanderings, and for many other pranks which are indeed peculiar to persons of his age and sex, but which he seemed to have the greater temptation to do, and which he did with more zest and temerity than other boys, because he had only half their time in which to do them. Tom Watts maintained that if a boy *was* a boy, then he ought to *be* a boy; and as for himself, if he had to be a girl a part of the time, he meant to double on them for the balance. By *them* he meant his Mammy, as he was wont to call his surviving parent. But she understood the method of doubling as well as he; for while she whipped him with that amount of good-will which in her judgment was proper, she not unfrequently cut short his gay career by reducing him to Susan's frock, or (if it was not ready for the occasion) to his own single shirt. On such occasions he would relapse at once into the old melancholy ways. If Thomas Watts had been familiar with classical history, I have not a doubt that, in these periods of his humiliation, he would have compared his case with that of the great Achilles whose mother had him kept in inglorious seclusion amid the daughters of Lycomedes. Yet, like that hero further in being extremely imprudent, no sooner would he recover his male attire than he would seem to think that no laws had ever been made for him, and would rush headlong into difficulties and meet their consequences. Tom, as his mother used to say, was a boy of a "tremenjuous sperrit." But it had come from her, and enough had been left in her for all domestic purposes. In every hand-to-hand engagement between the two, Thomas was forced to yield and make terms; but he resolved over and over, and communicated that resolution to many persons, that if he ever did obtain his liberty, the world should hear from him. His late father having been to a degree connected, as we remember, with the legal profession, Tom had learned one item (and that was probably the only one that he did learn sufficiently well to remember) of the law: that was, that young men of fourteen who had lost their fathers might go into court and choose their own guardians, and do other things besides. How he did long for that fourteenth birthday! The more he longed for it the longer it seemed in coming. He had gotten to believe that if it ever should come, he would have lived long enough and had experience enough for all, even the most difficult and responsible purposes of human life.

But events that must come will come, if we will only wait for them. In process of time, which to the hasty nature of Tom seemed unreasonably and cruelly long in passing, he seemed to emerge from the frock for good and all. The latest inducement to a preparation for this liberty was a promise that it should come the sooner provided he would improve in the care that he was wont to take of his clothes, for he had been a sad fellow in that item of personal economy. When this inducement was placed before him, he entered upon a new career. He abjured wrestlings with other boys, and all other sports and exercises, however manly, which involved either the tearing of his attire or contact with the ground. He even began to be spruce and dandyish, and the public was astonished to find that in the matter of personal neatness Tom Watts was likely to become a pattern to all the youth of Dukesborough and its environs. His roach grew both in height and in sleekness; and when his hat was off his head, Tom Watts was the tallest-looking boy of his inches that I ever saw.

Resolute as was the Widow Watts, she had respect for her word, and was not deficient in love for her offspring. Besides, it was getting to be high time for Tom to go to school, if he ever was to go. Now, in a school, I maintain, if nowhere else, it is undeniably to be desired that everybody's sex should be put beyond doubt. Even a real girl in a school of boys, or a real boy in a school of girls, it is probable would both feel and impart considerable embarrassment. This would doubtless be much increased in case where such a matter was in doubt. There is no telling what a difference an uncertainty in this behalf would make, not only in the hours of study, but even to a perhaps greater extent in those of play. I have lived in the world long enough to feel justified in saying that suspicions and doubts are more efficacious than facts in producing embarrassments and alienations. Oh! it is no use to say anything more upon the subject. Mrs. Watts had sense enough to have respect for public sentiment; and when Tom was ready for school, Susan's frock had to be laid aside. However, Mary Jane, who was a fast grower, went into it, with the taking of only a little tuck, and nothing was wasted.

Tom Watts, therefore, avowedly and notoriously, for good and for all and forever, became a boy. When he stepped out of Susan's frock for the last time, and stepped into a new pair of trowsers which had been made for the purpose of honoring the occasion, he felt himself to be older by many years; and if not as sleek, was at least as proud as any snake when, with the incoming Spring, he has left his old skin behind him and glided into the sunlight with a new one.

The neat habits which he had adopted from policy, he continued to practise, to his mother's great delight. It was really a fine thing to observe the care he took with his clothes; and the manly gait he as-

18

sumed would have led unthinking persons almost to conclude that the having been confounded so long with the other sex had begotten a repugnance for the latter which might never be removed. Such was the rapidity of his strides towards manhood, that some females of his acquaintance not unfrequently spoke of him as Mr. Thomas Watts; while others went further, left off the Thomas altogether and called him Mr. Watts.

But time, which is ever making revelations that surprise mankind, was not slow to reveal that Mr. Watts had not yet been fully understood. He had been going to school to Mr. Cordy for several weeks in the winter, and was believed to be making reasonable progress. He had now passed his thirteenth year, and had gone some distance upon his fourteenth. He had long looked to that day as the commencement of his majority. A guardian (or as he was wont to say, a *gardzeen*) was an incumbrance which he had long determined to dispense with. This was not so much, however, because there would be not a thing for such an official to manage except the person of Mr. Thomas himself, as that he had no doubt, not a shadow of a doubt in fact, that such management would be more agreeable, more safe, and in every way better in his own hands than in those of any other person of his acquaintance.

Mr. Cordy's school was in a grove of hickory and oak at the end of the village opposite to the one at which Mrs. Watts's cabin stood. At the hither end of this grove was another small school of girls, kept by Miss Julia Louisa Wilkins. She was from Vermont, and was a young lady of about twenty-eight years, very fair, somewhat tall, and upon the whole a rather good, certainly a cheerful-looking face. For I should remark that Dukesborough, which ever held Augusta in view, had in the pride of its ambition abolished the system of mixed schools, and though the number of children was rather limited to allow of great division, still Dukesborough would have, and did have, two institutions of learning. Miss Wilkins had under her charge about fifteen girls, ranging from eight years old to fourteen. Prominent among them were Miss Adeline Jones, Miss Emily Sharp, Miss Lorinda Holland, Miss Jane Hutchins, and Mr. Watts's elder sister, Susan.

Mr. Watts's relations to this Institution (for it was thus that the mistress insisted that her establishment should be styled) seemed to have been started by accident. One morning, as with lingering but not unmanly steps he was passing by on his way to his own school, he spied Miss Wilkins through the window in the act of kindling a fire. As her face was turned from him he had the opportunity, and he used it, to observe her motions for several moments. Whether because the kindling wood was damp, or Miss Wilkins was not expert, I would not undertake at this late day to say. But the fire would not make a start ; and the lady, apparently bent upon getting warm in some way, threw down the tongs, gave the logs a kick, and abruptly turned her back upon the fire-place. Observing Mr. Watts at that instant, and possibly suspecting that he was a person of an accommodating disposition, she requested his assistance. He yielded promptly, and it did Miss Wilkins good to see how quickly the blaze arose and the genial warmth radiated through the room. The artificial heat at once subsided, and she smiled and thanked him in a way that could not soon be forgotten. Then she inquired his name, and was surprised and gratified to know that so manly a person as he was should be the brother of one of the best and most biddable girls in her school.

This accident, trifling in appearance, led to consequences. Mr. Watts had frequent opportunities of rendering this same service, and others of an equally obliging nature. These gave him access to the Institution in its hours of ease ; and the care that he took of his clothes, and the general manners that he adopted, were reaching to a height that approached perfection. If the roach on the summit of his head was not quite as high as formerly (a depression caused by his having now a hat to wear), it was not any less decided and defiant.

Yet, he never seemed disposed to abuse his privileges at the Institution of Miss Wilkins. Although he was there very often, he usually had little to say to any of the young ladies, and seemed to try to have the utmost respect for all the mistress's rules and regulations in regard to the intercourse of her pupils with the opposite sex. It must be admitted that Mr. Watts had not advanced lately in his studies to the degree that was promised by his opening career. But Mr. Cordy was a reasonable man, and, upon principle, was opposed to pushing boys along too fast. Mrs. Watts, although not a person of education herself, yet suspected from several circumstances that her son was not well improving the little time which she could afford to send him to school. But his deportment was such an example to the younger children that she had not the heart to complain, except in a very general way.

Of all persons of Mr. Watts's acquaintance, his sister Susan was the only one who seemed to fail to appreciate his manly habits. She used to frown dreadfully upon him, even when he seemed to be at his very best. Sometimes she even broke into immoderate laughter. While the former conduct had no influence, the latter used to affect him deeply. He would grow very angry, and abuse her, and then become even more manlike. But when Susan would think that he was carrying matters into extremes, she would check him somewhat in this wise :

"Now lookee here, Tom ; if you talk to me that way, I shall tell Ma what's the matter with you ; and if you don't quit being such a man, and stop some of your foolishness, I'll tell her anyhow."

Threats of this sort for a time would recall Mr. Watts at least to a more respectful treatment of his sister. Indeed, he condescended to beg her not to mention her suspicions, although he assured her that in these she was wholly mistaken. But Susan did know very well what he was about, and it is probable that it is high time I should explain all this uncommon conduct. The truth is, Susan had ascertained that so far from having the repugnance to ladies that had been feared at first might grow out of his remembrance of the long confusion of the public mind touching his own sex, Mr. Thomas Watts had already conceived a passion that was ardent, and pointed, and ambitious to a degree which Susan characterised as "perfectly redickerlous."

But who was the young lady who had thus concentrated upon herself all the first fresh worship of that young but manly heart? Was it Miss Jones, or Miss Sharp? Was it Miss Holland, or Miss Hutchins? Not one of these. Mr. Thomas Watts had with one tremendous bound leaped clear over the heads of these secondary characters, and cast himself at the very foot of the throne. To be plain, Mr. Watts fondly, entirely, madly loved Miss Julia Louisa Wilkins, the mistress and head of the Dukesborough Female Institution.

Probably, this surprising reach might be attributed to the ambitious nature of his father, from whom he had inherited this and some other qualities. Doubtless, however, the recollection of having been kept long in frocks had engendered a desire to convince the world that they had sadly mistaken their man. Whatever was the motive power, such was the fact. Now, notwithstanding this state of his own feelings, he had never made a declaration in so many words to Miss Wilkins. But he did not doubt for a moment that she thoroughly understood his looks, and sighs, and devoted services. For the habit which all of us have of enveloping beloved objects in our hearts, and *making* them, so to speak, understand and reciprocate our feelings, had come to Mr. Watts even to a greater degree perhaps than if he had been older. He was as little inclined and as little able to doubt Miss Wilkins as to doubt himself. Facts seemed to bear him out. She had not only smiled upon him time and time again, and patted him sweetly on the back of his head, and praised his roach to the very skies; but once, when he had carried her a great armful of good, fat pine-knots, she was so overcome as to place her hand under his chin, look him fully in the face, and declare if he wasn't a man, there wasn't one in this wide, wide world.

Such was the course of his true love when its smoothness suffered that interruption which so strangely obtrudes itself among the fondest affairs of the heart. Miss Susan had threatened so often without fulfilment to give information to their mother, that he had begun to presume there was little or no danger from that quarter. Besides, Mr. Watts had now grown so old and manlike that he was getting to be without apprehension from any quarter. He reflected that within a few weeks more he would be fourteen years old, when legal rights would accrue. Determining not to choose any "gardzeen," it would follow that he must become his own. Yet he did not intend to act with unnecessary notoriety. His plans were, to consummate his union on the very day he should be fourteen; but to do so clandestinely, and then run away, not stopping until he should get with his bride plump into Vermont. For even the bravest find it necessary sometimes to retreat.

Of the practicability of this plan he had no doubt, because he knew that Miss Wilkins had five hundred dollars in hard cash — a whole stocking full. This sum seemed to him immensely adequate for their support in becoming style for an indefinitely long period of time.

As the day of his majority approached, he grew more and more reserved in his intercourse with his family. This was scarcely to be avoided now when he was already beginning to consider himself as not one of them. If his conscience ever upbraided him as he looked upon his toiling mother and his helpless brothers and sisters, and knew that he alone was to rise into luxury while they were to be left in their lowly estate, he reflected that it was a selfish world at best, and that every man must take care of himself. But one day, after a season of unusual reserve, and when he had behaved to Miss Susan in a way which she considered outrageously supercilious, the latter availed herself of his going into the village, fulfilled her threat, and gave her mother full information of the state of his feelings.

That resolute woman was in the act of ironing a new homespun frock she had just made for Susan. She laid down her iron, sat down in a chair, and looked up at Susan.

"Susan, don't be foolin 'long o' me."

"Ma, I tell you it's the truth."

"Susan, do you want me to believe that Tom's a fool? I know'd the child didn't have no great deal of sense; but I didn't think he was a clean-gone fool."

But Susan told many things which established the fact beyond dispute. In Mr. Thomas's box were found several evidences of guilt. There was a great red picture of a young woman, on the margin of which was written the name of Miss Julia Louisa Wilkins. Then there was wrapped carefully in a rag a small piece of sweet soap, which was known by Susan to have been once the property of Miss Wilkins. Then there were sundry scraps of poetry, which were quite variant in sentiment, and for this and other reasons apparently not fully suited for the purposes for which they were employed. Mr. Watts's acquaintance with amatory verses being limited, he had recourse to his mother's hymn-book. Miss Wilkins was assured how tedious and tasteless were the hours. Her attention was directed alternately to Greenland's icy mountains and India's coral strand. She was informed that here he was raising his Ebenezer, having hitherto thus safely come. But immediately afterwards his mind seemed to have changed, and he remarked that his home was over Jordan, and suggested that if she should get there before he did, she might tell them he was a-coming. Then he urged Miss Wilkins to turn, sinner, turn, and with great anxiety inquired why would she die? These might have passed for evidences of a religious state of mind, but that they were all signed by Miss Wilkins' loving admirer, Thomas Watts. Indeed, in the blindness of his temerity he had actually written out his formal proposition to Miss Wilkins, which he had intended to deliver to her on the very next day. This had been delayed only because he was not quite satisfied either with the phraseology or the handwriting. As to the way in which it would be received, his ardent soul had never entertained a doubt.

"Well, well!" exclaimed his mother, after getting through with all this irrefragable evidence. "Well, well. I never should a-blieved it. But I suppose we live and larn. Stealing out of my hime-book too. It's enough to make anybody sick at the stomach. I know'd the child didn't have much sense; but I didn't know he was a clean-gone fool."

Yes, we lives and larns. But bless me, it won't do to tarry here. Susan, have that frock ironed all right, stiff and starch, by the time I git back. I shan't be gone long."

The lady arose, and without putting on her bonnet, walked rapidly down the street.

"What are you lookin for, Mrs. Watts?" inquired an acquaintance whom she met on her way.

"I'm a-looking for a person of the name of Mr. Watts," she answered, and rushed madly on. The acquaintance hurried home, but told other acquaintances on the way that the Widow Watts have lost her mind and gone ravin distracted. Soon afterwards, as Mr. Watts was slowly returning, his mind full of great thoughts and his head somewhat bowed, he suddenly became conscious that his hat was removed and his roach rudely seized. Immediately afterwards he found himself carried along the street, his head foremost and his legs and feet performing the smallest possible part in the act of locomotion. The villagers looked on with wonder. The conclusion was universal. Yes, the Widow Watts have lost her mind.

When she had reached her cabin with her charge, a space was cleared in the middle by removing the stools and the children. Then Mr. Watts was ordered to remove such portions of his attire as might oppose any hindrance whatever to the application of a leather strap to those parts of his person which his mother might select.

"Oh, mother, mother!" began Mr. Watts.

"No motherin o' me, Sir. Down with 'em," and down they came, and down came the strap rapidly, violently.

"Oh, Mammy, Mammy!"

"Ah, now! that sounds a little like old times ; when you used to be a boy," she exclaimed in glee as the sounds were repeated amid the unslackened descent of the strap. Mrs. Watts seemed disposed to carry on a lively conversation during this flagellation. She joked her son pleasantly about Miss Wilkins, inquired when it was to be and who was to be invited? Oh, no! she forgot ; it was not to be a big wedding, but a private one. But how long were they going to be gone before they would make a visit? But Mr. Watts not only could not see the joke, but was not able to join in the conversation at all, except to continue to scream louder and louder, "Oh, Mammy, Mammy!" Mrs. Watts, finding him not disposed to be talkative, except in mere ejaculatory remarks, appealed to little Jack, and Mary Jane, and Polly

Ann, and to all, down even to the baby. She asked them, Did they know that Buddy Tommy were a man grown, and were going to git married and have a wife, and then go away off yonder to the Vermontes? Little Jack, and Polly Ann, and baby, and all, evidently did not precisely understand; for they all cried and laughed tumultuously.

How long this exercise, varied as it was by most animated conversation, might have continued if the mother had not become exhausted, there is no calculating. Things were fast approaching that condition when the son declared that his mother would kill him if she didn't stop.

"That," she answered between breaths, "is — what — I — aims — to do — if — I can't git it — all — all — every — spang — passel — outen you."

Tom declared that it was all gone.

"Is you — a man — or — is you — a boy?"

"Boy! boy! Mammy," cried Tom. "Let me up, Mammy — and — I'll be a boy — as long — as I live."

She let him up.

"Susan, whar's that frock? Ah, there it is. Lookee here. Here's your clo'es, my man. Mary Jane, put away them pantaloonses."

Tom was making ready to resume the frock. But Susan remonstrated. It wouldn't look right now, and she would go Tom's security that he wouldn't be a man any more.

He was cured. From being an ardent lover, he grew to become a hearty hater of the principal of the Dukesborough Female Institution, the more implacable upon his hearing that she had laughed immoderately at his whipping. Before many months she removed from the village, and when two years afterwards a rumor (whether true or not we never knew) came that she was dead, Tom was accused of being gratified by the news. Nor did he deny it.

"Well, fellers," said he, "I know it weren't right; but I couldn't keep from being glad ef it had a-kilt me."

THE ORGAN-GRINDER.

"The poor man's dearest friend,
The kindest and the best."

WHEN I am thinking of those old times at Dukesborough, my mind often recurs to a person whom, although not a resident of that neighborhood, yet, as I never saw him elsewhere, I have always associated with it. He made a very deep impression upon me : so much so, indeed, that I have had, ever since I knew him, something like a fondness for his class. I am not likely, and I am sure that I have no desire to lose the old feeling that this one led me to feel. The music sounded so strange and mournful the first time I heard it in the grove at our gate, and the man was so strange looking, so pale and wan, that even now, in my old age, whenever I hear one of his class, especially if he be a foreigner, I feel much of the impressions of the old days. Many pence have I given to organ-grinders in my time, and I expect to give more as long as I continue to live.

They are so poor and so taciturn, and seem so harmless. Since I have read in the books and found to be true what my poor friend used to tell me about the great old bards, and after them the minstrels, my mind became fond of connecting these poor wandering musicians with those famous characters of bygone ages, and thus I learned to pity and to respect them as the last representatives of a class some of whom were illustrious and all of whom were beloved.

There seems to me ever an unchanging sadness, not only in their appearance and deportment, but in all their music. The plaintive airs they bring from their homes across the sea, are not less sad than those, whether they be meant to be lively or plaintive, which they find

19

among us. Indeed, the very saddest of all to my ears are those which strive to be gay. Upon their poor instruments and with their poor renderings, not only do the latter lose their native gaiety, but the effort to preserve it imparts a sadness which is sometimes piteous. When a man has to make merry in order to get bread to eat, and when the bread comes slowly and in insufficient quantities even after the merrymaking, the latter must lose most of its power to make us laugh. So I seldom can pass one of these persons without dropping into his till the mite which I cannot easily keep when I consider how much more the gain will be to him than the loss will be to me. Then I have found that such trifling losses in due time bring me gains in many ways. And then again, these little contributions, perhaps, I make as often as otherwise out of regard for the·memory of· an old friend.

The individual of whom I am speaking had an air and a gait superior to most of those of his class whom I have seen since. His features were well formed and handsome, and his eyes were of extraordinary brightness. His clothes, though very thin and worn, were well fitting and had once been fine. It was on a day late in October that I first saw him. We resided about four miles from Dukesborough, near the public road; our house surrounded by a grove of oak and chestnut trees. We were at dinner when for the first time I heard that strange music. I was startled by what seemed to be no earthly sounds, and with an exclamation, looked at my father. My mother, too, was surprised; for though she had heard such before, it had been seldom, and never at any place nearer than Augusta.

"Oh," said my father, "I forgot to tell you that I saw an organ-grinder in Dukesborough yesterday, and that I supposed he would be along here to-day. Indeed, I asked him to stop as he should pass up the road."

We went out, and there he stood. He made a respectful salutation to us, and continued turning his instrument. I looked and listened with an interest I never had felt before. Young as I was, I could see in his pale face the signs of deep suffering. By his side was a sweet-looking little girl six or seven years old, who sang two or three little songs in her native tongue. She, too, was pale and thin. Poverty and wandering and suffering in many ways had imparted a serious and oldish expression, which, however, was not inconsistent with uncommon beauty. Her sadness was most tender, and contrasted much with her father's sternness, which sometimes even appeared almost ferocious. I say sometimes; this was not always. While he turned his organ his teeth occasionally would become set, and his eyes wandered up and down the road. I noticed that he frequently lifted and gazed with painful interest at his left hand, which had lost its last two fingers; and then I noticed that when the child, whose eyes at such times were fully turned upon him with tender anxiety, would address him, his features would at once relax their rigidity, and he would answer her cheerfully and even gaily.

We gave them their dinner. Immediately afterwards the man rose to depart; but my father, noticing how much they needed rest, invited them to remain for the afternoon and night. The man seemed surprised and touched by the invitation. He looked concernedly at the child, and they spoke a few words together in Italian. How sweetly to my ears sounded those first words I had ever heard of this language! At first the invitation was declined, but upon my father's pressing it upon them, and especially upon his urging that the child needed rest, her father concluded to remain.

There was in the corner of the grounds a double frame-house, in one room of which the overseer slept. In the other, besides a box of tools which were kept for plantation uses, was a bed, which stood there for the service of poor travellers who might happen to be overtaken by night before they could reach the village. In this the two were lodged. As long as it could be done without too great embarrassment, my father kept them in our sitting-room. Finding that the Italian spoke English very well, and suspecting that he had been a great sufferer, he tried to obtain some knowledge of his history; but the man seemed so averse to allusions to himself that nothing could be elicited from him. But I well remember how charmed I was in listening as he spoke of Italy, its skies and vineyards, and then of the deep sea over which he had crossed, and the large cities he had visited here. On the next morning, when he was ready to depart, my father took his hand with cordiality and 'thus spoke:

"You have not always been what you are. You have had great sufferings of some sort. I hoped last night you would tell me something about them, supposing it possible that I might relieve you in some small degree. I will help you if I can at any time. Whatever you may need, come to me for it hereafter."

The poor man looked into my father's face, and then he began to weep. In a moment more he brushed his eyes, and hastily lifting his organ, without a word of thanks or farewell he led his child away. My father looked long and compassionately towards him.

"He has indeed suffered much. So has the child. Neither of them can bear such a life long. He is evidently a man of education, and has seen better times. I wish he had stayed. But I suppose we must all pursue our destiny."

It was about the middle of January following that my father and I were returning late in the afternoon from a walk in one of the fields where the hands were at work. We were crossing the public road, near which several wagons laden with cotton were encamped for the night. The day was very, very cold. Just as we were passing we heard the sounds of an organ, and looking to the camp, which was in the corner of a grove opposite our dwelling, we observed the Italian. The child was not with him. A very marked change had occurred in both his manner and appearance. His health had evidently much declined, but his restlessness and sternness were gone, and his countenance wore an expression of contentment and even of happiness. When he saw my father he suddenly stopped, placed his wounded hand upon his closed eyes for a moment, then removed it and looked dreamily at us. The next moment his face put on a sad smile.

"Oh, yes," he said, "it is the good Signor. I hope it has been well with him."

He then came up to me, took my hand, and seemed to be trying to call up something of which I reminded him. Then he let me go, and a shiver passed throughout his frame. I attributed this to the extreme cold, and started to ask him about the child; but my father looked at me to be silent, and then in a tone which had almost as much of command as of invitation proposed to go to the house. The Italian, without hesitation, lifted his organ upon his back. He did this with much difficulty, for he was very weak and cold, and my father assisted him. Little was said as we approached the house. My father, suspecting what were his thoughts, made only such general remarks as required little or no participation on his part. When we entered our sitting-room, I observed that he was more careful in the disposal of his organ than he was before. He placed it as gently as he could in a corner of the room, carefully covered it with a coarse green cloth, and then sat where he could see it all the while. He frequently looked at it, and with evident tenderness. When he took his seat by the fire he shivered most violently, as one usually does when coming out of extreme cold.

Orders were given for supper to be hurried. When it was ready we ate it ; and my heart has been seldom so touched as by the sight of the struggle which he made between the anxiety to gratify a hunger that was excessive and the fear of being thought ignorant of good manners. After supper he seemed to need rest so sorely that we sent him to his old room, after first having it well warmed. When he entered this room he looked abstractedly around him for a moment, and seemed to be considering where he should place his organ, which he had taken with him from the mansion. At last he seemed to be satisfied with a position which could be seen as well from the place where he was to sit and from the bed when he should be resting upon it.

The next morning the cold had increased. The sleet had fallen during the night, and the trees and the earth were covered with ice. The Italian rose betimes ; and we were awakened by the sound of his organ, which he was turning as he sat in the door of his chamber.

"I thought I should give you a matin-song the morning before I should leave, in return for food and rest," he said cheerfully to my father as he went to summon him to breakfast.

"Thank you : it was very sweet. But we cannot let you go this morning."

The man looked a little alarmed.

"Oh, no," continued my father, "not yet. After a while you can go. But now you need more rest, and it is cold."

He said nothing, but after breakfast he rose again and was making ready to start. My father laid his hand gently upon his organ as he essayed to raise it, and then said :

"Listen to me, my friend. I am neither a proud man nor a very rich one. I have been poor, too ; and now that I am so no longer, I like to assist when I can those who need some things which they have not. Where are you going? Are you going home?"

He looked at my father and answered with what would have been a sarcasm if it had not been so sad :

"Men like you must know that men like me have no homes."

"But you have had a home, and you are not one to endure what you are suffering now. You are sick ; indeed you are ill. You do not need much, and it will not cost me much to bestow what you do need. You do not, I repeat, need much ; but you need it sorely, and you need it now : I do with you as I would have you do with me if I were sick and in need, and you had a shelter to offer me from this cold. In the name of Heaven I beg you not to hinder me in a purpose which I owe even more to Heaven than to you."

Noticing that he wavered, my father continued his urging, and said that besides he would like for me to hear him speak more about his native country and of the Italian music and poetry; that if he would stay for a few days only, besides getting the rest that he so much needed, he could benefit me to such a degree that the obligation, if any, would really be on our part. He looked fondly upon me, and I asked him to stay. Several times I asked him.

"And thou? Dost thou so desire indeed?"

"Yes," I answered.

"Then I remain — but for a little while — a few days."

Although he had consented to remain, yet for a day or two he seemed restless and abstracted, with only a few intervals of serenity. During this time he preserved much of the constraint and reticence which he had heretofore practised. My father was very delicate in his conversation and deportment, and after a day or two more our guest began to seem as if he was among those who really felt a kindly interest for him. He became especially fond of me. At all hours, when about the house, except at meals, he sat in his own room. I spent much of the time with him there, and he would play for me, and talk with me with increased freedom. Although he was more and more cheerful, yet his physical condition did not improve. He ate little, and we began to notice that as night came it brought with it a fever. It would pass away by the morning, and his cheeks grew more and more sunken. By degrees he became more communicative, and at last my father succeeded in leading him to speak of himself.

It was on the night of the fifth day of his sojourn. At supper he seemed less disposed to be silent than ever before, and even showed a desire to be chatty. One or two playful remarks he made to my mother, of whom hitherto he had been shy. He readily accepted her invitation to linger in our company, and after we had been sitting together for some time around the bright log-fire, and had talked of general matters, in answer to the desire delicately expressed by my father he began to speak without reserve.

His name was Antonio. He had been an advocate of Brindisi, his native place, enjoyed a reasonable success, and married a young lady of good family who had lost their fortune. They were both much devoted to music, she to the piano and he to the violin and violoncello.

This devotion had been too much for their income, and it was not long before the means which he had accumulated before marriage were nearly exhausted. After seven years the lady died, leaving a young daughter six years old. Grief for her death, and the small hope of being then able to return in that place to the old habits of business, determined him to remove to America with his child, and pursue the profession of a musician. Of his success in this scheme he had not entertained a doubt, because, as he modestly assured us, he was considered, especially as a violinist, inferior only to the most distinguished performers of his native country.

In pursuance of this purpose he had arrived in New York the last winter. But for the humane intentions with which my father had led him to speak of himself, he would have repented when he noticed the pain and even the anguish with which for a while he spoke of his subsequent adventures. He had stopped, on account of his slender means, at an obscure tavern in the lower portion of the city. On the first night after his arrival an adjoining house caught fire while its occupants were asleep. He was aroused by the screams of his hostess, who had been the first to discover it, and had called to him for assistance in rescuing the family who were domiciled in the burning building. The flames raged with such rapidity that the rescue depended solely upon himself. He succeeded in saving them (a widow and three young children), but at the imminent risk of his own life. The poor woman, after emerging with her children, so bemoaned the loss of her household goods, and especially of a small bag of silver, that he re-entered in order to recover it. He reached with difficulty the chamber in which it was kept, seized it, opened the window, threw it down, and other means of escape being now cut off, he essayed to let himself down from the same window. While hanging upon the sill, and as he was waiting for the women to place underneath some bedding upon which he could alight, the sash suddenly dropped upon his left hand, and before he could be released its two lower fingers had been lost.

I can never forget his looks or his words while he spoke of his feelings upon that night.

"The loss of those fingers," he said, as he lifted his disabled hand, "was the loss of the only thing in this world belonging to me that was of value to me or to any other person. I knew that, and felt it all as I was hanging to the window. I do not — will the Signor — and the

Signora pardon me?—sometimes I forget all this—I tried to forget
it—and—yes, I think I shall forget it soon."

He rose abruptly and walked several times across the room. My
father begged him to be seated, and let us speak of something else.

"No, no, no!" he resumed, becoming calmed, and retaking his
seat. "No; the Signor has been kind—oh so kind!—and he must
hear. As I was hanging by those fingers, and tried in vain to release
them with my right hand, I remember how I calculated how much
they were to me, and what ruin their loss would bring upon me,
and—"

He paused a moment, and in the lowest and most solemn tone
asked:

"I had a little child with me here? Yes, yes, she was with me
here. Does the Signora remember the child?"

My mother bowed her head.

"Yes. Teresa. Her name was Teresa. A pretty child she was:
but we will not speak of that now. I believe I was saying that I
calculated as I was hanging at the window what the loss of those
fingers would bring. I did not feel any other pain. There was no
pain except in my heart. I remember thinking while I was hanging
there how much I would give if that were my right hand instead of my
left; and I remember that I thought, although I knew that I was even
in much danger of losing my life, yet if I could make my two hands
exchange places, I would be happier, up there hanging by the window,
than any other man ever had been or ever could be. Oh! I felt that I
could better afford to lose both my eyes and both my feet than those
two little fingers. My agony when I felt them giving way was greater
than it had been when I saw my wife breathing her last. I remember
that I then compared this feeling with that. and how strange it all was.
At last my own weight and the struggles I made tore me from them,
and I fell into the arms of those who had arrived in time to assist in
breaking my fall. I rose immediately, and attempted to climb the
wall in order to recover what I had lost. But I could not, and in a
few moments the flames had enveloped all. While I was hanging
there I heard Teresa's screams, and I wondered if she were thinking
that the only thing belonging to her father that was of value to her
was about to be lost. When I had thus descended, the child then
screamed with delight, and I pitied her out of the depths of my soul."

After an interval of several moments, in which he labored with his memories, he resumed his narrative. There was much of detail which I omit. When the poor man had gotten thus far, he seemed to be fond of dwelling upon the incidents of his history. After trying in vain to find employment in New York, he removed to Philadelphia, and thence to Baltimore. The most of his countrymen, though disposed to assist, had other claims upon their charity, and besides were of small means. He was forced to sell his musical instruments in order to pay his board-bills, and then as a last resort he purchased the hand-organ which he then carried. Laboring under the sense of degradation in being reduced to the poor place of an organ-grinder, he was without the art even to make that available except for the procurement of the barest necessaries. His greatest anxieties were of course for his child.

"I had hoped," he said, "to bring her up to be a distinguished singer; and she would have been, had means been afforded for her education. When I found that the dear child, instead of this, must labor with me at what I then thought was so poor an occupation, and labor for subsistence not only for herself but for me, my heart was crushed. To think that she must wander up and down with me, and sing for bread to listless and often to vulgar ears the little songs that her mother had taught her!—How variously and capriciously the rich conduct themselves to the poor such as me! Sometimes my heart has been filled to overflowing with gratitude by the reception of kindness which seemed almost like the Mother of Christ. At other times I have gone mad; yes, entirely mad—no, not quite, but almost mad—from the insults which our poverty has received. I have seen two ladies, both of whom were beautiful, and when Teresa looked to them for compensation for her little song, and the one began to open her purse, the other laughed at her for her weakness, and with insulting words to us, dragged her companion away; and then my little one would look into my eyes, and I would look into hers, and I would see that she was fast growing as old as her father in the knowledge of the world, and in misery. Oh! the thoughts that used to pass through my mind as I have been standing out in the cold : and how cold, cold my darling used to be! She would never tremble, or she would strive not to tremble; but she was so cold! At first I was near going mad. But for her sake, I think I should have gone mad. To think, only to think, if I had gone mad! Would that not have been piteous?—Will the good Signor and the Signora listen while I tell them some of my

20

thoughts in this first estate, and before I could understand — could understand —? Yes, I can tell of those thoughts now since my mind is so much better. At first I came near going mad. That would have been so piteous that I was saved from it. Praised be the Holy Virgin, Mother of God!"

He lifted his eyes towards heaven with an expression of profound gratitude and fervent devotion. Then, with a strange sad smile, he continued:

"I knew nothing of the hand-organ, and had always regarded it as a very poor instrument of music. It was so poor, and its tones were so different from what I had been accustomed to hear and to make, that I almost abhorred myself for having to carry it within the sound of human ears. But having lost my fingers, and with them the faculty to play upon the violin, I must carry it. My own ears became so wounded by its jarring sounds, that for a long time they became to be deaf to all others excepting the voice of Teresa. For hours and hours in the cold days in the streets of those Northern cities, I have turned, and turned, and the discordant notes have grown louder and louder, until the sounds of human voices, the feet of horses, the wheels of wagons, were drowned, and I could not have heard the roar of the cannon, or the thunder, or the hurricane. And yet I heard at such times, sounds which other ears heard not. Mine ears heard the cries of the poor of all lands, crying in their several tongues for bread. They have heard the wailings of exiles, of the desolate and bereaved of all conditions. They have heard the screams of the condemned of all prisons, and even the shrieks of every sinner in hell!"

While he thus spoke, although his eyes were lustrous and his pale cheek grew red, yet his voice was low and calm.

In the succeeding autumn he had wandered with his child to the South, dreading to encounter again the rigors of a Northern winter. As the alms which he had been receiving in the Southern cities were becoming too small for his wants, he went up occasionally into the country, and it was on one of these visits that we first saw him. For some time after telling us of these things, he remained silent and looked constantly and solemnly into the fire which was now subsiding. Afterwards, he suddenly turned his eyes and said:

"But have I told about the child, Teresa?—the beloved and the beautiful? No. Then I must tell it. Indeed, yes, I was near going mad. But I know I was saved from that, because it would have been so piteous.— But the Signor now sees me alone. I have been alone, except with my organ, for nearly a month. I had grown to be afraid after the danger of madness passed, that I should die and leave the child alone; for, although I have been constantly going, yet I think I have been sick somewhat. Yet I was afraid I might die. But that would have been too piteous, and I did not. In the cold days of December, when the snow was on the ground and when the damp was on the straw where we slept, the thin clothing of Teresa could not resist the cold by day and by night. And then she took a pneumonia. I sat by her side for six days, and then she was better. But one day as the sun was setting, the child who had been gay for some hours was talking to me of our home across the sea, and then she said that she had seen in her sleep her mother, and that she was more beautiful than before, and was clothed all in white, and a star was upon her forehead, and she carried a palm in her hand, and her face was shining, oh so gladly, so gladly! And then the child kept repeating these words, 'Oh, so gladly, so gladly,' and her voice grew lower and lower; and then she whispered one time, 'Oh, so gladly, so gladly;' and then she ceased, and then I took her hand and looked into her face."

He lowered his own voice now, and I never saw so solemn and sad a countenance as when he whispered:

"She was gone from me — gone beyond the seas and beyond the clouds." He paused a moment and looked curiously from one to another of us.

"I believe I told that she died? Yes, yes. Poor little child! It had been so cold. But I was so lonely afterwards."

Then his face became bright and he resumed.

"But now, will the Signor believe that since I have been alone, I have learned to love my organ? One must love something. Now what is the strangest of all things to me is this, that as soon as I came to love and appreciate it, it brought to me no more those horrid sounds. Its tones have become indescribably sweet to me. I cannot tell how it is; but for the poor airs which it made formerly, it has substituted others, some old and some new. When I play upon it now I hear the sweet sounds of my native country, and they have taken a more perfect melody than of old. There come to me the songs of the reapers on breezes scented with the new-mown hay. There come the carols of the birds from amid the orange trees: I hear the song and the oar of the boatmen. Then I hear the low lullaby with which the mother of Teresa sang her to sleep upon her lap when the evening was come. Is not that strange? And my organ, sometimes it becomes, oh so gay, and it sings me songs of cavaliers, and recites me the lays of the minstrels of olden days. One afternoon I was playing in the street of the pretty city on the river. I was standing before a costly mansion, and there came from my organ one of the old ballads of the Trouvères, and it sounded so gaily that a fair maiden came to the window, and she listened and smiled ; and then she sent her page to me, and I was led into the dining-hall, where the fire was burning so bright and warm. And then she gave me wine, and made a nosegay of flowers and gave them to me, and while I praised poesy she listened, and was exceeding beautiful.— But now will all hearken to me? Within these last days, this organ, it has been giving forth airs that are unlike those I have heard before. They are so solemn. They are of low tone ; so low, indeed, that one can scarcely hear them. They come as when standing on the shore of the Adriatic I have heard the solemn murmurs come from afar over the waves. Then, sometimes, I hear sounds sweeter yet and more solemn, as it were a harp companied by soft feminine voices ; and they seem to come from the air above me.— So I must have loved my organ. Holy Virgin! what must I have done if I had not grown to love something after Teresa left me."

My parents seeing that through grief and want he had become partially bereft of reason, became more and more assiduous and tender in their care of him. He became quite reconciled to remain with us, and although he seemed not to be conscious of it, he would have been unable to travel with his organ. He grew quite fond of me, and told me many things of the old bards and heroes, of knights and ladies of the chivalrous ages. He would carry his organ to the door of his chamber and play for a while in the early morning, and again at the twilight. After a few days the weather became much more mild, and he and I would walk together in the grove and up and down the road. He was so gentle that I could lead him anywhere I chose.

Early one bright morning, just as the sun arose, I was awakened by the sound of his organ. I arose, dressed myself, and went out to him.

"Good day! good day!" he answered gaily to my salutation ; "Beautiful is this day! See the sun how he shines! I awakened early and came out to meet him. Wilt thou not listen for one song of my organ? It is gay in the jocund morning: in the evening it will be sad."

He turned the handle, and was playing an air that I had often heard. As he played, he looked at me inquiringly.

"Dost thou not recognise it? Ah, the boy is too young to have studied the music and the legends of the brave old days! That is the great Richard, and Blondel the minstrel. Shall I repeat the words along with the air? I do not sing, thou knowest; but I will rehearse. Dost remember the scene? Yes, I have told it to thee. It is before a castle of the Duke of Austria. The King, upon his return from Holy Land, has been taken captive, and is imprisoned in this castle. Blondel has been seeking him in all lands, for thou knowest that the minstrels had access to all places. This song the King and Blondel had composed together, and they would sing, as the muses of old times loved most the song, in alternate verses. When the minstrel played the former part, then he heard the other part from within the castle walls. Now listen to the minstrel:

'Your beauty, lady fair,
  None view without delight;
But still so cold an air
  No passion can excite:
Yet this I patient see
While all are shunned like me.'

And now thus comes the reply:

'No nymph my heart can wound,
  If favor she divide,
And smile on all around,
  Unwilling to decide:
I'd rather hatred bear
Than love with others share.'

It was thus that Blondel found the beloved master whom he had sought so long."

Two days after this, when I arose and went to his chamber, although he was up and sitting at the door and the morning was even sweeter than before, the gaiety which he usually seemed to feel at this hour was away, and his face was full of solemnity. I led him into the grove. We went slowly, for he had now grown very weak. The wagons were going along in unusual numbers this morning. He looked at them attentively, and as we neared the road he lifted his cap reverently from his head, held it in his hand, and turning to me, said in subdued tones :

"It is a funeral procession."

"No," I answered.

"It must be a procession. See how solemnly they are marching! Lo! there are two processions! Yes, yes! there are two processions! One is going up and one is going down. The dead, even like the living, travel in differing ways. Yes, yes! there are two ; and one is going up, and one is going down."

I led him back again, and, by my father's directions that I should not leave him, I stayed with or near him throughout the day. In the afternoon he lay upon his bed. He had said nothing to me since the morning, but had lain through the afternoon looking alternately at his organ and out upon the sky. My father frequently passed near the door, but none of us spoke.

The sun was setting. Through the window the invalid could see it. He watched it until it was down. He then turned to me and said:

"And now the good Signor thy father may come. All may come." We all sat in the chamber.

"It is good that ye be here. I had no music the morn.

"I was weak and aweary.

"But now before the sunset I have been listening to my organ. Is it not strange?

"The music was low, but mine ears did hear.

"Not the gay sounds.

"But the tranquil.

"The songs of the reapers.

"Oh! I could scent the new hay.

"The carols of the birds.

"In the orange trees.

"The songs that come from the air above me.

"The voice of Teresa.

"And Teresa's mother.

"Along with heavenly harpings."

He lay awhile silent.

"Wilt thou take my hand, Signor?" My father was about to take his right hand.

"Not that : the other."

Then my father took his left. He smiled and said:

"Thanks! thanks and blessings for all — and forever.

"Hist!" said he, suddenly, "Hearest thou not? Hearest thou?"

"Yes," answered my father.

"And seest thou? and seest thou? Behold! they are at the door! They have returned to me."

An ineffable gladness was upon his face.

My father laid his lacerated hand upon his breast, and as he took the other to place by its side, the wanderer joined those silent messengers, and departed to the abodes beyond the seas and beyond the clouds.

We buried him behind the garden among our own dead; and my father, as long as he lived, tended his grave like the rest.

MR. WILLIAMSON SLIPPEY AND HIS SALT.

"Sale omnes superare."

CICERO.

THE Slippeys had never been any great things. The Dukesborough people as a general thing used to look down upon the Slippeys. Somehow all of them did poorly. Poorly in their raising ; and when they grew up, they all, boys and girls, married poorly. Anything like improvement seemed to be impracticable to any of the name. This was the way with the first set. Old Jimmy Slippey, the father of the family, all of whom were extremely like him, persuaded himself in his old age that he had been a model of a parent ; and he became disgusted with his children for having fallen so far short of his great example. Quite late in life, however, Mrs. Slippey, the last Mrs. Slippey (for she was the second who had enjoyed the honor of that name), who was much younger than her husband, gave birth unexpectedly to another son. He was named Williamson.

Even while yet a baby, Williamson seemed to give such uncommon promise that his father, although he said that he should never live to see it, used to foretell that this son of his old age would make such a career as would lift up the Slippeys in good time out of their obscurity, and be an honor to his family when he himself should be in his grave. Among other evidences of precocity was that afforded by the surprising speed and facility with which he cut his teeth. On one occasion in particular, when he was only a few months old, while his father was fondly caressing the three which had appeared in front, he slyly, as it were, sucked his finger off, and with another quite away to one side bit it with such violence that Mr. Slippey cried out with mingled pain and delight. And not only so, but as the latter ever afterwards declared, he smiled and even winked when he did it. Now, the question was if he did these things in infancy and with his own folks, what would he do at manhood and with the world at large? The old gentleman pondered on these things, and in the fulness of assurance he was often heard to say that people need not be surprised if Williamson should some day become a public man.

The fond parent was right in saying that he should not live to see these things. Indeed, Dukesborough itself was destined to fall before the time of Williamson Slippey's highest greatness. Yet the old gentleman, even in dying, adhered to his hopes and opinions; and bequeathed to his favorite child, who was yet in his shirt, the bulk of his estate. This consisted mainly of a small, brown, aged, short-tailed pony named Bull.

Interesting as his boyhood and youth and young manhood may have been, yet I cannot linger among them. If it would not have done to begin with the history of Diomede from the death of Meleager, nor with the Trojan war from the double egg of Leda (*vide Epistola ad Pisones*), neither will it now do to narrate all the events in the life of Mr. Williamson Slippey that were preliminary to that high career which, at a later period and in an unusually excited state of society, he was destined at least for a short time to lead. The facts are, however, that he had had some few ups and many downs in the interim between childhood and the period which I propose to select for the purpose of holding him and his business up to the public view.

This was in the winter of 1863–4. At this time Mr. Slippey was in the city of Atlanta. Indeed, it seemed to me that there were very few persons (at least among those who were old enough and not too old to travel) who were not in the city of Atlanta at some time or other during the late war. In those days, if you wanted to see specially and soon any particular person whose whereabouts you did not certainly know, your best plan was to go to Atlanta and walk about the railroad depôt. If you did not see him at once, the chances were that he would arrive by the next train. We had never expected, it is true, to see Sherman. And, indeed, many persons did not see him, for they had to leave before he reached there, and did not return until after he was gone.

21

As for Mr. Williamson Slippey, he had been residing there for five or six years before the war, and had kept a little store, of which he was very proud. If old Jimmy Slippey, when he was prophesying such great things of this son, foresaw thus far into the future, he must have been right in feeling that this last paternity had already made amends for the disappointments of all the preceding ones.

In politics, Mr. Slippey had been an original secessionist. The fact was, Yankees were settling in Atlanta too fast. Then Mr. Slippey had no idea that there would be any war ; and even if there should be one, he reflected that, according to the best of his recollection (although he looked younger), he was over or very nearly over forty-five years of age. Besides, furthermore, there was no doubt that in times of war people came to town oftener than in times of peace, they bought and consumed more merchandise, and, upon the whole, such times were better for the mercantile business. So Mr. Slippey became a secessionist out and out, saying boldly, often and often, that consequences might be consequences.

Although his business was avowedly and mainly grocery, yet he watched the general market, and was in the habit of keeping a few other things besides : a small lot of cutlery, mostly pocket-knives ; a few saddles and grindstones ; some tubs and wagon whips ; and even a trifling supply of assorted candy and nails. For having caught a customer in the general line, Mr. Slippey seemed to feel it to be his duty to accommodate him in these special articles instead of sending him all over town for them. By such and like means he was making a little more and more every year ; and when the war broke out, Mr. Slippey might have been said to be a growing man.

"Williamson Slippey *is* a 'growin' man, certing shore," used, in point of fact, to say Elias Humphrey, a small farmer in the neighborhood. He had backed up Mr. Slippey as well as he could ever since he had been at Atlanta, and carried him many a customer in a small way. Mr. Humphrey had predicted that Mr. Slippey would grow after a while, and sure enough here he was growing.

"Jest as I said he would," Mr. Humphrey often remarked triumphantly.

At a very early period in our late struggle, which I am sure every Southern man and woman, boy and girl, of this generation is likely to remember as long as they live, the attention of the Southern public began to be directed to the subject of salt. And I must remark in passing, that probably at no time in the history of commerce has that one subject received greater attention than during our late struggle. Old as I was at the time, and having been a considerable reader of books for one of my age, yet I found that I had had no idea of how much general attention would or could be bestowed upon the single article of salt as was the case in our late struggle. Of course that is all over now. I know that very well; and it is not my intention now to bring up the heart-rending scenes which I often witnessed, and which were caused mainly by the want of salt; and I will end what I had to say upon the general principles appertaining to that subject, by expressing the sincere hope that never again in what time is left for me to live, may I, and my friends and neighbors and countrymen of the South generally, be so pinched for salt for ourselves and our cattle, our sheep and hogs, and even our goats (what few we had), as was the case in our late unfortunate struggle. We may have war again. I am well aware of that. The universal Yankee nation have grown lately to be a mighty nation for fighting; and therefore I think it is highly probable that we shall have other wars. But I do think that an old man like me, who has seen more than one war (although all former ones were as nothing when compared with the last), and who may be said to be disgusted with wars in general, may be allowed, even in this connection, to express the hope that if other wars are to come, some arrangements will somehow be made by somebody by which the people everywhere can be supplied with salt at living prices, and man and beast will not be so put to it in order to obtain it as was the case in our late unfortunate struggle. There was probably not a single old smoke-house in the whole Confederate States whose floor was not dug up for at least three feet, thereby rendering it yet more accessible to thieves and rats. I remember well in the case of my own — however, I forgot that I was to stop. I will stop, and merely remark in conclusion that the disposition to talk overmuch, which I sometimes suspect to be coming upon me, as I have often noticed in men of my age and even younger, and which I have thus far been careful to avoid — this disposition, I say, I never feel more sensibly than when I am thinking of how we of the South were cramped about salt during the time of our late most unfortunate struggle.

Mr. Slippey had always managed, even before the war, to make a little something upon salt. He had usually cleared from eighteen and three-quarters to thirty-seven and a half cents a sack. Bagging,

Mr. Slippey had grown to be a little afraid of. He had been "burnt" once, as he expressed it, by bagging. But salt, he used to boast that he understood through and through. Now it so happened that when we were into the war for good, he had about a hundred sacks on hand. Salt went up with such rapidity that it soon reached ten dollars a sack. It would seem that now was a good time for Mr. Slippey to sell out. But did he do it? Not he. Not the first sack. Instead of this Mr. Slippey went about buying more salt. Indeed, he sold out everything he had *but* salt. He seemed determined to stake everything, even to his reputation as a merchant, upon salt. For he had predicted that if this war should continue, salt would go a great deal higher yet. Indeed there was no telling where salt would go. Thus things went on until the summer of 1863, when Mr. Slippey, yet holding on to his stock, prophesied publicly and above board that salt would go up to one hundred and fifty dollars. True, he was laughed at, and by some persons abused. But having said it, Williamson Slippey stuck to it.

Like all other prophets (mere uninspired prophets, I mean) he wished his predictions verified. When the summer had passed, and while the fall was passing, Mr. Slippey was excited to a degree probably beyond anything that had ever been noticed in the town in similar circumstances. It seemed as if we were going to have a late fall. Mr. Slippey had rather hoped that winter, his business season, was going to set in sooner than usual. Instead of this, he thought there had never been such a late fall!

Meanwhile, our public troubles seemed rather to promise an early adjustment, and most persons were highly gratified by the prospect. As it interfered with his predictions and his business, Mr. Slippey was not. He was not the man to be willing to be made a fool of. Conscription had taken all the men below thirty-five. Like other men over that age, he thought that was a very fine thing, and though this business might be carried yet further, still, according to the best of his recollection as to his own age, it was not likely to reach him. Yet the fall lingered, and while it lingered he came near selling off his stock. But the idea of eating his own words in that way was so revolting to his feelings, and he thought he knew the universal Yankee nation so well, that he concluded to hold on.

Didn't he say so? A winter campaign is decided on. Didn't he say so? The salt-works will not be competent to supply the necessary demand. Didn't he say so? The railroads will not be able to afford transportation for what the salt-works can furnish. Now, watch the figures if you like. Salt, sixty dollars a sack! Seventy! Eighty-five! One hundred! That will do. Everybody gets hopeless, and nobody cares a red where it goes now. So, without anybody's remonstrance, it went on up to one hundred and fifty dollars, and Williamson Slippey was numbered among the prophets.

Now Mr. Slippey thought he might afford to sell. During the year he had done but a small business in that way, and that mostly by way of barter for his family expenses. These were extremely moderate in spite of the high price of everything. He had economised while accumulating his stock to a degree that showed genius. He carried matters to such extremes that his wife, who was by no means an extravagant woman, and some grown-up daughters tried to hold him back by representing that unless they could do so, he and they must all perish together. These ladies did not suppose, nor did the public, that he ever treated himself to any luxury. They did not dream that every night of his life he was in the habit of making, at his store where he slept, a whiskey-stew, and then drinking it up alone.

It was about the middle of December. A cold spell had set in. Salt was in high demand. Mr. Slippey had been selling briskly for some days. Late one afternoon, Mr. Elias Humphrey, his old friend, came into the store. Lately, Mr. Humphrey had not been much about there. The fact is, Mr. Slippey had grown so far above him that his society was not as welcome as formerly. Mr. Humphrey had noticed this, and governed himself accordingly. But he wanted a sack of salt, and, like the rest of his neighbors, had put off buying until his little pen of hogs was ready to be killed. He had not made any cotton, and the summer drought had cut short his crop of corn. He had therefore but little money. You think that man did not have the effrontery, trusting to old friendship, to try to borrow a sack from Mr. Slippey? He stated his case. He spoke with the earnestness of a man who felt that it was needed to ensure success. He looked around at the great heaps of salt-bags (and he knew that there were many others in the cellar or elsewhere), and wound up with an effort to convince Mr. Slippey that one single sack would hardly be missed from such a vast pile.

"Jest one leetle bit of a sack, Slippey."

Mr. Slippey at first believed that Mr. Humphrey was joking. But he looked closely at him and saw that he was in earnest.

"Have you any peach brandy, 'Lias?"

"No."

"But you know who has some?"

"Yes; some of the neighbors has some, but they ask a mighty big price for it."

"What?"

"Twelve dollars a gallon."

"Gracious! that *is* high. But you can get it cheaper. You can get it for ten."

Mr. Humphrey did not think he could; but supposing he could?

"Well then, if you can, you can make thirty dollars."

"How?" inquired Mr. Humphrey doubtingly.

"If you will bring me twelve gallons of good peach brandy (I want it in case of sickness, you know) I will let you have a sack of salt. That is thirty dollars less than the price of salt to-day, and the price will be twenty dollars higher next week."

"But I can't raise the money. You won't lend me a sack then?"

Mr. Slippey could not quite do that. It would not — ah — be treating his brother merchants right. If it wasn't for treating his brother merchants wrong, he would do it. Positively he would, but for that.

Mr. Humphrey looked hard at his old friend, and it was on his mind to say some bitter things. His lip trembled in the effort to repress his feelings. But he did repress them, and walked quietly away. Mr. Slippey was troubled somewhat. To turn off in that way a man that had befriended him looked hard. He watched him as he went in and came out of several stores. Once or twice he thought of calling him back and putting a sack down to him at half price. He did try to do it. But he could not; and when he found that he could not, he quit trying.

Oh what a glorious stew Mr. Slippey had that night! It was about nine o'clock when he began it. He was not in the habit of beginning until about half-past nine; mostly because he would not have liked to be interrupted in a matter that was not one of business, and in which he needed and desired no companion. But all the time during the afternoon and in the evening he had been troubled by thoughts of Elias Humphrey, and he wanted to think of a more agreeable subject. Salt was such a subject; but somehow Mr. Humphrey had become mixed up with that. So he turned away from it and set his mind upon whiskey-stew.

The night was cold and he had a splendid fire. Still he mended it a little, and after carefully closing, as he believed, the door of his store, he presently brought out from a corner where they stayed, and where nobody suspected that such things were, a demijohn, a pewter mug and spoon, a tea-kettle, and a little round sugar box. Mr. Slippey had taken to stew only since the war began. Yet no man of the largest experience knew better how to mix things than he did. He took pains, I tell you. He stirred and tasted even the sugar and water before he poured in the whiskey. For he had ever been a dear lover of sugar, owing partly, as he used to confess, to the fact of how little of that article he was accustomed to get when he was a boy.

"Nobody," he would often say blandly, after he had become great, "nobody loved it better than I did, and got it sildomer."

When he had gotten the sugar and water right, then he poured in the whiskey. He stirred and tasted, and stirred and tasted, until it was exactly right. By the time it was finished it was capital! He would stir and taste even while it was simmering over the coals. Just at the instant when it would have boiled, he took it off the fire. Hot as it was he took a little sip immediately, gave a slight cough, smiled, and ejaculated "Hah!" He then filled the mug, put it on the table, drew up his arm-chair, and stroking gently the leg which was next the fire, and throwing the other across the table, he began to sip with the deliberation of a man who feels that he has something good which he wishes to last a long time.

Mr. Slippey sipped and thought how good it was. He sipped and surveyed the vast piles before him, as they lay in the rear part of his store. He sipped and wondered why he had not taken to stew before. He had once been a great temperance man, even a Knight of Jericho. Nay, that man used to make speeches in a small but violent way, especially against moderate drinkers, whom he used to style, every single one of them, first-lieutenants of the devil. But he now believed that of all the things that he had ever done this was the most foolish. The fact was, Mr. Slippey had had no idea how good whiskey-stew was until he had tried it.

"My opinion is," said Mr. Slippey then and there to himself, yet in audible tones, "my opinion is that there ain't nary man, nor nary woman in the world that wouldn't love a sweetened dram."

Whereupon he took a whole mouthful, and his very eyes seemed to cry with delight.

Again Mr. Slippey surveyed the heaps of salt, and by this time all unpleasant thoughts of Mr. Humphrey having departed, he began to make all sorts of inward speculations upon the salt question and upon the war. For he had studied both these subjects closely; the former for its own sake, and the latter for the sake of the bearing it might have upon the former. He had read everything he could find upon the subject, even to allusions to it in the Bible, and had come to the conclusion that salt was a much more important article than he had once supposed. He began away back at the salt-mines of Lymington. Wasn't that a slim business? And wasn't the same thing here a slim business? He laughed scornfully at the pitiful turn-out the salt companies were making. Pshaw! they never can do anything. Fossil-beds and brine-springs are the things for salt. Cheshire and Worcestershire are the places for salt. If you want *salt*, go to Cheshire and Worcestershire. But the question is, how will you get there? And then the question will be, how will you ever get back again with your salt? Only to think now of how much Mr. Slippey would be worth if he had a monopoly of those fossil-beds and brine-springs for one year, and then could run the blockade! Five hundred thousand tons of salt! Not sacks! Tons! How many sacks make a ton? What would it all amount to at present prices? Why, it went far up into the billions! He wouldn't take time to work it up just now; but he shouldn't be surprised if it went up somewhere among the trillions. Goodness alive! Mr. Slippey could buy out the Rothschilds and own them every one. Blame them old Jews! They shouldn't hold up their heads in the presence of Mr. Slippey.

But then if that amount of salt were here, the price might fall. No, upon reflection it should not. He would keep it in different places and make it look scarce, and by Gracious! he wouldn't sell a sack without getting his price. Everything and everybody, people and cattle, might die of the murrain before he would fall in his price after going to the expense and risk of working the fossil-beds and brine-springs of Cheshire and Worcestershire for one whole blessed year, and then running the blockade. Mr. Slippey was indignant at the bare idea of lowering the price. Fool with him much about it and he would raise it higher yet!

But the Governor might seize it.

"There now!" exclaimed Mr. Slippey aloud. "Old Brown *is* a mighty seizer, that's a fact; and he is sot on gettin' salt wharsomever he can for them miserable old poor people up in Cherokee."

He took another sip and reflected.

Let him see now. How would it do to take the Governor into — ah — a sort of partnership? Oh the mischief! That won't do. Old Brown was born with a prejudice against merchants. By Gracious! he would seize the salt and Mr. Slippey too, and lock them both up in the Penitentiary.

But let him see again. How would it do to put salt to the Georgia people at half price, and compel the rest of the Confederacy to make up the loss?

But wouldn't the Confederate Government seize? The Confederate Government! Thunder.! No. It had more money now than six yoke of oxen could pull down a mountain, and was still grinding out more every day and every night. Pshaw! if he could keep old Brown down he could manage the Confederate Government easy enough.

But a speedy peace would cut these profits down? A speedy peace, indeed! Mr. Slippey had no fears on that subject. He would take all them chances.

Mr. Slippey was a happy man as he rubbed his leg and sipped his stew. While going again over his calculations as to the value of one year's product of the fossil-beds and brine-springs, his mind became a little fatigued, and he thought he would rest a moment and take another sip. It was near the bottom, and the undissolved sugar had made a sort of mush that seemed the very perfection of earthly sweets. As he sat there leaning back in his chair, resting, and sipping and sucking, he was fast getting to the conclusion that he was the happiest of mankind.

But how fickle is fortune, especially in the times of great revolutions! How suddenly she sometimes changes her garments! Just as Mr. Slippey was about to extend his hand and take hold upon this felicity, there suddenly but noiselessly appeared before him, leaning against a pile of salt, the tall form of Mr. Elias Humphrey. This unexpected occurrence so surprised Mr. Slippey that he could not find words with which to make a single remark by way either of remonstrance or of interrogation. Mr. Humphrey seemed for a moment to expect some such remark. But Mr. Slippey was so slow in beginning that he began himself. In the same sad tone in which he had spoken in the afternoon, possibly even more sad, he reminded Mr. Slippey of some of the favors which he had conferred upon him, and mildly reproached him with ingratitude in refusing the loan of a single sack of salt at a

22

time when of all others in his life he, Mr. Humphrey, most urgently needed it.

Mr. Slippey began to feel a little, a very little better, for at first it occurred to him that this must surely be Mr. Humphrey's ghost. As soon as he heard his well-known voice, although his language was certainly much improved, he became partially reassured. He was on the point of asking him to take a seat, and of telling him that he had been thinking about the matter in order to see if some arrangement could not be made. But while he was getting ready to say all this, his visitor with even an increased sadness of tone and exaltation of manner and expression, informed him that he knew what he was going to say, but that it was now too late.

"Williamson Slippey, don't you see where you are and where you are going?"

Mr. Slippey looked around and concluded that he was in his own store-room, before a warm fire, in his own arm-chair, by the side of his own table, on which was a mug with the remains of what was a most excellent whiskey-stew, and that he was not going anywhere just then. He would probably have denied about the stew, but there was the demijohn, which he had forgotten to hide; and then somehow Mr. Humphrey looked as if he would be hard to fool. So Mr. Slippey was making up his mind to answer this double question by putting another to Mr. Humphrey; and that was, how *he* came where *he* was? It was right here that Mr. Slippey thought he clearly had Mr. Humphrey. But he was so slow in making up this answer that Mr. Humphrey began upon him again.

"Williamson Slippey, you are the most altered man I ever saw. Five years ago you came to this place, a poor, little, insignificant fellow, and put up a little store. It was such a little thing that none but poor men like me traded with you. I helped you along in various ways. You have forgotten them now, and I have not come here especially to remind you of them. What I did for you I did because, poor as I was, I wanted to see you do well. I knew that there was not much in you any way; yet I knew you were poor, and I did think you were honest, and even somewhat kind-hearted."

In spite of Mr. Slippey's growing discomfort, he was touched by these remarks; for he had never before heard Mr. Humphrey (whom he considered an unlearned man) employ such expressive language. Mr. Slippey, at the allusion to his former virtues, felt his eyes to be growing a little moist. Mr. Humphrey continued:

" You used to seem to be satisfied with reasonable profits upon your merchandise, and to be willing to allow to other people fair prices for what they might have to exchange. Indeed, I have sometimes known you to give little things in the way of charity. And then, Slippey, you certainly were a sober man. You can't deny that, for you know that I have often heard you when you would be trying to make little bits of temperance-speeches."

Mr. Slippey looked at the demijohn and then at the mug. As he could not deny, he thought, as the lawyers do sometimes in hard cases, that he would confess and avoid.

" Ca — case — case o' sickness, 'Lias. Ca — case —"

But Mr. Humphrey paid no attention to his plea.

" But now, since this unhappy war has come, you have gradually grown to be an entirely different man. You have speculated, and speculated, and speculated. The more money you have made the stingier you have become, even to your own family, and the more hard-hearted to the world. You have prophesied about the blockade not being raised, and about the continuance of the war, and the prospective rise in the price of salt, until you have not only become bereft of every sentiment of charity for a poor man, even one who has befriended you as I have, but this night, yes this very night, you are a traitor and an enemy to your country."

Mr. Slippey seemed not to have the remotest idea of what to say in answer to such talk as this. He felt that somehow he had lost his opportunity in the beginning, and that Mr. Humphrey had gotten the advantage of him so completely that now it seemed useless to try to recover it. He could only throw back his head, and with eyes and mouth gaze at, and, as it were, take in Mr. Humphrey. The latter, conscious of his advantage, pushed on.

" Yes, sir, I repeat it, you are a traitor to your country. You have been afraid, actually afraid, that the blockade would be raised, and that poor men like me would be able to get those things which if they do not get they must die. The cries of the sick and the dying, not only of those who are dying from pestilence and wounds, but from that more unhappy malady the longing for home; the anguish of old men and women and children for the absence and death of sons and husbands and fathers, and the miseries of all the poor for the want of corn and meat and clothes and shoes,— all these are nothing to you. You have speculated in many ways. But lately you have been confining your operations to salt : to salt, of all things the most needed and the hardest for poor people to get. You have bought up salt until you actually lie to your own wife both as to the quantity which you have and the places where you keep it. Not satisfied with what you have and the ruinous prices at which you sell it, you sometimes try to imagine that you are the sole proprietor of all the fossil-beds and brine-springs of Cheshire and Worcestershire."

Now Mr. Slippey thought that if there was anything that he would have been willing to swear to, it was that Elias Humphrey had never heard of Cheshire and Worcestershire, or of fossil-beds and brine-springs ; and he was getting confirmed in a suspicion which he had that the latter had been in the store long before he had exhibited himself. Mr. Slippey therefore had some vague notion of saying to Mr. Humphrey that he did not consider such conduct exactly fair. But still he could not but feel that the advantage was yet on the side of Mr. Humphrey, and that the latter was using it with a skilfulness that was becoming very oppressive.

"Ah, yes," resumed Mr. Humphrey, now lifting his right arm, "you have dealt in salt until every thought of your mind and every impulse of your whole nature are of nothing but salt. Everything you look at and everything you think about are connected in your mind with salt. If you could you would turn your own wife and children into salt, believing that thus they would be of more value to you than as they are now. You are in a worse condition than the poor wife of the exiled Lot. She was changed into salt only for disobedience in turn- ing to look back once more upon the graves of her fathers and the home of her youth. You have become a living, moving pillar of salt, because a disastrous war has made this necessary article of life pre- cious as gold ; and aside from the riches you make out of it, you love to be pointed at by the lean hands of the poor, and hear of them saying, ' *There goes a man of* SALT.' "

Mr. Slippey began to perspire.

"Quotin' Scripter on me to boot ! " he feebly muttered. Mr. Hum- phrey had now gotten so far above him, and he saw he had heretofore so far underrated him both as to the amount of his information and his powers of speech, that he became completely hacked. Mr. Hum- phrey continued his pursuit.

"Hard-hearted man, and proud ! Hard-hearted as Abimelech, son of Jerubbaal, who murdered his seventy brethren, and having taken

Shechem and slain its people, beat down the city and sowed its deso-
lated streets with salt! And proud! Yea, this poor little salt merchant expects to be famous, even as David gat him a name when he
returned from smiting of the Syrians in the Valley of Salt, being
eighteen thousand men."

Mr. Slippey began to feel as if the roots of his hair would not be
sufficient to keep it from rising from his head and leaving it perfectly
bald.

"And then to think," Mr. Humphrey went on —"only to think how
utterly mean and contemptible you have become! What an arrant
coward! What an egregious liar! Before the war and before conscription you used to like to be considered a smart young fellow. But
you have lately been growing older and older with a rapidity unprece-
dented in human life. You have gotten into the habit lately of speaking
of yourself as an aged man, weary with cares and the weight of years.
Ahead of conscription in the beginning, you intend to keep ahead of
it to the end. As soon as it was hinted that if the war should continue
another year the Governor would call out the militia up to fifty-five
years of age, you went right to work talking about things that happened
before you were born, and saying that younger men than you must
fight the battles of the country. You mean to keep ahead of conscription and yet keep up the activity of a man of business. If it were
necessary for your purposes, you would be as old as the Wandering
Jew. And you have this advantage of the enrolling officers: you
come of such a low family, and your father was so mean and poor
and ignorant that there was no family Bible in which to record the
date of your birth, and there is not a respectable man living, at least
in this neighborhood, who has ever concerned himself enough about
you to know anything of your age. All this you know, and you glory
in it. And yet you don't see where you are and where you are going."

Here Mr. Humphrey paused, and looked as if he intended to move
himself in some direction. Mr. Slippey, hacked as he was, now
thought surely he must say something.

"Ta — take — take a — take a seat, 'Lias, which — I should say —
Mister, Mister Humphrey. Ta — take a — seat — and let me — ex — explain."

Mr. Humphrey, instead of complying with this request, moved off a
little to one side and stopped. Mr. Slippey, without moving his
body, merely turned his head and looked at his visitor with a sort of

cock-eyed expression. It was extremely inconvenient, and made him perspire more and more.

"Tha — thake a — theat — pleathe — won't you thake a —"

Mr. Humphrey, without heeding these words, came at him again in this wise:

"But you could not do all this without some compunctions. To repress these you have taken to intemperance — to whiskey-stew, forsooth! Day after day have you been tossed to and fro in the maddening vortex of speculation, never resting, never seeking rest. Only when the night has come, forsaking the couch of the wife of your bosom, forsaking the society of the children who have been born to you, and who, if properly nurtured and admonished, might have become swift and unerring arrows in the full quiver of a stout and virtuous old age, you have been coming to this miserable hole in order to steep your reason and your conscience in the fumes of a fiery fluid that is consuming the last substance of your vitality. The amount and the quality of the whiskey that you have consumed within the last six months are perfectly shocking to humanity. When the old-time whiskey gave out or got too high for your mean, stingy soul, you began on blackberry. That got too high, and you went to potato. Mean as that was, you went lower yet: to tomatoes and persimmon. Oh, how you have cheated the poor people in this neighborhood out of persimmon whiskey! A little pocketful of salt for a big bottleful of persimmon whiskey! And then, lower yet, China-berry! China-berry! Who but the men of this generation would ever have thought of making whiskey from China-berries?—China-berries which only cows and robins eat; thus taking away the principal article of food from the innocent Robin-Redbreast, the sweet songster of the grove."

These words about the robin affected Mr. Slippey to tears. He saw himself to be so much worse than he had believed that he began to despise himself. Yet he could but feel that some little injustice was done him in this last charge, having acted from, as he thought, no wanton disregard of the wants of that favorite bird.

"Tha — thake a — theat — Mith — Mith — Humph — and let me exth — exthpl —"

But Mr. Humphrey was deaf to his entreaties.

"And now, within the last week, you have descended to the very bottom of this last infamy, and taken to *Sorghum:* to SORGHUM! I repeat it," almost roared Mr. Humphrey, "of all vile potations, the

vilest, Sorghum ; the very most fatal device which war and the evil
spirit have concocted together for the ruin of this unhappy country.
There you sit even now with an exhausted mug of stew made of sorghum four days old ; and to say nothing of your looks, which are
wretched in the extreme, the very odors you and your mug and demijohn dispense are such that were the very vulture here, the vulture
that loves to riot in corruption, and had he the opportunity of preying
upon your dying carcass, he would consult the dignity of his bill, turn
his head, plume his dusky wings, and fly away to distant shores."

Great drops of sweat now formed upon Mr. Slippey's face, and were
coursing one another down his nose.

" And now," asked Mr. Humphrey with earnest compassion, " don't
you see where you are and where you are going ? No he don't. The
miserable creature don't ! Oh Williamson Slippey, don't you see that
you are dying and going to *perdition ?* "

The poor man had had no idea of being so near his earthly end.
Notwithstanding his advance of all conscriptions, both past and prospective, he yet had felt within himself the supplies of a life of many
years to come, and in his blindness had believed that sorghum-stews
were furnishing strength far behind his age. But now these words fell
upon his ears with the import of doom. His heart ceased to beat.
His tongue could no longer articulate. Earthly objects were fading
from his vision, and with unutterable horror he beheld the approach
of the eternal burnings. Oh for a little more of life ! Oh for the
opportunity of repenting and of distributing his salt among the poor !
Too late ! On the fires came rolling and roaring. Feet foremost Mr.
Slippey glided to meet them.

" Oh ! Oh !! Oh !! Oh !!! Oh !!!! " screamed the unhappy man,
and gave it up.

At least so he believed.

But Mr. Slippey fortunately was mistaken. He was not quite dead,
although the fire and the sorghum-stew had come near finishing him.
He had fallen to sleep and to dreaming, and had subsided in his
chair until his head was hanging over the arm next the fire. Its
weight and that of his other upper parts had pushed one leg so far in
that direction that his trowsers caught the blaze and his calf began to
burn. The fire and the shriek awoke the sleeper, and it was half a
minute before he could convince himself that he was not where Mr.
Humphrey had said he was going. With many a slap and some kicks,

having found out the state of things and extinguished the flames, he went with speed to the door, opened it, and thought that the cool night-air never had felt so fresh and so nice.

The next morning Mr. Slippey was observed to have on a new pair of trowsers and to limp slightly. On that day he sold out his whole stock except two sacks, which before night were in Elias Humphrey's smoke-house. In a very short time Mr. Slippey with his family started off in a southwesterly direction from Atlanta, and it was supposed succeeded in getting to Texas, whither he seemed to be bound.

INVESTIGATIONS CONCERNING MR. JONAS LIVELY.

"I well believe
Thou wilt not utter what thou dost not know,
And so far will I trust thee."

SHAKSPEARE.

"Man is but half without woman."

BAILEY.

CHAPTER I.

ALTHOUGH Mr. Bill Williams had moved into Dukesborough, this exaltation did not seem to interfere with the cordial relations established between him and myself at the Lorriby school. He used to come out occasionally on visits to his mother, and seldom returned without calling at our house. This occurred most usually upon the Sundays when the monthly meetings were held in the church at Dukesborough. On such days he and I usually rode home together, I upon my pony and he upon a large brown mare which his mother had sent to him in the forenoon.

Ever since those remote times I have associated in my memory Mr. Bill with that mare, and one or another of her many colts. According to the best of my recollection, she was for years and years never without a colt. Her normal condition seemed to be always to be followed by a colt. Sometimes it was a horse-colt and sometimes a mule; for the planters in those times raised at home all their domestic animals. And what a lively little fellow this colt always was; and what an anxious parent was old Molly Sparks, as Mr. Bill called the dam! How that colt would run about and get

23

•

mixed up with the horses in the grove around the church; and how the old mare would whicker all during the service! I knew that whicker among a hundred. Mr. Bill used always to tie her to a swinging limb; for her anxiety would sometimes cause her to break the frail bridle which usually confined her, and run all about the grounds in pursuit of her truant offspring. Mr. Bill had also to sit where he could see her in order to be ready for all difficulties. I used to be amused to notice how he would be annoyed by her cries and prancings, and how he would pretend to be listening intently to the sermon when his whole attention I knew to be on old Mary and the colt. Seldom was there a Sunday that he did not have to leave the church in order to catch old Mary and tie her up again. This was a catastrophe he was ever dreading, because he really disliked to disturb the service; and he had the consideration when he rose to go to place his handkerchief to his face, that the congregation might suppose that his nose was bleeding.

While we would be riding home, the conduct of that colt, if anything, would be worse than at the church. His fond parent would exert every effort to keep him by her side, but he would get mixed up with the horses more than before. Twenty times would he be lost. Sometimes he would be at an immense distance behind; then he would pretend, as it seemed, to be anxiously looking for his mother, and would run violently against every horse, whether under the saddle or in harness. Old Mary would wheel around and try to get back, her whickers ever resounding far and wide. When the colt would have enough of this frolic, or some one of the home-returning horsemen would give him a cut with his riding-switch, he would get out upon the side of the road, run at full speed past his dam and get similarly mixed up with the horses in front. If he ever got where she was he would appear to be extravagantly gratified, and would make an immediate and violent effort to have himself suckled. Failing in this, he would let fly his hind legs at her, and dash off again at full speed in whatever direction his head happened to be turned. Mr. Bill would often say that of all the fools he ever saw, old Molly and her colt were the biggest. As for my part, the anxiety of the parent seemed to me natural in the circumstances; but I must confess that in the matter of the quality usually called discretion, while the young of most animals have little of it usually, I have frequently thought that of all others the one who had the least amount was the colt.

Yet I did not intend to speak of such a trifling matter, but was led to it unwarily by the association of ideas. Mr. Bill often accepted our invitations to dinner upon these Sundays, or he would walk over in the afternoon. Although he liked much the society of my parents, yet he was fondest of being with me singly. I was certainly more appreciative of his conversation than they were. With all his fondness for talking, there was some constraint upon him, especially in the presence of my father, for whom he had the profoundest respect. So, somehow or other Mr. Bill and I would get away to ourselves, when he could display his full powers in that line. This was easily practicable, as never or seldom did such a day pass without our having other guests to dinner from among those neighbors who resided at a greater distance from the village than we did. Our table on these Sundays was always extended to two or three times its usual length. My parents, though they were religious, thought there was no harm in detaining some of these neighbors to dinner and during the remainder of the day.

Mr. Bill had evidently realised his expectations of the pleasures and advantages of town-life. It seemed to me that he was greatly improved by it. He had evidently laid aside some of his ancient awkwardness and hesitation of manner. He talked more at his ease. Then he gave a more careful and fashionable turn to his hair, and, I thought, combed and brushed it oftener than he had been wont. His trousers too were better pulled up, and his shirt-collar was now never or seldom without the necessary button. I was therefore somewhat surprised to hear my father remark more than once that he did not think that town-life was exactly the best thing for Mr. Bill, and that he would not be surprised if he would not have done better to keep at home with his mother. But Mr. Bill grew more and more fond of Dukesborough, and he used to relate to me some of the remarkable things that occurred there. About every one of the hundred inhabitants of the place and those who visited it, he knew everything that by any possibility could be ascertained. He used to contend that it was a merchant's business to know everybody, and especially those who tried to conceal their affairs from universal observation. He had not been very long in Dukesborough before he could answer almost any question you could put to him about any of his fellow-citizens.

With one exception.

This was Mr. Jonas Lively.

He was too hard a case for Mr. Bill. Neither he nor any other person, not even Mrs. Hodge, seemed to know much about him. The late Mr. Hodge probably knew more than anybody else; but if he did, he did not tell anybody, and now he was dead and gone, and Mr. Lively was left comparatively unknown to the world.

Where Mr. Lively had come from originally people did not know for certain, although he had been heard occasionally to use expressions which induced the belief that he might have been a native of the State of North Carolina. It was ascertained that he had done business for some years in Augusta, and some said that he yet owned a little property there. This much was certain that he went there or somewhere else once every winter, and after remaining about a month, returned, as was supposed, with two new vests and pairs of trousers. At the time I began to take an interest in him, in sympathy with Mr. Bill, he had been residing at Dukesborough for about two years; not exactly at Dukesborough either, but something less than a mile outside, where he boarded with the Hodges, occupying a small building in one corner of the yard, which they called "The Office," and in which before he came the family used to take their meals. He might have had his chamber in the main house where the others stayed but for one thing; for besides the two main rooms there were a couple of low-roofed shed-rooms in front, only one of which was occupied by Susan Temple, a very poor relation of Mr. Hodge. There were no children, and Mr. Lively might have had the other shed-room across the piazza but for the fact that it was devoted to another purpose. Mr. Hodge —

But one at a time. Let me stick to Mr. Lively for the present, and tell what little was known about him.

Mr. Lively was about fifty-one or two years of age. Mr. Bill used to insist that he would never see fifty-five again, and that he would not be surprised if he was sixty. I have no idea but that this was an over-estimate. The truth is that, as I have often remarked, young men like Mr. Bill are prone to assign too great age to elderly men, especially when, like Mr. Lively, they are unmarried. But let that go.

Mr. Lively was about five feet five, quite stout in body, but of moderate-sized legs. He had a brown complexion, brown hair and black eyebrows. His eyes were a mild green, with some tinge of red in the whites. His nose was Roman, or would have been if it had been longer; for just as it began to hook and to become Roman it stopped short, as if upon reflection it thought it wrong to ape ancient and especially foreign manners. He always wore a long black frock-coat, either gray or black trousers and vest, and a very stout low-crowned furred hat. He carried a hickory walking-stick with a hooked handle.

Mr. Lively had come to the neighborhood about two years before and taken board at the Hodges'. He had never seemed to have any regular business. True, he would be known sometimes to buy a bale of cotton, or it might be two or three, and afterwards have them hauled to Augusta by some neighbor's wagon when the latter would be carrying his own to market. Then he occasionally bought a poor horse out of a wagon and kept it at the Hodges' for a couple of months, and got him fat and sold him again at a smart profit. He was a capital doctor of horses, and was suspected of being somewhat proud of his skill in that line, as he would cheerfully render his services when called upon, and always refused any compensation. But when he traded, he traded. If he bought, he put down squarely into the seller's hands; if he sold, the money had to be put squarely into his. Such transactions were rare, however; he certainly made but little in that way. But then he spent less. Besides five dollars a month for board and lodging, he furnishing his own room, if he was out any more nobody knew what it was for.

He was a remarkably silent man. Although he came into Dukesborough almost every day, he had but little to say to anybody and stayed but a short time. The greater part of the remainder of the day he spent at home, partly in walking about the place and partly in reading while sitting in his chamber, or in the piazza between the two little shed-rooms in the front part of the house. He never went to church; yet upon Sundays he read the Bible and other religious books almost the livelong day.

In the life-time of Mr. Hodge he was supposed to know considerable about Mr. Lively. The latter certainly used to talk with him with more freedom than with any other person. Mrs. Hodge never was able to get much out of Mr. Lively, notwithstanding that she was a woman who was remarkably fond of obtaining as much information as possible about other persons. She used to give it as her opinion that there was nothing in Mr. Lively, and in his absence would talk and laugh freely at his odd ways and looks. But Mr. Hodge at such times (when he felt that it was safe to do so) would mildly rebuke his

wife. After Mr. Hodge had died, the opinion became general that
no person was likely to succeed him in Mr. Lively's confidence, and
there was a good deal of dissatisfaction upon the subject.

Mr. Bill Williams felt this dissatisfaction to an uncommon degree.
Being now a citizen of Dukesborough, he felt himself strongly bound
to be thoroughly identified with all its interests. Any man that
thus kept himself apart from society and refused to allow everybody
to know all about himself and his business, was in his opinion a
suspicious character, and ought to be watched. What seemed to
concern him more than anything else was a question frequently
mooted as to whether Mr. Lively's hair was his own or was a wig.
Such a thing as the latter had never been seen in the town, and therefore the citizens were not familiar with it; but doubts were raised
from the peculiar way in which Mr. Lively's hung from his head, and
there were others besides Mr. Bill who would have liked to see them
settled — not that this would have fully satisfied him, but he would
have felt something better. Mr. Bill desired to know all about Mr.
Lively, it is true ; yet if he had been allowed to investigate him fully,
he certainly would have begun with his head. "The fact of it ar," he
maintained, "that it aint right. It aint right to the Dukesborough
people, and it aint right to the transhent people. Transhent people
comes here goin through, and stops all night at Spouter's tavern.
They ax about the place and the people ; and who knows but what
some of 'em mout wish to buy propty and come and settle here? In
cose I in ginerly does most o' the talkin to sich people, and tells 'em
about the place and the people. I don't like to be obleeged to tell
'em that we has one suspicious character in the neighborhood, and
which he ar so suspicious that he don't never pull off his hat, and that
people don't know whether the very har on his head ar his'n or not.
I tell you it aint right. I made up my mind the first good chance I
git to ax Mr. Lively a few civil questions about hisself."

It was not very long after this before an opportunity was presented
to Mr. Bill of chatting a little with Mr. Lively. The latter had
walked into the store one morning when there was no other person
there except Mr. Bill, and inquired for some drugs to give to a sick
horse. Mr. Bill carefully but slowly made up the bundle, when the
following dialogue took place :

"I'm monstous glad to see you, Mr. Lively ; you don't come into
the store so monstous powerful ofting. I wish I could see you here

more ofting. Not as I'm so mighty powerful anxious to sell goods, though that's my business, and in course I feels better when trade's brisk ; but I jest nately would like to see you. You may not know it, Mr. Lively, but I don't expect you've got a better friend in this here town than what I am."

Mr. Bill somehow couldn't find exactly where the twine was ; he looked about for it in several places, especially where it was quite unlikely that it should be. Mr. Lively was silent.

" I has thought," continued Mr. Bill, after finding his twine, "that I would like to talk with you sometimes. The people is always a inquirin of me about where you come from and all sich, and what business you used to follow, jest like they thought you and me was intimate friends,— which I am as good a friend as you've got in the whole town, and which I spose you're a friend of mine. I tells 'em you're a monstous fine man in my opinion, and I spose I does know you about as well as anybody else about here. But yit we haint had no long continyed convisation like I thought we mout have some time, when it mout be convenant, and we mout talk all about old North Calliner whar you come from, and which my father he come from thar too, which he ar now dead and gone. Law ! how he did love to talk about that old country ! and how he did love the people that come from thar. If my father was here, which now he ar dead and gone, he wouldn't let you rest wheresomever he mout see you for talkin about old North Calliner and them old people thar."

Mr. Bill handed the parcel over to Mr. Lively with as winning a look as it was possible for him to bestow. Mr. Lively seemed slightly interested..

" And your father was from North Carolina ? "

" Certinly," answered Mr. Bill with glee ; " right from Tar River. I've heern him and mammy say so nigh and in and about a thousand times, I do believe." And Mr. Bill advanced from behind the counter, came up to Mr. Lively, and looked kindly and neighborly upon him.

" Do you ever think about going there yourself ? " inquired the latter.

Mr. Bill did that very thing over and ofting. From a leetle bit of a boy he had thought how he would like to go thar and see them old people. If he lived, he would go thar some day to that old place and see them old people.

From the way Mr. Bill talked, it seemed that his ideas were that the North Carolinians all resided at one particular place, and that they were all quite aged persons. But this was possibly intended as a snare to catch Mr. Lively, by paying in this indirect manner respect for his advanced age.

"Oh!" exclaimed Mr. Lively, while he stored away the parcel in his capacious pocket, "you ought to go there by all means. If you *should* ever go there, you will find as good people as you ever saw in your life. They are a peaceable people, those North Carolinians, and industrious. You hardly ever see a man there that has not got some sort of business; and then, as a general thing, people there attend to their own business and don't bother themselves about other people's."

Mr. Lively then turned and walked slowly to the door. As he reached it, he turned again and said:

"Oh yes, Mr. Williams, you ought to go there and see that people once before you die; it would do you good. Good-day, Mr. Williams."

After Mr. Lively had gotten out of the store and taken a few steps, Mr. Bill went to the door, looked at him in silence for a moment or two, and then made the following soliloquy:

"Got no more manners than a hound. I axed him a civil question, and see what I got! But never mind, I'll find out somethin about you yit. Now, aint thar a picter of a man! Well you cars a walkin-stick: them legs needs all the help they can git in totin the balance of you about. And jest look at that har: I jest know it aint all his'n. •But never do you mind."

After this, Mr. Bill seemed to regard it as a point of honor to find Mr. Lively out. Hitherto he had owed it to the public mainly; now, there was a debt due to himself. He had propounded to Mr. Lively a civil question, and instead of getting a civil answer had been as good as laughed at. Mr. Lively might go for the present, but he should be up with him in time.

It was perhaps fortunate for Mr. Bill's designs, as well for the purposes of this narrative, that he was slightly akin to Mrs. Hodge, whom he occasionally visited. However, we have seen that this lady had known heretofore about as little of her guest as other people, and that, at least in the life-time of Mr. Hodge, her opinion was that there was nothing in him. True, since Mr. Hodge's death she had been more guarded in her expressions. Mrs. Hodge probably reflected that now she was a lone woman in the world, except Susan Temple, who was next to nothing, she ought to be particular. Mr. Bill had sounded his cousin Malviny (as he called her) heretofore, and of course could get nothing more than she had to impart. He might give up some things, but they were not of the kind we are considering. He informed me one day that on one subject he had made up his mind to take the responsibility. This expression reminded me of our last day with the Lorribies, and I hesitated whether the fullest reliance could be placed upon such a threat. But I said nothing.

"That thing," he continued, "are the circumsance of his har: which it ar my opinion that it ar not all his'n: which I has never seed a wig, but has heern of 'em; and which it ar my opinion that that har ar a imposition on the public, and also on Cousin Malviny Hodge, and he a livin in her very house — leastways in the office. I mout be mistaken; ef so, I begs his pardon: though he have not got the manners of a hound, no, not even to answer a civil question. Still I wouldn't wish to hurt a har of his head; no, not even ef it war not all his'n. Yit the public have a right to know, and — I wants to know myself. And I'm gittin tired of sich foolin and bamboozlin, so to speak; and the fact ar, that Mr. Lively ar got to 'splain hisself on the circumsance o' that har."

The next time I met Mr. Bill he was delighted with some recent and important information. I shall let him speak for himself.

CHAPTER II.

MR. BILL had come over to our house one Sunday to dinner. I knew from his looks upon entering that he had something to communicate. As soon as dinner was over, and he could decently do so, he proposed a walk to me. My father was much amused at the intimacy between us, and I could sometimes observe a quiet smile upon his face when we would start out together upon one of our afternoon strolls. As I was rather small for nine, and Mr. Bill rather large for nineteen years old, I suppose it was somewhat ludicrous to observe such a couple sustaining to each other the relation of equality. Mr. Bill seemed to regard me as fully his equal except in the matter of size, and I had come to feel as much ease in his society as if he had been of my own age. By his residence in town he had acquired

24

some sprightliness of manner and conversation which made him more interesting to me than formerly. This sprightliness was manifested by his forbearing to call me Squire persistently, and varying my name with that ease and freedom which town-people learn so soon to employ. This was interesting to me.

When we had gotten out of the yard and into the grove, Mr. Bill began:

"Oh, my friend, friend of my boyhood's sunny hour, I've been nigh and in about a dyin to see you, especially sence night afore last — sence I caught old Jonah."

"Have you caught him, Mr. Bill?"

"Caught him! Treed him. Not ezactly treed him neither; but runned him to his holler. I told you I was goin to do it."

Seeing that I did not clearly understand, Mr. Bill smiled with delight at the felicitous manner in which he had begun his narrative. We proceeded a little farther to a place where a huge oak-tree had protruded its roots from the ground. There we sat, and he resumed:

"Yes, Sir, I runned him right into his holler. And now, Squire, I'm goin to tell you a big secret; and you are the onliest man, Phillmon Pearch, that I've told it, becase, you see, the circumsances is sich that it won't do to tell too many people nohow; becase you see Mr. Lively he ar a curis sort o' man, I'm afeard. And then you know, Philip, you and me has been thick and jest like brothers, and I'll tell to you what I wouldn't tell to no monstous powerful chunce o' people nohow. And ef it was to git out, people, and specially other people, mout say that — ah — I didn't — ah — do ezactly right. And then thar's Cousin Malviny Hodge. Somehow Cousin Malviny she aint — somehow she aint ezactly like she used to be in Daniel Hodge's life-time. Wimming is right curis things, Squire, specially arfter thar husbands dies. I never should a blieved it of her arfter what I've heern her say and go on about that old feller. But wimming's wimming; and they ar going to be so always. But that's neither here nor thar: you mustn't let on that I said a word about him."

I felt flattered by this the first confidential communication I had ever received, and promised secrecy.

"Well, you see, Squire Phil, I axed Mr. Lively as far and civil question as one gentleman could ax another gentleman, becase I thought that people had a right and was liable to know *somethin* about a man who live in the neighborhood, and been a livin thar for the last two year and never yit told a human anything about hisself, exceptin it mout be to Daniel Hodge, which he are now dead and gone, and not even Cousin Malviny don't know. Leastways didn't. I don't know what she mought know now. Oh wimming, wimming! They won't do, Philip. But let 'em go. I axed Mr. Lively a civil question. One day when he come in the sto' I axed him as polite and civil as I knowed how about gittin a little bit acquainted along with him, and which I told him I was friendly, and also all about my father comin from North Calliner, thinkin may be, as he come from thar too, he mout have a 'sorter friendly to me in a likewise way, ef he didn't keer about bein so monstous powerful friendly to the people in ginerl, which the most of 'em, you know, like your folks, they mostly come from old Firginny. You see I sorter slyly baited my hook with old North Calliner. But nary bite did I git — no, nary nibble. The old fellow look at me mighty interestin while I war a goin on about the old country, and arfter I got through he smiled calm as a summer evenin like — so to speak — and then I thought we was goin to have a good time. Instid o' that, he axed me ef I war ever expectin to ever go thar, and then said that I ought to go thar by all means and see them old people ; and then he sorter hinted agin me for axin about him bein from thar, becase he was mighty particler to say that them old people in ginerly was mighty fond o' tending to their own business and lettin t'other people's alone. Which I don't have to be kicked down stairs befo' I can take a hint. And so I draps the subject ; which in fact I was obleeged to 'drap it, becase no sooner he said it he went right straight immejantly outen the sto'. But, thinks I to myself, says I, I'll head you yit, Mr. Lively. I'll find out sumthin about you, ef it be only whether that head o' har ar yourn or not."

"Is it a wig?" I asked.

"Phillimon," said Mr. Bill, in a tone intended to be considered as remonstrative against all improper haste —"Phillemon Pearch, when a man ar goin to tell you a interestin circumsance about a highly interestin character, so to speak, you mustn't ax him about the last part befo' he git thoo the first part. If you does, the first part mout not have a far chance to be interestive, and both parts mout, so to speak, git mixed up and confused together. Did you ever read Alonzo and Melissy, Phil?"

I had not.

"Thar it is, you see. Ef you had a read Alonzo and Melissy you

would not a ax the question you did. (In that novyul they holds back
the best for the last, and ef you knowed what it was all goin to be
you wouldn't read the balance o' the book ; and which the man, he
knowed you wouldn't, and that made him hold it back. And which I
war readin that same book one day, and Angeline Spouter she told
me that nary one of 'em wan't goin to git killed, and that they got
married at the last, and which then I wouldn't read the book no longer,
and which I war gittin sorter tired anyhow, becase I got very little
time from my business to be readin novyuls anyhow.")

I was very sorry that I had asked the question.

"No, Philmon, give every part a far chance to be interestin. I
give Jonas Lively a far chance ; but the diffic-ulty war he wouldn't
give me one, and I tuck it. I'm goin to take up Mr. Lively all over.
He ar a book, Sir — a far book. I'll come to his har in time."

Mr. Bill readjusted himself between the roots of the old oak so as
to lie in comfort in a position where he could look me fully in the face.

"You see, Squire," he continued, " Cousin Malviny Hodge, she ar
sort o' kin to me, and we always calls one another *cousin*. The
families has always been friendly and claimed kin, but I don't blieve
they ever could tell whar it started, but it war on Cousin Malviny's
side, leastways John Simmonses, her first husband, who his father he
also come from North Calliner. I used to go out thar sometimes and
stay all night ; but I haint done sich a thing sence Mr. Lively have
been thar. One thing, you know, becase he sleeps in the office, and
the onliest other place for a man to sleep at thar is the t'other shed-
room on the t'other side o' the pe-azer from Susan Temple's room,
and which about three year ago they made a kind of a sto' outen
that. The very idee of callin that a sto' ! It makes Mr. Bland laugh
every time I talk about Cousin Malviny's sto'. I jest brings up the
subject sometimes jest to see Mr. Bland laugh and go on. Mr.
Bland, you know, Philip, ar the leadin head pardner, and one of the
funniest men you ever see. Mr. Jones ar a monstous clever man, but
he ar not a funny man like Mr. Bland, not nigh."

This compliment of Mr. Bill to his employer I considered proper
enough, although I could have wished that he had made fewer remarks
which appeared to me to be so far outside of the subject. But I knew
that he lived in town, and I think I had a sort of notion that such
persons had superior rights as well as superior privileges to mere
country people. Still I was extremely anxious on the wig question.

Mr. Bill had told me strange things about wigs. He assured me that they were scalped from dead men's heads, and I did not like to think about them at night.

"But," continued he, "as I was a sayin, they aint been no convenant place for a man to sleep thar sence they had the sto', as they calls it, exceptin a feller was to sleep with Mr. Lively; and I should say that would be about as oncomfortable and ontimely sleepin as anybody ever want anywhar and stayed all night. And which I've no idee that Mr. Lively hisself would think it war reasonable that anybody mout be expected to sleep with him, nor him to sleep with any other man person. When a old bachelor, Philmon, git in the habit o' sleepin by hisself for about fifty year, I spose he sorter git out o' the way of sleepin with varus people, so to speak, and — ah — he ruther not sleep with other people, and which — ah — well, the fact ar, by that time he aint fitten *too* sleep with nobody. I tell you, Phlimmon Pearch, befo' I would sleep with Jonas Lively, specially arfter knowin him like I does, I would — ah — I'd set up all night and nod in a cheer — dinged ef I wouldn't!"

Mr. Bill could not have looked more serious and resolute if he had been confidently expecting on the night of that day an invitation from Mr. Lively to share his couch.

"Hadn't been for that," he went on, "I should a been thar sooner than I did. But arfter he seem so willin and anxious for me to go to North Calliner, I thinks I to myself I'll go out to Cousin Malviny's, and maybe she'll ax me to stay all night, and then she can fix a place for me jest for one night: I sposen she would make a pallet down on the flo' in the hall-room. So Friday evenin I got leaf from Mr. Jones to go away from the sto' one night. He sleep thar too, you know, and they warn't no danger in my goin away for jest one night. So Friday evenin I went out, I did, to supper, and I sorter hinted around that if they was to invite me I mout stay all night, ef providin that it war entirely convenant; specially as I wanted a little country ar arfter bein cooped up so long in town — much as I loved town I had not got out o' all consate for country livin and country ar, and so forth."

Mr. Bill showed plainly that he knew all about how to bamboozle Cousin Malviny, and country folks generally.

"Cousin Malviny were monstous glad to see me, she say; and I tell you, Squire, Cousin Malviny are right jolly lately. She look better and younger'n any time I seen her sence she married Hodge ten year ago. Oh, wimming, wimming! But that's neither here nor thar; you can't alter 'em, and let 'em go. Cousin Malviny said her house war small but it war stretchy. I laughed, I did, and said I would let it stretch itself one time for my accommidation. Then Cousin Malviny she laughed, she did, and looked at Mr. Lively, and Mr. Lively he come mighty nigh laughin hisself. As it war, he look like I war monstous welcome to stay ef I felt like it. As for Susan Temple, she look serious. But that gurl always do look serious somehow. I think they sorter puts on that poor gurl. She do all the work about the house, and always look to me like she thought she have no friends.

"Well, be it so. I stays; and we has a little talk, all of us together arfter supper; that is, me and Cousin Malviny and Mr. Lively. Which I told you he had no manners, becase he don't pull off that hat even at the table. Oh well, he moutn't. But never mind that now; give every part a far chance to be interestin. We has a talk together, and which Mr. Lively are in ginerly a better man to talk to than I thought, leastways at his own home. That is, it ar Cousin Malviny's home in cose; but I tell you, Phlimmon Pearch, she look up monstous to the old man these days. Oh, wimming, wimming! But sich it ar, and you can't alter it. Mr. Lively and me talk freely. He ax me freely any question he mout please. Our convisation war mostly in his axin o' me questions, and me a answerin 'em. He seem to look like he thought I did not keer about axin him any more: which he did see me once lookin mighty keen at his head o' har. And what do you sposen he done then? He look at me with a kind of a interestin smile, and said I ought by all means to go some time and see old North Calliner. And somehow, Squire, to save my life I couldn't think o' nothin to answer back to him. I knowed he had caught me, and I tried to quit lookin at his old head. The fact of it is, ef Mr. Lively say old North Calliner to me many more times, I shall git out o' all consate of the place and all them old people over thar. Cousin Malviny she sorter smile. She look up to the old man more'n she used to. But you can't alter 'em, and t'aint worth while to try. But I, thinks I to myself, old fellow, when I come here I owed you ONE; now I owe you TWO. You may go 'long.

"Well, arfter a while, bed-time, hit come, and Mr. Lively he went on out to the office; which, lo and behold! I found that Susan had made down a pallet in Cousin Malviny's room, and I war to take Susan's room. I sorter hated that, and didn't have no sich expecta- tion that the poor gurl she have to sleep on the flo' on my account; and I told Cousin Malviny so, and which I could sleep on a pallet myself in the hall-room. But Cousin Malviny wouldn't hear to it. Susan didn't say yea nor nay. They puts on that gurl, shore's you ar born. But that aint none o' my business, and so I goes in to the little shed-room. And arfter all I war right glad o' that arrangement, becase it give me a better chance for what I wanted to do, and was detumined *too* do ef I could. I war bent on findin out, ef I could find out, ef that head o' har which Mr. Lively had on his head war his'n. That's what I went out thar for. I had axed him a civil question and he had give me a oncivil answer, and I war bent on it now more'n ever, becase I couldn't even look at his head without gittin the same oncivil answer and bein told that I ought to go and see North Calliner and all them old people thar, which I'm beginnin not to keer whether I ever sees 'em or not, and wish daddy he never come from thar. But I runned him to his holler."

Mr. Bill then rose from the ground. What he had to say now seemed to require to be told in a standing attitude.

CHAPTER III.

" AND now, Philip, I'm comin to the interestin part; I'm a gainin on it fast. That man ar a book — a far book. If I war goin to write a book I should write a book on Jonas Lively and the awful skenes, so to speak, o' that blessed and ontimely night. But in cose you know, Philipmon, I don't expect to write no book, becase I haint the edyecation nor the time. But now, lo and behold! it war a foggy evenin, and specially at Cousin Malviny's, whar you knows they lives close onto Rocky Creek. Well, no sooner I got to my room than I slyly slips out onto the pe-azer, and out into the yard, and walks quiet and easy as I kin to the backside o' the office, whar thar war a winder. I war detumined to get thar befo' the old feller blowed out his candle and got to bed. I had seed befo' night that a little piece war broke out o' the winder. I didn't like ezactly to be a peepin' in on the old man, and I should a felt sorter bad ef he had a caught me. But you see, Squire, he didn't leave me no chance. I had ax him a civil question; it war his fault and not mine. My skeerts is cler."

It was pleasant to see my friend thus able to rid himself of responsibility in a matter in which it was rather plain that blame must attach somewhere.

"So I crope up thar, I did, and found that he had let down the curtin. But I tuck a pin and draw the curtin up to the hole in the glass, and then tuck my pen-knife and slit a little hole in the curtin, so I could go one eye on him. I couldn't go but one eye; but I see a plenty with that — a plenty for one time. In the first place, Phlim, thar aint a man in the whole town of Dukesborough exceptin me that know Mr. Lively ar a smoker. I don't blieve that Cousin Malviny know it. As soon as I got my eye in the room I see him onlock his trunk, which it war by the head o' his bed, and take out a little tin-box, which it have the littlest pad-lock that ever I see: and then he onlock it with a key accordin, and he tuck out the onliest lookin pipe! I do blieve it war made out o' crockery. It war long, and shape like a pitcher; and it had a kiver, and the kiver it war yaller and have little holes, it 'pear like, like a pepper-box; and which it have also a crooked stem made out o' somethin black; and ef it warn't chained to his pipe by a little chain I'm the biggest liar in and about Dukesborough! Well, Sir, he take out this pipe, and then he take outen the trunk another little box, and which it have tobarker in it, all cut up and ready for smokin. Well, Sir, he fill up that pipe, and which I think it hilt nigh and in and about my hand-full of tobarker; and then of all the smokes which I ever see a mortal man smoke, or mortal woming either, that war the most tremenjus and ontimeliest! It ar perfecly certin that that man never smoke but that one time in the twenty-four hours. I tell you he war *hongry* for his smoke; and when he smoke, he smoke. And the way he do blow! I could farly hear him whistle as he shoot out the smoke. He don't seem to take no consolation in his smokin, as fur as I could see; becase sich everlastin blowin made him look like he war monstous tired at the last. Sich vilence can't last, and he got through mighty soon. But he have to git through quick for another reason; and which I ar now goin to tell you what that other reason ar — that is providin, Squire, you keers about hearin it."

Notwithstanding some capital doubts upon the legality of the means by which Mr. Bill had obtained his information, yet I was sufficiently interested to hear further, and I so intimated.

"Yes, I thought," Mr. Bill continued with a smile, "that may be you mout wish to hear some more about his carrins on. That man ar a book, Philyermon Pearch—a far book. Well then, to perceed on with the perceedences of that awful and ontimely night, Mr. Lively he have no candle more'n a inch long. Outen that same trunk he tuck out another box. I never see sich a man for boxes; he have more boxes than clothes, certin. I see two or three more boxes in that trunk. What war in 'em Mr. Lively know—I don't; but in that other box what I'm a speakin about now I see at least fifteen little pieces o' candle about a inch long. Mr. Lively have tuck out one o' them candles and lit it for to see better how to go to bed by. He have a fire; but he want more light, it appear like. That candle it can't last so mighty powerful long; but it have got to last jest so long for him. I never see jest sich a man befo'. Interestin as he war a smokin, it war nothin to his goin to bed. Arfter he put up his pipe, and fix his boxes back and lock up his trunk, he begin to fix hisself for goin to bed. And which it, in cose, ar a single bed, as by good rights, accordin to all human, reasonable understandin, it ought to be."

Mr. Bill regarded me in silence for a moment with an expression which I understood to be perfectly serious.

"I should say, Philerimon Pearch, that bed of Jonas Lively by good rights it ought to be a single bed. Ef Mr. Lively was to ever have to sleep with anybody, and—well—I don't know. It's a ontimely world, and they aint no tellin what people will do; and you can't alter 'em, and it aint worth while to try. But that's neither here nor thar. At the present Mr. Lively certinly do occupy a single bed, and which I say by good rights he ought to."

These parenthetical remarks sounded very mysteriously to my ear, and seemed to convey, I suspected, an admonition to some person in particular, or perhaps to the world in general.

"It war a monstous plain bedstead, and which I have heerd Cousin Malviny say, when she used to laugh at him, and didn't seem to look up to him like she do here lately, which she used to say he made it hisself. It have a shuck mattress, with one blanket and one quilt; but nary piller, nor nary sheet. That ar a bed which it ar monstous easy to make it up, and which Mr. Lively, he say, Cousin Malviny used to say, he didn't wish nobody to pester it and rather make up

25

his own bed hisself. So now Mr. Lively he perceed to git ready to go to bed, ef a body mout call sich a thing a bed. The first thing he do, it ar to pull his little table up agin to the foot of his bed. Then he pull off his boots. That ar perfecly natral, of cose : yit I sposen he war goin to pull off his hat first; which it war the onliest thing I mostly wanted to see, and was a waitin *too* see. But no hat off yit. And what do you think he do with them boots?"

I ventured to guess that he put them under the bed or against the wall.

"Not a bit of nary one. No, Sir. *Make a piller of 'em.* Yes, Sir, he twist 'em up and wrap 'em up in a old newspaper, and put 'em under his mattress for a piller. Some people mout be called extravigant ; but it wouldn't be Jonas Lively. Then what you sposen that man pull off next?"

"His coat. No, his hat!"

"Never!" answered Mr. Bill emphatically, "nary one. It war his *briches!* And now about them briches. • I always thought, Cousin Malviny thought, everybody in Dukesborough, includin the surroundin country and the whole neighborhood, we all thought that Mr. Lively have two par of briches, one black and one gray. Well, Philipmon Pearch, I ar now prepard to say, ef I mout so speak, that Mr. Lively have not got but one par of briches : leastways exceptin you mout call it two par when one par is linded with t'other par, and t'other par is linded with them par. For that's jest the fact o' the case : they ar linded with one another. He have 'em made so. People that lives in town, my honest friend, they sees a heap o' things. That man ar a book — a far book.) And now thar stand Mr. Lively in his prisent and ontimely sitovation ; and he do look *lively*, I tell you."

Mr. Bill chuckled, and winked and rubbed his hands at this remark, and evidently felt that none other than an inhabitant of Dukesborough, or some other equally extensive and densely populated place, could have perpetrated so brilliant a pun. It was the first I had ever heard, and I could but remark how much Mr. Bill had improved.

"And now I'm goin to tell you another thing. I tell you, Philip, I aint near done with Jonas Lively. He ar a book — a far book. You mout think now, and specially in cold weather, that Mr. Lively mout war draws. It look reasonable. *But no draw!* But I tell you what he do war. He war the longest shirt that I ever see to a man person of his highth. It come plum down below the bone of his knees. I could but notice, after Mr. Lively pulled off his briches, how small was his legs, speakin comparative.   Yit don't you blieve I ezactly sees Mr. Lively's legs.   And becase why?   Does you give it up?"

Of course I did.

Mr. Bill looked at me with an expression partly humorous and partly compassionate, and then ejaculated:

"Stockens!!   Yes, Sir, stockens!   The onliest tiem I ever knowed a man person to war stockens, exceptin in a show, where them that wars 'em wars 'em for you to laugh at him fur warin 'em. And them stockens comes up ezactly perpendicler to the very pint whar his long shirt retches down to, and they fits him tight.   As for Mr. Lively's legs, I wouldn't wish to do injestice to no man's legs, but they're the littlest and spindlest legs that ever I see to car what they have to car.   Them legs mout a had calves to 'em, but I never see 'em.   I don't say he never had calves ; I merily say I never see 'em.

"When Mr. Lively take off his briches he turned 'em wrong side outerds and thar is another par, and then he lay 'em keerful on the table with the top part todes the bed ; and then arfter he take out of his pocket his big red pocket-hankercher, he take his coat off and lay it keerful on top o' his briches, collar fomost.   And now he ar ready to take off his hat, and I perceed to the interestin part o' the subjick."

Mr. Bill rubbed his hands afresh and his dull eyes almost watered while he was describing this operation.

"When he ar ready to take off his hat he sit down on the bed, poke his hands under his har like he war goin to scratch, and it appear like he war onfastenin somethin on top o' his ears ; and then he bob down his head, give a sudding jerk, and lo and behold ! here come Mr. Lively's hat carrin with it every har upon the top o' Mr. Lively's head !   Oh, Philip, I war satisfied.   I always spicioned he war a wig, and now I knowed it, becase thar I seed his har in his hat, and his round, slick, ontimely old head a shinin befo' me.   And oh, *ef* it don't shine, and *ef* it don't do him good to rub it !"

And Mr. Bill laughed, and shed tears and laughed, making the grove ring.   He wiped his eyes and resumed.

"But, jest like his smokin, he ar mighty soon through that operation also.   And then he tie his head in that pocket-hankercher, and slip his hat and its con-tents under the bed.   So thar stand Mr. Lively ready for bed ; and ef you didn't know it war him, but some body was to tell you it war a person of the name of Lively, you couldn't say, ef it was to save your life, whether it war Mr. Lively, or Miss Lively, or the old lady Lively. If it warn't for his westcoat you would say it war a woman person, becase thar's his long shirt, which it looks like a gowen; and notwithstandin his legs is oncommon small, thar's his stockens. And ef it warn't for his long shirt and his stockens you would say it war a man person, becase thar's his west-coat. As it ar, your mind ar in a confusion and a state o' hesitatin doubt which ar highly amusin. I don't speak o' myself, becase I knowed him, and seed him as he shucked hisself, and I follered him thoo and thoo the varous — ah — tranmogifications — so to speak — o' that blessed and ontimely evenin."

"But didn't he take off his waistcoat?" I inquired.

"Yes, indeed: but whot for? Jest to turn her over and put her on agin, which dinged ef she aint jest like his briches in bein linded with itself. I tell you, Phlinimon, a little more and that man would a been linded with hisself."

Mr. Bill again laughed and shed tears.

"But what makes him sleep in it?"

"Thar now! becase westcoats is cheaper'n blankets. Leastways westcoats by theirselves is cheaper than westcoats and blankets put together."

Mr. Bill announced this with as much emphasis and gravity as if it had been a newly discovered principle of political economy.

"And now Mr. Lively ar ready for bed, as I war a sayin; and he know he got to go quick, becase his little piece o' candle are most gone. So he take up his walkin-stick, and liftin up the kiver creep in slow and gradyul."

"His walking-stick?"

"Yes, Sir," answered Mr. Bill with immense firmness, "his walkin-stick, and which he have a use for it. Didn't I tell you he war a book? With that stick he smoove down his shirt in the first place, and then he tuck that blanket and that quilt under hisself good, turnin hisself about, and he poke here and pull thar on top o' hisself, under hisself, on both sides o' hisself, till he look snug and tight as a sassenge. When he ar done with that business, lo and behold! he retch down that stick and hook it on to his coat under the collar, which thar it ar a waitin for him, and he pull it up slow and gradyul, lettin the tails hang jest immegeantly over his toes. You say prehaps, leastways you mout say, that his arms and hands is yit unkivered. And sich it ar. But I now ax the question whar's his briches ? Don't you forgit, my honest friend, whar I told you he put them briches, which I mout call 'em the double briches — don't you forgit whar I told you he put 'em when he pulled 'em off o' them interestin and ontimely legs o' his'n. With that same hooked stick he retch down, he lift up them briches, he fetch them briches up, he turn and wrap them briches in more ways than you could tie a rope, all about his arms and his neck and his jaws. And then finnally he ar the snuggest man person, take him up and down, by and large, over and under — he ar the snuggest person, man person I say, that ever I went anywar and see, be it — I takes the responsibility to say it — be it wheresomever or whomsoever or whatsomever it mout. Mr. Lively are a good calker-later. It warn't more'n fifteen seconds arfter he had fixed hisself when his little piece o' candle gin out and he war a snorin, and I tell you he knocked it off perpendickler. By this time I war tolerble cool, ⌐ and I crope back to the house and went to bed. And I thinks I to myself, Mr. Lively, you are one of e'm. You ar a book, Mr. Lively — a far book. We ar even now, Mr. Lively; and which I laid thar a long time a meditatin on this interestin and ontimely case. I ax myself, ar this the lot o' them which has no wife and gits old in them conditions, and has no har on the top o' thar head? Is it sich in all the circumsances of sich a awful and ontimely sitovation? Ef so, fair be it from William Williams !"

Mr. Bill delivered this reflection with becoming seriousness. Indeed he looked a little sad, but whether in contemplation of possible bachelorhood or possible baldness I could not say.

"The next mornin we was all up good and soon. When we went to breakfast I felt sorter mean when I look at the old man, and a little sort o' skeerd to boot. But he look like he have got a good night's rest, and I have owed him somethin, becase I have ax him a civil question ; and so I thinks I, Mr. Lively, you and me's about even — only I mout have a leetle the advantage. When I told 'em all good-bye, I told the old man that I'm a thinkin I'll go to old North Calliner some o' these days and see them old people ; and which I tell you he look at me mighty hard. But what struck me war to see how Cousin Malviny look up to him. But wimming's wimming, Philiminon. You can't alter 'em, and it aint worth while to try."

CHAPTER IV.

MRS. MELVINA HODGE being destined for a more distinguished
part in the Lively Investigations than might have been supposed
at first, I feel as if I ought to mention a few of her antecedents.
She resided near Rocky Creek, about a mile from Dukesborough.
Some years before the occurrence I am now narrating she was
Miss Melvina Perkins, or rather Miss Malviny Perkins, as she preferred to be called.   Judging from what she was now, she must
have been good-looking in those early years.   She had been married
first to a Mr. Simmons, who, as we have heard Mr. Bill Williams
say, was related to his family.   Some five or six summers had passed
since this first marriage when Mr. Simmons died.   However ardently
this gentleman may have been beloved in his life-time, the grief which
his departure produced did not seem to be incurable.   It yielded to
Time the comforter, and in about another year her name was again
changed, and she became Mrs. Malviny Hodge.   ·

Persons familiar with her history used to remark upon the different
appearances which this lady exhibited according as she was or was
not in the married estate.   As Miss Perkins and as the widow
Simmons, she was neat in her person and cheerful in her spirits to a
degree that might be called quite gay ; whereas in the marriage relation
she was often spoken of as negligent both in her dress and her housekeeping, and was generally regarded as being hard to please, especially by him whose business it was and whose pleasure it ought to
have been to please her the most.   Mr. Daniel Hodge had frequently
noticed her with her first husband, and apparently had not seen very
much to admire.   The truth was he had rather pitied poor Simmons,
or thought he had.   But when about three or four months after the
latter's death he happened to meet his widow, Mr. Hodge saw such
remarkable changes that he concluded he must have grossly misjudged
her.   A more extended acquaintance, in which she grew more and
more affable and sprightly and generally taking in her ways, tended
to raise a suspicion in his mind that so far as his previous judgment
of her was concerned it was about as good as if during all that time
he had been a fool.   Mrs. Malviny Simmons had a way of arranging
a white cape around her neck and shoulders, which with her black
frock had a fine effect upon Mr. Hodge.   This is a great art.   I have

noticed it all my life; and old man as I am, even now I sometimes feel that I am not insensible to the charm of such a contrast in dressing among women, who having been in great affliction for losses, have grown to indulge some desire to repair them in ways that are innocent.

This new appreciation of Mrs. Simmons increased with a rapidity that actually astonished Mr. Hodge; the more because he had frequently said that if he ever should marry it certainly would not be to a widow. But we all know what such talk as that amounts to. In the case of Mr. Hodge it was not long before he began to consider with himself whether the best thing he could do for himself might not be to hint his admiration of that white cape and black frock in such a way as might lead to other conversation after a while; for he had a house of his own, a hundred acres of land, and three or four negroes; and he was about thirty years old. I say he began to consider; he had not fully made up his mind. True, he needed a housekeeper. But he remembered that the housekeeping at Simmons's in his life-time was not as it ought to have been. His memory on this point, however, became less and less distinct; and when he thought upon it at all he was getting into the habit of late of laying all the blame upon Simmons. To be sure, poor Simmons was in his grave, and it wouldn't look right to *talk* much about his defects, either of character or general domestic management. Mr. Hodge was a prudent man about such matters generally, and always wished to do as he would be done by. But he could but reflect that Simmons, though a good enough fellow in his way, was not only rather a poor manager, but not the sort of a man to inspire a woman, especially such a one as Mrs. Malviny Simmons now evidently appeared to be, to exert her full powers whether in housekeeping or anything else. In thinking upon the case Mr. Hodge believed that justice should be done to the living as well as the dead, and that in the married life much depended upon the man. This view of the case gradually grew to be very satisfactory, and even right sweet to take. Not that he would think of doing injustice to Simmons, even in his grave; but facts were facts, and justice was justice; and it was now certainly too late to think about altering the former in the case of Simmons. So poor Simmons had to lie where he was, and be held to responsibilities that probably he had not anticipated.

So Mr. Hodge began to consider. He knew there was no harm in merely speculating upon such things. He knew himself to be prudent, and generally accurate in his judgments. But it was his boast, and always had been, that whenever he was convinced that he was wrong he would give it up like a man. This had actually occurred; not very often, it is true, but sometimes; and he had given it up in such a way as to confirm him more and more in the assurance that he was a person who, though little liable to delusion, was remarkably free from prejudice and obstinacy. Probably the most notable instance of such freedom that his life had hitherto afforded was the readiness with which he gave up the erroneous opinions he had previously formed of Mrs. Malviny Simmons, and put the blame of what seemed her shortcomings where it belonged.

Mr. Hodge was thus considering the possibility of what he might propose to do some of these days, say a year hence, when Mrs. Simmons might reasonably be expected, young as she was, to be taking other views of life besides those which contemplated merely the past. Mr. Hodge knew that there was plenty of time for the exercise of the most matured deliberation. But somehow it happened that he began to meet the lady much more frequently than heretofore. Mr. Simmons having left his wife in very limited circumstances, she resided alternately with one and another of her own and his relations. These people, though kind, yet seemed all to be more than willing that Mr. Hodge should have the benefit of any amount of her society. The consequence was that Mr. Hodge, having such opportunities, was enabled the sooner to bring all his thoughts to a head; not that he contemplated immediate action, but was becoming more and more fond of musing upon future possibilities. But one day he had looked upon the white cape and the black frock until he was led to express himself in terms that implied admiration. It was intended merely as a hint of what might come some of these days. One word brought on another. It would be impossible to describe how Mrs. Malviny Simmons looked and how she talked. Mr. Hodge was not a man of many words, and it gratified him when she assisted and accelerated his thoughts, and even almost put into his mouth the very words which, though not intending such a thing just then, he had been considering that he might employ some of these days. Things went on with such rapidity that before Mr. Hodge knew what he was about he had the cape in his arms, and was assured that it and the person it belonged to were his now and forever, "yea, if it might be for a thousand year."

Surely, thought Mr. Hodge, no man since the days of Adam in the garden had ever made so tremendous an impression upon a woman. He did not know that it was in him to make such an impression. However, we don't know ourselves, he reflected ; and there *is* a difference in men just as in everything else.

One week from that day Mr. Hodge succeeded to Mr. Simmons, and Mrs. Malviny went to keep house for Mr. Hodge on Rocky Creek. There was little in the married life of Mr. and Mrs. Hodge that would be very interesting to relate. I before intimated that Mrs. Malviny was most interesting in those seasons when she was unmarried. The beginning was splendid, but the splendor was evanescent. Mr. Hodge was surprised to notice how soon his wife relapsed into the old ways and the old looks. He never should have expected to see that woman down at the heels. But the laying aside the black frock and putting on colors seemed to have had a depressing influence upon her tastes. As for the housekeeping, Mr. Hodge had to admit to himself that plain as things were when old Aunt Dilcy, his negro woman, attended to them, they were not as well ordered now. Then Mr. Hodge found that, in spite of his conscious superiority to her former husband, he had apparently no greater success in his efforts to please. At this Mr. Hodge gradually began to feel somewhat disgusted. He never had thought much about Simmons in his life-time ; now his mind would frequently revert to him, and he began to suspect that Simmons was a cleverer man than he had credit for. It seemed strange and somewhat pitiful generally that he should have died so young.

But Mr. Hodge knew as well as anybody that matters could not be altered now, and he determined to do the best he could. He worked away at his farm, and in spite of difficulties made and laid up a little something every year. No children were born of the marriage ; but he did not complain. They had been married several years when the parents of Susan Temple having died and left her with nothing, the relatives generally thought that as Mr. Hodge, who was as near akin to her as any, and who had no children of his own, ought to give her a home. Susan was just grown up, and though plain was a very industrious girl. Mr. Hodge suggested to his wife that as the business of housekeeping seemed rather troublesome they might take Susan for that business, giving her board and clothes as compensation. At first Mrs. Hodge came out violently against it.

26

Such, however, had long been her habit of treating all new propositions of her husband. He was, therefore, not surprised ; and indeed was not seriously disappointed, as he was acting mostly for the purpose of satisfying his conscience regarding his orphaned relative. He said nothing more upon the subject then ; indeed, he had been ever a man of but few words, and since his marriage he had grown more so. Mr. Hodge had seemed to find from experience that the more talking he did the less influence he had. Words, he found, were not the things to employ when he wanted her to do even necessary offices. After all his previous disclaimers to that end, Mr. Hodge was suspected by more persons than one of having some obstinacy ; and it grew with the lapse of time. He kept his pocket-book in his pocket, and his own fingers opened and shut it. Mrs. Hodge maintained to his face that he was hard-headed as a mule and too stingy to live. He appeared to her most obstinate when she would labor in vain to lead him into discussions upon the justice of her causes of complaint against him generally. One day she did a thing which Mr. Hodge had been once as far from foreseeing as any man who ever married another's widow. Mr. Simmons, with all his imperfections, was a man who would sometimes allow to his wife the satisfaction of leading him into a little domestic quarrel, and to make it interesting would try to give back as good as he got, so to speak. I am well aware that such an expression is not warranted by good usage ; but I cannot stop now to look for a better. Besides, I think that some liberty of expression ought to be allowed to a man at my time of life.

However, to return to Mrs. Hodge. One day when Mr. Hodge was about finishing his dinner, his wife, who had finished hers some time ago, having but a poor appetite on that occasion, was complaining in general terms of her own hard lot. Mr. Hodge ate away and said nothing. Once he did look up towards her as he reached his hand to break another piece of bread ; and as he contemplated his wife's head for a moment, he thought to himself if she would give it a good combing the probability was that she would feel better. But he said nothing. The lady did expect from his looks that he was going for one time to join in the striving which had hitherto been altogether on one side. Finding herself disappointed, she brought forth a sigh quite audible, and evidently hinted a more tender regret for the late Mr. Simmons than she had exhibited even in the first period of her affliction for his loss. She did not exactly *name* Mr. Simmons, but she spoke of what a blessing it was for people to have people to love 'em and be good to 'em ; and that some people *used* to have 'em, but they was dead and gone now ; and people didn't have 'em in these days — no, not even to talk to 'em. And then Mrs. Hodge gently declined her head, gave a melancholy sniff with her nose, and looked into her plate as if it were a grave and she were hopelessly endeavoring to hold conversation with its occupant. Mr. Hodge was on his last mouthful. He stopped chewing for a moment and looked at his wife, then he gave a swallow and thus answered :

"Oh! you speakin about Simmons. Yes, Simmons war a right good feller ; pity he died so young. Ef Simmons had not a died so young, some people might a been better off."

And then Mr. Hodge rose, put on his hat, and walked to Dukesborough and back. When he returned, Mrs. Hodge was in better humor than she had been for weeks and weeks,

CHAPTER V.

ON the night immediately succeeding this little misunderstanding, Mr. and Mrs. Hodge happened to meet upon a subject on which they agreed. It was perhaps a lucky thing that the subject was broached that night. It would be difficult to say in whose mind the idea first occurred of having a little bit of a store in one of the little shed-rooms. It was so convenient, in the first place. Their house was within only a few steps of the road, on the top of the first hill just this side of the creek ; and the little shed-rooms were in front, with little windows opening towards the road. On the night aforesaid Mr. Hodge and his wife seemed disposed to be chatty. Mr. Hodge was gratified that the allusions to his predecessor had so soothing an effect. They talked a while about their having no children, and both agreed that it seemed to be the lot of some families not to have them. And then it occurred to them that it was a pity that the two little shed-rooms could not be put to some use. True, they had been keeping a signboard which promised " Entertainment for man and horse ;" but the stand was too near Dukesborough, where the great Mr. Spouter lived and reigned. Besides, Mrs. Hodge had sometimes had her feelings hurt by occasional side remarks of what few guests they did have about the height of the charge, which, though reasonable enough generally speaking, seemed high when compared with the supper, the bed, and the breakfast. This business, therefore, for some time had seemed to be discouraging.

On the night aforesaid, however, it seemed a fortunate accident that the conversation gradually drifted about Dukesborough, its rapid growth, and the probability that in time it would grow to be an important place. Already people were coming to the stores from six or seven miles around ; and it was believed that the store-keepers, especially Bland & Jones, were making great profits. Threats had been made that unless they would fall in their charges they might hear of opposition. While talking together upon these things, Mr. and Mrs. Hodge seemed almost simultaneously to think that it might be well, in all the circumstances, to convert one of the little shed-rooms into a little store. The more they turned this idea over the more it seemed good, especially to Mrs. Hodge. She was for going into it immediately. Mr. Hodge thought he wanted a little more time for reflection. He did have a few hundred dollars which he had accumulated by honest work and good economy ; but he was without mercantile experience, and people had told him that merchants some-times break like other people. Besides, he should not think it prudent to neglect the farm, and that required most of his attention. But Mrs. Hodge suggested that she could attend to the store her own self. She could do it, she knew she could. He could go on and attend to the farm, and spend what time he could spare from that in the store. Mrs. Hodge reasoned that her husband had sometimes com-plained that she invested too heavily even in the purchase of neces-sary articles ; and here was an opportunity of getting all such things at home and not have to pay out one cent for them, except of course what little was paid out for them in the beginning, and that would be lost sight of in the general profits of the concern.

Mr. Hodge reflected.

What about the housekeeping ?

Mrs. Hodge in her turn reflected.

Where was Susan Temple ?

There now ! If ever one question was well answered by pro-pounding another, it was in this case. Mr. Hodge admitted this to himself. It was a matter he had himself proposed once to do, to take Susan to keep house. The truth was, the house ought to be kept by somebody; and Susan, though a plain girl, was known to be neat and orderly and industrious, and understood even most of the things about a kitchen. Mr. Hodge thought to himself that as his wife's talent did not seem to be in housekeeping, it might not be wrong to let it make a small effort in the mercantile line. And so they agreed.

This was all right. Susan was so thankful for a home that she did her best, and any sensible and honest person would have been obliged to see and admit that the housekeeping improved. Everything was kept clean and nice. Mrs. Hodge, however, thought that if she gave Susan too much credit for this change it might spoil her. It was the way with all such people, she thought. So she took all the credit to herself, and would occasionally remind Susan of what would have become of her if they had not taken her and put clothes upon her back. Susan ought to be very thankful, more so than she seemed to be in fact, that she had not been left to the cold charities of an unfeeling world. To make things under this head perfectly safe, Mrs. Hodge sometimes insisted that Susan ought to be ashamed of herself for not doing more than she did, considering what was done for her. Susan, doing everything as it was, would seem to look about as if to find something else to do. Not being able to find it, she would get very much confused, and seem to conclude that she must be a very incompetent person.

But the store. Mr. Hodge went all the way to Augusta. Mrs. Hodge would have liked to go too; but it was thought not necessary for both to go. So Mr. Hodge went alone, and laid in his stock. A hundred dollars well laid out would buy something in those times. Such a sum goes a precious little way these days. He brought home with him some pieces of calico and skeins of silk, a few hats, a smart box of shoes, nails, a barrel of molasses, and one of sugar; some coffee in a keg, two or three jars of candy, mostly peppermint; some papers of cinnamon, a reasonable number of red pocket-handkerchiefs, any quantity of pins and needles, a good supply of tobacco and snuff, and one side-saddle. Mrs. Hodge had urged and rather insisted upon the last article. Mr. Hodge hesitated, and seemed to think it not a perfectly safe investment; but he yielded. In addition to this stock Susan made ginger-cakes and spruce-beer. These sat on a shelf outside the window, except in rainy weather. Mr. Bill Williams once brought me one of these cakes, and I thought it was as good as I ever ate.

Mr. Hodge, being a man somewhat adroit in the use of tools, made his own counter and desk and shelves. It was a great time the night on which the goods arrived. It was after dark when they came, but there was no going to bed until those goods were opened and set in their places. And oh, how particular they were in handling! Susan must positively be more particlar, and quit bein so keerless, because them things cost money. Susan got to be so particular that she even handled the tobacco-box and the coffee-keg as if they were all cut glass. When she took the pieces of calico one by one into her hands and put them on the shelves, you would have thought every one was a very young baby that she was lifting from the cradle and laying upon its mother's breast. When the box of shoes was opened Susan declared that they actilly *smelt* sweet, that they smelt the sweetest of anything in that sto' exceptin the cinnamon. Mrs. Hodge's feelings were too deep to allow very many words; but she let Susan go on. Much as Mrs. Hodge admired everything, she was most deeply affected by the side-saddle. The seat had a heart quilted into it of red stuff. This was so becoming that Mrs. Hodge declared, and made Susan admit, that it was the loveliest picter that ever was seen. She said that that picter wer the picter of her own heart, and which it had been on a new side-saddle for she didn't know how long. But still — Mrs. Hodge didn't say any more about it then. She merely kept caressing the heart softly with her hand until Mr. Hodge placed it on a small board-horse which he had made for the purpose, and set it in a corner.

When all was finished they took a good look at everything, and it was the unanimous opinion that nobody could have had any reason to expect that that shed-room could have been made to look like it did then. If that store wasn't carefully locked and bolted that night, there never was one that was. Susan, who lodged in the other shed-room, lay awake for hours — she declared she did — a thinking on it all; but as for her part, she owned it was mostly about the shoes and the cinnamon.

There was some talk about the store in the neighborhood for a while. Some were for it and some against it. The Dukesborough merchants were all of the latter party. Mr. Bland asked, if Hodge wanted to set up in opposition, why didn't he come into town like a man? It didn't look fair to be having a store away out there and be a farming at the same time. But when he heard what the stock consisted in he pretended to laugh, and people said that it would never come to anything. Still some people said that Mr. Bland fell a little in tobacco and shoes.

A person in going along the road and looking upon this store, might have imagined that, apart from the cake and spruce-beer, it had been established mainly for the purpose of supplying country people with such little things as they would be likely to forget while in town. Indeed, after the novelty had passed away it gradually relapsed into such a state of things. It was seldom that a customer stopped while on his way into town. Mrs. Hodge's hopes and reliance were mainly on the outward bound. When any of these would call, she was wont to meet them with an expression of countenance which seemed to ask, "Well, what is it that you have forgotten to-day?" Like other merchants, Mrs. Hodge, who gradually became the principal person in the concern, studied the chances and possibilities of trade ; and her husband at her suggestion laid in his stock in the fall, principally of such articles as a person might be expected to overlook while making purchases of other more important things. He added largely to his stock of pins, and went very extensively upon combs and buttons.

The side-siddle seemed hard to get off. But Mrs. Hodge at the very start, on learning the cost, had declared that it was entirely too cheap ; and she asked for the pricing of that herself, and she thought she was warranted in putting it at a high figure. She had offers for it. The heart in the seat had attracted several ladies, and once it was within a half-dollar of going. But Mrs. Hodge, so far from falling, intimated an intention upon reflection of rising, and that drove the customer away.

Upon the whole, things went on right well. Mrs. Hodge certainly improved in spirits ; but of course she never could attain to that state of contentment which Mr. Hodge could have wished, and which at first he did fondly anticipate. In the matter of dressing herself she looked up a little, and there was about her person not unfrequently the odor of mingled cinnamon and peppermint. And it must be remarked that the displeasure that it seemed inevitable for her to indulge at intervals was now divided between Mr. Hodge and Susan Temple, with the greater share to the latter. Susan did not reflect nigh as often as she ought what it was to her to have a home and clothes upon her back. The girl knew she ought to do it, and was everlastingly trying to do it, and filled herself with reproaches for her own ingratitude to her Aunt Malviny. Mr. Hodge didn't express any opinion upon the subject, but seemed to be satisfied with taking care of himself the best he could. His attention lately had been restored mostly to his farm.

In one of his trips to Augusta he brought back with him Mr. Lively. He had made his acquaintance some time before, and had mentioned the fact that the gentleman had talked about coming to take board with them, and even went so far as to propose, in such an event, to pay as much as five dollars a month. This sounded well. Mrs. Hodge had an idea that the having a boarder might make the house come to be regarded more as a public place; and so she said that, as for herself, she was willing. So Mr. Lively came. When he did come, she thought he was certainly the queerest person that she had ever seen. She looked at his hair and then at his nose and legs, and then at his hair again, from which he never removed his hat, not even at meals. But he was a boarder, she knew, and was entitled to privileges. She tried to pick him; but Mr. Lively was a man of some experience and would not be picked. Mrs. Hodge being satisfied that it was best for Mr. Lively to know at once that she was a person of consideration, berated Susan the very first night of his arrival for her carelessness and general worthlessness.

Messrs. Hodge and Lively seemed to get along together very well. The latter, like the former, was a man of few words; and as time lapsed they seemed to have something of a friendship for each other. On the contrary, Mrs. Hodge seemed to have less and less regard for her boarder according as he and her husband seemed to like each other the more, and was often heard to say that in her opinion there was nothing in Mr. Lively. Whatever estimate Mr. Lively placed upon her he never told to anybody; but he went along and acted as if Mrs. Hodge and whatever might be her thoughts about him were not at all in his way. As time passed Mr. Hodge would often sit with Mr. Lively, and talk with him with some freedom of his business and other matters. Small as was Mr. Hodge's business comparatively, he was careful of his papers and always kept them locked up in his desk.

On one of his return trips from Augusta Mr. Hodge spent a little more time than usual at his desk in looking over his papers and one thing and another; but when he came out he seemed to be very well satisfied. The next day he was taken sick. Little was thought of it at first ; but in a day or two he took on a fever, which looked as if his time was coming. Mr. Hodge himself did not seem to be aware of the state of the case until it was too late to leave any special directions about anything. At the last he did rouse himself a little, looked very hard at Mr. Lively, and muttered a few unintelligible words about " my desk," and Mr. Lively's being " mighty particular," and such things. But at last he had to give it up, and then Mr. Hodge carried his succession of Mr. Simmons to extremes.

CHAPTER VI.

So now here was Mrs. Malviny a widow for the second time. The late Mr. Hodge was mourned becomingly by all the household. Even Mr. Lively was seen to brush away a tear or two at the funeral ; but Mrs. Hodge and Susan did the most of the actual crying, and they cried heartily. Both felt that Mr. Hodge's continued absence from that house was obliged to make a difference.

The question now was what must be done. Mr. Lively seemed to think that Mr. Hodge must have left a will, so he and Mrs. Hodge in a day or two went together and looked carefully over the papers ; and although Mr. Lively followed Mr. Hodge's last confused directions, nothing could be found. Mrs. Hodge had nothing to do but to heir the property ; and as there were no debts, it was considered not worth while to take out letters of administration. Seeing that she was obliged to take the responsibility of all this business, she submitted, and was very meek, remarking that now she was nothing but a lone woman in the world, property was no great things in her mind. But she thought she could be kind to Susan Temple. Of course Susan was nothing to her, and it was an expense to feed her and put clothes on her back ; still she might stay there on the same terms as before. People should never say that she had the heart to turn off a poor orphan on the cold charities of the world. Susan was very thankful, perfectly overcome with gratitude indeed, and continued to do everything ; and, like Alexander the Great, would almost weep that there was nothing more to do. As for Mr. Lively, he somehow had got used to the place and didn't feel like going away at his time of life to seek a new home. Mrs. Hodge also disliked the idea of turning

27

away one that had been so good a friend of the family ; and indeed, with all the business upon her hands, it did look like that one who was nobody but a poor lone woman in the world should have some friend near enough to go to sometimes for advice, instead of being everlastingly running to a lawyer and they a charging all that a poor lone woman could make. Mr. Lively seemed gratified, and thus matters settled down ; but all seemed to miss poor Mr. Hodge.

And now many years had elapsed since Mrs. Hodge had been a widow before. She reflected upon it. Yet she was thankful that she could bear up under this repeated infliction as well as she did, and that she was as strong and active as any person who was a mere lone woman in the world could be expected to be. The amount of business now upon her hands would require as much strength and activity as could be commanded. Her looking-glass had somehow got broken some time since, all but one little piece in the corner of the frame. Mrs. Hodge gave what was left to Susan, remarking that as for herself she had very little use for such things. Some time afterwards, however, she reflected that even the lonely and desolate should go neatly, and that it always did require more pains to dress in black. Even Susan admitted this to be true, and she fully justified her Aunt Malviny in the purchase of a new dress.

Weeks passed, and then some months. Mrs. Hodge's strength and activity grew so that she began to feel as if they might be as good as ever. Mr. Bill Williams and others, including Mr. Lively, had heard her say that, although she knew it must be so, yet she did not feel any older than she did when she married Mr. Hodge. It was perfectly plain to see that Mrs. Hodge was not willing to be considered one day older than she really was, notwithstanding what she had been through ; and that if she had to grow old she intended to do so by degrees. Mrs. Hodge's face certainly did look somewhat thinner than it did in those former years ; but it began to participate in the general recovery, and to have a peachiness which occasionally extended over the whole jaw. Remarks *had* been made about that peachiness, the various directions it took, and the varying amount of surface it overspread at different times. She heard of some of these remarks once ; they made her very mad, and she said that the color of her cheeks was nobody else's business.

The rest of Mrs. Hodge was entirely satisfactory. She had always been a very good figure of a woman, and even now, from her neck down, she was apparently round as a butter-ball. And how spry she was in her walk! In this respect she could not be beat. I do think that when she was walking rapidly, her usual gait, and had to pass any unpleasant obstruction, she would lift her skirts as adroitly as any lady I ever knew. And then she rode a horse remarkably well, for now she had laid aside the old side-saddle and took the one with the heart in the seat. The new one would not sell at the price demanded, and the old one was not comfortable.

This restoration of her youth seemed to do away with the melancholy in which her married life had been too prone to indulge. She even became somewhat gay. I do not mean wild; there was not a particle of what might be called wildness about her. But apparently she had made up her mind not to yield herself up to useless regrets for what could not be helped, to do the best she could as long as she was in the world, and to stay in it as long as she could. When persons come to these conclusions they can afford to be cheerful, and sometimes even a little gay. Mrs. Hodge had lost one husband. Many a woman does the same and then gives up; and although some of them reconsider and take back, yet others give up for good. Mrs. Hodge had put herself right on this point in the beginning. She refused to give up at Mr. Simmons's departure; and then, when another man who was at least as good, and even better, presented himself, she had nothing to take back, and we saw how it all ended. People said, as they always do, that it was heartless; but this gave her no concern. And if it had, there was Mr. Hodge to help her bear it. This experience seemed to be of value to her in this second bereavement. The course she had pursued in that first extremity was so judicious and turned out so well that the fact is, Mrs. Hodge began to ask herself what she might do provided another person of the opposite sex should make a remark similar to that which Mr. Hodge had made, and which had so momentous consequences.

But now, here was the difference. Men are more slow to make remarks of that sort to ladies of forty or thereabouts who have already had two husbands, than to those of five-and-twenty who have had but one. Mrs. Hodge noticed this, and it made the peachiness of her cheeks increase at times to such a degree that it extended up to her very eyes. Yet the more she thought upon the probability that another person might succeed to the position which Mr. Simmons first and Mr. Hodge afterwards had vacated, the more she believed that an extraordinary amount of happiness might result in such case to all parties. She thought to herself that she had experience, and with sensible persons that was worth at least as much as youth.

I have often heard it remarked, and indeed my own observation, I rather think, affirms, that when a lady who has been married, especially one who has been married more than once, is making up her mind to do so again, she makes it up with some rapidity. We remember of Queen Dido, who was a very respectable widow for her day and generation. By-the-bye, she was one who gave up when her first husband died. Yet, after listening to another man talk nearly all night long, mainly about himself, she began to make up her mind on the very next day; and about nine o'clock, or at any rate soon after breakfast on the day after, she *was* married — or what she called married. *He* did not, it seemed; and acted very badly, I always thought, for in no long time after he ran away and left her, and then she did give up for good.

But to return to Mrs. Hodge. Knowing that she did not have as much time as before she began to cast about, and her ears were opened to pertinent remarks which any single gentleman might be disposed to make. But both widowers and bachelors were scarce; and what few there were either were young or had their thoughts upon younger ladies, or possibly did not understand the nature of Mrs. Hodge's feelings.

At first she had not thought much about Mr. Jonas Lively. True, he stayed there and looked somewhat after out-door business, and even advised occasionally about the store. For Mrs. Hodge still thought it best to keep up the store, though upon a scale somewhat more limited than before; and in the multitude of the business matters now devolved upon her, she could not give her undivided attention as before to this single one. Susan Temple, therefore, who had been anxious, as we have seen, to find additional work, looked after the store, and Mr. Lively gave a helping hand sometimes. Useful as Mr. Lively was, he had not been thought of at first except as a mere boarder and friend of the family. Besides his general want of attractiveness, Mrs. Hodge knew too much about him. I am satisfied that a too long and intimate acquaintance between two persons of opposite sexes is not favorable to marriage connections. You seldom know a girl to marry her next door neighbor's son. A notable instance, I admit, was that of Pyramus and Thisbe. They did make the effort to marry each other, and probably would have succeeded but for a very hasty and fatally erroneous conclusion of the gentleman touching a matter of fact. But even taking this to be a true history and not a mere fable, I have been inclined frequently, while contemplating this peculiar case, to maintain that the strong attachment of these young persons to each other, residing as they did in contiguous houses, was owing mainly to the fact that their respective families so assiduously kept them apart, and thus they were able to court each other only through a comparatively small hole in the dividing wall. But such cases are very uncommon, even in extraordinary circumstances. My opinion is that, as a general thing, persons who desire to marry well, and have no great things to go upon (if I may be allowed to use such an expression), do best by striking out at some distance from home.

But I must positively try to stick closer to Mr. Lively and Mrs. Hodge. I hope I shall be pardoned for these digressions. The fact is, that a man of my time of life has seen so much of the world, to say nothing of what he has read in books, if like myself he have been a reading man, that he has picked up some useful experience and observation which it may be his duty to communicate even in such narrations as I am now writing, although the occasions for such communication may sometimes appear to be inopportune. We do not know always what is best to do in such matters. That is a remark, I am aware, that might be applied to very many other matters of various sorts. That man does well who, whether in writing or speaking, succeeds in avoiding both extremes, the one of having too many words and the other of having too few. While I have never had any great apprehension of falling into the latter, I think that I may say that few men of my age have coasted around the former more assiduously than I have. And thus I can easily return from this digression to Pyramus and Thisbe, and the reflections their case induced, to Mr. Jonas Lively and Mrs. Malviny Hodge.

I repeat that, besides his general want of attractiveness, Mrs. Hodge knew too much about Mr. Lively to be capable of entertaining a very hasty and violent thought of raising him ·to the succession of the couple of gentlemen who had gone before. For two long years and more they had lived in the same house, and long before this period Mrs. Hodge had contended that, with the exception of his hair, she already knew all about Mr. Lively that was worth knowing. Except in this matter of the hair it would have been difficult to say in what both she and Mr. Lively had failed to find each other out in all this time. We never knew much of his opinion respecting her, but we know that hers respecting him fell far short of extreme admiration.

But time was moving on, and in spite of Mrs. Hodge's own youthful gaiety and activity, she had learned to give up some of that ardent appreciation which, in her younger days, she had set upon mere external appearances. It had come to be generally understood that Mr. Lively had property somewhere or other to the amount of several thousand dollars. He was neither young nor handsome. But Mrs. Hodge reasoned with herself. She remembered that she had had already two young and rather good-looking husbands ; and even if she had been younger herself, she could not be expected to go on at this rate and marry an unlimited number of such men. So, to be plain with herself, she thought she ought to be satisfied with what she had already enjoyed of these blessings ; and to be yet plainer, she thought she might go further and fare worse. It has always been a matter of remark with me what an amount of prudence some women can exert under the cover of unlimited frivolity. But I have no idea of pursuing this thought any further now.

Such was the state of things at the period when I first introduced Mr. Lively to the reader. Mr. Bill Williams had noticed, as he thought, that his cousin Malviny was beginning to look up to Mr. Lively.

Nobody knew Mr. Lively's views, either of Mrs. Hodge or of the general subject of marriage. He had never been heard to say whether he would or would not marry in certain or in any contingencies. But if he intended ever to marry, it was high time he was thinking about making arrangements. This was all that people had to say about it. When Mrs. Hodge began to collect her scattered thoughts, they converged upon him with the strength and rapidity usual in such cases. She had no doubt that this would be an easy conquest. Indeed her shrewd mind had guessed that this was what Mr. Lively had been staying there for all this while. But she charged him in her mind with being rather slow to take a hint, after having several times pointedly driven Susan out of the room, and with her looks invited Mr. Lively to tell what she knew must be on his mind. Mr. Lively at first seemed slow to notice all this, and he was equally slow to notice how much the character of the breakfasts had improved of late. A little bit of a something nice would be sitting by his plate every morning. This was for the most part some small fish, a string of which Mrs. Hodge would frequently purchase from a negro or poor white boy who had caught them the night before from the creek. These would usually just be enough for Mr. Lively. Mrs. Hodge and Susan would never accept of any, and the former thought that Mr. Lively ought not to have misunderstood the glance and the smile with which she would decline. Sometimes there would be also beside his plate a little sprig of something or other, mostly cedar. But he would forget to take it up and fix it in his button-hole. Women do not like for such favors and attentions to pass unregarded. Mrs. Hodge began to be vexed, and speak sharply to Mr. Lively and Susan alternately about her opinions of both. She would say to Mr. Lively that in her opinion Susan was the most good-for-nothing hussy that anybody was ever troubled with ; and she told Susan more than once that Jonas Lively was the blindest old fool that ever lived, and that he didn't have sense enough to ask for what he wanted, and what he ought to know he could get for the asking.

Mr. Lively, never or seldom having been the object of any woman's pursuit, was slow to understand Mrs. Hodge. The truth was he had become warmly attached to the place, and he was very anxious to stay there and make it his home. At first he did not clearly see Mrs. Hodge's plans. But there are some things which even the dullest understandings may be forced to take in after a while. By degrees he began to open his eyes, to look around him, and to appear to be pleased. The single attachment of such a woman as Mrs. Malviny Hodge ought not to be a thing that could be rudely cast aside by such a man as Jonas Lively. When, therefore, Mrs. Hodge began to press matters a little, Mr. Lively showed very plainly that he was *not* a fool. And Mrs. Hodge *had* began to press matters. She had even gone to expense. She sat down one night and counted up what she had spent upon him in strings of fish and other luxuries, and found that it amounted to eight dollars and something. Extravagant as this was, she determined to go further, especially as her instincts had taught her that there were some signs of intelligence and reciprocation. Mr. Lively had lately gone upon his yearly trip to Augusta and had returned earlier than usual with some improvement in his dress. This was an excellent sign. Besides, he was growing more communicative with his hostess, and occasionally had a kind word even for

Susan. Things began to look well generally, and as if that was one undivided family, or ought to be and would be.

CHAPTER VII.

THE cordial relations in the household of Mrs. Malviny Hodge became much more decided after a little incident that occurred one morning before breakfast. Mrs. Hodge had not yet risen from her couch; she had always contended that too early rising was not good for the complexion. Susan, who had other things to think about besides complexion, always rose betimes and went to her work. On this morning, at about sunrise, she was sweeping the store and readjusting things there generally. Susan was an inveterate sweeper; she had made a little broom of turkey-quills, and was brushing out the desk with it. One of the quills being a little sharpened at the end by constant use, had intruded itself into a crack and forced out the corner of a paper which had been lodged there. She drew the whole out, and seeing that it was one of Mr. Lively's letters, as it was addressed to him, at once handed it to that gentleman, who happened to be standing by the window outside and had just remarked what a fine morning it was. Mr. Lively took the letter, wondering how he could have been so careless as to leave it there. He opened it, looked at the beginning for a moment, and then at the end; then remarking that it was all right, and that he was much obliged to Susan, he went to his office. At breakfast Mr. Lively said that he believed he would ride to the court-house that day, as he had not been there in some time, but that he would surely return at night. Mrs. Hodge merely remarked that she *had* given orders for a chicken-pie for dinner; but to-morrow would do as well, she supposed. Oh yes, certainly; or Mrs. Hodge and Susan might have it all to themselves. Oh no, no; they could have it to-morrow.

That night when Mr. Lively returned and came into supper, there was a sight for the eyes of a man who had ridden twenty miles and gone without his dinner, except a couple of biscuits which Mrs. Hodge had put with her own hands into his coat-pocket in the morning. On that supper-table were not only fried eggs, but two sorts of fish, perch and horny-heads. Mr. Lively had an appetite, and these dishes looked and smelt exactly right.   Uncle Moses, Aunt Dilcy's husband, had been made to quit his work for the afternoon for the express purpose of having those fish for supper.   Mrs. Hodge looked at them and at Mr. Lively.   She said nothing, but there was expression in her countenance.

"Ah, indeed?" inquired Mr. Lively, as he took his seat.

"Yes, indeed," answered Mrs. Hodge.

Even Susan looked gratified; she had fried them every one.   In spite of his intense satisfaction, Mr. Lively was a little pained that the ladies should compel him to eat more than as an honest man he considered his proper share.   He insisted and insisted, not only that Mrs. Hodge, but that Susan should take some ; and at last he declared that if they didn't, he would stop eating himself.   He maintained that people oughtn't to try to kill a person that liked them as well as he did the present company, by trying to make him eat himself to death, and that, as for his part, that he wasn't going to do it, because he felt more like living on in this little world now than he had ever done.   Being thus pressed, she compromised.   She agreed that she would take an egg and a horny-head, or maybe two horny-heads ; but she declared that she wouldn't tech a pearch : they was for Mr. Lively, and him alone.   Susan had to come in that far also ; Mr. Lively insisted upon it.   She tried to get off with one very small little bit of a horny-head ; but it was no go.   Mr. Lively maintained that there was enough perch for all, and he made them both come squarely up.

Oh it was all so nice !   Mr. Lively was quite chatty for him.   His visit to the county-town, the ride and the supper, had all enlivened him up smartly ; but after all, he didn't see that the county-town had any very great advantage over Dukesborough.   Dukesborough was coming along ; there was no doubt about that.   As for himself, he would rather live where he was living now than at the county-town, or indeed any other place he knew of; he hoped to end his days right where he was.   It would have been too indelicate for Mr. Lively to look at Mrs. Hodge after these words, and so he looked at Susan.   Both the ladies looked down ; but it was all *so* pleasant.

By the time supper was over, as it had been delayed for Mr. Lively's return, it was getting to be his bed-time ; but it didn't look right to be hurrying off after such a supper as that.   Besides, Mr. Lively of late had been in the habit of lingering in the house a little longer of

28

evenings than formerly — no great deal, but a little. On this occasion it might have been foreseen that he was not going to rush right away from that society.

"Well," said Mr. Lively, when he and Mrs. Hodge had taken their seats before the fireplace, and Susan was clearing away the things, "Well, they *ware* fine! I pity them that don't live on any sort of water-course. Fish air blessings, certain, even when they air small. Indeed, the little ones air about the best, I believe; because they air as a general thing always fried brown, and then a person don't have to be always stopping to pull out the bones. Those we had for supper ware fried *ex-zactly* right."

Mrs. Hodge was a woman who liked appreciation even in small things. "I'm glad you think so, Mr. Lively. I told Susan to be very particler about 'em, because I thought you loved to have 'em brown."

"Yes," said Mr. Lively, with some emphasis; "always when they air small and you don't have to stop to pull out the bones."

"Yes, and you may well say *bones*," replied Mrs. Hodge —"fish-bones in particler. Fish-bones is troublesome, and even dangous sometimes. My grandfather had a aunt that got one in her throat outen one o' them big fish they used to have in them times, and it come nigh killing her at the first offstart; and it never did git out that anybody ever heerd of. And she used to have a heap of pains for forty years arfter, and she said she knowed it was that fish-bone, and that it run up and down all over her; and even when she was on her dyin bed with the rheumatism, and I don't know how old she war then, she declared that it was nothin but that fish-bone that was a killin her."

"My! my! your grandfather's aunt!" exclaimed Mr. Lively, and he could not have looked more concerned if it had been his own grandfather's aunt instead of Mrs. Hodge's who had come to such a tragical end. But he reflected perhaps that for some time past that relative had been relieved of her sufferings, and then he looked towards the table where Susan was rapidly clearing away the things.

"Be in a hurry there, Susan," said Mrs. Hodge, in a mild but admonitory tone.

"Yes; fish and such-like's blessins; but yit —" Mrs. Hodge couldn't quite make it out.

Susan hurried matters, I tell you.

"Oh yes, indeed," suggested Mr. Lively.

"Yes," Mrs. Hodge admitted; "but still fishes and — livin on water-courses, and — everything o' that kind's not the onliest things in this world."

"Oh no, indeed," hastily replied Mr. Lively. "But still — I suppose, indeed I think — of course thair must be — and — " But Mr. Lively at that moment couldn't think of what else there was in the world.

"Yes, indeed." Mrs. Hodge, having thus recovered, could proceed a little further. "Fishes and such-like's blessins, I know; I don't deny it. Of cose it is to them that loves 'em, and to them I spose it's very well to live on water-courses. Yit them and everything else is not all to every person."

"Oh no, no; by no means." Mr. Lively would not wish to be so understood.

"Not all," continued Mrs. Hodge; "particler that a person might wish in a vain world. No, fair be it to them that has loved and lost, and loved and lost again, and might love again once more, and that forever and eternally!"

Pen cannot describe the touching solemnity with which these words were uttered. Mr. Lively was extremely embarrassed. He had not intended to go very far that night; matters were so recent. He looked very much puzzled, and seemed to be trying to make out how an innocent remark about water-courses could have led them away so far into dry land.

"Susan," he called out confusedly, and looked around. But Susan had cleared off everything and gone to bed.

Mrs. Hodge waited a moment to see if Mr. Lively intended to avail himself of this good opportunity of saying anything specially confidential; but he was too confused to get it out. So she thought she would venture a remark about the weather that might reassure him.

"It's right cool these nights, Mr. Lively."

This made Mr. Lively almost jump out of his chair. He had been remarking only a day before how warm it was for the season, and according to his feelings there had been no change since that time. He answered as well as he could:

"No, I don't — yes — it's right cool — that is, it's *tolerable* cool. I suppose — that is, I expect it *will* be *quite* cool after a while. A — yes — I think a good rain — and a pretty strong wind from the northwest now — would — ah, help — and ah — "

"Yes, indeed," assisted Mrs. Hodge; "and it's about time that people war getting ready for winter. Thar isn't anything like people's bein ready to keep theirselves warm and comfortable in the cold, cold winter."

Mrs. Hodge shrugged her shoulders as if winter was just at the door, and then she hugged herself up nice and tight.

"Yes, oh yes," answered Mr. Lively, somewhat circularly; "we all don't know. But still comforts — yes — of course — and especially in the winter-time."

Mrs. Hodge looked down, her hands played with a corner of her pocket-handkerchief, and she thought that she blushed. Mr. Lively, concluding possibly that he had carried matters far enough for one evening, rose up and broke away. That night he was more desirous than ever to make that place his home as long as he lived, if he could; and he rather believed he could.

Although matters did not advance with the rapidity that might have been expected, yet it was very plain to Mrs. Hodge, and even to Susan, that Mr. Lively saw and appreciated the whole situation. Mrs. Hodge knew that he was a steady and rather a slow man, but persistent in his purposes, and somewhat peculiar in his ways of compassing them. He could neither be driven nor too violently pulled. His growing cheerfulness and the new interest he took in everything about the premises showed that his expectation was to make that his permanent home. He even went so far one day as to say that the house needed repairs, and that it must have them before very long. Mrs. Hodge and Susan looked at each other and both smiled. Susan seemed to be gratified about as much as anybody, poor thing; for of late, Susan seemed to be on some little better ground with her aunt. Thus it is that a new and very strong feeling towards one dear object disposes us sometimes to feel kindly towards all.

It was delightful to see how pleasant and affable Mr. Lively could be; slow as he might be, he was perfectly affable and pleasant. Mrs. Hodge would have been pleased to see Mr. Lively more ardent; but she knew that was not his way, and upon the whole she was very well satisfied.

Matters grew more and more interesting every day. All parties were perfectly sociable. Improvements were constantly going on in Mr. Lively's dress. A great box came for him one day from Augusta, and the next Sunday Mr. Lively came out in a new cloth suit. Both

Mrs. Hodge and Susan declared at breakfast that he looked ten years younger; that pleased him highly. It seemed that thoughts upon marriage had suggested to him the notion of going back to his youth and living his life over again. But how would you suppose Mrs. Hodge looked when, after breakfast, Mr. Lively brought in a long paper bundle, laid it on the table, and then took out and handed to her one of the finest black silk dress-patterns that had ever appeared in that neighborhood?— and not only so, but buttons, hooks-and-eyes, thread, lining, and binding! Nor had that kind-hearted man forgotten Susan, for he handed her at the same time a very nice white muslin pattern. "Oh my goodness gracious *me*, Mr. Lively!" exclaimed Mrs. Hodge; "I knew it; but — but — still I — I didn't — expect it." Susan was overpowered too, but she couldn't express herself like her Aunt Malviny. But she took the pattern, and blushed all the way round to the back of her neck. It was Susan's first present.

And now those dresses had to be made up right away. Mr. Lively required that in the tone of a master, and he intimated that there were other things in that same box. Mr. Bill Williams was not so very far wrong when he said that man was a book.

People now began to talk. Already Mr. Bill had hinted to several persons how his Cousin Malviny appeared to look up to Mr. Lively. This started inquiry, and the new clothes and youthful looks convinced everybody that it was so. Mrs. Hodge began to be joked; and without saying yea or nay, laughed and went on. Susan was approached; but Susan was a girl, she said, that didn't meddle with other people's business, and that if people wouldn't ask her any questions they wouldn't get any lies — a form of denial which in old times was considered almost as an affirmative. So here they had it.

Matters had come to this stand when Mr. Lively determined to make a decisive move.

CHAPTER VIII.

IT so happened that my parents had made a visit, taking me with them, to my father's sister, who resided about a hundred miles distant. We were gone about a couple of weeks, and returned on a Saturday night. I wished that the next day might have been the one for the monthly meeting in Dukesborough, as I was anxious among other reasons to see Mr. Bill and inquire about the parties on Rocky Creek. The next afternoon I was walking alone in the grove, and was surprised and pleased to see him coming up the road towards me. I walked on to meet him.

"Why, Philip, my dear friend, you've got back, have you? I'm so glad to see you. Mammy said you was all to git back last night, and I thought I'd jest walk over this evenin like, and see if you had come shore enough. And here you are! In cose, you've heerd the news?"

No; we had got back last night, and had seen no person but the negroes. What news?

"About the old man Jonis. You haint heerd the news? Goodness gracious! I'm *so* glad. Come along, Squire. I'm *so* glad."

Mr. Bill did look even thankful. We went together to our tree.

"And you haint heerd it? Goodness gracious! I thought it would a been all over Georgy before this. Let's set down here. Philip Pearch, I think I told you that Jonis Lively war a book. I won't be certing; but I think I did."

He certainly did.

"Is it all over?" I asked.

Mr. Bill smiled at the very idea that I should have expected to get it out of him in that style.

"Don't you forgit what I told you, Philip. Let every part have a far chance to be interestin. Law me, law me! I'm *so* glad you haint heerd it."

Mr. Bill *fixed* himself as comfortably as possible among the roots of the old tree, and thus began :—

"Well, you know, Squire, I told you that I seed that Cousin Malviny war lookin up mighty to-wards the old man. Which I sposen I oughtn't to say the old man now; but let that go. I seed that she war lookin up to him, and I knowed that she war thinkin about changin her conditions. I knowed that she had change 'em twice already befo'; and I knowed that wimming, when they git in sich a habit, you needn't try to alter 'em. When Cousin Malviny have made up her mind, she take right arfter Mr. Lively. Mr. Lively, it seem, war at first surprise, and he rather hold back. It appear like he war hard to understand Cousin Malviny. But the more he hold back, the more Cousin Malviny keep movin up. He see Cousin Malviny keep sprusen up; but he think he know sich things is common with widders, and he have no sich idee that she war sprusenin up so for him.   But byn-bye Mr. Lively begin to sprusen up hisself, and to git new clothes, you know; and he war monstous free and friendly like with Cousin Malviny, and begin to talk about what ought to be done about fixin up the house and things in ginilly; and it seem like he and Cousin Malviny war movin up tolerble close: and I haint seed Cousin Malviny so spry and active sense she war a widder befo', and that war when I warn't nothin but a leetle bit of a boy.

"Well, things kept a goin on, and everybody see that they war obleeged to come to a head, and that soon, becase people knowed they was both old enough to know thar own mind; and both of 'em a livin in the same place, everything was so convenant like.   Mr. Lively begin to spend his money free.   He have bought new clothes for hisself, and he have bought a fine silk dress for Cousin Malviny, and he even went so far as to give a right nice muslin to Susan.   Oh he's a book!   The very day you all went away a man come thar from Augusty and fotch a bran-new gig, and two fine bed-stids, and a bureau, and cheers.   And he never say a word to Cousin Malviny till they got thar, and he have all the furnitoor put in the office; and Cousin Malviny war delighted, and didn't ax him anything about it, becase she know he war a man of mighty few words, and didn't do things like t'other people nohow, and didn't keer about people axin him too many questions — and which I could a told her the same. When all this got thar people know what was a comin: leastways they think they do.   As for me, I war lookin out every day for a invite.

"And now, lo and behold!   The next mornin I war woke up by day-light by wheels a rattlin; and our nigger-boy, who war makin me and Mr. Jones's fire, he went to the door, and he come back and he say that it war Mr. Lively in a new gig, and he have a female in thar along with him, and which she have on a white dress and a veil, but which he know it war Cousin Malviny Hodge, and they went a scootin on.   Thinks I to myself, and I says to Mr. Jones, what's the reason they can't git married at home like t'other people?   And Mr. Jones he say that considerin they war both tolerble old people they was in a monstous hurry from the way the wheels was a rattlin; and which they minded him of what old Mr. Wiggins said in his sarmints about rushin along Gallio-like, a keerin for none o' these things.   Shore enough they goes on to Squire Whaley's at the two-mile branch, and thar they git married.

"I have just git up from breakfast at Spouter's, when lo and behold! here come that gig a driving up nigh and in and about as fast as it come by the sto'. I know that they was in for a frolic that day, and was bent on havin of it, and I laughed when I see 'em a comin. When they got to the tavern door, Mr. Lively he hilt up his horse, and it war nice to see how spry the old man hop outen the gig and hand out his wife. And she, why she farly bounce out, and bounce up and down two or three times arfter she lit! I says to myself, Cousin Malviny she think now she about sixteen year old. She have on her white veil till yit, and clean till she got in the house.

"'How do you do, Mr. Williams?' says he to me when I follered in. 'A very fine morning,' says Mr. Lively. Says I, 'How do you do, Mr. Lively; or mout I now say Cousin Jonis? A fine mornin indeed, I sposen, to you, Sir, and 'specially for sich pleasant bizness. I wishes you much joy, Mr. Lively, and also Cousin Malviny. But,' says I, 'I did spect a invite, and I wants to know what made you two run away in that kind o' style; for I calls it nothin but runnin away? Why didn't you have the frolic at home, Cousin Malviny?' says I. And then she ansered me. I tell you, Philinipinimon, she ansered me!"

Mr. Bill paused, and seemed waiting for me to question him further. "Why didn't they marry at home, then?" I inquired.

"Ah, yes; well mout you ax that question, my friend of the sunny hour. When you ax that question yur talkin sense. Well, I'll tell you. *One* reason why they didn't was becase they couldn't."

"'They couldn't?'"

"Couldn't. Onpossible. Jest as onpossible as if it had been a bresh-heap and it afire."

"But why not?"

"Becase Cousin Malviny wouldn't a been willin." This was answered almost in a whisper.

"Well, that is funny."

"Fun to some people and death to the t'others."

"Why, I should think she would rather marry at home."

"*She,* I think you said, Philip?"

"Yes. *She.*"

"Well, Philmon Pearch, will you jest be kind and condescendin enough to tell me who it is you're speakin about at the present?"

"Why, Mrs. Hodge, of course!"

"Oh!" exclaimed Mr. Bill in apparently great surprise. "Oh yes; Cousin Malviny. Yes. Well I sposen Cousin Malviny, reasonable speakin, she mout ruther git married at home, providin in cose that people has got homes to git married at. I should ruther suppose that Cousin Malviny mout some ruther git married at home."

"Well, why didn't she do it then?"

"Do what?" Mr. Bill seemed to be growing very much abstracted.

"Get married," said I quite distinctly.

"Git married! Ah yes. Git married. To who, Philip?"

"To Mr. Lively. What's the matter with you, Mr. Bill?"

Mr. Bill slowly elevated his eyes until they looked into the zenith for a moment, and then he lowered them again.

"Oh! Mr. Lively! Well, when Mr. Lively *he* got married, you see, Philip; when Mr. Lively *he* got married, Cousin Malviny *she warn't thar.*"

I could have put both my fists into Mr. Bill's mouth, and there still would have been room.

"What!" I exclaimed. "Didn't Mr. Lively marry Mrs. Hodge?"

Mr. Bill rose upon his feet, bent his head and knees forward, and roared:

"Na-ee-ii-o-oh-woh!"

"What! Then they didn't get married after all?"

"Yes they did."

"Why, what do you mean, Mr. Bill? Did Mr. Lively get married?"

"Certing he did. Ef any man ever got married, Mr. Jonis Lively got married that same mornin."

"Who did he marry then?"

"Se-oo-woo-woosen!"

"Who?"

"See-oo-woo-woosen, Tem-em-pem-pemple. Susan! Temple!"

"Susan Temple!"

"Yes, *Sir*, it war Susan Temple; and I didn't have not the slightest concate of sich a thing tell she lift up her veil and I see her with my own blessed eyes spread out in all her mornin glories, so to speak. Didn't I tell you, Philerimon Pearch, that that blessed an ontimely old feller war a book? I'm not so very certing, but I ruther *think* I did."

"But what about Mrs. Hodge? What did she say?"

29

"Ah now," said Mr. Bill sadly, "now, Philip, yur axin sensible questions, but monstous long ones. You must let me git over that first awful and ontimely skene befo' I can anser sich long questions as them about poor Cousin Malviny. Them questions is civil questions, I know, and I shall anser 'em; but they're mighty long questions, Philip, and a body got to have time. Ain't he a book? Come now, Philippippimon, my honest friend, you ax me questions; and far play, I axes you one. Ain't he a book?"

I could but admit that if ever man was, it was Mr. Lively.

CHAPTER IX.

I HAD to let Mr. Bill expatiate at length upon his surprise and that of the public at this unexpected match before I could bring him to the finale. Mr. Bill admitted that he was at first not only embarrassed, but speechless. He never had expected to live to see the day when he should be in that condition before Susan Temple. But such it was. We never know what is before us. The longer a man lives to see anything, the more he finds that it is a solemn fact that he can't tell what he may live to see. He had never been so minded of that as at the present; "leastways" on that blessed and "ontimely" morning. Mr. Bill was very sorry that Miss Angeline Spouter had not been at home to share in his astonishment; but she had gone the evening before to spend the night with Miss Georgiana Pea, friendly and intimate relations having been fully restored between these ladies.

"When I got so I could open my mouth," said Mr. Bill, "in cose I feel like I ought to say somethin, even ef it war but a few lines, and — ah — some perliminary remarks — so to speak. So I goes up to Mr. Lively, I does, and I says to him: 'Mr. Lively,' says I, 'you has took us all by surprise. And you more so, Susan,' says I; 'which I sposen I ought to say Miss Lively, but which it ar so onexpected that I begs you'll excuse me.' And then I ax 'em ef Cousin Malviny know of all sich carrins on. Then Susan she looked skeered. And I tell you, Philippimon, that gurl look right scrimptious with them fine things on and them shoes. But Mr. Lively war cool as a summer evenin like, and he said that he sposen not. Then he say that he had stop to git his breakfast, him and Susan, and that arfter breakfast

they was goin out thar; but also that he war first goin to git Mr.
Spouter to send Cousin Malviny word what had become of 'em, and that
they war all safe. And then I tells Mr. Lively that ef it suited him
I would go myself. I tell you, Philip, I wanted to car that news out
thar myself. Mr. Lively he sorter smile, and say he would be much
obleege ef I would. I hurries on to the sto', tells Mr. Jones what's
up, and gits leave to go to Cousin Malviny; and I mighty nigh run all
the way out thar.

"Cousin Malviny war standin at the gate. When I git about
twenty yards from her I stop to catch a little breath. Cousin
Malviny holler out to me: 'Has you seen 'em, Cousin William?' I
tried to be calm and cool, and I ax Cousin Malviny to be calm and
cool. And I says, 'What's the matter, Cousin Malviny? Ar anything wrong out here? Seed who?' 'Susan,' says Cousin Malviny,
'and Mr. Lively, and Uncle Moses.' 'Uncle Moses!!' says I;
'have Uncle Moses gone too?' 'Yes,' says Cousin Malviny; 'I
sent Moses on John mule to look for 'em when I heerd they was
gone.' At the very minnit here come old Uncle Moses a trottin on up
on John mule; and I don't know which war the tiredest and solemest,
John or old Uncle Moses. Cousin Malviny ax Uncle Moses what
news. 'Bad, Missis,' said Uncle Moses, 'bad nuff. You see, Missis,
when you tole me git on top o' John an take arter 'em, Missis, I
thought fust they was gwine todes Agusty, for he did start off that
way; but, Missis, time I got to the creek and t'other side whar the
roads forks, I gits off, I does, offen John, and looks close to the
ground to find track of 'em an' which road they tuck. Day hit jest
begin to crack a leetle bit; and bless your soul, Missis, they hadn't
been thar. I rode on back tell I got to our cowpen right yonder; and
shore nuff they has been done got down, let down the draw-bars, gone
round the cowpen, let down the fence up yonder ontoo the road agin,
back up yonder and gone on todes Dukesborough. I tracks 'em in
that field thar same as Towser and Loud arter a possum.'

"Cousin Malviny tell Uncle Moses to let possums alone and go
on. 'Yes, Missis. I war jest tellin how they let down our draw-bars
and went through behind the cowpen yonder, an got ontoo the road
agin an whipt on to town.' But, Philip, I couldn't stop for Uncle
Moses to tell his tale; it war always astonishin to me how long it do
take a nigger to tell anything. So I tells Uncle Moses to go 'long
and put up his mule, and feed him to boot, and hisself too, as I seed

they was both of 'em hongry and tired, and that I knowed all about
it and would tell Cousin Malviny myself. And so I did tell her the
upshot of the whole business. And oh, my honest friend, ef you
ever see a person rip and rar, it war Cousin Malviny; she come nigh
and in an about as nigh cussin as she well could, not to say the very
words. But which you know Cousin Malviny ar a woming, and kin to
me — leastways we claims kin; and you musn't say anything about it.
When I told her they was comin back arfter a little, she declared on
her soul that they shouldn't nary one of 'em put their foot into her
house ef she could keep 'em from it; and it look like, she said, she
ought to be mistiss of her own house. Well, I war nately sorry for
Cousin Malviny, an I ax her ef Mr. Lively have promise to marry
her. Cousin Malviny say that no, he didn't in ezactly them words;
but he have bought furnitoor, an' talk in sich a way about the place an'
everything on it as ef he spected to own it hisself; and she war
spectin him to cote her, and then she war goin to think about it
when he did ax: not that she keerd anything about him no way; and
now sense he had done gone and made a fool o' hisself, and took up
with that poor, good-for-nothin Susan Temple, he mout go; and as
for comin into her house, she would set old Towser and Loud arfter
him first. Now I knowed that war all foolishness; and specially
about them dogs, which I knowed they was bitin dogs, and which I
wouldn't a gone out o' that house that night I stayed thar ef I hadn't
knew that Uncle Moses have went possum-huntin; but which I told
Cousin Malviny that them dogs warn't goin to pester Mr. Lively nor
Susan, becase they knowed 'em both as well as they knowed her.
We was inside the gate, and we was jest a startin to go to the house
when here drive up Mr. Lively and Susan. 'Here, Towser, here,
Loud!' hollers out Cousin Malviny, 'here! here!' Says I to Cousin
Malviny, 'Cousin Malviny, ef them dogs bites anybody here to-day,
it's agoin to be me; and I hopes you will stop callin 'em.' But bless
your soul, my friend Philipiminon, them dogs was round by the
kitchen, and they heerd Cousin Malviny and they come a tarin and
a yellin. As soon as they turned the corner o' the house, I seed they
thought I was the person they was to git arfter. I jumps back, I does,
and runs through the gate and shets it. 'Sich 'em, Towser! Sich
'em, my boys,' says Cousin Malviny — the foolishest that I think I ever
see any sensible person ever do sense I war born; but Cousin
Malviny, all the eyes she had war upon Mr. Lively, and he war a ,

gittin out of the gig, cool and calm, and he give Susan the reins to hold. 'Sich 'em, my boys!' kept hollerin Cousin Malviny, outen all reason. Well, Sir, lo and behold! while old Towser war at the gate a rippin and a roarin to git out, Loud he run down about thirty steps whar thar war a rail off the yard fence, and he lit over and he come a chargin. I says to myself, ef here aint a responsibility nobody ever had one, and the only way I has to git outen it is to clime that gate-post. So I hops up, one foot on a rail of the fence, hands on the gate-post, and t'other foot on one of the palins o' the gate. I war climbin with all that bein in a hurry that you mout sposen a man in my present sitooation would know he have no time to lose. I has done got one foot on top o' the fence, and war about to jerk the t'other from between the gate palins, when old Towser he grab my shoe by the toe, inside the yard, and the next minute Loud he have me by my coat-tails outside.

"At this very minute Mr. Lively have farly got down from the gig; and when he seed Loud have me by my last coat-tail (for he have done tore off t'other), he rush up, gin him a lick with his hickory-stick, and speak to Towser, and they let me go. Bless your soul, Philip! I war too mad to see all what follered. Both o' my coat-tails was tore pretty well off; and hadn't been for my shoes bein so thick, and tacks in 'em to boot, I should a lost one of my toes, and maybe two. When I got sorter cool I see Mr. Lively tryin to show Cousin Malviny a paper, and call her *Aunty*. When she hear Mr. Lively call her Aunty, Cousin Malviny, who have been a ravin all this time, she say that war too much; and then she go in the house, and sink in a chair and call for her smellin vial, and tell 'em to put her anywhar they wants to, ef it even war her grave. She give up farly and squarly.

"Come to find out, Mr. Lively, while I war gittin back my temper and bein sorter cool — for I tell you, boy, I war never madder in my life — Mr. Lively have been a tellin Cousin Malviny what I'm now a tellin you, that that place and everything on it belong to him now as the husband o' Susan; and which they have jest t'other day found Hodge's will, which he have hid away in that desk; and which Hodge he give everything thar to Susan and Cousin Malviny jintly, for Cousin Malviny's death, and arfterwards the whole to Susan; and which he have pinted Mr. Lively his Ezecketer; and which that ar a law word, Philipip — a meanin that somebody arfter a man dies have got to tend to the business in ginerly.

"And now, Philip, I tell you that Mr. Lively ar a right clever old man arfter all. He ar from old North Calliner, shore nuff; and away long time ago he have a plantation thar, and he war goin to marry a gurl over thar, long time ago, but she took sick and died. And then Mr. Lively, he got low sperited like, and sell out and move to Augusty and buy propty, and make more money and buy more propty, tel he got to be worth twenty thousand dollars at least calclation. Did you ever see such a man?

"Well, he got tired livin in sich a big place, and he want to git back in the country. But somehow he don't feel like goin back to old North Calliner; and then he git acquainted with Hodge, and he heern about Dukesborough, and so he come here. Well, arfter Hodge he died, Cousin Malviny, you see, she think about changin her conditions again, and they aint no doubt but she take arfter Mr. Lively. She deny it now; but wimming can't fool me. Well, Mr. Lively he git somehow to like the place and don't want to go away from it; but he see somethin's obleeged to be done; and he have always like Susan, becase he see Cousin Malviny sorter put on her so much. Hodge war sorry for Susan too, and he use to talk to Mr. Lively about her; and he tell Mr. Lively that ef he died he war goin to 'member her in his will. But shore enough they couldn't find no will, and Mr. Lively he sposen that Hodge done forgit Susan; and so Mr. Lively he make up his mind to cote Susan, and ef she'd have him he mean to buy out the propty even ef he have to pay too much for it. So he go to cotin Susan the first chance he git; and Susan, not spectin she war ever goin to be coted by anybody, think she better say *yes*, and she say yes. It war a quick cotin and a quick anser. But lo and behold! Susan found in the sto' one day a paper, and she give it to Mr. Lively; and Mr. Lively see it war Hodge's will, as I tell you. But this didn't alter Susan; for when the old man told her about it, and say he'd let her off ef she wanted to, Susan say she don't want to be let off; and you now behold the conshequenches.

"And now, Philip, what make I tell you he ar a right clever old feller ar this: when Cousin Malviny ar sorter come too, and understan herself and the sitooation she war in, Mr. Lively call Susan in; for I tell you that gurl war not for gittin out o' that gig till matters got cooler. And then Mr. Lively tell Cousin Malviny that she mout stay right whar she war, and that he war goin to fix up her house, and she mout keep her same room, only it should have new furnitoor, and he would fix another room for him and Susan; and he war goin to find everything hisself, and she shouldn't be at no expense; and ef she got married he would give her more'n the will give her in money, and she mout will away her intrust into the bargin and he would pay it in money; only Mr. Lively say that sto' must be broke up, and he will pay her down in cash twice what the stock war worth. Arfter all this, Cousin Malviny gin up for good and call for Susan. Susan went to her, and they hugged; and Cousin Malviny she laughed, and Susan she cried. I could but notice them two wimming. One of 'em was a laughin and one was a cryin; and which I couldn't see the use nor the sense of nary one. But wimming's wimming, and you can't alter 'em.

"But it war time I war leavin and goin back to my business. Thar business war not mine. I bids them wimming good-bye; and I axes Mr. Lively, ef it war not too much trouble, to see me throo the gate and safe from them dogs; becase I told Mr. Lively I didn't want to hurt them dogs, but I wanted 'em not to be pesterin o' me no more. Mr. Lively he go with me about a hundred yards; and as I war about to tell him good-bye, I says to Mr. Lively, says I, 'Mr. Lively, it 'pear like you has plenty o' money; and I don't sposen that you think people ought to lose anything by 'tendin to *your* business, when it's none o' theirn. Well, Mr. Lively, it seem like somebody by good rights, reasonable speakin, somebody ought to pay for my coat-tails; for you can see for yourself, Mr. Lively, that ef this coat ar to be of any more use to me, it ar got to be as a round jacket; and all this bizness whar it got tore — and I come monstous nigh gittin dog-bit — war none o' mine, but t'other people's; and it seem like I ought to git paid by somebody.' Mr. Lively smile and say 'of cose,' and ax me about what I sposen them coat-tails was worth; and I tells him I don't think two dollars and a half was high. And then, Philip, ef he didn't pull out a five-dollar bill and give me, I wish I may be dinged!

"And then, Philip, what do you sposen that blessed and ontimely old man said to me? Says he, 'Mr. Williams, you did lose your coat-tails, and come very nigh bein badly dog-bit while lookin on at business which, as you say, was not yourn. You've got paid for it. When you war out here before, Mr. Williams, you took occasion to look at some other business — oh, Mr. Williams, I saw your tracks, and you told on yourself next mornin at breakfast. Towser and Loud war then gone with Uncle Moses possum-hunting. Sup-pose they had been at home, and had caught you in the dark at my window, Mr. Williams? Don't say anything, Mr. Williams; but let this be a lesson to you, my young friend. There's more ways than one of paying for things. I advise you, Mr. Williams, not to talk about what you saw that night to any more people than you can help. I am not anxious to fool people, Mr. Williams, and haven't done it; but I would ruther people wouldn't *dog* me about. You see how unpleasant it ar to be *dogged*, and what Loud got for meddlin with your coat-tails. But *he* didn't know any better. *You* do, or ought to. Let Loud's be a example to you, Mr. Williams. Good-day, Mr. Williams.' And he left me befo' I could say a single word.

"Now, Philip, I war never so much nonplushed in all my born days; and which when he talk about how Loud mout be an ezample, I knowed what he mean, becase which I don't have to be knock down stairs befo' I can take a hint. But you see, Philip, under all the circumsances I thinks it's maybe best not to say anything about the old man's har. Not as I keer for Mr. Lively's old hickory-stick, becase thar's plenty o' hickories in the woods; but, Philip, it mout git *you* into dif-ficulties; and ef it was to do that, I should jest feel like I ought to take the responsibility, and I should do it. So let's keep still. I haint told nobody but you and Mr. Jones; and he ar a man of mighty few words anyhow, and he aint goin to talk. So less let the old man go, and not interrupt him, and wish him much joy of his young wife. Poor Cousin Malviny! But she look peert as ever. I see her yistiday, and she look peert as ever. But wimming's wimming, Philip, and you can't alter 'em."